Books by Traci Hall

MURDER IN A SCOTTISH SHIRE
MURDER IN A SCOTTISH GARDEN
MURDER AT A SCOTTISH SOCIAL
MURDER AT A SCOTTISH WEDDING
MURDER AT A SCOTTISH CASTLE

And writing as Traci Wilton

MRS. MORRIS AND THE GHOST
MRS. MORRIS AND THE WITCH
MRS. MORRIS AND THE GHOST OF CHRISTMAS PAST
MRS. MORRIS AND THE SORCERESS
MRS. MORRIS AND THE VAMPIRE
MRS. MORRIS AND THE POT OF GOLD
MRS. MORRIS AND THE WOLFMAN
MRS. MORRIS AND THE MERMAID

Published by Kensington Publishing Corp.

Murder
at a
Scottish
Castle

TRACI HALL

Kensington Publishing Corp.
www.kensingtonbooks.com

ISBN: 978-1-4967-4438-8 (ebook)

ISBN: 978-1-4967-4437-1

First Kensington Trade Paperback Printing: February 2024

10 9 8 7 6 5 4 3 2 1

Printed in the United States of America

I'd like to dedicate this book to my readers for making this writing dream a reality—with a special shout-out to Kathleen Dannecker Nixon, for giving me the real scoop on Scottish terriers, pictures included. Your Geordie is so cute.

Acknowledgments

I still pinch myself that I am an author and that my career is telling stories. It is a literal dream come true.

I am so grateful to John Scognamiglio and the team at Kensington for bringing me into the fold. My thanks always to Evan Marshall, the best agent in the world.

To my family, and to my close friends who are family by choice. I am blessed!

Chapter 1

Paislee Shaw winced as the Juke's tire hit a large rock in the barren field designated as a car park for the annual end-of-summer bagpiping event at Ramsey Castle.

"Mum!" Brody complained from the back seat.

"Careful, lass," Grandpa Angus groused from the passenger side. "Cannae afford tae chip me teeth!"

"Sorry!" Her grandfather's teeth were his pride and joy as they all belonged to him.

The clock on the dash read nine, and there was only one other vehicle parked as the competition didn't start until noon. A van with CLAN MACTAVISH stenciled across the side had various musicians climbing out to help unload instruments and gear.

She, along with Grandpa, Brody, and their Scottish terrier, Wallace, had arrived early to meet Dowager Countess Grant, who'd arranged to carry Paislee's cashmere knitted goods in the new gift shop.

After the contest, a feast of roasted meats for two hundred folks would be prepared by Lord Patrick Grant, who was right proud of his barbecue—for good reason. She'd never had better. She'd attended the annual event off and on since her youth, though not as often when Brody was little. Now that her son was older, she didn't worry about him running into the field, or falling off the metal stands, and she could relax a wee bit.

Paislee parked and turned off the engine. "Everyone out and on their best behavior," she said. "It's important we Shaws make a brilliant impression."

She eyed Grandpa, who had a tendency to wander off, and then Brody, who was twelve and constantly distracted, and finally, she met the near-black gaze of Wallace. The pup chuffed. Of the three, he was the best behaved, though it had taken much training to get beyond his willful terrier streak. Recalling the scuffles of last year, she told Brody, "No wrestling, no jumping, no hitting."

"Mum, you never lemme have any fun," Brody said. "I'm no wean!" He was in jeans and trainers with a comic book figure on his T-shirt, his auburn hair tousled but clean, his hand on Wallace's blue collar.

"I get paid extra tae ruin your life, don't you know?" Paislee was only half-listening as she dropped the keys into her handbag.

"He'll be fine," Grandpa announced. "You dinnae need such a tight hold on the lad. Boys will be boys."

Paislee only half-listened to that, too. The pair occasionally ganged up on her, so she'd had to put her foot down. "Grab everything you need," she instructed as she slid out.

She ruled the roost at the Shaw home. Aye, they could share their opinion, and heaven help her they did, but hers was the final vote. Bedtime, bath time, brushing teeth, homework, and chores. If she gave even a smidge, Brody wanted more.

It was the way of things, Fordythe Primary's headmaster, Hamish McCall, assured her, but it was a point of tension with Brody in S1 and no longer attending primary school.

Grandpa's moodiness was a thing of the past since he now knew that his son Craigh was alive and living undercover in America. He cooked, which was a timesaver. He had strong opinions and liked his newspaper folded a certain way, but they got on quite well. He worked four afternoons a week at Cashmere Crush, giving him a bit of income and her a much-needed assistant.

Odd as it may be, Paislee felt like her late gran approved of the situation.

It had rained cats and dogs earlier that morning, a normal occurrence in lush Nairn, but for now the September sky was clear. The air smelled fresh after the deluge. Wallace raced around the SUV, sniffing at the damp earth.

"Brody, he needs tae be on a lead. We don't know what other dogs might be here."

"Mum, he hates it."

"That was the deal: you keep him on the leash, or he was tae stay home. You promised. No going back on your word now."

Brody blew out his breath but attached the leather lead to Wallace's collar. Paislee had one job in this world, and that was to raise a fine young man. Everything else in her life was secondary to that goal since she'd chosen to be a single parent.

"Thank you." Brody came to Paislee's shoulder, but Doc Whyte predicted that Brody would be tall, like her da. He and Grandpa both had brown eyes, while hers were light blue. Besides their red hair, she and Brody had a similar chin that tilted toward stubborn.

"Welcome," Brody mumbled, giving Wallace enough of the leash to run ahead after a bird, with him following close.

How on earth did Brody already have dirt on his shoes? *Och.* Paislee pulled her gaze away and opened the back hatch.

Ramsey Castle loomed to her right. This structure had been around since 1820, built after the previous building had burned. To make sure that didn't happen again, the walls were thick stone meant to last. It was imposing, as were the tall doors banded with metal to withstand any enemy. It looked medieval, like a proper castle.

"Can I help?" Grandpa tilted his blue tam over his silver-gray hair at a rakish angle.

"Aye, please!" Paislee selected a box of scarves and gave it to him, leaving the two bulkier boxes for herself.

He whistled and pretended to drop it.

Paislee gasped. "Grandpa!" Had it been too heavy? "Let me."

"I'm fine." Grandpa's back stiffened because she hadn't realized he'd been kidding. "Jokin' with ye."

"Now's not the time!" Paislee gathered the other two boxes and shut the hatch. Her specialty items were the finest cashmere and a dredging in the mud wasn't remotely amusing after the hours she'd poured into each. "Should we go tae the front door?"

"I dinnae see another entrance," Grandpa said.

"The dowager countess told me tae park in the field." Paislee balanced both boxes and her handbag. Lady Shannon Leery had championed Paislee's bespoke cashmere clothes and accessories, suggesting them to her friend. This had resulted in a golden opportunity to showcase her finer goods and add an income stream besides the online orders and her storefront.

"It was kind of Shannon tae put me in touch with the dowager countess, wasn't it?"

"Aye. Lady Leery is a special woman," Grandpa said. He'd known the beauty all his life and held her in high regard.

Paislee glanced at her grandfather over the top of the boxes, her stomach tight. "What if the dowager countess doesn't like what I've brought?" They'd discussed over the phone a few items to begin with.

"You have a braw talent with yer knitting needles, lass, so dinnae fash." Grandpa winked at her, his glasses slipping down his nose.

"Ah. Thanks, Grandpa."

Paislee had dressed in boots for a day outdoors on the castle property, paired with a lightweight, thigh-length floral jumper she'd knitted from merino wool over leggings rather than jeans. Lydia Barron-Smythe, her best friend in the world, had suggested the outfit.

They followed a gravel path toward the front of the castle. She'd been inside several times but not since the sunroom had been remodeled for the gift shop.

"Have you been here before?" she asked her grandfather.

"Not in many a year," Grandpa said. "Used tae hunt with the previous earl, Dermot Grant."

"Well, now it's Robert Grant who is Earl of Lyon," Paislee said. "And Patrick does the hunting. The dowager countess hinted that the men aren't embracing modern improvements, but she sounds like a force of her own. Something she and Shannon have in common."

On either side of the gravel path was a carpet of verdant grass. Paislee led the way, pausing as they neared the tall double doors of the castle. It had no stoop, and barrels overflowed with late summer flowers, creating bold color. The blossoms didn't soften the medieval doors.

Wallace sniffed a red geranium and snapped at a bee. Paislee noticed actual mud on Brody's shoes and worried he'd track dirt inside. "I'd like you tae stay here while we go in. Try tae keep the dog away from the flowers. We'll be right out after delivering the cashmere."

"Sure." Brody studied the metal bands on both tall wooden doors like a scientist with a magnifying glass. "Can we get doors like this?"

"I don't think they'd match our house," Paislee said with a laugh. They had, thanks to Gran, an older standalone home, two stories with a back garden for Wallace and Brody to run around in. Two bedrooms and a bath upstairs; a long bedchamber downstairs, with a bathroom. Lounge, kitchen, and covered back porch.

No castle, but perfect for them.

"Those metal straps probably kept oot the battering rams." Grandpa held the Cashmere Crush box in one arm and peered closer. "See that dent? These doors mighta been in the action."

"A battering ram?" Brody asked, joining Grandpa for another look.

"Maybe a cannon or two." Grandpa nodded. "Castles had tae be strong against the enemy. A fortress." He connected the iron knocker to the metal plate. The sound reverberated.

"That's pure barry," Brody gushed. "Let's ask the earl aboot it."

Robert Grant would play in the piping competition as his family had done for decades, providing food and drink afterward in celebration. There would be twelve bands competing in total for a small cash prize.

The front door opened. A pretty lass in a blue maid's uniform widened it. "Welcome tae Ramsey Castle!"

Behind the maid was Dowager Countess Sorcha Grant, a tall woman with sable-brown hair, green eyes, and lean, lightly made-up features. According to the research Paislee had done online, the DC was sixty-three. While Paislee had been to the castle before she'd never officially met the family.

Grandpa removed his tam. He was seventy-six and his heart belonged to her granny, but that didn't stop him from appreciating the ladies.

"Paislee Shaw! Come in, come in. Cinda?" The dowager countess gestured for the maid and another woman standing near, a cute blonde with an upturned nose, to take the boxes.

Paislee released her hold to Cinda and turned to Brody, who waited near the threshold with Wallace. "Stay around here—we'll be back shortly."

"No need," the dowager countess said. "Boys and dogs are more than welcome in this castle. I've two sons and a daughter—grown now, but they once brought a newborn calf inside because they were worried aboot it being too cold. What a mess! The calf survived and it did my heart guid tae see them care."

Brody smiled at Paislee with a glint in his eye, then bobbed his head toward the dowager countess. He stomped his feet before entering. "Thank ye!"

The castle floors were stone and covered with thin rugs that were probably easy to clean. A cow? Brody better not get any ideas!

"I'm Cinda Dorset." The blonde tapped the lid on the top box. "I manage the gift shop."

Paislee feared that she'd made a mistake bringing everything to the front doors. "Was there a different entrance?"

"You couldnae have known! It's around the back tae the right, and we've just added gravel for a dedicated parking area," the dowager countess said. "Making the gift shop accessible with its own door."

The woman was very kind, Paislee thought. Down to earth. Like Shannon Leery, though Shannon dressed fancier and was twelve years older than the dowager countess.

"Not tae worry," Cinda said with a sunny smile. "We'll cut through the castle."

Paislee brought her hand to her heart, relieved she hadn't made a faux pas after telling Brody and Grandpa to be on their best behavior. "Thank you." She gestured to Grandpa. "This is Angus Shaw, my grandfather, and my son, Brody."

"Nice tae meet you. Call me Sorcha," the dowager countess said. "And the pup?"

"Wallace," Brody answered.

Paislee was glad Brody didn't call her Sorcha, despite the invite to be familiar.

The interior of the castle was wood and stone. A chandelier overhead and lots of electric lamps created abundant light. There was a large fireplace to the right, and a closed door. To the back of the room was a wide staircase leading to the second and third floors, with an open gallery.

"This way," Sorcha said. She went to the left, following a narrow hall. "Downstairs is the kitchen; after the original house burned because of a kitchen fire, this one was built from rock quarried near the river. Tae the right as we go are various public rooms—library, an office, a lounge. Everything in use. The family's private rooms are upstairs."

Paislee peeked into each as discreetly as she could, loving the history of this home. It felt alive and vibrant, due to the extravagant lighting. She'd hate to pay their energy bill.

Grandpa and Brody strode ahead of her, and Wallace heeled at Brody's side—something new they'd worked on with the trainer because of Lydia's wedding a few months ago. Cinda walked with her, while the maid and Sorcha led the way.

Paislee offered to take one of the boxes, but Cinda shrugged her off with a wink. "I've got it," she said.

They arrived at the end of the hall and turned right, the only way to go, and continued along the length of the house until they reached the far corner.

"Here we are!" The dowager countess opened a door that had been painted white and they went inside. The glass walls from the sunroom allowed natural light, which helped lift one's spirits even on a dreary day. Plants crowded the many shelves and a door led to an outdoor sitting area with a round table and benches; the car park was marked by gravel so new it sparkled. Beyond that were fields yet to be harvested, a barn, and a greenhouse.

"How spectacular," Paislee said.

Cinda deposited the boxes on a long counter, as did the maid. "As ye can see, we have plenty of room. We plan tae sell jams from fruit harvested here at the castle, sausage from Lady Leery, jerky from our own venison. Patrick oversees the process. The dowager countess has collected a book of recipes still used today from their Grant ancestors."

"A cookbook?" Grandpa asked with interest.

"Aye." Sorcha removed the lid of a box, taking out a fine-as-silk cashmere shawl in the Grant red, green, navy, and lighter blue tartan. "Oh! This is lovely."

Grandpa elbowed Paislee as if to say *I told you so.* It warmed Paislee to see the admiration in Sorcha's eyes. Cinda's, too. "Thank you. I brought two jumpers, shawls, and several scarves."

Paislee showed the items, the softness of the cashmere beneath her fingers a testament to the quality. It was more expensive, but worth it to the right buyer.

"These will fly off the shelves!" Cinda held up a scarf. "Starting with me. I'm fair fond of cashmere."

"We'll see aboot that," Sorcha said with a look at the blonde that wasn't so fond.

"Mum!" a feminine voice called somewhat impatiently. "Where are ye?" The door pushed all the way open and a sturdy lady with the same sable-brown hair and green eyes as Sorcha stopped short when she saw that her mother had company. "Oops!"

The dowager countess tisked. "Here I am, Lissia. Lissia, meet Paislee, Angus, Brody, and the dog is Wallace. She's the knitter we've hired tae fill the shelves with tempting goods. Feel this cashmere."

Lissia's cheeks colored with a hint of embarrassment. "Sairy for yelling like a dairy maid. Hallo." She walked across the room, fitted out in a Grant tartan kilt with a white shirt and navy-blue jacket. Was she also in the band?

"See?" Cinda touched the scarf to Lissia's flushed cheek. She smelled of the fresh outdoors—rain and grass.

"Ooh!" Lissia said. "This is nice. And in the Grant tartan? Yer right, Mum. These will sell withoot a problem. Should tick Robert off." She grinned at the idea of her older brother being upset.

Sibling rivalry? Different views of where the castle was headed?

Sorcha's lips twitched in a smile. Lissia must be an ally. "And where were you, my pet?"

"Ootside, saying a wee prayer that it willnae rain us oot today." Lissia scrunched her nose and told Paislee and Grandpa, "Robert's in a snit aboot Jory and Clan Cunningham winning last year. The *only* thing that will make it right is for him tae regain the title as champion. Doesnae matter that we're all in the band—he takes it personally."

"Robert is the earl," Cinda said, as if that forgave everything.

"Clan pride," the dowager countess proclaimed.

Lissia twirled her finger in the air. "The Grant clan will not let the fans doon."

"You're in the band?" Brody inched closer to Lissia. "A bagpiper?"

"Naw." Lissia smiled at Brody and tapped invisible drumsticks to the counter. "I play the snare drum."

Brody, thoroughly impressed, gave a wistful sigh. "That's amazin'. I want tae be a drummer!"

"Do you play? I was a bairn when I first started, wasnae I, Mum?" Lissia turned to Sorcha, who nodded.

"You were. Following in your da's footsteps." Sorcha patted Lissia on the shoulder. "He'd be proud."

"Brody wants tae be a footballer." If he wanted to try a musical instrument, Paislee would support that. Better the drums than the bagpipe, to her way of thinking. The music was fine, but pipes could be screechy if not done properly. She'd been a screecher, and never pursued it.

"I'll show ye sometime," Lissia offered. "Right now, I need tae confer with Robert over a bit of timing on the roll at the beginning attack. It would *kill* Robert if Jory and the Cunninghams won two years in a row. Where is he?"

"Robert's in the music room," the dowager countess said. "I thought I'd give the Shaws a tour of the property after we finish here, if you want tae find us. Consignment okay with you, Paislee?"

It was a leap to leave the expensive items without pay, but worth the risk in terms of a new income stream. "Aye."

Lissia left, along with the maid. Cinda showed Brody and Grandpa toys, trinkets, and a calendar with castle photos going back to the original wooden structure, while Paislee filled out paperwork for the items to stock. She overheard her son ask Cinda about battering rams.

Before long, Sorcha straightened. "Well, I believe that's it. We'll both profit by this arrangement. Robert doesnae like tae discuss the cold fact that running a castle takes money, especially as we change with the times."

"Shannon says the same," Paislee said.

"She's a dear friend who has helped me bring ideas tae fruition, on a larger scale of course, than the Leery estate." Sorcha rounded the counter. "Care tae see the grounds?"

Paislee checked her watch—not even an hour had passed. A

private tour by the dowager countess was not something she'd turn down. "If it's no bother?"

"Nane. Cinda, if you dinnae mind pricing the items?" Sorcha gave directions to her employee in a firm tone.

"Aye. So nice tae meet you all!" Cinda headed to the counter while they exited.

Brody raced out with Wallace as if he'd been cooped up for years. Paislee bit her tongue to keep from telling him to calm down. He'd been very engaged and well-behaved so far. Did she have his recent birthday to thank?

Sorcha's long legs in brown pants easily covered ground. She wore a plaid red-and-beige shirt tucked in, and a narrow brown belt revealed a slender waist. "You can tell by the scent that we have cows, horses, and sheep. Lots of deer. Fish in the river. The trees are harvested for firewood. We're almost completely self-sufficient, except for electric. Robert has a conniption each time I suggest solar panels."

A dark-haired man on a horse followed by two hounds sped by them to the barn and out of sight.

"Who was that?" Brody asked. "He's so fast! Was it the earl?"

"Naw. My other son, second child of three, Lord Patrick Grant." Sorcha's voice held pride. "He's provided the meat for our barbecue later."

"Does he play in the band, too?" Grandpa asked, tam once again on his head. The sky was overcast, the morning cool, but at least it wasn't raining.

"No. Patrick is no musician—I'm not, either. We do other things, like hunt and manage the accounts," Sorcha said in a teasing tone. "We all know our duties here at the castle."

Sorcha crossed to the greenhouse and opened the door. Inside, a man with a weathered face, as if he lived permanently outdoors, bowed over a row of greens. A knit cap covered black hair threaded with a hint of silver strands.

"Finn McDonald, groundskeeper and gardener." Sorcha entered fully. Steam frosted the glass panels of the greenhouse from their breaths.

"Hi!" Paislee said.

Finn looked up and tipped his head. He might have smiled but it was hard to tell. "Hallo. Shall I leave . . . ?"

"Dinnae go," Sorcha said. "I'm just showing the Shaws around. Paislee will be a frequent visitor now that her items are in the gift shop. Are the stands already up for folks tae watch the performance?"

"Aye." Finn pinched a green leaf and pocketed it, moving on to the next plant. "Me and the lads did it this morn."

"It was pouring!" Brody said.

"If I was tae stop an activity because of a sump o' rain, I'd never get anythin' done," Finn remarked with a twinkle in his eye.

"Thank you, Finn." Sorcha turned and gestured them back outside. "Finn is my right-hand man on this place. He knows each blade of grass. Patrick manages the cattle and horseflesh while Robert tends tae the castle property. Lissia and I manage the inside, like the kitchen and staff. We are a well-oiled machine here at Ramsey."

There was no mention of Cinda.

They left and Sorcha headed toward the trees: evergreen, firs, chestnut, oak. Paislee recognized everything except for something that resembled very tall bamboo.

"What are those?" Grandpa asked.

Sorcha saw what he pointed at. "Giant Reed."

"Giant Weed?" Brody repeated.

"No." Sorcha laughed good-naturedly. "The name is Giant *Reed*. It's been grown for use on the bagpipes since the first records in the Ramsey Castle logbooks."

"What for?" Grandpa asked, giving his beard a scratch.

"The reeds. I dinnae play"—Sorcha raised both hands—"but Dermot, and now Robert, insist that the natural cane reed makes the warmest sound." She briefly brought her finger to her lips. "I zone oot when they go on aboot them. I've asked him tae put them in the gift shop along with the clan history. He's not behind it yet but he'll see that every wee bit of income helps."

Paislee nodded, understanding that very well.

They reached the edge of the forest, guarded by tall reeds and pine trees. Grass was springier beneath her feet. Wildflowers grew in pink and yellow clusters. Moss covered the trees.

Wallace strained against Brody's hold to chase a fat red squirrel waving his tail like a matador teasing a bull. "Brody!" Paislee warned. Too late. Wallace got loose, barking ferociously after the wily squirrel.

Brody darted for the trailing leash grip but missed and followed Wallace into the forest. The trees covered him from view as they ran. Paislee's blood pumped with adrenaline—she hated not being able to see her son, or their dog.

"Stay here a second." Sorcha strode after them while Paislee and Grandpa waited. The three returned within moments that felt like a lifetime.

Sorcha had Wallace's lead in one hand, and her other on Brody's shoulder. "Those squirrels are excellent foragers," she said. "They get nuts. Berries. Mushrooms. Even the poisonous ones."

"They could die if they eat them!" Brody said, his eyes round with worry.

"Nope. Squirrels can digest the poison, but it would make your pup sick." Sorcha handed Brody back the lead. "Need tae be careful, is all."

Wallace, panting, lowered his head when Paislee gave the terrier the stink-eye. "Did he get into something poisonous?" She had the veterinarian, Dr. Kathleen McHenry, on speed dial.

The dog's black muzzle was flecked with dirt and grass. The gloating squirrel chittered from the treetop.

"No. Wallace was just pawing at the tree tae get tae the squirrel. Let's stop at the barn so Wallace can drink from the trough." Sorcha moved away from the forest.

"Thank you," Paislee said. "Brody learned about mushrooms on a field trip when he was eight. Do you remember?"

"Not really," Brody said. "So, I just stay away from all of them. Yuck."

"Finn harvests them and other herbs," Sorcha said. "Our chef makes a divine brandy and wild mushroom soup that will be in the cookbook. I might sell food doon the line as well."

"It sounds wonderful," Paislee said. "Mushroom soup is delicious, but my true favorite is a cock-a-leekie soup that my granny made."

"Oh?" Sorcha tucked her hand into her pants pocket. "I'd love tae exchange recipes."

"Sure." They stopped at the barn, where Wallace drank his fill. Bagpipes and drums sounded as the musicians warmed up before the competition.

Sorcha glanced at her watch. "We'd best get back. Warm-ups start at half past eleven, competition at noon. Meri is adamant that her schedule be followed."

"Meri?"

"Meri McVie. The judge," Sorcha said. "She gives 'no-nonsense' a whole new look. Dinnae get me wrong," the dowager countess stated, "I admire a strong woman. You must be tae succeed in this world." She tapped her rose-tinted mouth. "But there is nothing wrong with a touch of lipstick."

Chapter 2

Various melodies started, then stopped, as the bands warmed up. Sorcha hurried her step, urging them along. "I cannae play a note, but I love tae hear them perform." Her lips twitched as she squeezed her thumb and forefinger together. "I may've placed a wee wager on my favorite. Have you one, other than Clan Grant?"

"Clan Campbell," Paislee said. "Our friend Jerry McFadden plays the bagpipe, so I always cheer for them. They were third last year."

"That Jory Baxter was an upset." Sorcha glanced at her watch. "Robert raged aboot it for months. He never expected tae lose the title tae a newcomer. If the Campbells had won, aye, he wouldnae have taken it tae heart as he did."

The piping community had been stunned over Clan Grant's loss. It was all Jerry had talked about for a week afterward, how Jory had come from nowhere, young and talented. Part of the competition allowed each band to choose their star for a small solo performance, and Robert had led his clan to the win for years.

"Jerry said that Jory was new tae the Clan Cunningham band, wasn't he?" Paislee asked.

"Aye," Sorcha said. "Clan Cunningham had never been close tae the top before Jory Baxter. Robert wondered if Clyde Cunningham had brought in a ringer tae win."

"What does that mean?" Brody asked. "A ringer?"

"Someone who is verra good at what they do," Sorcha explained. "Being acquired for the sole purpose of winning."

"Is that against the rules?" Paislee asked.

"No." Sorcha shrugged. "Just came as a surprise."

"Must one be a member of the clan in order tae be in that particular band?" Grandpa asked.

"I believe it's recommended but I dinnae ken how closely it's followed. Meri would," Sorcha said. "The members of Clan Grant, besides Robert and Lissia, are farmers or tenants on Ramsey Castle land."

"So, I couldnae join Clan Grant, with Lissia?" Brody asked, sounding despondent.

Sorcha laughed. "Brody, for you, me lad, we'd find a way. The truth is that the entire Grant band has practiced their fingers tae the bone." She rubbed her hands together. "I'm looking forward tae their well-earned win today. Go on ahead now"—she waved them toward the outdoor tiered stands with a canopy against the rain, and opened the door to the gift shop where Cinda waited—"I've a few last-minute things tae take care of."

"Thank you for everything!" Paislee said.

The Shaws followed the non-melodic fits and starts of instruments being tuned to the left of the castle and a gigantic expanse of green lawn. Brody and Grandpa were on either side of her. Wallace, on her naughty list for chasing the squirrel, didn't once tug against the lead in Brody's hand.

They reached the edge of the field and Paislee paused in wonder at the explosion of bright hues. The sun broke from behind a cloud to shine on brass and metal fittings. Twelve bands were to compete, between eight and ten players, each with matching kilts in a variety of tartans.

"Well, isnae that something," Grandpa said with amazement in his tone.

"It's impressive." Paislee smiled at a few familiar faces. Bag-pipers, drummers, and the band directors gathered in clusters. Each group was here to perform their best.

Three stands had been erected for spectators and the band members who would sit and watch the others when they weren't playing.

"Hey—there's Jerry." Grandpa stepped toward Jerry McFad-den, member of Clan Campbell, sporting a kilt in green, blue, and black. When Jerry wasn't delivering her yarn, he rocked the bag-pipes. His light brown hair matched his thick mustache.

Jerry saw them and lowered his bagpipe. "Bonnie day after all for the competition," he said as they neared him. "I was a wee bit worried during the downpour this morning."

"God's way of giving the cows a bath," Grandpa said sagely. "How are you part of the Campbell clan?"

Jerry placed his pipes at his shiny black brogues. "My mother is a Campbell cousin. Why do ye ask?"

"Sorcha told us it was a rule," Grandpa said.

"Sorcha, is it?" Jerry teased.

Paislee laughed when Grandpa turned red.

"She gave us a tour," Brody said. "Mum's got her cashmere in the gift shop."

"Well, that *is* nice," Jerry said.

"I hope it means I'll need tae increase my order of cashmere." Paislee smiled. "We'll see. But today is not about that—today is about you and the competition. How are you feeling regarding the outcome?"

"Verra well." Jerry leaned toward them. "We've mastered a new tune tae land the number one spot. I was voted by my mates tae be our soloist this year."

"What aboot the other bands?" Grandpa asked. He gestured with his head to the musicians around them.

"The Grants will come oot strong, too, due tae old-fashioned practice, but I think Clan Cunningham is rattled." Jerry nodded to the stand at their right. "Jory Baxter and Clyde Cunningham were arguing over something."

"Who is Clyde?" Grandpa asked.

Brody was jerked to the side as Wallace saw another dog—also on a lead, thank heaven. Paislee put her hand on Brody's shoulder and arched her brow.

"Clyde Cunningham is the pipe major, or band director. He organizes the group and keeps tempo. He's responsible for turning in the program tae the judges, and also the liaison between the band and the GHB—Great Highland Bagpipe—Competition Council." Jerry dipped his head toward a short man with copper hair in the Campbell tartan. "That's Mattias Campbell, our pipe major. Keeps us in line. Though they dinnae play a physical instrument during competition they are crucial tae the performance."

Brody couldn't hide his eagerness to explore, so Paislee tapped Jerry on the arm. "Good luck tae you. Where will you be sitting? We'll cheer you on."

"This stand behind us. If you've a mind tae place a wager, I think we've got a guid chance at the win. Thanks!" Jerry picked up his pipes and joined the group around Mattias.

Paislee and Brody, with Wallace, went to the stands and scored a seat on the second row, near the end. There were three stands surrounding a circular field, with enough seating for two hundred.

"Can I go play, Mum?" Brody pointed to a group of other kids his age kicking a football around in the barren field, well within her eyesight.

"Sure. But leave Wallace here, please."

Brody reluctantly handed her Wallace's lead.

"Maybe you can take him later," Paislee said.

"Awright!" Brody ran off.

Wallace chuffed as his boy joined the others and sat with his furry back to the bands. A protest? Paislee opened her handbag and dug around for a dog treat. "Here you go."

Wallace snapped up the biscuit and swallowed, then returned to his vigil. She poured water into a pop-up water bowl and placed it in the grass for the dog along with a chew toy. She returned to her seat next to Grandpa, content that Wallace would alert her if anything happened to Brody, and focused on the circular field.

At noon on the dot, judge Meri McVie stepped into the center field. She had a sharp, fox-like face and naturally orange hair, with brown eyes behind silver-framed glasses that gazed at the spectators steadily. White shirt beneath a black jacket, a blue and light-green kilt, and a badge attached to a ribbon around her neck proclaimed her position.

Meri blew her whistle to get everyone's attention, though the competitors were ready to go. Each clan had grouped together. The Campbells were on the first two rows below Paislee and Grandpa, along with Clan Buchan, Clan Lincoln, and Clan MacTavish.

Across from Paislee, Clan Grant took an entire two rows, and above them sat Sorcha and Cinda. Sorcha had changed her clothes and now wore a Grant tartan blazer over navy-blue slacks. Clan Douglas, Clan Sinclair, and Clan McKinley waited their turns. On the third stand was Clan Cunningham, Clan Cameron, Clan Graham, and Clan Fraser.

"Hello!" Meri said in a clear voice. "Welcome tae this year's Ramsey Castle Competition."

Applause sounded.

The kids huddled around the stands to see the beginning. Paislee gave Brody his water bottle and offered a granola bar that he declined.

"Let me go over the rules." Meri read from a clipboard she held. "Each band will play for fifteen minutes or less, but no more. The songs must match what has been turned in tae the judges—myself, and Connor Armington." The second judge was much older, seventy to Meri's fifty, and his jacket didn't quite button over his belly. "If they dinnae match, that team will be disqualified."

Murmurs could be heard on the benches.

"Last year's champion will be the final act of the day. Clan Grant will perform second tae last, and Clan Campbell third." Meri raised her pointed chin and lowered the clipboard. "This is my tenth year of judging this competition. Each year the talent exceeds expectations. It's my privilege tae announce the first of our twelve bands: Clan MacTavish!"

The clapping was loud as Meri left the grass to stand on the edge of the circle, her posture perfect. Connor also had a clipboard. The judges walked around and made various marks as the band played. The MacTavish kilts were red with sky blue and black, the shirts white, the jackets sky blue. They were a newer band and so had placed at the bottom to start.

Clan Fraser played next. The band's kilts were a robin's-egg blue with red and gray, the jacket gray over a white shirt. It seemed that each outfit would have to be custom-made to fit the person and Paislee wanted a closer look at the way the arms fit for ease of movement, whether at the drums or the bagpipes. The horizontal and vertical patterns allowed for a large variety in the tartan.

The difference between a plaid and a tartan was the replicated pattern in the fabric at the vertical and horizontal ends tied to a specific clan, whereas plaid described a crisscross of any sizes or colors.

Finally, it was time for Clan Campbell: Jerry's team. So far Meri hadn't called anyone out for breaking the rules, though Paislee wouldn't know. She thought everyone sounded wonderful, and her hands were sore from applauding so enthusiastically.

In the last four hours, Brody had come for water or snacks but mostly had stayed with his new mates. She admired how he could make friends like that. She'd always been shy.

Grandpa finished his water. "Shouldae brought me flask," he said, smacking his lips. "Dinnae suppose you've anythin' stashed in that bag of yours?"

"I do *not* have whisky, Grandpa. That would be correct." Paislee didn't mind the occasional dram but wasn't much of a drinker. Her vice was chocolate.

"That handbag is big enough for a whole keg," he remarked.

She glanced at Grandpa, then back at the field. Her bag was large, roomy, and perfect for all the items needed on an outing. "I have an extra water bottle, if you'd like that."

"No thanks. I'll wait for the guid stuff." Grandpa scratched his bearded chin. "There *will* be the guid stuff, eh?"

"Drinks will be served with the meat afterward, aye." In years past, an outdoor eating area had been set up next to several large barbecues. There were kegs of beer and whisky both, tea as well as coffee, and, of course, cases of Irn-Bru, Scotland's number one soft drink.

"I'd expect no less at a castle," Grandpa said.

"Did you ever play the bagpipes, Grandpa?"

"A wee bit." He touched the brim of his tam. "Enough tae know it's best left tae the professionals."

"Jerry called it a GHB."

"Aye." Grandpa pointed to Jerry as he took his position on the field with his bandmates. "The Great Highland Bagpipe. The leather bag collects air, they each have two tenor drones—the shorter pipes there—and the big one over Jerry's shoulder is called a great drone."

"I don't see the reeds Sorcha was talking about," Paislee said.

"Oh, you wouldnae," Grandpa said. "They're inside the instrument."

"I had tae learn the recorder in primary, and so did Brody. P3." Paislee smiled at Grandpa as she remembered the awful noise her son had made, and she'd been no better. "You're lucky you weren't with us then. It was a racket."

Grandpa chuckled. "Do you think he'll really want tae learn the drums?"

"I'm praying he'll forget when he's playing football next weekend," Paislee said.

"That's the way of it," Grandpa agreed. "Boys have short memories."

"Shh! It's starting." To her delight, Jerry was positioned close enough that Paislee could watch him play. She was proud of him for being chosen to perform a solo.

Clan Campbell had ten members: four drummers and six pipers, with one pipe major, Mattias Campbell. Jerry's solo was amazing. The breaths he took, the way he held the leather bag, the gold trim on the drones . . . he created magic that moved her deeply.

Someone—not Jerry—missed a note but recovered quickly. In this tight competition, there had been very few mistakes, even with the less experienced bands.

When it was over, folks stomped their feet to the bottom rung of the bench, cheering the Campbell performance.

"That was great!" Paislee's heart raced with excitement.

"Hard tae believe such an awkward instrument can create such beauty." Grandpa doffed his tam. "In the right hands. I'm glad I left that dream behind."

Clan Campbell exited the field to much applause.

Next was Clan Grant. Eight performers in their group, with Robert at the lead. Lissia wore the snare drums just as proudly as her brother held the Great Highland Bagpipe.

The dowager countess, on the opposite stands from Paislee, stood and clapped.

Robert Grant, every inch the Earl of Lyon, bowed toward her. "This set is dedicated tae our mother, Dowager Countess Sorcha Grant, our biggest supporter."

Sorcha Grant bowed in return. "Many thanks for the tribute, my darlings." She scanned the crowd as if looking for someone . . . Patrick? He wasn't there to share in the moment.

Finn McDonald watched from the sidelines, his arms crossed before him as he scowled at the rowdy crowd around Jory Baxter's team. Clan Cunningham fans chanted Jory's name even though the Grants were on the field.

Cinda, next to Sorcha, showed her support by wearing the Grant colors in a bold red blouse with green, navy-blue, and light-blue accents. She kept glancing toward Jory's group, too. Would she be loyal to Clan Grant, or did she favor the other team?

Paislee didn't recall Jory Baxter being better last year, so she was glad she didn't have to judge and could simply enjoy the music. She turned her attention to the grass as the band director for Clan Grant raised a hand.

The eight band members seemed to puff their chests and shoulders in unison.

White shirts, red, green, navy-blue, and lighter blue kilts, navy socks, and shoes. They wore fitted navy jackets. The overcast sky kept them cool—still no rain, a minor miracle considering how the day had started.

Paislee sat forward, her hands over her knees.

When the Grants performed, the sound was heavenly. Lissia was a master with her drum strokes, soft to loud, urgent to casual. Her maple drumsticks created a snappy sound. Oh, and how Robert played, taking the lead, letting everyone know as he stepped toward Jory and Jory's team that he was here to win. To reclaim his crown.

How could Jory beat Robert, who appeared blessed by the angels as he piped today? When it was over, Paislee was so overcome that she had to wipe a tear from her cheek before she bolted upward to clap her hands until they stung.

"That was lovely. So lovely," she said.

Grandpa stomped his feet with approval, his large hands clapping hard. "They have tae win. How could anybody be better? Not a single bloody mistake in either set."

They looked at the judges, who each wrote on their clipboards. Were they as swept away?

It took several moments for the crowd to hush, and finally Meri had to blow her whistle to quiet them down.

"And that was Clan Grant! Robert Grant, Lissia Grant, and the Ramsey Castle crew," Meri announced. Her clipboard was to her chest as if to conceal any notes she'd taken from curious eyes.

"Well played!" Connor, the other judge, commended as the Grants strode, heads high, off the grass to the stands.

Sorcha, from the top row, blew the Grants a kiss.

Paislee peered over her shoulder. Wallace was still watching Brody as he played football with his new mates—nothing wrong.

She turned back to the field. High fives and cheers slowed as everyone resumed their seats.

It was time for Jory Baxter and his team, Clan Cunningham. Clyde Cunningham was the pipe major. He had brown hair and wore it long in front, short in back. Paislee guessed he'd be in his forties.

Paislee felt very confident that there was no way Jory and his team could do better than what they'd just heard.

It took a while for Clan Cunningham to find their marks. She wondered if they were made nervous by the previous talent, or if they were unaffected. The energy pulsed.

Jerry and the Campbells were seated on the first rows, with the other clans. She heard them murmur that Robert would be impossible to beat, and surely the Campbells would be second place.

At last, Clan Cunningham was in formation. They were just as impressive as the previous bands had been. Their kilts were black and red rows, with thin white stripes, black socks and shoes, and black shirts. The black jacket was fitted.

The ten players of their group were an even split of five drums, five pipers, with Jory at the lead. Two of the snare drummers were women. Pretty lasses, slender yet strong. There was a large bass drum, and two medium-sized drums that Grandpa said were tenor drums.

Clyde faced them and dramatically raised his pipe major's mace, holding the stick high.

A few hoots from the stands made it to the field.

Jory Baxter had vocal supporters in the crowd, though the event was on Grant land; Scots were fierce in their rights to their own opinions, laird of the manor or no. A man (or woman) had to earn any respect.

Tension weighted the air, like a summer storm right before the rain broke free.

Jory, as last year's champion soloist, had booted Robert from the top spot, bringing Clan Cunningham the win. It was coveted for the right to brag of being best, with a nominal cash prize. Sorcha had said this was about clan pride.

Robert was a handsome man of forty years and Jory just thirty. Robert had been classic in looks, sable-brown hair and clean-shaven. Jory was raven-eyed with black curls to his shoulders, caught back out of his way with a leather hair tie. His profile was sensual, his hands as he held the bagpipes, steady.

Paislee watched, throat dry, as Jory brought the mouthpiece of the blowpipe to his full lips. How the muscles in his arms flexed as he held the black leather bag to his body as sensual as a lover, his fingers caressing the chanter. Silver flashed around the drones. Paislee swallowed and fanned her face.

The others on his team waited for him to begin, the "attack" beginning with the pipes rather than the drums, and then the band was as one. Like the other clans, it was talent collected and re-turned, a thing of beauty.

She broke from the spell to see Lissia and Robert, seated below Sorcha. Lissia glared at Jory, though Robert kept his gaze noncommittal. The arrogant lord of the castle unaffected by the riffraff.

Cinda kept glancing at Robert, then Jory and the Cunningham performers. Who did she favor?

The tune finished. The crowd went wild with applause, but it wasn't over just yet. They had another song to play, their last one. This would be Jory's solo. Jory smirked toward Robert, Lissia, and Sorcha with no respect.

Jory breathed in and put his lips on the mouthpiece. Eyes closed, he blew into the blowpipe.

And then . . . his face turned a dark reddish purple.

He fell, stumbling into his other players. They oohed in alarm and paused—this wasn't part of the performance. Should they continue? The female snare drummers slowed their strokes of sticks to the round tops.

Jory swerved, his eyes fluttering closed, as he landed on his back.

The awkward musical instrument hit the ground with a clatter as the drones knocked together. The kilt hiked up to his hips.

It was true that men wore nothing beneath them, and Jory briefly flashed the crowd before the tartan settled at his muscular thighs.

His bagpipes made an awful screech, matched by Cinda Dorset's scream.

Chapter 3

Jerry, on the first row below Paislee, jumped toward Jory. Grandpa clasped his hands over his knees. Paislee looked behind her to make sure that Brody was all right. Wallace whined as if he knew something had just happened but kept his gaze on his boy.

Brody was fine, the kids unaware of the commotion.

Jerry knelt by Jory and discreetly pulled the man's kilt down to his knees. The green, blue, and black Campbell kilt and the red and black of the Cunninghams', competitors in their battle uniforms, overlapped on the grass.

Grandpa stood, hands on his hips, beneath the canopy. He angled forward as if to see better and Paislee feared he might fall.

Jory dragged in a ragged breath as he sprawled on his back. Jerry tilted Jory's chin up. What could cause a young man in his prime to pass out like that? Stroke? Heart attack? Lack of air from the bagpipes?

With a groan, Jory stirred but didn't speak.

Jerry shifted and accidentally put the toe of his brogue on Jory's bagpipes when he backed up from the man. It screeched like a furious cat. He picked it up and studied the instrument in confusion. The brunette female snare drummer knocked into Jerry on her way to Jory and he dropped it again.

"Sairy," Jerry said. He placed the bagpipes on the bench seat out of the way.

"What's wrong with Jory?" the young lady asked. Her plastic over-the-shoulder drum carrier made it awkward to get around Jerry and impossible for the lass to kneel.

Paislee brought out her phone. "I'm calling emergency services." Nobody argued, and she dialed 999, giving the address and the information that Jory had collapsed during a bagpipe performance at Ramsey Castle.

People crowded around to find out what was happening, but Meri blew her whistle and instructed everyone to back up.

"An ambulance is on the way," Paislee shouted to her.

"Guid." Meri leaned over and touched Jory's wrist and then his throat, nodding to Jerry.

Paislee sagged in relief. Jory was alive and had probably just fainted from lack of air. The bagpipes took skill to master properly.

He'd won last year and seemed to know his stuff, so it didn't make sense that he wouldn't know how to breathe. However, he was young, and maybe had pushed himself too hard.

Why didn't he wake up, then?

Robert clambered down the metal seats to the grass. This wasn't the arrogant lord playing the pipes with his clan but instead a man with concern for his fellow bandmate. He defied Meri's instructions and stood near Jory's body.

"What happened?" Robert demanded.

"I dinnae ken," Jerry said. "He was playing and then just passed oot."

"That's what I saw as well," Meri said. "Please, back up and give Jory some air."

"Where's Clyde?" Jerry asked. "His champion is doon."

Paislee looked across the crowd of people and saw Clyde on the phone, arguing and tossing one hand to his side.

"Unbelievable!" The blond female snare drummer scowled toward Clyde, who was oblivious and still on the phone.

Meri's gaze narrowed on the band director. Clyde was acting very strangely. Jerry had been quick-thinking to keep Jory's bag-pipes on the bench where they wouldn't get stepped on.

Her drum and carrier to the side, Lissia left her perch on the tiered seats, followed by Sorcha and Cinda, who spoke with Mattias Campbell. Lissia, though, made her way to Jerry with worry in her green eyes.

"Hey, Jer," Lissia said. "What's up with Jory?"

Jerry gave a concerned shrug. "I've no idea."

It made sense that they'd know each other as the piping bands were a community despite the competition element. Lissia kept glancing at Jory with more emotion than her older brother showed. The daughter of the castle had more leeway perhaps to show her feelings?

At last, Paislee heard sirens. That was enough to bring Brody running and he joined her, Grandpa, and Wallace at the stands, standing next to the seat. She was anxious to know that Jory would be fine.

"Grandpa, go see what's going on," Paislee said, sending Angus into the fray despite Meri's request that everyone stay seated and calm. Calm was impossible considering last year's champion had fainted.

"Aye. I'll be back." Grandpa adjusted his tam and descended the seats with much agility for a seventy-six-year-old man.

The ambulance parked on the pristine grass, creating ruts. Jerry, Robert, Sorcha, Cinda, and Lissia hovered around the edges of the playing circle. Grandpa stood next to Meri and Connor. Patrick, followed by his hounds, arrived on horseback, jumping down with grace and strength.

"What's going on?" Patrick demanded.

"Where have ye been?" Sorcha asked quietly. "I asked you tae support our band while they played."

"I never promised. I'm helping with the venison," Patrick replied. He made his way to the half circle around the medics and Jory as the team put Jory on a stretcher. "Wassup?"

"Jory fainted." Cinda scooted close to Patrick and rested her fingers familiarly to his arm. "Before they finished their set."

Patrick scoffed, glanced at his mother, and shrugged Cinda off. "Fainted? Some champion," he said. "Well. Guess that means the Grants win, eh?"

Meri and Connor both appeared appalled at the brutal assessment by Patrick Grant.

Lissia scuffed the grass with her brogue as if wishing she could disappear. "Eejit."

Patrick bristled at his sister's remark. Cinda glared at Lissia. Lissia didn't seem to care about Cinda's opinion any more than Sorcha had.

Robert folded his hands before him, his jaw clenched. "What happens next?" The earl turned to Meri, then Connor. "A rematch?"

Meri blew out a breath and then conferred with Connor. They were still talking in whispers as the medics loaded Jory's figure into the ambulance.

The female snare drummers for Clan Cunningham, now divested of their drum-carrying apparatus, offered to drive to the hospital.

The brunette sent Clyde a scorching look of disapproval and then told Meri, "Jory rode with me and Cass, so we'll take him home. Jory's health is more important than the competition."

Cass, the blond drummer, agreed, scrubbing tears from her eyes.

"Of course," Meri said immediately. "Jory's health matters most. Will ye be all right tae drive?"

"I'm fine," the brunette said, wiping her cheeks. "Let's hurry, Cass."

The rest of Clan Cunningham seemed more interested in a rematch than how Jory was faring. Clyde was finally off the phone.

What had that been about? What was more important to the man than his star piper going down?

Paislee had a bird's-eye view from her spot on the tiered seats. The brunette called to Clyde, "We'll phone as soon as we know anything. Could ye stay off yer mobile? Rude!"

Clyde's throat and forehead colored a rusty pink at being called out by his teammates. "Yeah. Thanks."

"You'll need tae find another way home," Cass said. "Could ye load our drums?"

"Aye." Clyde strode their way, his hands to his sides. "Sairy aboot that. I'm sure Jory's awright. I'll catch a ride with Ewan in the van with our equipment."

Paislee, eavesdropping, wondered if she should tell them about Jory's bagpipes but they'd turned away. Clyde walked with the lasses toward the car park in the field. Jerry had kept the pipes from being trampled and would no doubt return them when things settled down. Paislee scanned the area for Jerry's familiar face but didn't see him.

The ambulance drove away with a flash of lights and sound, leaving the folks milling around the lawn with an instant of uneasy silence.

Robert Grant, once again every inch the Earl of Lyon, put two fingers in his mouth and blew. The piercing noise garnered everyone's attention.

Meri stepped closer to Robert, peering up at him, her wild carrot-orange hair flattened on one side as if she'd repeatedly patted it down. "I've never had this happen tae me durin' a competition." She scanned her rulebook. "It clearly states that if the team cannae finish, they forfeit."

Gasps and boos echoed around the lawn.

Robert raised his hand to quiet the reaction. After a moment's consideration he said, "I'd be willing tae offer a do-over for the top three teams within the month, once Jory is back in full health."

Lissia and Patrick donned matching sour expressions. Some of the other competitors complained that it wasn't fair. It should be all twelve teams if they were going to do it over again, not just last year's top three.

"Just take the win," a female member of Clan MacTavish said. "'Tis the rules."

Some of her band members disagreed. It was a mixed bag of responses and Paislee felt bad for Meri, who seemed like she just wanted to do the right thing.

Robert shook his head. "Given the importance of the title, my clan and I wouldnae feel right aboot winning in such a way."

Lissia gritted her teeth but didn't argue. Paislee figured Lissia thought it would be just fine to accept the win, but as earl, Paislee could also see why Robert would want to be fair to everyone.

"And who says you'd win?" Mattias Campbell challenged. Paislee liked his spunk.

"We havenae tallied our points," Meri said. "The competition was verra close this year. We'll check with the GHB Council tae verify what can be done."

"What do you think, Connor?" Robert asked.

"The council will need tae approve this, aye, but let's take a show of hands for who agrees tae the rematch and vote on it," Connor declared in a tone that suggested this was highly irregular.

Grandpa watched the proceedings, smoothing his beard in speculation. Why would he care if there was a do-over, or if the Grants won? Unless he'd found a way to make a small wager?

Jerry had suggested they'd be a solid pick for a win.

Paislee didn't bet. She didn't have anything against it, but she rarely had extra funds to do so, not to mention that Gran had looked down on it.

Meri rocked back on her heels with a nod toward Connor. "If the clans could gather in their groups, it will make it easier tae see a show of hands for a vote."

Within moments, they were in groups of eight or ten, except for the Cunningham clan, who was missing three of its members.

Meri asked, "Clan MacTavish—raise your hands if you would agree tae a rematch."

Their pipe major stepped forward. "We think all twelve teams should get another shot."

Applause sounded from a majority of the clans.

Meri and Connor conferred.

Meri returned. "Aye. All twelve of the clans, tae be fair."

Robert grimaced, no doubt seeing a great expense with food and drink by hosting so soon again. Would he regret not allowing the champion, whoever it might have been, to win by forfeit? How strong did he believe that he'd beat out the Campbells?

The pipe major of Clan MacTavish lifted the director's mace. "Aye. We'll be here."

By the time the voting had reached Clan Campbell and Clan Grant it was clear that there would be a complete rematch if the council approved.

Sorcha, Robert, Lissia, and Patrick had been talking, and now Robert stepped forward, his arms at his sides.

"Let's continue the feast tonight," Robert said graciously. "Instead of a winning team, we will celebrate everyone's talents. My brother Patrick, along with our chef, has made a barbecue suited for kings. Venison, steak, and of course, whisky!"

That got the highest round of applause yet.

"And what of Jory?" Jerry asked, his brow lifted. He'd taken a seat sometime during the discussion. He didn't seem quite as willing to let it go, probably because he'd been first by Jory's side. Paislee knew from her own experience how that marked a person.

"We'll raise the first toast tae Jory and his health," Robert said smoothly. "Let's go around tae the back of the castle—follow the scent of roasted meat!"

Finn McDonald and the dowager countess led the way. Patrick handed Cinda the reins to his horse, and he joined Lissia and the other Clan Grant band members. Cinda watched him leave, stars in her eyes.

Paislee, Brody, Wallace, and Grandpa brought up the rear as she wanted to be out of the crush. When she looked down at the bench where Jerry had been sitting, she realized that Jerry and Jory's bagpipes were gone.

"Grandpa, did you see what happened tae the bagpipes?"

"Naw. Not since Jerry saved them," Grandpa said.

She hoped they weren't lost. Besides the cost, they'd be a personal object, fitted just right for Jory. As personal as her favorite style of knitting needles but a good deal more expensive.

The smell of barbecue made her stomach rumble. Most of the time she preferred fish and vegetables to beef, but it was a treat on occasion. There was something rather primitive about meat prepared over a fire.

They followed the last of the band members to a large open-air covered area perfect for outdoor parties. It could easily seat two hundred or more with wooden tables for eating, and higher serving tables with platters of food and kegs of drinks.

Brody flicked his fingers toward his mates, all clustered together at a table. "Can I eat with them, Mum?"

Paislee checked out the situation, seeing them supervised, loosely, by other parents. "Aye. Be good. I'll keep Wallace for you."

"Why cannae he come?"

"After you finish. Wallace has a special diet that can't be ruined by fatty meat." It was bad enough that the terrier was better than a broom when it came to catching crumbs beneath the table.

"The dog has a diet," Grandpa scoffed. "Nothin' wrong with sturdy animal bones. It's guid for him."

"They can splinter and catch in his throat," Paislee cautioned.

Brody scowled, but then nodded and joined his mates. Wallace whined. Paislee patted the pup's head. "I'll make sure you get some lean pieces of venison."

Wallace lay down on the stone slab of the dining area with a whine.

"Dinnae blame ye, boy," Grandpa said. He looked at Paislee. "Ye're making the dog a sissy."

"Keeping the dog healthy," Paislee countered. She eyed the lines for food. "Why don't you go first, Grandpa? I can wait here. Unless you want me tae get both our plates?"

"I'm no bairn ye need tae coddle, lass." Grandpa straightened his tam over his silver-gray hair. "Want *me* tae get *you* a plate? Mibbe something soft, like porridge?"

Oh! That's what she got for just trying to be nice. Paislee exhaled. "No, thank you."

Grandpa returned with a paper plate piled high with meat, not a single vegetable to be seen. He sat opposite her and smacked his lips, daring her to say a word.

She kept her mouth shut. "Can you watch Wallace?"

"Aye." The dog lead was tied to the wooden bench and the pup watched her actions with a legitimate canine pout.

"Thanks." Paislee joined the end of the queue, and it was as if there hadn't been a dent in the massive platters of roasted beef or venison.

She chose several ribs and then a leaner selection with no bones for Wallace. Next, she added roasted potatoes, mushrooms, and corn. A fresh salad of tomato and herbs, and last, a bannock. She took two, knowing that Grandpa would enjoy a piece of the flatbread to sop up the juices from his carnivore feast.

On her way back to the table, she saw Brody and a group of kids all telling jokes as they ate. It made her happy to be part of this community, as he was, too.

Upon her return, Paislee noted that a woman from Clan Mac-Tavish had joined them and brought two mugs of whisky for Paislee and Grandpa.

"How sweet!" Paislee sat opposite Grandpa. Clan MacTavish took up the rest of the table. Most of the instruments had been put along the back partition wall made of lattice. Bagpipes had different kinds of cases, hard to soft, and same for the drums.

"My pleasure," the lass next to Paislee said. "I'm Nettie. Thanks for sharing your table!" Her eyes were the exact hue of her sky-blue jacket, her hair a soft brown styled to her chin.

"Paislee. Nice tae meet you." Paislee handed Grandpa a bannock. He accepted with a grin, already happy with the whisky and the company.

She bit into the tender meat, feeling Wallace's eyes on her as if he'd never had a meal in his life. She shredded the cooled leaner cuts and put them aside on an extra plate she'd grabbed for the purpose.

"Slowly! Taste it!" she said. Wallace waited until her hands were free and then dove in. It was gone in seconds, and he whined at her for more.

"He didnae savor a bite," Grandpa laughed.

"He didn't. I'm lucky tae have my fingers." When she'd bought the adorable puppy to fill the hole left by Gran's death, he'd stolen her heart with his dark eyes and soft wiry fur. She hadn't cared about the terrier's temperament. Like many human Scots, the Scottish terrier was fierce, loyal, willful, and loving. Dr. Kathleen McHenry, the veterinarian, had suggested a trainer when Wallace was at the pet clinic for eating socks the first week they'd had him.

Now, six years later, Wallace was much better behaved than many dogs and she credited that to Dr. McHenry. The lifespan for the breed was twelve to fifteen years, so long as he didn't eat any more clothes. He had a special diet to keep from gaining weight, which would hurt his short legs. Wallace was a loved member of her family.

"More whisky?" Nettie asked Grandpa and Paislee. "I'm going for a refill. I'm not driving, and the earl brews his own. Cannae get it anywhere else."

"None for me," Paislee said. She'd been so busy eating that she'd barely touched her drink. "Thanks, though."

"I'll help you," Grandpa said, getting up.

"You're a dear," Nettie said.

Her grandfather blushed.

Paislee hid her smile behind a bite of roasted mushroom. The herbs were grown in the wild as well as in the greenhouse. Maybe one day when she wasn't so busy, she could put a few pots in the back garden for some container vegetables.

When Grandpa returned, Paislee went for just a few more of the roasted veg and another bannock, perusing the tables for Brody.

Ah, he was done eating and playing a game of catch with the other kids by the barn.

It was good that he was having fun and independent. It hurt a wee bit as she realized he was loosening his attachment to her. As it should be. He was twelve now and next year he'd be a teen. Her heart ached. Trying to hold onto time was as impossible as catching rain in a sieve.

Paislee shifted with her plate. There were Lissia and Cinda, in conversation about how Patrick had excelled with the roasted meat. Cinda's eyes sparkled as she watched Patrick. At the far end of the long table, Sorcha and Robert exchanged heated words.

Clan Cunningham members sat at their own table, the director often checking his phone. Clyde was no doubt waiting for word about Jory. Was he finally worried? She didn't have a high opinion of the pipe major.

She checked her watch. It was seven in the evening. It had been three hours since Jory had collapsed to the grass.

Jerry and the other Campbell clan members were not as joyful as some of the others. Did they feel that they'd lost today by not forcing a forfeit?

Jerry saw her looking and waved, no usual smile for her as he dug into his food.

She was going to ask him what was wrong but then decided against it. A room of competitors wasn't the place for a private conversation. She trusted that he would take care of Jory's bagpipes, knowing the importance of the instrument, even if they were competitors.

Clyde's phone rang and the director answered with a loud, "Hallo?"

Clyde turned very pale. His next words were murmurs as he frowned and asked more questions. "Are ye okay?"

Clyde gulped and jumped up to the table, knees visible in his red-and-black kilt as he cleared his team's plates with an angry foot. His longish hair in the front flopped over his eye.

"What's wrong?" his bass drummer asked. The big man scowled at the meat on his shirt from Clyde, then brushed it off. "It better be guid."

"Jory Baxter is dead." Clyde pointed with fury toward Robert. "You have some explaining tae do."

Chapter 4

Paislee turned to Robert, who rose quickly from his spot at the table. Lissia and Patrick, even Sorcha, stood in unison, as a family. As a clan. They all had sable-brown hair, and green eyes that sparked with adrenaline.

"What do ye mean?" Patrick growled. He was one of the few not in a kilt but in dark denim. "The Grants arenae responsible for your boy not knowing how tae hold his pipes."

Clyde Cunningham quaked with emotion at the insult and almost slid off the table to the ground, using his phone to jab Patrick's chest. "Jory was no neophyte."

Cinda gasped, her hand to the collar of her red blouse.

Robert squared his shoulders and moved menacingly closer to the director. "Get back from my brother."

Clyde lowered the phone.

Color tinted Patrick's cheekbones. Embarrassed that Robert had intervened? Angry at Clyde? Patrick pushed the director backward. "What happened tae him?"

"He's dead, mate." Clyde stumbled into his own table and the bass drummer steadied him. "Gone."

Paislee stepped backward into a table piled with cans of Irn-Bru. She couldn't believe the handsome bagpiper was dead.

"How?" Robert asked.

"I dinnae ken." Clyde wiped his damp forehead with the back of his hand. "The lasses are a mess." He shook his phone. "They had tae leave him at the hospital and dinnae understand what happened. They were told tae go home, so they will."

Paislee recalled how fast Jory had dropped to the grass. It made no sense for a seasoned piper to run out of breath.

"Mum!" Lissia said, pointing to two police officers led by Finn McDonald. They must have parked and walked around the castle rather than drive.

Paislee didn't recognize these officers, and DI Zeffer wasn't there. She wondered if she would see him again since his business in Nairn had concluded after putting the Norwegian counterfeit ringleader in jail.

Paislee denied the tiny spark of interest in where Zeffer might be. She blamed any thrill on the fact that when they were together, there was usually danger. In spades. She'd gone out to dinner twice with Hamish McCall. They were learning to be friends again now that Brody was no longer in primary school, which was just her speed.

Sorcha turned as Finn, escorting a tall constable, called for her attention. "Constable Thorn, milady."

Dowager Countess Sorcha Grant folded her hands before her, an indomitable lady of rank. Her blazer of red, green, navy-blue, and blue tartan was like a suit of armor. "Welcome tae Ramsey Castle," she said firmly.

The constable touched the brim of his hat. "I bring news aboot Jory Baxter. He is deceased."

The dowager countess gave no indication of her feelings as she nodded. "We just heard from Clyde, the pipe major for Clan Cunningham. It's terrible."

"We have some questions," the constable said.

"Of course." Sorcha reached her arm to the side and gestured to a table away from the food and diners. "Let's sit where it's quiet."

Paislee looked for Brody, who hadn't noticed the police at the castle as he played football with his new pals.

She returned to the table with Grandpa and sank to the bench, troubled. The MacTavish clan had moved closer to the action and sat with Clan Fraser, their robin's-egg blue kilts and gray jackets melding nicely with the MacTavish colors. She couldn't help being drawn to patterns, hues, and fabrics.

"Hey." Paislee blew out a breath as she put her plate of food down.

"Did ye hear Jory's dead?" Grandpa murmured as he leaned toward her. He must have had several whiskies as his whisper boomed around her.

"I did." She pointed to the police officer talking with the dowager countess, Constable Thorn. Another was chatting with Clyde, taking notes.

"Och!" Grandpa turned back around to Paislee. "When did they arrive? Sneaky."

"An investigation," Paislee said quietly.

"Killed?" Grandpa sipped his whisky. "Poor bastard."

"Grandpa!" After a few drinks, he let curses fly like a sailor.

"What?"

"Never mind." Paislee shook her head, still in disbelief. "We only know that Jory is dead, not how, or why. I can't believe it."

"It's a shame," Grandpa said. "Jory was just mediocre. I bet a fiver that the Campbells would win, but the Grants had it in the bag. Robert was quite the star. Doesnae matter now."

She'd also thought Jory's skill on the pipes was fair. Not as good as Jerry's or Robert's, from what she could tell. "Let's not speak ill of the dead."

Grandpa nodded and wiped his beard with a napkin. Wallace got to his feet and shook his body, alert, possibly sensing the mood in the room changing. The laughter had gone, and people seemed worried.

"I'll see what's goin' on," Grandpa said. He stood and the bench shifted.

"I'll go, too." Paislee rose and realized that folks were split between watching the constable converse with the dowager countess, and the officer with the director.

"Wonder how he died, then?" Grandpa said.

"I'd like tae know. He was fine, then his face turned a bright color, then he dropped."

"And flashed his jewels tae any who were lookin'," Grandpa said piously.

Paislee bit her tongue and scooped her hand to his elbow, steadying him. "He's gone, Grandpa. Be nice."

They made their way to the long table where Patrick, Lissia, and Cinda sat. Finn hovered near the end but didn't take a seat as the dowager countess returned. Constable Thorn followed her.

"I'd like tae speak with the earl next, if I may," the constable said.

"Certainly!" The dowager countess donned a look of confusion. "Why, Robert was just here a minute ago! Patrick, do you know where your brother went?"

"I'm sure he'll be back." Patrick exuded charm as he smiled and stood. "Can I get you something tae drink, Constable?"

"No," Constable Thorn replied curtly.

Robert had been at the table seconds ago. Had the dowager countess distracted the policeman so that Robert could slip away? But why? Nothing untoward had happened—that Paislee knew of.

"We'd like tae see where the incident took place," the other officer said, Clyde at his elbow.

"Sure!" Lissia hooked arms with her mother, a unit. "Mum and I can show you."

"Thanks." Constable Thorn was polite—barely. They were investigating how Jory died and needed to collect information as well as evidence.

"I told Constable Smith here all aboot the rivalry between Robert and Jory," Clyde said, his chin raised defiantly.

"What is there tae tell?" Patrick's confident smile didn't budge and for the first time, Paislee could understand Cinda's infatuation. "It's normal in a competition for things tae get heated."

"Heated?" Constable Thorn asked.

"Not heated," Patrick retreated. "Just normal back-and-forth banter. If you're not a winner, you're a loser."

Paislee didn't care for that line of thought when it came to games.

"And Robert Grant lost," Clyde said.

"That was last year. We were going tae win today," Lissia said. "We'd *practiced* nonstop as one does tae prepare when competing."

"Nothing unusual in that," the dowager countess said. "Are you sure we cannae get you something tae drink? Water, tea?"

"Nothing," Constable Thorn said.

"Is there a monetary prize for the winner?" Constable Smith asked.

"Nominal at best." Lissia chuckled. "It's a pittance."

"It's aboot the clan pride," Clyde said.

"Jory wasnae a Cunningham, if that's the case," Patrick pointed out, his goal to needle Clyde clear.

"How did he get added tae your band, then?" Constable Thorn asked Clyde.

"We *are* Cunninghams," Clyde said. "My cousin Ewan Cunningham discovered Jory two years ago playing at a pub and invited him tae join our team. As the pipe major, I control timing as well as lead the band. The position is as important as the instruments."

"Is it?" Patrick asked, sounding doubtful.

The pipe major lifted a fist and shook it toward Patrick. "I dinnae like you. Arrogant as your brother."

"Calm doon, mate. I dinnae play in the band, so it was a serious question." Patrick turned to Lissia. "Is it?"

"Aye." Lissia gave a begrudging nod.

"My mistake." Patrick shrugged. "So. Jory wasnae a Cunningham and has no tie tae the Cunninghams. Is that against the rules?"

"It's not a hard-and-fast issue," Meri said, having overheard the question. "It's recommended for clan unity that they be family, but there is no way tae enforce that every member is a blood tie."

"I see," Constable Thorn said.

"Lissia and I will take the officers tae the field where Jory fell," the dowager countess said to Patrick. "Perhaps it's best if you stay here tae oversee our guests."

"Yeah. I'll be here," Patrick said. He turned to everyone watching, without pretense. "Eat and drink, friends. We will find oot what happened before long."

Grandpa wandered to the long table with the platters of food. "I'll be right back," Paislee told him. "I'm going tae walk Wallace and check on Brody."

"Aye. Cannae believe the kids havenae noticed the commotion," Grandpa said.

"I'm glad of it." Paislee walked Wallace across the lot to where the youth were playing. She could see the stands and the grass in the dusky evening but not clearly. It would be dark before long.

Constable Thorn seemed to be in deep discussion with Sorcha.

She was mildly surprised to see DI Zeffer's blue SUV come through the open castle gates, beyond the field of parked cars, to the barn and the outdoor area. He parked before the barn next to the police cars.

Tall lights had been placed around the open-air seating area. Paislee and Wallace quickly returned to Grandpa, who was seated at the table with a fresh tumbler of whisky, and Nettie. About half of Clan MacTavish had gotten up to chat with other band members. A member dying during a competition was an awful first.

DI Zeffer shielded his eyes and narrowed them to the table where she sat. She braced her body as if she'd been caught misbehaving.

He strode toward her and stopped abruptly. "Paislee."

"DI Zeffer!"

She wasn't sure that he'd be taking the cases around Nairn as his reason for being in Nairn was now drinking margaritas in the Keys. Wallace chuffed to see the DI. A hello?

His blue suit fit him to perfection. His eyes were the color of sea-glass green, his hair russet and shiny, kept trimmed. "I heard that you'd called in the emergency for Jory Baxter."

"I did."

"I decided tae pick up the case."

"It's a homicide, then?" Grandpa asked.

Clan MacTavish—those who'd heard Grandpa—gasped.

"No," the DI assured them, smiling his white shark's-tooth smile at them all. "It's an unusual death, which means we have protocol tae follow. Questions tae ask. Dinnae fash, now, I doot you're in danger."

Nettie blushed becomingly.

Grandpa swirled the liquid in his cup.

Paislee refrained from rolling her eyes.

"What happened tae poor Jory, then?" Nettie asked.

"We dinnae know. It's under investigation." Zeffer smoothed the lapels of his suit. The man had style no matter the emergency.

"Oh." Nettie leaned forward to smile at him, batting her lashes. The sweet lass was a bit of a flirt.

"What can you tell me aboot what happened?" Zeffer tilted his head invitingly.

"Not much," Nettie said. "We were all excited aboot performing at the castle. Everyone is always so nice. And it was thrilling tae see who would win of the top three. We arenae as experienced as the others. Just a Grade V. Amateur. The best is Grade I."

Yep, Nettie was flirting with Zeffer, all right. And Zeffer was encouraging it!

"Did you have a favorite?" Zeffer asked. "I hear the side bets are where people can make money."

"I was hoping Jory would win, actually," Nettie said.

"Is he a better piper than the others?" Zeffer asked.

"Who cares, right? He's lovely tae look at." Nettie grew serious. "Or, he was. Did he pass oot? Faint? I heard some of the others wonder if he was on drugs."

"Drugs?" Zeffer alerted like Wallace tracking the red squirrel earlier that day. So much had happened since. "Do you know what kind, if he did them?"

"No! It's just a rumor. Everyone's curious how he died, that's all," Nettie said.

Zeffer pursed his lips. "There's nothing I can tell you aboot that. Is there anything unusual you remember aboot Jory's performance today?"

"No," Clan MacTavish chorused.

"Was it as guid as last year?" Zeffer asked.

"I think so, though he didnae get a chance tae finish," Nettie said.

Another member of Clan MacTavish spoke up. "I think Clan Grant might have won. Robert went all oot."

This statement got many nods from the group.

"Thank you. If you think of something else, here is my card." Zeffer placed it on the table and Nettie snatched it up.

Zeffer moved his gaze to Paislee. "Can I talk with you a second?"

"Sure." She stood, not wanting to converse in front of his new gushing fans.

When they stepped away from the table, Wallace with Grandpa, Zeffer winked. "Miss me?"

"No," Paislee said.

"I dinnae believe you." Zeffer tucked his mobile into his slacks pocket.

"You should." Paislee sniffed. "What can I help you with?"

Zeffer slowed as they reached the end of the open-air room where the instruments had been stacked. The lattice partition acted as a wall and gave them a decent view of the crowd. "I'd like your take on what happened, since you called the emergency in. Who was there, and what they did."

Paislee nodded. "Jerry McFadden was a hero and acted right away. Jory collapsed and Jerry was prepared tae do CPR if needed."

Zeffer lost all teasing. "Who else?"

"Meri McVie, the competition judge. She asked everyone tae stay back and give Jory some air. Jerry moved Jory's bagpipes tae keep them from being trampled."

"Where are they now?" Zeffer asked.

"I don't know," Paislee said. "Jerry would make sure the instrument was safe. He told me before the competition started that Clyde Cunningham, the Clan Cunningham pipe major, had argued with Jory." She raised her hand. "I have no clue about what."

Zeffer scanned the room of musicians. "Where is he?"

"Jerry or the director? One of the other constables already talked with Clyde, anyway," Paislee said.

Zeffer crossed his arms to study her in the dim light. "Let's start with Jerry. Do you play?"

"God, no." Paislee shuddered. "You?"

"Not a note." Zeffer half-smiled. "Lead the way tae Jerry!"

Paislee maneuvered around the tables. The crowd was drinking but not eating as much, which meant that folks were loud and boisterous.

Jerry wasn't happy when Paislee arrived at the table that he shared with the nine other Clan Campbell members, and raked a hand through his hair. They were unique among the kilts as their tartan was predominantly green, blue, and black.

She noticed that the bands had stuck together during the meal with no crossover of mates sitting with a competing band.

"Hiya, Jerry," Paislee said. "Remember Detective Inspector Zeffer?"

Jerry cupped his tumbler of whisky. "Hey, DI Zeffer. How are ye?"

Zeffer nodded to those at the table, then returned his gaze to

Jerry. "I was wondering if you could tell me what happened today?"

Jerry clenched his jaw and then mumbled, "Aye."

"Should we stay?" Mattias Campbell asked. His copper hair was in all directions as if he'd been tugging at it.

"I dinnae mind if ye do," Jerry said. Clan Campbell murmured their agreement. He turned to the DI.

"You gave CPR tae Jory Baxter?" Zeffer asked.

"No. I was closest tae Jory when he fell," Jerry admitted with a shaky breath. "He never stopped breathing, but he wasnae with it, ye ken?"

"He was conscious the whole time?" Zeffer asked.

"I guess." Jerry's jaw clenched.

Zeffer pursed his lips. "Did he say anything?"

"No."

"So, Jory was just playing the bagpipes and then he passed oot," Zeffer said. "What happened tae the instrument?"

"I moved it oot of the way." Jerry scowled. "Folks were jostling around the field withoot a care. I tried tae give it tae his director, but Clyde was oblivious—on the phone." Jerry looked over his shoulder to Clyde, at the Cunningham table. "I thought he was calling for an ambulance, but Paislee did that. Why would Clyde take a call instead of check on Jory, his star piper?"

Paislee thought Jerry had an excellent point. Had he received a message? They'd all been asked to silence their cellphones for the performances.

"Where are the bagpipes now?" Zeffer asked.

"I tucked them oot of the way." Jerry hooked a thumb over his shoulder. "Clyde hasnae asked aboot them once. Not a top leader, in my opinion. Mibbe I'm being petty, with Jory dead now."

Paislee felt sorry for her friend.

"It does seem strange," Zeffer said. "Why dinnae you show me?"

"Aye." Jerry got up and frowned at Paislee as if she'd ratted him out for something. She'd have to explain that it hadn't been like that.

They walked to the corner of the area away from the fires and food where many other instruments in a variety of cases were stacked.

Jerry searched the array, then shook his head, befuddled. "It's a soft backpack style with his initials, JB, on the handle. It isnae here anymore!"

Chapter 5

"Where could the bagpipe have gone?" Paislee asked. "It's not like a flute or something small. The pipes, and the cases, are cumbersome."

Clyde joined them and narrowed his gaze. "I saw you glaring at me, Jerry. What's the problem?"

"Have you seen Jory's bagpipe?" Zeffer asked.

"No, but Ewan might have already put it on the equipment van." Clyde flopped his hair back. "Want me tae go ask?"

"You do that," Zeffer said. "But first, I have some questions for you."

"Okay?" Clyde shuffled nervously. "Dinnae ken what I can share that I havenae already told Constable Smith."

Jerry smoothed two fingers over his bushy mustache as he looked from Zeffer to Clyde. Paislee also stayed, curious as to what Zeffer, a skilled investigator, might get from Clyde.

Zeffer exuded the air of a cat toying with a mouse. "Did you know Jory long?"

"N–not really," Clyde stammered. "Well, two years. Since Ewan brought him onto the team."

"Would you consider him a guid piper?" Zeffer asked.

"Aye, the best. Better than Robert Grant, and I dinnae care

what else you hear aboot it. The two were on par in skill but Jory's youth gave him an edge." Clyde made a fist. "He had passion."

"Bollocks," Jerry said. "You're trying tae sway the DI like he hasnae any common sense. It was a competition. Robert won five years in a row, until Jory stole the win last year. This year, Robert wanted the crown back and made no bones aboot it."

"What's the prize?" Zeffer asked.

"A hundred pounds. Not much, but it's the braggin' rights, you see," Clyde said.

"Bragging rights," Zeffer repeated slowly. "Tae some folks a hundred is a lot."

"Not tae a man who owns a castle," Clyde said with derision.

"It might seem that way," Jerry countered. "These old places are a drain. That's what makes the ones still in operation so great."

"I agree, Jerry," Paislee said. "They have tae change with the times while operating on an old system that no longer serves them."

Zeffer turned to her with a smirk. "And what makes you so knowledgeable on castles?"

"The dowager countess took us on a tour," Paislee said. "She's doing her part tae modernize and will have a gift shop with things they make on the grounds for sale."

"And she just *told* you this?" Zeffer shifted his weight from one boot to the other.

"Aye." Paislee shrugged. "I'll be selling bespoke cashmere items, too."

"Hmm." Zeffer looked around the small group. "Let's stay on track, shall we? Jory just dropped on the castle lawn and died at the hospital. Did he have any enemies?"

"Besides Robert?" Clyde said.

"They werenae enemies," Jerry protested. "They were competitors. Besides, me and the whole clan saw you and Jory arguing before the day even started. Why dinnae you tell us what that was aboot?"

Clyde crossed his arms low to his hips. "Why are you on Robert Grant's side all of a sudden? Trying tae get in his guid graces?"

"I'd like to know what you and Jory were arguing aboot as well," Zeffer said. "Did you share that already with Constable Smith?"

"No." Clyde's gaze became shifty.

"Well?" Jerry prodded.

"It might have tae do with Robert Grant, and a wee side bet that Robert and Jory made," Clyde finally said.

"So?" Zeffer asked. "That's common enough."

"You're right, DI." Clyde raised his palms. "Nothing tae worry aboot." He gave Jerry a dark look.

"I consider Robert Grant a friend," Jerry said to Clyde. "But that's not what this competition is aboot. Robert and the Grant clan band were on point today. Our team made a mistake."

"Was Jory a friend?" Zeffer asked Jerry.

"Not really," Jerry said, his eye twitching.

"Was Jory a better piper than Robert?" Zeffer asked.

"No. I dinnae think so," Jerry said.

Clyde scoffed. "Easy tae say. We will never know now."

Paislee didn't trust the tension between the men from erupting into a fistfight. Clyde was a loose cannon.

Zeffer's astute gaze turned her way. "I didn't know Jory personally," Paislee said. "Lissia—Lady Lissia Grant—plays the snare drum in the band. She said that Robert practiced nonstop tae make sure he regained the title."

"Robert takes clan pride verra seriously," Jerry agreed. "But not tae the place where he was mental aboot it, you know?"

Zeffer turned back to Clyde. "Tell me again why you were arguing with Jory. Not just aboot the side bet Jory had with Robert. If there is more tae it, I *will* find oot."

Clyde clenched his jaw and indecision crossed his face. At last he said, "I think Robert accused Jory of cheating. That qualifies as mental tae me. Verra low behavior the day of the competition."

"What do you mean?" Zeffer asked.

"*Cheating?*" Jerry said at the same time as Paislee.

"Aye." Clyde braced his shoulders. "The phone call I took just as Jory fell? Well, I was talking tae a member of the GHB Competition Council tae see what the ramifications were of an accusation twelve months past." He raised both brows. "It no longer applies, and we can keep the win no matter what."

"Jory Baxter was on your team, mate," Jerry said huffily. "You'd ken if he cheated."

"I asked him," Clyde said. "That's what we were really arguing aboot, if you must know. He said not tae worry aboot it."

"Why did you think so tae begin with?" Paislee asked.

Clyde pushed his floppy hair back. "I received an anonymous letter earlier."

"I dinnae believe it," Jerry replied heatedly. "Robert wouldnae send a letter with an accusation like that. He's the kind of man tae sign his name tae something."

"Do you still have the letter?" Zeffer asked.

Clyde's mouth twisted. "It may have gotten a wee bit damp in the rain this morning—it was torrential. It wasnae readable anymore, so I threw it away. It was in my pocket."

"How can we believe you?" Paislee asked. "An accusation that you can't prove from an anonymous sender."

"I know how it sounds!" Clyde said. "I should have taken a picture of it, but, well, I wasnae expecting tae receive such an accusation, or tae be in a second downpour after already changing into dry clothes."

"I can check with the council that you called today," Zeffer said.

"No. I didnae use my real name, did I?" Clyde shrugged. "What if there was truth tae it? I know Jory wouldnae want tae give up the title. It bought his beer at the pub all last year. All of us, even. And aye, Jerry, there were times you were there."

"So?" Jerry turned pale. "I wasnae hanging oot with just Jory."

"Let me see your phone, Clyde," Zeffer said. "Incoming and outgoing calls will show the number."

Oh, yes, Paislee thought. Zeffer was quite good.

Clyde reluctantly showed Zeffer.

"Thanks," Zeffer said and copied the information down.

"Tell us what the letter said," Jerry suggested.

"Just that Jory had cheated during the competition last year and wouldnae get away with it this year," Clyde said, miserable. "I dinnae ken how he could have with everyone watching so closely. The judges. The competitors." He shook his head.

"It *would* be hard," Jerry agreed.

"What do the judges look for, exactly?" Zeffer asked.

"Tuning. Tone. Pipes and drums together with a blend of attacks and cutoffs," Jerry said.

Clyde raised a finger. "Tempo. Each band plays two sets. There must be a medley, tae prove skill in executing musicality. A tune tae show expression. No reading of music," he said. "I'm the pipe major and I didnae see anything untoward."

"I didnae notice but I wasnae looking for someone tae pull a fast one," Jerry said. "This is an honest competition and always has been. Robert wouldnae have anything tae do with an accusation like that."

"And were you going tae mention this letter, or let Jory win again this year?" Paislee asked Clyde.

"What do you mean?" Clyde shuffled back from her.

"You would lose a lot of respect in the piping community tae lead a winning piper in a competition who was caught being a cheat." Paislee didn't like cheaters.

"After twelve months, there is nothing tae be done. The title cannae be taken away." Clyde firmed his jaw. "This morning, I told Jory aboot the accusation, so he knew. He said he wasnae, and mibbe in this instance, this year, he wouldnae have, you know, if he knew someone was on tae him."

Zeffer nodded at Paislee. "Guid observation."

"Thanks."

"I'd love tae see those bagpipes," Zeffer said.

"Let me go check the van," Clyde said. He hurried away from the detective, Paislee, and Jerry.

"I'll follow him," Jerry said. "I dinnae trust the sleekit weasel." He was gone before Zeffer could say yes or no.

Paislee agreed with Jerry's assessment and faced Zeffer. "You're very good with your questions, getting Clyde tae tell you about the letter accusing Jory of cheating. Jerry'd wondered why Clyde would take a phone call at that time and was pretty upset by it. Jory's bandmates were too."

"It's odd tae care so much aboot a bagpiping competition," Zeffer said. "But I once had a case where a bloke was killed over spilled milk. There's no accounting for human behavior."

Paislee had sadly learned that the DI was right. "Do you think Jory was killed?"

Zeffer stepped away from the stacks of instruments, his air of superiority back in place. "Ha! Nice try, Paislee. Did you see anything else of note?"

"Not really." She walked at his side, her gaze automatically searching for Grandpa and Wallace at the table. Brody was still playing.

"Hmm. It's guid for you tae have your items in the castle gift shop. Very high brow," Zeffer teased.

"Thanks tae Lady Leery," Paislee said with gratitude. "She suggested it tae the dowager countess as a way tae expand their inventory, along with jams and a castle cookbook."

"You have impressive friends, Paislee. Lydia and Corbin Smythe. Shep and Blaise O'Connor. Arran and Mary Beth Mulholland. Lady Shannon Leery. And now a dowager countess."

Paislee blushed. "It's just my community. I was born and raised here, fourth generation at least." She changed the subject immediately. "You mentioned that you'd moved around?"

"Aye, after my da died my family did. I never considered settling doon." Zeffer lowered his voice. "How's your grandfather?"

"Much relieved since you found his son." They exchanged glances but didn't say the words of where Craigh Shaw was at, or why, or under what name he now lived. Some secrets were better kept close to the chest.

"That's guid."

Elbow-to-elbow, they reached the table where Grandpa sat with Clan MacTavish. Nettie had topped them all off again, bringing a jug of whisky to the table rather than the cups to the keg.

"You're driving?" Zeffer asked Paislee quietly.

"Of course," she assured him.

Zeffer checked the notes on his tablet. "Clyde talked with Constable Smith?"

"Aye." Paislee smiled at Zeffer. "You got more from Clyde."

"Smith is guid, but new. Makes him eager," Zeffer said. "He'll mellow a bit with time and experience."

Clyde raced back, Jerry on his heels, both men huffing for breath. They'd come from the field where the vehicles had been parked, which wasn't that far, so Paislee surmised the adrenaline was for another reason.

"Jory's bagpipes arenae there," Clyde panted. "Ewan just searched the entire van—he doesnae recall seeing them since Jory played today."

Jerry gulped air and bent over, hands braced on his knees.

"It was in the case?" Paislee asked. She had only seen the pipes out. The giant Cunningham bass drum player stood.

"Aye. I'd put them in myself." Jerry sipped air and slowly straightened. His large chest heaved. "I wanted tae teach Clyde a lesson."

"Misplaced?" Zeffer asked.

"Doubtful." Clyde scowled. "But we can search the stands and see if it was jostled oot of sight. I cannae think where else it might be."

"I'm telling you," Jerry said, "that I put the pipes in Jory's case and against the back wall with the other instruments."

"Let's ask right now if anybody's seen them. It's not a secret, is it, DI?" Paislee asked.

Zeffer considered this, then said, "No."

Paislee elbowed Jerry. "Make an announcement."

"Aye." Jerry whistled with two fingers in his mouth, the sound piercing. "Can I have your attention!"

"Is this aboot what happened tae Jory? Do you know?" asked

Cinda, sitting pressed with her hip next to Patrick's on a wooden bench.

"Not yet," Jerry said. "We're looking for Jory's bagpipe. I put them against the back wall, but they arenae there now."

"His bagpipe?" Patrick repeated as if not sure he'd heard right.

Paislee realized that Robert was not back yet from wherever he'd dipped off to when the police arrived. Constable Thorn wanted to speak with him and had made that clear. Would his family cover for him?

Patrick might not be wearing a kilt with the Grant tartan, but he had on a vest with the pattern, matching his mother's blazer, and his sister's kilt.

She had the feeling that they would.

"Aye," Jerry said.

"Clyde should know where they are." Cinda gestured with her mug to where Clyde stood with Jerry. "As the Cunningham Clan pipe major."

"I do not, and they arenae in the van," Clyde assured her and the rest of the avid listeners.

"That's strange," Mattias Campbell said. "I *know* Jerry had them. Tae avoid being stepped on in the field while Clyde was on the phone. Not tae be bothered with his own bandmate passed oot."

It was apparent to Paislee that Clyde did not have a lot of friends in this group. Cinda wanted it known that Clyde should have been taking care of Jory's things, and Mattias also wanted it clear that Clyde had been on the phone instead of helping his own teammate.

"That's so lucky that you thought tae do so," Paislee said.

"Yeah," Clyde said with a narrowed gaze at Jerry, "*lucky*."

Jerry puffed his broad chest at the man.

Jerry didn't like Clyde, either. Paislee hated to judge without knowing someone for herself, but if a roomful of people felt the same way, she would put up her guard.

The large bass drum player crossed his muscular arms, moving next to Clyde in a show of Cunningham Clan support. "This isnae the time tae blame anyone for misplacing them—we need tae find Jory's pipes. The man is *dead*."

"Right," Zeffer said. "Let's split up. Smith, if you will take a group of five and search the stands, I'll scout around here. Please, if you see them, call for me. Dinnae move them yourselves."

With that, Constable Smith gathered five volunteers and left the open-air eating area to search the ground around the stands. It was dark and the lighting provided wasn't that bright. The barbecue fire offered a dim glow.

"I'll help you," Paislee said.

Zeffer nodded. "I have a portable lamp in my SUV tae make this area bright as day."

"What's going on?" The dowager countess returned with Constable Thorn. "I saw Clyde and Ewan searching the Cunningham equipment van."

"Jory's bagpipes." Cinda scooted away from Patrick. "They're missing."

"That cannae be," the dowager countess said, in true confusion this time rather than the false face she'd worn previously.

"I'm afraid it's true." Zeffer shrugged. "For now. I'm DI Zeffer, milady. If I can be of any service."

He had just the right amount of respect for the title without being too rigid. He'd learned from Lady Leery that giving a little didn't mean losing control.

"Oh dear. Is it important?" Sorcha asked in a damsel-in-distress way that Paislee hadn't seen from the woman since they'd met.

"It might be," Zeffer replied smoothly. "If they dinnae turn up tonight, we'll be back tomorrow morning at first light."

Her jaw tightened.

"It's part of the investigation process," Zeffer said.

The dowager countess gave a regal sniff and turned her shoulder to Constable Thorn. "As your coworker has repeated tae me, over and over."

Paislee bit her lip to hide a laugh.

In the old days, the nobility would have separate rules and be held just a wee bit above the law. When she'd first met Zeffer, he'd been quite cool to Lady Leery. It seemed they'd each learned a little more since then.

The tall constable kept a neutral countenance as he scanned the room. "DI, I've already searched the stand where Jory was sitting with his team."

"Another look willnae hurt," Zeffer said. "And all of them, just tae mark the stands completely clear."

Constable Thorn nodded. "I've asked tae speak with Robert Grant, but he still isnae here."

"*The Earl of Lyon* retires early some nights," Patrick said.

"It has been a verra long, emotional day," Lissia agreed, adding a yawn to her statement.

Sorcha's expression was inscrutable, and Paislee admired her calm even as she wondered why they were covering for Robert.

"Mibbe tomorrow for an interview with him, as well," Zeffer suggested, catching on that Robert wouldn't be available tonight without a warrant.

"I will be oot at dawn tae hunt," Patrick said. "But back by noon."

"We wouldnae intrude, and dawn would be fine," Zeffer said. "I'm not much of a sleeper."

Patrick's eyes glittered.

"I'll go get a lamp," Constable Thorn said, backing away from them.

"Thanks," Zeffer said.

"Dawn willnae be necessary," the dowager countess demurred. Without promising that Robert would be there, she said, "I'll be home all day. Just knock and Finn or myself can escort you around the property."

Zeffer gestured to the wall of instruments. "This willnae take long."

Constable Thorn returned with a large battery-operated lamp that he switched on, showcasing the one lattice-style wall of the outdoor dining area.

Sorcha looked at Finn and said, "Perhaps it's time for the evening tae come tae an end."

With those words, the castle staff appeared from nowhere to clear plates and dishes, cups, and platters of food.

Zeffer didn't have to move the equipment as the pipers and drummers who had not already loaded their items into vehicles now grabbed them, under Zeffer's eagle eye, and departed. Paislee admired the bling and decoration on the cases, which were more personalized than the instruments themselves.

What had happened to Jory's case? She believed Jerry had put it with the others.

Jerry and Clyde were nose to nose, faces red, fists clenched. Mattias pulled them apart. "Go home, both of you. Sleep it off. Where are your pipes?"

Jerry grumbled. "Already loaded in the truck."

"Are you okay tae drive?" Mattias asked.

"Aye." With that, Jerry turned and left.

Clyde held up his hands and backed out of the dining area. "I'm going. Ewan's driving. God, Mattias, you're worse than an old granny."

Mattias gritted his teeth but didn't comment. The Campbell pipe major thanked Patrick, Lissia, and Sorcha for the event and left.

Paislee said her goodbyes and gathered Brody, Wallace, and Grandpa. Zeffer walked with them toward Paislee's Juke. "No bagpipes—if you think of where they might be, give me a call, would you?"

"Sure." Paislee shouldered her handbag, pulling her car keys from the side pocket.

"What do you know of Jerry McFadden?" Zeffer asked.

"He's a good guy. Delivers my yarn and has for years. Why?"

Zeffer didn't answer but melted back when they reached the car with a wave of his fingers. "Drive home safe, Shaw family."

"What's he want?" Brody asked warily once Zeffer was gone.

Paislee couldn't blame her son for being cautious around the detective inspector, who usually meant some sort of trouble. "He has questions about what happened tae Jory."

"The piper who went tae the hospital?" Brody's grip on Wallace's lead was firm as the hounds bayed in the night.

How was it possible Brody hadn't heard of Jory's death? Well, playing football with his mates, that's how.

"Uh. He died, love." Paislee unlocked the car but watched her son's face to see how he reacted to the news.

"What?" Disbelief crossed his young features. "No way!"

Wallace stopped and got up on his back legs to lean on Brody's calves, as if to see for himself if his boy was okay.

"It was an accident of some kind, but the DI will get it sorted." Brody patted Wallace's furry head. "I heard Jory passed oot but was fine."

"We thought that at first, too."

"And then . . ." Grandpa sliced his finger across his throat.

"Grandpa!" Paislee said.

"Sairy." Angus shrugged apologetically.

"It's not a laughing matter," Paislee said sternly, "or something tae make jokes about."

"Okay. I wasnae, anyway." Brody glared at his grandfather.

"I said I was sairy!" Grandpa sounded like Brody as a wean. Heaven help her if he regressed as Brody progressed.

"Let's all get in the car." She opened the back hatch but then shut it. The boxes for the gift shop had already been unloaded.

"Will the accident be in the paper tomorrow?" Brody asked.

Paislee got into the driver's seat and peered around to the back. Sunday's morning paper was full of news for Grandpa and Brody liked the comics. She was all about the sales. "I don't know. Why?"

"Well, it's a bad thing that happened but I'm supposed tae do a report on what we did over the weekend."

"Maybe you should focus on making new friends instead of Jory Baxter," Paislee suggested.

"It's more interesting than football."

"Death?"

"Aye."

Brody hadn't been watching the bands play, so hadn't seen Jory on the ground. Hearing about a death was less traumatic than seeing one.

She had the misfortune to know. "We'll talk about it in the morning."

"Mum! We all know that means *no*."

Chapter 6

Sunday morning in the Shaw house had changed since Grandpa had joined them. Paislee still made a big, hearty breakfast with Lorne sausage, but now she had someone to share the tea with; to discuss the news in the paper with.

Brody carefully spread orange marmalade on his toast. As much as she loved every second of Brody's boyhood, he wasn't much of a conversationalist—yet.

"More tea?" she asked Grandpa as she got up to refill her own mug.

"No, thanks," Grandpa said, not lowering the paper.

Now that Brody was twelve and in S1, she could see his quick wit and intelligence. Not that he was the smartest in the class, but she didn't see that as a setback.

Brody was thoughtful and kind. He played football well, and he still loved comics. Edwyn Maclean remained his best mate. Jenni was a friend and not a girlfriend, which was also fine.

School was mandatory until the age of sixteen, but more and more kids were sticking around for the education of S5 or higher (*Why not?* her gran had said to her), which prepared them for university outside of Scotland.

Depending on the hour, Brody's thoughts for his future changed.

A doctor, an astronaut, a footballer, or a race car driver. A drummer. He was clear that he didn't want to own a yarn shop, though he said it was fine for her. Not a teacher, either, like Mrs. Martin or Headmaster McCall.

The two times she and Hamish had gone out for dinner, Brody had been at Edwyn's overnight. Avoidance was easier than trying to explain.

Grandpa teased her and Lydia steered her toward new clothes that didn't scream *mum*. She *liked* being a mum, but understood what Lydia meant. Her best friend was beyond beautiful, and a loving, married woman now.

"Can I have the home adverts?" Paislee asked.

"Aye." Grandpa slid them across to Paislee and she scanned them as she ate a bite of sausage. "Lydia having any luck?"

"There's a place Lydia wants tae show me, so I'm hopeful."

Lydia had married Corbin Smythe and now both were hyphenated as the Barron-Smythes. She didn't want children of her own and spoiled Brody. Corbin was content with his army of Smythe nieces and nephews.

Lydia sold real estate and was the best estate agent around. Despite that, she and Corbin couldn't make a decision on a new home together and were "cramped" in Lydia's three-bed flat overlooking the Moray Firth.

Corbin wasn't complaining exactly but he'd made a few remarks about wanting his own office within the apartment. Lydia had offered to share but they didn't have the same design taste. He owned a successful tech business and rented a small office space, but since he'd already sold his home to buy a shared one, he was feeling the lack of privacy.

The difficulty in finding a new home was because Corbin had grown up loaded. Lydia hadn't but had worked hard for her money and was also rich. They couldn't agree on a combined house. She wanted three bedrooms, he wanted four. There were times as she listened to them get heated that Paislee was glad to be unmarried. The mistakes she made (while plenty) were her own.

Paislee eyed Brody over her big mug that said I <3 MUM on the side, a gift from Brody for her last year's birthday. This November, she'd be the big thirty. Lydia wanted to throw her a party, but Paislee was resistant.

"So. Any thoughts on how we should spend our Sunday Funday?"

Brody concentrated on a second helping of eggs and potatoes, snagging another piece of sausage. And toast. And orange marmalade, his favorite.

"I dunno. Edwyn has tae be with his dad for a comic book convention in Edinburgh. I think it sounds fun, but Edwyn says it's dull as mud."

"A comic book convention?" Grandpa lowered the business section of the paper he'd been reading. "Hmm. Is that where you get tae meet the comic book characters?"

"Is it?" Brody looked stricken. "I wanna go! Can we?"

"Maybe it's not that," Paislee said. Edinburgh was over three hours away and the Juke needed a tune-up. "I think Edwyn would have told you, right?"

"Yeah. I'll text him, though. He might not have known."

Paislee had acquiesced to a penknife for Brody's P7 graduation, which he loved. She and Grandpa had picked out a top-of-the-line model and had it engraved. She'd also said yes to a shared mobile since when Brody was gone, she wanted him to be able to call her. It wasn't the top of the line, but Brody was still glad to use it. Grandpa shared with him, not caring about a mobile. It was kept near the landline to be charged and not allowed upstairs at night.

"After breakfast," Paislee instructed. "And it's your turn for the dishes."

"All right," Brody grumbled, but there wasn't much heat.

"So. I know you have a paper tae write. How long will it take you? Should you get that out of the way before we go do something?"

At that, her son deflated over the table as if she'd stuck him with a pin and he was a balloon. "Mum! That's the worst."

Grandpa chuckled. "Mibbe you should be an actor."

Brody slowly straightened. "Naw. I want tae be a football star. Just like Patterson!" The young up-and-coming footballer Nathan Patterson had just signed with Everton, as a right-back, and it was all Brody could talk about.

"Let's concentrate on getting through today first." Paislee sipped her tea, content.

Brody sighed. "I can do my homework in an hour," he decided.

If he said an hour, Paislee allotted two. "What will you do it on?"

"Is that dead piper in the paper?" He'd been reading the comics. Brody enjoyed "The Broons" as much as she and Grandpa did.

"As a matter of fact," Grandpa said, "Jory did make this issue."

Paislee exchanged her mug for her fork and scooped eggs. "What does it say?"

Grandpa passed it over to Brody. "Why not read it aloud tae all of us?"

"All right." Brody nibbled his bottom lip as he concentrated.

Paislee smiled at her grandfather. Wily as a fox as he helped Brody with his reading and comprehension. They would talk about the article afterward.

"'Jory Baxter, age thirty-two, died at Ramsey Castle during the annual piping event on castle grounds. He was last year's champion, and many believed he was sure tae win this year as well. He has no kin in the area. His bandmates hope tae hold a mem . . . memorial service of some sort tae invite the bagpiping community.'" Brody looked up from the paper with dismay. "Do we have tae go?"

"Oh, no, I don't think so." Paislee had been to far too many funerals.

"Does it say how he died?" Grandpa asked.

Brody read the paragraphs next to a picture of Jory with the two snare drummers he'd been friends with to himself and shook his head. "No."

"Does it say when they might have the memorial?" Paislee asked.

"It doesnae give a date," Brody said with more confidence.

Paislee lowered her mug. "Is there anything you can use for a report?"

Brody scratched his nose. "It's too sad. No family, and no reason for him tae kick the bucket. I'd rather go fishin' and write aboot that, later."

Paislee smiled. It was true that Brody was putting off the assignment, but it showed a caring heart and that she very much approved.

Grandpa did, too. "Guid choice, lad."

Within an hour they'd finished breakfast, fed Wallace, and done the dishes. Paislee may have helped a wee bit with a rinse so that Brody could change his clothes for fishing.

Grandpa dried them and Paislee put them away in the cupboard. Paislee had made a rule of no mobile phones while they were eating at the table to keep a semblance of family time. She'd read it in a magazine of Lydia's and liked the idea.

"So. Fishing." Paislee shook her head.

"I know it's not yer favorite, lass, but you're a guid sport aboot it."

"I'd rather he be outdoors and active than worry about Jory's death. Do you think Zeffer has it solved yet?"

"Naw," Grandpa said. "It would be in the paper if he had."

"You're right."

By the time they'd finished in the kitchen, Brody rushed down the stairs, phone in hand. "Mum! Edwyn says they can leave me a ticket at the door! They get tae meet Ant-Man!"

As much as Paislee wanted to say yes, she knew Brody had homework. He tended to procrastinate when it came to doing his school papers.

He saw the look on her face and scowled. "Mum. I want tae go."

"You know what I'm going tae say." Paislee hardened her heart to his pleas. "When are they coming home? Edwyn has school, too."

"He already did his assignment," Brody said with a pout.

"Well." She felt like a heel, saying no. This might be a good time to give a lesson on procrastination. "Edwyn completed his work."

"It's a three-and-a-half-hour drive tae Edinburgh," Grandpa said. "There and back will be late."

"Aye. I know." Brody brightened. "I could do it in the car! If I write aboot Ant-Man, I'd get a top mark for sure."

Paislee thought of the check-engine light in the Juke. "I'm sorry, love. I just don't trust the car right now tae go that far."

Brody bit his lip and dragged himself woefully up the stairs, carrying all the worries in the world behind him. Wallace barked at her and then joined Brody.

"Well, that was awful," Paislee said. "Why didn't Edwyn invite him earlier? Then we could have planned for it, and he wouldn't have tae be disappointed."

"Because he's twelve?" Grandpa replied.

Paislee blinked tears from her eyes. "I feel terrible. Brody loves Ant-Man."

"It's the right thing, lass," Grandpa said. "We can still go tae the river and fish, and mibbe ice cream wouldnae be amiss?"

"Not a bad plan." Ice cream was something guaranteed to bring Brody out from a blue mood. That and pizza with extra cheese. He'd outgrown his love for cheese sandwiches.

A few minutes later, Brody came downstairs, cheeks red but his shoulders up. Wallace trotted at his side. "Mum, Edwyn said he'd get me an autographed poster, so that's okay, and then next time it willnae be last minute."

"Oh, brilliant." Her heart lightened.

Wallace scratched at the back door and Paislee let the pup out to chase birds and butterflies while marking his territory.

"That red squirrel yesterday was funny," Brody said, watching Wallace run. "He didnae want Wallace tae find his stash of food."

"I've never seen one with such attitude," Paislee agreed. "Maybe you could write about that?"

Brody frowned. "I'd rather go fishing and catch a gigantic trout. When me and Grandpa went last time, we didnae get anythin'."

In other words, not write the paper. Oh well, she'd already said yes. "Some days are like that."

"You gotta be patient," Grandpa said. "And you were. Today mibbe we'll catch two."

Brody laughed, good humor restored, and she hadn't had to resort to ice cream at all.

After a fun day on the River Nairn, the Shaws returned home with three large fish that Grandpa would filet and bread for fish and chips. Paislee was on potato-peeling duty.

Lydia called to check in about Jory and the event at Ramsey Castle, and the sad death of the piper. After covering the phone with her palm, Paislee asked Grandpa and Brody if she could invite Lydia and Corbin.

"Aye!" they both said. Lydia and Corbin were very well loved.

Paislee extended the invitation for a fresh-catch dinner. "If you want tae," she said. "We have plenty."

Lydia muted her phone and returned within a minute. "Corbin says yes. Didnae even think twice. I can bake like a dream but my cheffing leaves a little tae be desired."

"I think you cook just fine," Paislee said. "You're like me and do the basics. Grandpa takes it tae the next level."

She hadn't touched a fishing pole, but Brody and Wallace were covered in mud. She sent Brody up to shower and Wallace to the back garden where he would roll around in the grass. He had an appointment at the groomer next week, as she didn't dare tackle his wiry fur herself. She kept his coat short to avoid knots.

"How can I help?" Paislee asked her grandfather.

"Add another two potatoes for five total," Grandpa said, "and I'll do the filets."

Lydia and Corbin arrived within thirty minutes, bringing a bottle of Riesling from their honeymoon trip in Germany. The gorgeous couple radiated joy.

"Thanks for the invite!" Lydia said, kissing Paislee's cheek, then Grandpa's. Lydia had kept her longer curls a shade of caramel, her gray eyes lined expertly. She and Corbin wore matching denim jackets.

Paislee heard Brody's loud music over the gurgle of the pipes and the hair dryer, glad she didn't have a castle to heat but a cozy home. At least the energy bills were manageable.

"Hi! We brought another we really enjoyed." Corbin placed the tall bottle on the round table.

"Yum." Corbin and Lydia had spent two full weeks away and been home around a month or so. "I've loved everything so far." There'd been an oaky chardonnay, a tart pinot grigio, and now this sweet Riesling. Paislee was getting a German wine education without ever leaving Nairn.

"No offense, but I prefer me whisky." Grandpa went to the cupboard, reaching for the appropriate glasses. "Who will join me?"

"I'll take a whisky," Corbin said. "What smells so good?"

"It's the curry in the batter for the fish. Smoked paprika. A hint of pepper." Grandpa brought two tumblers to the table. "Paislee did the chips with ground sea salt and a touch of onion powder."

"Fancy." Lydia tapped his arm.

"Ta, Lydia," Grandpa said.

Paislee knew of all her friends, Lydia was his favorite.

Lydia was her favorite, too. Like Edwyn and Brody, they'd been fast friends since primary. She hoped that Brody and Edwyn would remain as close. There was something to be said for a mate who knew all of your secrets and loved you anyway.

Brody skipped the stairs as he raced down. "Aunt Lydia!" He

smelled of citrus shampoo as he clasped Lydia with a hug. He adored her, and Corbin. "Hi, Uncle Corbin."

"Hey, sport." Corbin pulled a packet of trading cards from the latest video game Brody was crazy about from his back pocket. "Guess what I found?"

"Thanks!" Brody said. "Do you have this game?"

"No," Corbin said. "But my nephews rave on aboot it. Swear it's the best ever. Should we check them oot?"

Brody and Corbin went to the couch in the living area with the TV and several armchairs along with a fireplace.

"Just a few minutes, eh?" Paislee wasn't houseproud and dreamed of a stainless-steel kitchen one day, but was grateful for this roof over their heads, thanks to inheriting it from her granny.

The fivesome sat at the table to eat. The fish tasted divine with Grandpa's spices and a homemade dipping sauce he'd just "whipped up."

"Delicious," Corbin decreed. "You could bottle this and sell it. Make a bloody fortune."

"You could." Paislee grinned at her grandpa. "Want tae be an entrepreneur? Maybe we could get it sold at Ramsey Castle."

"Listen tae them go on," Lydia said. "Hanging oot at the castle. And how was Sorcha?"

"Listen tae *you*, how was Sorcha?" Paislee laughed. "Dowager Countess Grant is quite the character."

"But she said Mum, me, and Grandpa could call her Sorcha, too," Brody said, eating a chip swiped in sauce.

"Oot of the mouths of babes." Corbin chuckled at Lydia's crestfallen expression. "You're still special, Lydia my sweet."

"She is amazingly generous with various charities and invites *everyone* tae be a little free with her name," Lydia admitted with a self-deprecating snicker.

"Brody chose wisely and did not take her up on the offer," Paislee remarked. "I was so proud I almost floated out of the gift shop."

"And how did it go?" Lydia demanded. "Sorcha must've been gobsmacked by the array of quality items you brought."

"She did like them, but . . ." Paislee wiped her fingers on a napkin.

"But?" Lydia sipped her wine.

"The new merchandise pales when you consider what happened tae Jory. Zeffer was there and asking questions."

Lydia's hold on the wineglass stem tightened. "Does that mean Jory was"—she gulped and mouthed over Brody's bent head—"killed?"

Chapter 7

"Jory's death is under investigation," Paislee murmured to Lydia before she and Corbin went home. Monday was a workday for them all, so they didn't stay late. "Zeffer went tae the castle today tae search for Jory's bagpipes, but I haven't heard anything."

"I wonder how Sorcha and the Grants will handle that?" Lydia chuckled. "Then again, the DI can hold his own."

They'd seen him get cases closed despite many obstacles. With her uncle Craigh's situation, he'd played the long game for years to catch the bad guy.

"That he can," Paislee agreed.

"Any chance you might sneak away from the shop tomorrow afternoon? Tae see a possible house." Lydia tucked a curl behind her ear, diamonds flashing from the lobe.

"I think so," Paislee said. Grandpa would be in at noon.

"Guid. After all the ones we've considered, this is a real contender. Corbin doesnae hate it, and neither do I." Lydia shrugged.

"Shouldn't you love it when you spend a wee fortune?" Paislee asked from the front stoop. The night air was cooler and had a hint of fall.

"Funny lass," Lydia said. She fluttered her fingers and followed Corbin outside to their car. Today, they were driving Corbin's latest toy, a silver SUV that could pose as a tank, if a tank had a leather interior and heated seats.

Paislee, grinning, shut the door and joined her family. Just as she was congratulating herself on a full day over with no major mishaps, she recalled Brody's assignment. He was watching a program and petting Wallace.

"Brody, love, come away from the telly and get your assignment done for tomorrow."

Brody blew out a breath but grabbed his backpack and a pen and paper. "I'd rather do it on the computer," he complained. "It's faster."

"Sorry. You must follow the directions tae the letter. Longhand, full page, proper paragraphs, and punctuation. Points off for any mistake. Do you remember that Gran taught English? We can't let her down."

"Agnes was the cutest teacher ever," Grandpa remarked. "All the students adored her."

"I dinnae adore my teacher, Mr. Hughes," Brody said with gusto.

"I suppose you dinnae." Grandpa poured himself a cup of tea. "Paislee?"

"I'm fine, thanks." Paislee was quite full after their dinner. She went to the basket of laundry and started to fold at the table as Brody worked. The kitchen was the heart of this home, and always had been. *Thank you, Gran. Things just couldn't be better.*

Tuesday, Paislee woke up to a good morning text from Hamish, wondering about dinner Friday or Saturday. He'd agreed with her to go slow and learn to be friends. Her priority would always be Brody.

Edwyn would be at her place Friday, there was a football game Saturday, and Brody would be at Edwyn's Saturday night. She'd call Hamish later. She scanned the pages of the paper but there was no further news about Jory Baxter's death.

Yesterday, Lydia had shown Paislee the house, which was perfect in every single way. An old home on the Firth with a view of the water, all remodeled and new. Old, for Corbin, new, for Lydia. Two large offices of equal size, three bedrooms. The master suite was luxury defined.

The garden had every variety of flowers. The couple who wanted to sell the house had given Lydia the name of the gardener and the housekeeper if Lydia was interested in keeping them on.

Lydia hemmed and hawed until Paislee had grabbed her by the shoulders and demanded to know what could possibly be wrong with the gorgeous home. Lydia had agreed that there wasn't anything and put in an offer.

They were discussing now whether to sell Lydia's flat or keep it as a rental income. Corbin thought it would be fair for her to sell it as he'd sold his, but Lydia, very savvy with her money, thought it might be best to keep the place and make it pay not only for itself but for other property down the line.

"And what are you going tae do with your day off today, Grandpa?" Paislee asked over breakfast of Weetabix and toast.

"Not a bloody thing," Grandpa said, stretching his arm out and shaking the pages of the paper in his hand.

Brody snickered. "Money for the swear jar!"

"Father Dixon has loved the donations since you've moved in, Grandpa," Paislee said, laughing.

"Agnes was a stickler for language at that." Grandpa shrugged. "I'll do it later, lad, just tae make sure I dinnae make any other mistakes today. You got your paper turned in all right?"

"Aye. Mr. Hughes knows that fishing spot himself and was impressed that we caught three on Sunday."

"Mr. Hughes doesnae sound so bad," Grandpa said.

"He's all right." Brody finished his cereal and "accidentally" dropped a piece of toast to Wallace on the floor beneath his chair.

The pup licked it up in the blink of an eye.

The clock ticked half past eight and school started at nine. The drive to secondary took an extra five minutes for fifteen, and Brody had to be in class at nine, or was considered tardy.

"We've got tae go, Brody, love."

He pushed his chair back. "I'm ready."

"Upstairs, please—wash the crumbs off your hands and face. Your teachers will think you're a vagabond."

"A what?"

"Like nobody cares."

"You dinnae have tae care so much, Mum."

"Now!" She pointed to the ceiling.

He raced up the stairs. Water screeched in the pipes as he turned on the tap in the sink.

"That sounds terrible," Paislee said.

"Those pipes are old," Grandpa said. "Old but sturdy."

"I don't have time tae worry about them. The Juke is due for maintenance and Eddy warned me that the brake pads are worn."

"I can take a gander," Grandpa offered.

Paislee didn't want her elderly grandfather changing brake pads. "It's okay, Grandpa. I have a budget."

Everything was on a budget—groceries, taxes, car maintenance, rent on Cashmere Crush, her shop on Market Street. Since the fiasco a while back, Lady Shannon Leery had promised that the rents wouldn't increase drastically.

Her son, Shawn Marcus, suffered from liver disease and had needed a transplant. He was now in recovery and dating Margot, the manager of the med center on their little block.

Paislee couldn't see it, as Margot was both beautiful and smart and Shawn neither, but to each their own.

Brody came downstairs and let Wallace out.

"Dinnae fash aboot the dishes. I'll do them," Grandpa said. "After I'm done with the paper. I'll let the dog in, too."

"Thank you!" Brody and Paislee said.

Grandpa might have his quirks, like folding the paper in three rather than rolling it back up again, but Paislee didn't care when compared to all the help he gave her.

He cooked, cleaned, and was companionship. He was also friends with James Young, who ran the leather shop next to Paislee's place. The pair hung out at the pub for darts or billiards and talked about the good old days.

Paislee dropped Brody off at school, knowing better than to offer a kiss or a hug or any visible gesture that would embarrass him. "Love you!"

"You, too," Brody said as he dashed from the car to the school. He had several friends waiting for him; one was Jenni. So sweet.

Paislee arrived at Cashmere Crush twenty minutes later. Tuesday was yarn delivery day and Jerry was already there, so she parked next to his truck.

He didn't seem happy as he glared at her through the windshield. She climbed the steps to the back door of Cashmere Crush. Trepidation filled her.

What could Jerry possibly be angry about? Jory had died on Saturday and there was no news, which she took as a good sign. Yet . . .

She hadn't heard a peep from Zeffer—not a surprise—and there'd been nothing in the paper, so she'd assumed things were progressing. Not all investigations led to a conclusion of murder. Sometimes awful accidents happened.

"Jerry!"

The burly man got out of the delivery truck, his mustache quivering. "Paislee. I'd like a word with you."

"Sure!"

He stalked toward her.

She could see he was angry, but she didn't feel fear. This was *Jerry*, for heaven's sake. "What about?"

"That bastard, Jory Baxter."

"Oh! Want tae come inside?"

"I suppose we'd better or it will be all over Nairn that you and I had a row."

Paislee unlocked the door. It was true that in small towns like this everyone knew everyone else's business. "Welcome."

Jerry followed her inside and she shut the door, then flipped on the overhead lights. Cashmere Crush smelled like wool and instantly comforted her. This was her livelihood. Because of Gran's encouragement, she was able to support herself and Brody even after Gran was gone.

And now Grandpa, too.

The pretty polished cement floor was easy to clean, the shelves for storage in the back full and organized. Paislee passed the small loo, armchair, and telly, until she reached the long counter with her register. Tossing her purse to the lower shelf, she folded her hands before her and smiled at Jerry.

He didn't smile back.

"What could be so bad?" Paislee tilted her head. "Aren't you always going on about it being a bonnie day?"

"Aye." Jerry's cheeks turned red beneath her gaze. "It's Zeffer."

"What about him?"

"He's like a tick on a sheep and willnae leave me alone."

Paislee sucked in a laugh so as not to hurt Jerry's feelings, but that was pretty accurate about Zeffer's ability to stick to things. "All right. Why?"

"He seems tae think I know more aboot what happened tae Jory and Jory's bagpipes than I'm saying and it isnae true." Jerry scraped his chin with rough, workman's fingers—no beard despite the thick mustache.

"I believe you." Paislee raised her hand in a calming gesture. "I was there." Jory had dropped, dead weight, and his pipes had hit the grass. Jerry had jostled them, and they'd squealed, so he'd moved them to the first bench of the stands for safety.

"Well, tell that tae the DI," Jerry said. "He's hounding me."

"How so?"

Jerry exhaled at finally being able to talk to her about what he perceived as a grievance that could be laid at her feet. "Why did you tell him that I was the one tae reach Jory first?"

"Zeffer asked!" Paislee shrugged. "It's not a secret, and you did a good thing. I told him you acted like a hero."

"I regret it!"

"How can you?" She shook her head.

"Something is up with how Jory died, and Zeffer wants tae blame it on me," Jerry said. "I dinnae ken anything!"

"What questions did he ask?" Paislee figured this might help her discover what Zeffer was after.

"He wants tae know if Jory was awake at all. Wants tae know why I picked up the blasted pipes. Keeps asking aboot Clyde being on the phone and the timing of everything."

A knock sounded on her front door. It was nine thirty, and she was usually open by now. "Hang on, Jerry. Let me get this."

He fumed but understood that this was her business. "Fine. I'll go get the yarn."

They each split in a different direction.

Paislee opened the door to see Elspeth Booth. Seventy-two, retired, with white hair and a love for needlepoint, she'd probably just dropped off Susan, her blind younger sister, at Margot's clinic. Susan answered the phones and dictated notes for Margot.

"Morning! Come in," Paislee said.

Elspeth entered ten steps' worth, then wrung her hands. "Susan wants a service dog. It's probably a guid idea and Margot is going tae help her since *my* help is the last thing Susan wants." She sighed, equal parts hurt and angry.

Susan resented needing another person and so the sisters grated, though they loved one another. Macular degeneration had stolen Susan's sight.

"What do *you* think?" Paislee asked. "Wallace filled a hole in our lives for us."

"I would do anything tae make Susan's life easier." Elspeth raised a hand to Jerry as he entered the back door. "Jerry."

"Elspeth. How are ye the day?" Jerry asked around the boxes he carried.

"Could be better. Anyway, I'm off tae walk the beach, but I just had tae vent." Elspeth headed out as quickly as she'd arrived. "See you at noon!"

With that, her part-timer left, and Paislee turned to Jerry as he placed two boxes on the counter: one of beige that she couldn't keep in stock, and another of dark brown and sage.

"Thanks." Paislee went to her register and wrote a check for the amount. "This looks lovely as usual. Now, where were we? Zeffer: 'a tick on a sheep.'" She couldn't wait to share that with Grandpa.

"Aye. I'm tempted tae drop in tae say hello tae Robert and search the castle grounds myself. Those pipes must be somewhere. Zeffer and his team didnae find anything. I spoke with Ewan last night at the pub. He said Constables Thorn and Smith combed through the Cunningham clan equipment van and interviewed each of the band members tae see if they had it by mistake."

"What about the lasses who went tae pick Jory up?" Paislee thought of how they'd called the pipe major out. "They were sure mad at Clyde."

"Ewan said everyone." Jerry slumped against the counter.

"I'm sorry."

"I'm sairy, too." Jerry smacked his palm to his chest, then pointed at her. "You have tae get me oot of this mess."

"*Me?*" Paislee couldn't be more surprised at his demand.

"Aye."

The day's first customer walked in. "Morning!"

"Good morning," Paislee said.

"I'll just browse," the customer said. "I love the colors of yarn in the window. Like a rainbow."

"No rush at all." Paislee wasn't the kind of salesperson to haunt a body who wanted to shop and take their time.

"There's nothin' in the paper," Jerry said, "since Sunday. How can there not be any new discovery tae report?"

"Investigations take time." Paislee wanted to comfort Jerry, but she knew nothing about Jory, or bagpipes.

"There's something else," Jerry said.

"What?" She listened to Jerry with one eye on the customer, who was feeling the various skeins: merino wool, cotton, alpaca, a blend of the natural fibers. Cashmere. She didn't sell acrylic. Her yarn had several thicknesses and textures, and of course she had every size knitting needle in stock.

"I've heard the rumor that Jory was cheating from more than one source," Jerry said loudly, to get her complete attention.

Paislee shifted toward him. "Zeffer knows this?"

"Aye. I was happy tae give him somewhere besides me tae look," Jerry admitted. "Not proud of it, but he's breathing doon my neck like a dragon."

He rubbed his nape.

"How is it possible tae cheat on the pipes?" Paislee wondered, not for the first time.

"Morally? Physically?"

"I'll leave the moral aspects tae the Above." Paislee eyed the ceiling. "Physically."

"I didnae see it, and neither did Ewan, but I'll ask around," Jerry said. "Find oot if there's a way."

Another customer walked in. The first woman brought six skeins of beige and a pattern book to the counter.

Jerry huffed.

"Stay in touch," Paislee said. "I have tae go." Business was very, very good, especially considering that it was almost the end of summer.

With a twitch of his mustache, Jerry conceded. "No wonder ye need a muckle of yarn."

Chapter 8

Thursday morning, the Juke took several tries before the engine caught. Once her pulse settled to normal, Paislee told Brody to remind her to make an appointment with Eddy for the car tune-up she'd been putting off.

It used to be she had no money or time, and now she had a wee bit of each, but it wasn't grand. She had to take care of her things to make them last. And she still hadn't confirmed with Hamish about Saturday night.

She was so distracted that Brody poked her arm and laughed. "Mum, you're driving tae Fordythe!"

"Och!" She tightened her grip on the steering wheel and banished Hamish. "Sorry. You can't be late—you'll have tae run inside like you're heading tae the goal line. We can't be tardy, ever."

"You're driving," Brody said righteously. "Want tae teach me?"

"Not until you're sixteen, and only after passing driving classes. You have tae earn the money for them. There won't be a free ride, laddie."

She was firm on that. Her folks had been the same. It taught responsibility, to her way of thinking. If you paid for something yourself, it had more value to you. Her first car had been barely legal with no fancy extras, but it had been freedom.

"I know, I know."

Paislee headed toward Brody's correct school. "I saw Jenni yesterday," she said casually.

"We're friends," Brody said. "We might date someday, but there's no pressure tae rush things. She wants tae go tae university in Edinburgh."

"She does?" Paislee asked. That might be a friendship worth fostering, her thoughts about Jenni warming.

"Aye. Tae be a fashion designer."

Or not. Well, this was the time to encourage dreams before the hard knocks in life came calling. Once one had a steady gig to pay the bills, then dream away.

"That's nice." Paislee turned into the school lot. "Here we are."

"Bye, Mum. Try not tae get lost on the way tae the shop."

"Smart alec."

Brody slammed the door with a grin. How could she be mad?

Paislee, with a teeny bit more concentration, drove to Cashmere Crush. Once inside, she unlocked the doors for business.

The steady increase allowed for three part-time employees: her grandfather, twenty hours a week; Elspeth, twelve; and Amelia Henry on Saturdays. Amelia also worked at the Nairn Police Station as a receptionist. They were good friends who all knitted—except for Grandpa, who thought that men knitting made them sissies.

She'd once pointed out that actor Ewan McGregor knitted to relax, but he called it a publicity stunt. When she'd discovered an article about how men used to be the ones to knit in Scotland, Grandpa said, "Thank heaven for modern times." She thought he was joking but it was hard to tell.

Bottom line? Grandpa refused to learn and would rather fish.

Paislee checked her website, happy that a gansey jumper order had come in overnight. The woman requested a size large for her husband, who would wear it sailing, so it needed to be weatherproof. His build was slim.

Gansey sweaters had no seams and were all in one piece. The customer requested a stitch pattern, which she enjoyed. Paislee said a quick prayer of thanks, thinking of Gran, and chose a dark blue merino wool. The durable yarn was water repellent, and the moisture-wicking properties meant it offered good insulation.

Just as she was getting started, the door opened. Paislee glanced at the time. Eleven. Grandpa would be here today at noon. The tourists would slow now until the holidays so he wouldn't need to work as hard, or at all, if he didn't want to.

He said he enjoyed it, and she wouldn't complain. He was good with customers—especially the female ones.

Lady Shannon Leery entered the shop and Paislee lowered the yarn with a welcoming smile. Shannon was a lovely woman in her seventies with a youthful face and a styled blond bob at her chin.

Paislee'd initially had no idea that her landlord, Shawn Marcus, was Lady Leery's son. Well over a year ago, he'd threatened to sell the shops on Market Street, breaking their prized leases, without his mother's knowledge—but that was in the past and she was willing to move forward. Gavin Thornton—originally Lady Leery's accountant, now her husband—had ensured Paislee and the others were protected from that happening again.

An ice cream shop was scheduled to open on the opposite corner of Paislee's place. She couldn't wait to welcome them to the block. Next to her was James Young, who specialized in leather repair, then Ned at the dry cleaners, Margot at the med center, and Jimmy and Lourdes at the office supply store. Lourdes managed the business while Jimmy ran an adult daycare from their home. The ice cream place would be perfect where the bakery used to be that had sold the most delicious raspberry scones.

Last she'd heard, Theadora Barr had left Scotland for France. Paislee wished her well.

Behind Shannon was the dowager countess, Sorcha Grant.

Her stomach tightened. Why would both noble ladies be in her small shop? She smiled past the butterflies doing cannonballs in her belly. "And tae what do I owe the honor? It's my lucky day!" Paislee came around the counter with her hand out to greet them.

"Nonsense," the dowager countess said. Though younger than Shannon by a little over a decade, Sorcha's skin was more lined, as if she didn't care about creams or makeup, beyond the required lipstick.

"If you've sold some items, I'd be happy tae bring more tae you." Paislee honestly couldn't imagine both women just dropping in. They had very busy lives. Nobility didn't mean leisure. From what she'd learned it was a hardworking position with a lot of responsibility, if taken seriously.

"I did sell two scarves," Sorcha said. She turned around to study the shelves of yarn and the layout of the shop.

"That's not why we're here," Shannon clarified.

"Okay . . . Please, have a seat. I'll plug the kettle in or get you a can of fizzy water." Paislee gestured to one of the high tables with stools.

The ladies sat and placed their handbags on a vacant stool.

"Nothing for me," Shannon said sweetly.

"Me either." Sorcha seemed to be playing second fiddle to whatever tune Shannon hummed.

Paislee kept smiling despite the apprehension. Why would they both be here? It had to have something to do with the cashmere goods at the castle, as that was the only connection all three of them had.

She cleared her throat. "Well, thank you again, Shannon, for suggesting my wares tae the dowager countess. Is there a problem?"

"Call me Sorcha. No problem at all!" The dowager countess rested her forearm on the high table. "They're so fine, they practically sell themselves. I've sold two, as I said earlier, and a jumper."

Paislee was on consignment, which meant that she'd get paid after items were sold. Since the car needed maintenance, keeping inventory at the castle climbed higher on her priority list.

"Wonderful!" She made a note on a piece of receipt paper.

Shannon patted the stool next to her and burst out laughing. "It's not nice of us tae drag it oot, but the truth is, we need your help."

"My help? With scarves? Shawls? I'm happy tae donate tae whatever fundraiser you might have."

"Not that! I'm talking aboot finding oot what happened tae Jory Baxter," Shannon said.

"Oh!" Paislee shook her head. "I can't do that. DI Zeffer is working the case and doing a bang-up job."

Sorcha's coral-hued mouth pursed in denial. "I disagree. He's searched my property twice since Saturday, upsetting Finn and Patrick. The dogs. They're strangers on the grounds, and it makes everyone twitchy."

"You helped me when my Shawn was in trouble," Shannon said. "I was just telling Sorcha how you kept Shawn from jail. Not that DI."

"I didn't, well . . . that was different." She'd been at Leery Estate that fateful day for a fieldtrip and witnessed firsthand what had happened to Shawn's cousin, Charles, shot by mistaken identity while Paislee and the Fordythe students had been there to view the gardens.

"How so?" Shannon asked. "You were there, Sorcha said."

"Jory collapsed in front of us all." Sorcha brought her thumb to her lower lip.

"That's true. Is it"—Paislee looked around the room, though the shop was empty other than them—"foul play?"

"I dinnae ken," Sorcha groused. "That DI Zeffer willnae say a word. Constable Smith is much chattier, but I still dinnae know anything after they're gone."

Paislee nodded. "Did they find the bagpipes?"

"No." Sorcha shifted on the stool. "They want tae question Robert and I just cannae allow it."

"Why not?" Paislee asked. "Robert didn't have anything tae do with what happened, did he?"

"Of course not!" Sorcha said.

"Then it's best tae let him answer questions and get the DI off your back." Paislee glanced at the sweater project, wishing she could work on that while they conversed, but it would probably be considered rude.

"Robert has some anger issues," Sorcha said in a soft voice. "He's been working on them with a therapist. If word got oot . . ."

Her brow rose in warning at Paislee, who raised her hands. "I won't say a thing."

"Shannon said you were discreet."

Paislee hated being in a position where she needed to be. "I don't understand why you need tae shield Robert from the police."

"I just dinnae know how Robert will react once he gets in a mood," Sorcha admitted. "As Earl of Lyon, Robert sometimes feels above the law. I've tried tae explain that isnae the case. If anything, we must be impeccable examples of what's right in our community." Sorcha twirled a simple gold band on her finger. "He swears he had nothing tae do with Jory or the bagpipes. Since Jory died at Ramsey Castle, we are under the microscope. I've poured blood, sweat, and tears into the property and operate with integrity."

Paislee nodded. The castle and the grounds oozed with prosperity.

Sorcha tilted her head. "Bring replacements for what I've sold tomorrow, and I'll prepare lunch. I should've brought the check with me, but I was in such a tizzy aboot Robert that when Shannon said how you'd helped, I practically dragged her oot the door."

Paislee remained by the register counter. How much did Sorcha know about what happened in truth?

"I've told Sorcha everything." Shannon's cheeks turned rosy. "Aila might be moving home tae the estate."

"Oh?" Aila Webster was the daughter that Shannon had kept hidden at boarding schools and brought home to the Leery Estate to donate a liver to Shawn when he'd been dying. It hadn't stopped him from drinking, and the transplant had failed.

"Aila lost the baby, and she and Graham split." Shannon gave a tremulous smile, her eyes welling with tears. "I dinnae ken if I will ever trust her completely, but she's apologized and promised tae never lie tae me again."

Having one child try to kill the other for an inheritance wasn't something Paislee was sure Shannon should forgive. "And what of Graham Reid?" The sculptor had been involved in the plot to murder Shawn but there'd been no jail time for either Aila or Graham.

"I dinnae care what happens to him." Shannon patted the stool next to her. Paislee reluctantly sat.

The affection Shannon had once held for her younger lover was dead.

"You know what it's like tae be a mum," Shannon said. "What wouldnae we do for our children?"

"I understand what you're saying, but is that good for you? Shawn?" Paislee pushed the memories of that day away and hoped that Shannon didn't repent her generous heart.

"Since Shawn's last liver transplant, he hasnae touched a drop of alcohol. Margot encourages him so much. I cannae thank her enough," Shannon said. "He's healthy and will inherit. I thought I'd have a grandbaby tae pin hopes on, but that isnae in the cards."

"Unless Aila marries?" Paislee asked.

Shannon briefly glanced down at the table. "Aila got the Leery genes, and her pregnancy was a miracle in the first place. She cannae have more. No, when I die, Shawn will get it all." Her mouth firmed. "I dinnae care if he burns the place doon."

"What?" Paislee asked, shocked. She knew what each plate and painting in the estate meant to Shannon.

"Shannon, you willnae always feel this way." Sorcha patted her friend's hand. "My Lissia is recovering from a broken heart, but she cannae drag her feet forever on choosing someone else. Our kids make us mental!" She kindly turned the attention away from Shannon. "Your boy is a dear, though, Paislee."

Paislee bowed her head. This whole idea of getting Brody to eighteen suddenly expanded to realizing he would never be done. What did that mean for her, personally?

Her head ached and she pinched her brow.

"Please say you'll come tae lunch? I'll tempt you with the wild mushroom soup I told you aboot. The recipe is from the second Earl of Lyon." Sorcha gave the words import.

Shannon rubbed Paislee's shoulder. "I'm sorry tae put more upon you, but I know how quick you are. You saved Shawn. I know you can help Robert."

Paislee tapped the high-top table. "Did Robert ever mention Jory cheating during a competition?"

"No . . ." Sorcha braced her shoulders.

"Did Jory *cheat*?" Shannon asked in awe.

"I don't know." Should Paislee share the news about what Clyde Cunningham had received? The note he believed Robert had sent?

Sorcha shook her head. "I dinnae see how he could have cheated in front of us all, but I dinnae play the pipes. I appreciate the art."

"That's right." Sorcha had placed a wager on Clan Grant. Paislee shifted on the stool. "Shannon, do you play?"

"No." Shannon tucked her sleek blond bob away from her smooth cheek.

"Clyde Cunningham claimed he'd received an anonymous letter that said Jory had cheated in last year's competition," Paislee said. "He wondered if Robert had sent it, which could be what the constables want tae ask Robert about."

"When was this?" Sorcha demanded.

"Saturday night," Paislee said. "Clyde wasn't quiet about it, so I'd wondered if you'd already heard."

"No," Sorcha said. "You must tell that tae Robert tomorrow. An anonymous letter? Did you see it?"

"No. Clyde said he threw it away." Paislee sighed.

Shannon heaved an insulted breath. "Tossed it, after an accusation like that?"

"I dinnae believe it," Sorcha said.

A part of her questioned it, too. Paislee considered her options. Shannon Leery had championed Paislee's bespoke goods, so she felt it would be rude to not help when asked. "I'll share with Robert what I know over soup. As Shannon can tell you, DI Zeffer is fair. Shawn should have gone tae him, and it would have saved some trouble."

"Is that so, Shannon?" Sorcha asked quietly.

Shannon smoothed her bob. "Shawn was in a mess over his head, I willnae lie—but not guilty of murder. Paislee may have a point, though Shawn wasnae thinking clearly. He was ill."

The noble ladies exchanged a glance, and then Sorcha cleared her throat. "I contacted Meri McVie and Connor Armington, the judges, about whether or not we should host the rematch of the competition."

"What do they think?" Paislee was curious about that, too. It would cost a lot of money to host the entire event again.

"Connor said he hadnae heard any news from the council yet, but Meri . . . well, she was downright evasive," Sorcha said. "Meri can cause trouble for the whole Clan Grant piping band with the GHB Competition Council. Robert said the rules are verra strict."

"Robert should talk with the police about Clyde's accusation," Paislee said. "By not addressing the problem full on, he seems . . . uncooperative."

Sorcha paled. "Clan pride is of the utmost importance tae our family. I will ask Robert if he sent that note tae Clyde as soon as I get home."

Shannon touched the blue cashmere scarf around her throat that Paislee had made for her. A reminder of how Shannon had connected Sorcha and Paislee for the gift shop? It wasn't only that, but Shannon sent people to Cashmere Crush whenever she had a chance. *Och.*

Paislee used to think that having a noblewoman on her side was a good thing, and hoped she didn't come to regret it. "That's probably best."

"I have another wee favor tae ask." Sorcha reached into her pocket and pulled out a business card with Meri McVie's judging information on it.

Like now. "What's this for?"

"I was hoping you could talk tae her," Sorcha said. "I'd arranged tae meet her for lunch today at the Lion's Mane but forgot that I have another appointment."

"Today?" Paislee asked. These two! The pub was just across the street and did have the best fish and chips around—besides Grandpa's—but that was not the point. Had this been their intent all morning?

"I would really appreciate it," Sorcha said, oozing sincerity. "Meri knows something that she's not willing tae tell me, but I'll wager the full price of a cashmere jumper that she'll talk with you. She knits, did you know?"

Shannon put her hand on Paislee's wrist. "If you cannae, well . . ." Noble disappointment hung in the air. "I understand."

Paislee drowned in guilt. She obviously needed to work on this skill in her interactions with Brody. "What time did you say?"

"Noon?" Sorcha sounded hopeful.

"Fine." Paislee exhaled and shook her hands. "I'll meet her for lunch. I'll see what she says, but it's not like I can question her without setting off alarms. She's expecting you, and getting me, plain Paislee Shaw."

"You are not plain, dearie, not the least," Shannon said. "Will you call Sorcha after?"

"If I learn anything useful and have time. No promises."

Sorcha passed money across the table. "For lunch, my treat. Let her know that I was in shopping for items for my gift shop and had tae run. Convey my apologies while connecting over yarn. I'm sure you'll be wonderful."

"You know your stuff," Shannon said.

Paislee was beginning to regret her kind streak.

Just then, some customers walked in, locals, who recognized the noble ladies from the various charities they did within the Nairn community.

Sorcha and Shannon each kissed Paislee on the cheek, praising her items and promising to be back. "And Paislee, love, I'll see you at the castle for lunch tomorrow," Sorcha said just before the door closed.

Well, that was good for business, she wouldn't lie. The women each bought a sweater and gushed about literally bumping into a dowager countess and a lady.

Grandpa arrived at five till noon. "Hiya!"

"Hello," Paislee said, still disgruntled. "You will never believe what happened this morning." She told him in a huff.

"Us old folks are crafty." Grandpa chuckled. "Enjoy your lunch!"

"Thanks!"

She headed across the street to the neighborhood pub. Meri McVie, with her carrot-orange hair, was easy to spot and already seated at a booth for two.

Paislee came around and sat across from the judge. "Hi, Meri! I'm Paislee Shaw."

Meri looked confused. "Hello?"

"Sorcha Grant was just over at my yarn and sweater shop, Cashmere Crush. She was called away and couldn't meet you for lunch, so she sent me over tae join you. She mentioned that you were interested in knitting?"

"Oh, I dabble, here and there," Meri said. If the judge had knitted the scarf she was wearing of a tight plaid weave, she wasn't bragging but could about her skill level. "Have we met?"

"At the competition." Paislee set her handbag next to her. "I'm friends with Jerry McFadden."

"Sure. I know Jerry." Meri smiled. "He's a guid man. Oh yes! You called for the ambulance."

Paislee didn't need to look at the menu. "Have you eaten here before?"

"Aye. Not so much now that I'm watching my cholesterol." Meri's eyes twinkled behind the frames of her silver glasses. "It's a real hardship, turning fifty. This will be a treat."

The waitress came over and they each ordered the fish special for lunch.

"Water for me," Paislee answered for a drink. Meri chose a light draft.

"So." Meri tapped the table when the drinks were brought. "Forgive me if this is oot of line, but did the dowager countess really have an emergency?"

Paislee blushed a fiery red, thanks to her pale skin and her penchant for honesty. She sipped her water to cool down.

Meri's mouth twitched and she drummed her short fingers on the table. "I can assume that means no. If I had tae continue with this line of thought, that means that when the DC questioned me aboot the rematch for the competition, she had an ulterior motive."

Paislee exhaled, wishing she could slide under the small table. "I can't speak tae her motives." Meri was smart so Paislee decided to share what she knew and hope for answers. "She wants information about what happened tae Jory, and tae know if her son is involved."

Meri arched a carrot-orange brow, her lips compressed into a thin line.

"Clyde received an anonymous note that Jory was cheating," Paislee continued. "Clyde said so himself, no rumor."

"Well, then." Meri drank and smacked her thin unpainted lips. "Since we're being straight with one another, I *also* received an anonymous letter, saying that Jory had cheated in the previous year."

Paislee sucked in a breath. Maybe Clyde's letter had been the real thing and not made up. "Any idea who sent it tae you?"

"No. I wondered who would benefit from such an accusation, I dinnae mind saying. Would the Grant clan get ahead? Would Robert have a reason tae send one tae both Clyde and myself?"

Paislee shifted on the hard bench. "Clyde was on the phone that day and it really ticked Jerry off, as well as the other Cunningham bandmates."

"I'd wondered myself! Do you know who he was talking tae?" Meri asked.

"Yes. He told me and Jerry, and DI Zeffer, that he wanted to make sure that the GHB committee couldn't take away the prize from the previous year."

"What a dobber," Meri said. "Selfish! I should mark Clyde down for having a mobile phone on the field. That is definitely against the rules."

Paislee considered that. "Clyde gives off a shady vibe, more so than Robert Grant."

Meri gave a quick laugh. "You're so right. But Clyde had a reason tae protect Jory from scandal."

"Why is that?"

Meri drank deeply from her beer, scooting to the end of the bench to say, "Clyde had put a lot of faith in Jory's abilities tae play the pipe. Called in favors tae get him noticed at smaller competitions."

"I see—any tarnish on Jory would rub off on him," Paislee said. "No different than the Grants and clan pride." It didn't answer who would send the notes. "One man has a castle, the other doesn't."

Meri pursed her lips and eyed Paislee over the top of her beer glass. "Clyde and I have had words before aboot being sneaky. Not cheating, exactly, but just pushing the rules tae the edge with a last-minute tune change or musician lineup. I know he had some cash behind the scenes on Jory winning the crown this year."

"A lot?" Paislee didn't understand wasting good money.

"We try tae put the hammer doon on it, but folks love tae gamble." Meri ruffled her orange hair. "I guess Clyde had a guid sum at stake if Jory lost—but not as much as Robert Grant. When Sorcha Grant called me aboot the rematch, she'd suggested that we cancel the event. Well, wouldnae that erase any bets? Which makes me wonder if Robert, the Earl of Lyon, did send the letters. Fifty thousand pounds isnae chump change."

Fifty thousand pounds!

Chapter 9

Fifty thousand pounds was an unreal amount. "Wait . . . Robert gambled, too?" Paislee recalled Sorcha saying she'd placed a small bet on Clan Grant. Even Zeffer knew about the side bets, but surely nothing that equaled fifty thousand pounds. That was a fortune.

"That's how the bigger names make extra money on the side," Meri said. "Connor told me Robert lost five thousand pounds last year when Jory took the win. They'd won the prior six years, so it wasnae a big stretch tae imagine. Robert is verra good, so is Lissia—the whole Clan Grant team works together."

The waitress brought their fish and chip specials. Steam wafted up from the golden batter on the fish, the tang of the chippy sauce sharp and tempting to Paislee's nose. Her mouth watered and she folded her napkin over her lap.

"Yum," Meri said, breaking a piece of white, flaky haddock. "This is so guid and yet so bad for me."

Paislee blew on a corner of steaming fish before popping it in her mouth. "Fifty thousand is a big leap from five. Was he hoping tae recoup his losses?"

Meri ate a chip. "I'm not sure. I dinnae imagine that the castle has an influx of cash. Property rich."

Like Lady Shannon Leery and the Leery Estate. "I am too cheap tae risk money on anything that wouldn't be a sure thing."

"Frugal!" Meri countered. "Aye, me too. No castles or the folks on them that I'd be responsible for—just me and my cat. That's plenty!"

"Sorcha said that you like tae knit?" Paislee said.

"I do! Believe it or not, I used tae play the pipes until I hurt my shoulder, so now I judge. I'm thinking of hanging up me badge, though. Cannae catch a cheater? What guid am I?"

"I don't think I'd trust an anonymous letter," Paislee said. "There's no proof, no evidence. *How* could someone cheat?"

"I've racked my brain, and Connor's, too, but the rules for the Great Highland Bagpipe competition are simple and havenae changed for a hundred years. The point is tae prove yer skill level. The money is small tae make it aboot talent, not cash."

"Yet, folks bet." Paislee swiped a chip through the sauce. "Do you still have the anonymous letter?"

"Naw. I gave it tae Constable Thorn on Monday. What aboot Clyde? Did he turn his in, too?"

"No." Paislee kept her tone neutral. "His letter supposedly got destroyed in the rain Saturday morning."

"It was torrential," Meri said thoughtfully. "I hope it provides a clue, but it was verra basic. Could have been printed oot from any-where."

"What did it say?" Paislee tilted her head. "If you don't mind telling me."

Meri hesitated but then shrugged. "Just that Jory Baxter had cheated in previous championship at Ramsey Castle and would probably do it again." She reached for her beer. "I didnae see a damn thing."

"It might not be true. Don't be so hard on yourself." Paislee sighed. "So, given your experience, Meri, would it be possible for Jory tae have knocked himself out, by not performing properly?"

"I dinnae think so. Yes, beginners can cause themselves tae faint. Respiratory fatigue." Meri touched her heart. "The more one practices, the stronger your lungs are. I was taught that you should blow"—she puffed her cheeks—"up tae a hundred and twenty-five

percent, and squeeze the bag"—she pressed her elbow to her side—
"at a hundred and twenty percent, tae be able tae play longer. Jory
was no beginner."

Paislee sipped her water. "It would be the best-case scenario if
he'd just fainted from not breathing properly. Nobody's fault."

"So why did he die, then? Dinnae why it's taking so long tae
get answers aboot what happened tae the poor bloke!" Meri said.
"A young man in his prime."

"It's so sad. These things just take time," Paislee replied. "Sorcha didn't tell me about Robert gambling. Could it be a problem?"
No, the dowager countess had deflected with anger issues. Did Sorcha know that Robert gambled?

"I havenae heard anything like that," Meri said. "Connor didnae convey concern when he shared what he'd heard."

"From who?" Paislee asked.

Meri shook her head. "I didnae ask. I will."

"Okay." Paislee sipped her water. "Sorcha wanted tae know if
you were going tae hold the rematch . . ."

No performance, no debt.

Meri sat back, her meal mostly finished. "I'm simply not sure.
Connor and I are biding our time tae see how tae handle the event."

Was that code for depending on Jory's cause of death? Sorcha
had figured that Meri was being evasive.

"We've already tallied the winners, if we move forward with
Clan Cunningham's forfeit," Meri said. "But the GHB Competition Council has said that because Jory Baxter died, the rematch
could be scheduled with the remaining members of Clan Cunningham performing, if Connor and I agree. That's a big deal for the
council. They're sticklers for the rules and verra anti-change."

"Did you let Sorcha know?" Paislee asked.

Meri placed her fork across the plate. "Naw. I would appreciate
it if you didnae share that with any of the Grants. Well, with anybody part of the competition, not even Jerry."

Paislee buried her curiosity about who the winners were. "I won't, but you should make sure tae give the police every bit of information."

"I'll stop at the station after we're done," Meri said. "It will give me a chance tae ask aboot the letter."

"Good. I'm having lunch at Ramsey Castle tomorrow," Paislee said. "Can I mention that you also received an anonymous note?"

Meri tapped her lower lip. "Since the constables already know, I suppose there's no harm in that."

"I agree. Sorcha said she'd ask Robert today if he'd heard that Jory had cheated, and about the anonymous letter to Clyde. What do you think of Robert?" Paislee finished her chips, her stomach pleasantly full.

Meri dabbed her mouth with a napkin. "I know him from the decade of judging the competitions. He's a hardworking man. A wee bit arrogant but not too bad considering he was born tae be an earl. I wouldnae have pegged him as a gambler if Connor hadnae told me—again, I dinnae ken if it's a problem. We would have heard, aye?"

It amazed her how many people had secrets, and what they would do to protect them. "I will keep an open mind, then. I do like Sorcha very much, for that same reason. She's not afraid tae work hard. She was very proud of all they've accomplished on the property." Which made her remember the missing pipes. "Do you know if they've found Jory's bagpipes yet?"

"Nope." Meri tapped the table. "Cannae imagine why anybody would toss them. They're worth a tidy sum."

What if they held a clue to how Jory might have cheated, or how he died?

Paislee wiped her hands and mouth, dropping the napkin over her plate. "I have a weekly Knit and Sip night on Thursdays—tonight, actually. Would you like tae try it out? Just a bunch of knitters for a blether."

Meri wore a pleased smile that softened her foxy features. "That sounds fun. What do I bring?"

Paislee felt good about including the judge. "A drink or dish tae share, and whatever project you're working on."

"I might stop by."

"Six tae nine." Paislee waved at the waitress for the bill. "So, is there anything else you can tell me tae navigate lunch at the castle tomorrow? I won't mention the council's tentative approval, only that you also received a letter accusing Jory of cheating."

Meri burst out with a laugh. "I like you, Paislee. A straight shooter. I prefer my games tae be on the piping field." The judge hummed beneath her breath. "What if the pipes and what happened tae Jory are related somehow, which is why they're missing?"

What if . . . ?

The waitress swooped by and Paislee paid for both of their lunches with a hefty tip from the money Sorcha had given her.

"The dowager countess's treat," Paislee said.

Meri stood and adjusted her scarf. "Give her my thanks."

The pair exited the pub, Meri to her car and Paislee to walk across the street. "Don't forget the station!"

"On my way. Bye, Paislee." Meri left.

Paislee hoped that Meri would join the group tonight. She'd done her good deed toward Zeffer's investigation by sending Meri with the news of the council agreeing to a rematch. She sent a text to Hamish saying that she looked forward to Saturday. It was his turn to choose the restaurant.

Nose to the phone, she reached for the handle of her shop, but Zeffer stood there, blocking her way.

"Look oot!" Zeffer gave the front of his suit an exaggerated brush. "Shouldnae text and walk. You could hurt yourself."

"But I didn't." Paislee arched a brow. "I didn't run into you, either."

"You didnae, but just barely." Zeffer's hair was perfectly styled, as was his blue suit; this one had a very faint pinstripe. "Most fortuitous."

"Is there a reason you're in front of my shop being a public nuisance?"

His eyes flashed with humor. "There is, actually."

Oh! That could be great news. "Did you find out what happened tae Jory?"

Zeffer half-smiled. "Perhaps."

Ugh. She refrained from stomping her foot. She was almost thirty, for heaven's sake, and she didn't need to react to his pushing her buttons. *One, two, three.* Calm.

"Okay." She reached around Zeffer to open the door.

"Okay?" he asked.

"Tell me or not." Paislee shrugged. "Up tae you."

Zeffer's shoulders sagged. "Take all the fun oot of it."

"Good." She gripped the handle. Zeffer didn't move, which brought them chest to chest. Her breaths came faster.

"I saw you with the judge from the competition," Zeffer said, so close his breath, warm and cinnamon-scented, brushed her cheek.

"So?" Paislee backed up. "Meri might be joining our Knit and Sip night."

"And here I thought you'd be digging for information aboot Jory and what happened tae him." Zeffer clucked his tongue behind his teeth.

"Why would I do that?" Besides the fact that she had two people demanding she help them . . .

"It's your nature tae help." His sea-glass green gaze bore into hers.

She swallowed hard. "And yours tae annoy me."

His smile widened. Her pulse sped. She put her handbag over her arm to add space between them.

"Why are you here, DI?"

Zeffer raised his palms. "Have you heard from Jerry today?"

"Not since he dropped off my yarn on Tuesday." Paislee grinned. "He compared you tae a tick on a sheep."

Zeffer stopped smiling.

Score one for Paislee. Then, considering there was a dead piper, she grew concerned. "Why? Is Jerry okay?"

"I want tae question him further," Zeffer said, "but he's taken some personal time off."

"Tae get away from you, probably." Paislee rolled her eyes. "I hope he succeeds."

"He was with Jory at the end," Zeffer said.

"Doing his human duty tae help a fellow man. Why are you harping on him? Jerry wouldn't hurt a fly."

"I wouldnae be so sure." Zeffer patted his biceps. "He's a big man used tae working on a farm. Hauling heavy boxes. Manual labor."

"So? He didn't wrestle Jory tae the ground. Jory quite literally dropped tae the grass. That's it. Jerry didn't get near him until he was already down."

"See? That's guid tae know."

"I already told you that, and so did he," Paislee said with exasperation. "Did you find Jory's bagpipes?"

"Jerry was the last person tae see them." Zeffer tucked a thumb in his jacket pocket. "We only have his word of what happened. I had a team searching the castle grounds Sunday and Monday, but nothing has turned up—so far. Patrick Grant threatened the need for a search warrant if we dinnae hurry up."

"I'm going for lunch tomorrow," Paislee said, just to tweak Zeffer. She was invited, he was a pest. "The dowager countess invited me." Goods sold meant money in her account.

"Why?" Zeffer demanded, sounding concerned. "You shouldnae go tae the castle."

Paislee bristled, disliking it very much when he told her what to do. "I am in no danger. I don't play the pipes. I don't even gamble.

I'm going tae eat an earl's recipe for mushroom soup and restock my scarves in the castle gift shop."

Zeffer groaned and put his palm to his forehead as if she caused him physical pain. "You need not meddle in this investigation."

"I don't meddle!" She heard the defensive tone in her voice and once again strove for calm.

"Did you or did you not talk aboot Jory's death with Meri?" Zeffer asked.

"We did," Paislee said. "We also talked about Clyde and the anonymous letter. Meri got one, too, and already turned it in."

"There's nothing tae find on that letter," Zeffer said. "Not a print, not a clue. Clyde thinks Robert could've sent it from the castle."

"What if Clyde is covering his own story about the anonymous note that no longer exists? I would believe Meri more than Clyde," Paislee pronounced. "He's shady. Clyde had money on his clan winning the competition."

Zeffer tapped his chin. "Five thousand pounds. He told me."

"And Robert Grant?" Was the amount of fifty thousand pertinent? "Not a big deal according tae just about everyone including you. Even Grandpa had a fiver on the Campbells tae win."

"Fifty thousand is a verra big deal."

So, Zeffer already knew about the large wager. Paislee put her hand on the door. "Is that all?"

Zeffer shook his head. "You're impossible."

"Me?" Paislee put her fingers to her chest. "I've got work tae do, DI. You should probably go tae the station. Meri is sharing information about the competition that you might find helpful as we speak."

Tension heightened between them. "Be careful, Paislee, all right? Dinnae walk and text. You've got tae be aware of your surroundings. Danger could be anywhere."

"Is that all you wanted tae tell me?" Paislee asked.

"No. If you hear from Jerry, please have him call me." With

that, Zeffer strode toward Nairn Police Station and didn't look back.

Disgruntled, Paislee went in, simmering with indignation until she realized what he was really trying to tell her without being able to do so. Danger. Was Jory a victim?

The matter of Jory's demise was put aside as a rush of customers came in, keeping her and Grandpa busy until five. Grandpa took the Juke and picked up Brody, and the pair went home for dinner while she stayed at the shop. Lydia would drive her home after Knit and Sip.

Lydia arrived first of the ladies, looking divine in a new pale yellow and charcoal suit that showed off her figure and her gray eyes. She carried a covered container of appetizers that were usually fun recipes she found in her glossy magazines.

"I cannae believe we actually found a house," Lydia said. "I'm eyeing things in my flat wondering if I should move it or keep it. How much do I love my holiday throw pillows? Is it worth packing tae the new place? I need a purge."

"If you offer it as a rental, it could be fully furnished and then you don't have tae move anything except your clothes and personal items."

Lydia threw her slender arms around Paislee. "This is one of many reasons why I love you."

They laughed and set up the tables. Paislee nodded toward the container. "What did you bring?"

"Roasted pears and Gruyère cheese with toast squares. I was in a hurry."

Of course, she was. "I can't wait tae try it." Paislee's lunch was wearing off after her busy afternoon. Appetizers like these made a perfect dinner.

Lydia straightened two stools. "Have you heard anything more aboot Jory Baxter?"

"Well, Shannon Leery and Sorcha Grant stopped in this morn-

ing, totally creating a lunch date for me at the pub with Meri McVie."
Paislee was over being annoyed as she liked the judge. "Meri might
be joining us tonight."

"Wait. You had two of the local nobility *just stop by?*" Lydia
raised her phone and showed the lack of messages from Paislee.
"You should've texted me."

"It's been busy." Paislee brought paper plates and napkins from
the back storage area and gave them to Lydia, who placed them
next to the pears. "I had customers at the time and it went over
pretty well."

"I bet! And no picture? No social proof that my bestie is the
premiere yarn *artiste* around?" Lydia demanded.

"Yarn artiste?" Paislee laughed so hard her stomach hurt. "That's
great, Lyd. I'll have tae tell Sorcha about that tomorrow when I go
for lunch at the castle tae deliver more items for the gift shop. I
guess she sold several things already."

"That's really splendid, Paislee. I'm so proud of you." Lydia
paused and studied Paislee closer. "Is there anything more tae it?"

"Maybe," Paislee admitted. "Zeffer has his sights on talking
with Robert and Jerry. You know how intense the DI can be. Jerry
took a few days off tae avoid him, and Robert is protected by family evasion."

"That doesnae sound guid for Jory. He sure was a hottie. Handsome and talented?" Lydia shook her head.

Paislee put out a dish of wrapped candy. "There are anonymous
accusations of Jory being a cheater during last year's competition.
No proof, though, which makes his missing bagpipe—pipes?—
important."

"Those arenae a wee instrument tae hide!" Lydia typed something into her mobile and read, "The word 'bagpipes' can be singu-
lar as well as plural. Sairy, love. Even the internet cannae decide."

Laughing, Paislee tossed a hard candy at Lydia.

Mary Beth Mulholland burst in on a wave of floral perfume and
happy vibes. "Paislee! Lydia!" The woman was as kind as anyone

Paislee had ever met. She and her husband, a solicitor named Arran, had twin daughters who were two years younger than Brody and were still at Fordythe, where Hamish was headmaster.

"Mary Beth! So nice tae see you."

Lydia arched a groomed brow at Paislee but stepped back. Any more of Jory would have to be tabled until it was just the two of them. Since Lydia was driving her home, there would be plenty of time.

For now, Paislee welcomed her knitters.

Elspeth arrived, carrying a quiche, wine, and her latest needlepoint. She had a small crush on Grandpa that would never go anywhere as Grandpa loved Agnes. They both enjoyed the mild flirtation, though.

"How's Susan and the therapy dog idea coming along?" Paislee asked.

"Well, she really loves your Wallace, but online research said terriers dinnae make guid service dogs," Elspeth said. "Susan wants a bigger dog that can help physically guide her if needed. She and the dog will both need training. It's a big commitment."

"That makes sense, though," Paislee said.

"Susan wants a dog?" Mary Beth pulled a dish of warm soft pretzels from her bag and set them on the table to share. "That's terrific. Our Niles is a treasure. He's a golden Lab. I can get the name of the breeder if you'd like."

"Susan's started the application process for a service dog tae suit her needs, now, and ongoing," Elspeth said, "but thank you anyway."

Blaise O'Connor arrived in time to hear the last part of the conversation. "I dinnae want a dog. Cats are fine with me. More independent." Her daughter, Suzannah, was at private school, and her husband, Shep, was a golf pro in Nairn. "Hi, everyone! I brought spinach dip and naan bread. Oh, are those fresh pretzels?"

On her heels were Amelia and Meri. Amelia's hair was dyed black with blue tips and kept short. Big, dark blue eyes. She and Meri were the same height and similar build.

"We have a newcomer!" Amelia said.

"Hi, Meri!" Paislee called, glad to see her. "Everyone, this is Meri McVie. She's a judge for the bagpiping competitions."

Amelia got a chair for Meri, who had a bag over her arm. Meri set it on the seat and pulled out a bottle of whisky, a skein of rainbow yarn, and circular knitting needles. "Last, sliced fruit and cheddar cheese."

Lydia took the food and brought it to the high-top table with the other treats. "Welcome, welcome!"

Paislee was proud of her knitters for making Meri feel at home, but the judge was a wonderful addition right away. Like Blaise had been, in the flow.

The night flew by with conversation, and jokes, and light-hearted gossip that hurt nobody. Elspeth had them in stitches about Widower Mann at the retirement home across the street and his usual shenanigans with a new lady every other night. There was a pause in the conversation as they replenished snacks and drinks.

"Lydia, you have news!" Paislee said. If she'd just bought a house, it would be all she could talk about.

"What?" Lydia sipped her wine—a chardonnay from Germany that she'd purchased a case of.

"A home," Paislee said. "That's a pretty big deal."

The ladies all laughed kindly. Lydia's wedding had been a nightmare, but now was a new beginning—the hunt for a place together had been a stretch of compromise.

"Where?" Blaise asked. "By me?"

"Not the golf course," Lydia said. "But the bay. An older home."

"What?" Elspeth said in surprise. Lydia was all about new.

Lydia sipped again. "It's a gorgeous home that's been completely gutted and has all modern appliances. Modern colors, modern furniture. Old architecture." She shrugged.

"It's beautiful! Ladies, just wait until you see the gardens," Paislee said.

"I'm glad you found something, my dear. Marriage is compromise," Mary Beth said.

"It is," Blaise agreed. "Are you married, Meri?"

"Single for me," Meri chimed in. "I like things my way." She raised her tumbler and they all cheered.

Paislee agreed with that sentiment.

Before she knew it, the night was over. Meri promised to come back the following week. Not one word was spoken about Jory Baxter's death, or the Grants. Meri could keep a secret, and Paislee liked that about her. Yes, the knitter-judge was a find.

On the way home, Paislee continued the conversation with Lydia about Jory, Ramsey Castle, and Robert Grant. "Do you know him, Lyd?"

"Not really. I am more familiar with Sorcha, as she's on many of the charities we do at the agency. Why?"

Paislee sent a message to the shared mobile that she was on her way home. Brody gave a thumbs-up emoji back, and she pocketed the phone.

"Sorcha told me Robert has a temper and she's not sure how he'll act if pressed by the constables, which is why the family is keeping him under wraps. I'm not sure I believe her, but she'd promised tae ask Robert if he'd sent the letter, as Clyde believes, or if he suspected Jory of cheating. Thanks tae Shannon, Sorcha thinks I can convince Robert tae cooperate with the police over a bowl of soup."

Lydia was quite familiar with what had happened at the Leery Estate. Her bestie sighed. "Could Robert have written the notes?"

Paislee rested her elbow on the armrest of the Mercedes. "I don't know. I think losing fifty thousand pounds on a bet is a big deal."

"For me, too," Lydia said. "It's no way tae keep your money."

"So, does Robert have a gambling problem? Would that debt be erased if the event is canceled? Meri said that Sorcha had suggested a cancellation over the phone." Paislee turned to look at Lydia, her beauty not dimmed by nighttime shadows. "Why would Clyde throw away the letter accusing Jory of cheating? Makes no sense tae me."

"I dinnae feel comfortable with you being at the castle," Lydia said. For once, she didn't laugh after she said the words.

Paislee reached for her phone. "I am no damsel in distress needing tae be saved. If anything happens, I'll have my mobile on speed dial tae the station."

"You sound tough, Paislee." Lydia parked her Mercedes in front of Paislee's old home, which didn't have a single remodel. "I miss your rose-colored glasses."

The comment sent a pang to her heart at her loss of innocence. "Don't worry. I'll be fine."

Chapter 10

"*I'll be fine.*" Paislee regretted those words the following Friday morning when it did more than the customary shower. Scotland supposedly had at least one hundred words for rain. This happening outside was all of those combined, from *daggle* (to fall in torrents) to *yillen* (a windy shower of rain).

Water bounced like hail off their old roof and created puddles in the back garden. The street was flooded up to her calves. Thank heaven for Wellies. Like the storm on Saturday, she hoped it would clear before she had to drive to the castle.

Lydia had texted numerous suggestions on what to wear today, but cute boots and a sundress were out. Paislee just might stick with her bright pink Wellies—the color was perfect for lifting one's mood on a *dreich* day.

Grandpa woke up grumpy, saying his muscles ached. Brody dragged his feet, too, and even Wallace had a droopy tail.

"Look at us sad sacks," Paislee said. She tried to tease her crew into smiles, but they weren't budging.

Grandpa tried to snap the damp paper as he drank strong tea. Brody scraped his spoon across the bottom of his cereal bowl. She arched a brow and he stopped.

"Grandpa, would you like me tae cancel the lunch at the castle today? You can stay home and rest."

"*I* want tae stay home and rest." Brody scowled.

"Brody, when you reach the golden age of seventy, I will give you permission. Until then, rain will not keep either of us home," Paislee declared.

"I will be there." Grandpa's voice was gruff. "A hot shower will loosen these old bones. Golden years, my arse."

"Grandpa! Swear jar," Brody said—no teasing this time.

"I don't mind canceling," she said. It wouldn't be a fun outing with the rain so bad. Her grandfather being under the weather was a terrific excuse—er, reason to cancel.

Grandpa glared at her. "I'm fine."

"All right, all right." She held up her hand. "Anything in the news about Jory?"

"No. I woulda said."

Paislee quickly finished her toast and stood, bringing her dish to the sink. "Okay, then. If you leave Wallace on the back porch, he'll be dry and warm."

"I know," Grandpa said.

"Brody. Are you still having Edwyn stay over tonight? You must be excited about the game tomorrow."

"We'll see," Brody grouched. "The rain makes the ball too slippery."

"Since when?" Rain was a fact of life and the kids had always played in it.

"Since now." Brody brought his empty bowl to the sink.

"Brush your teeth," Paislee said.

"I know!"

Brody ran up the stairs and she heard the sink turn on above their heads. She squinted her eyes at the ceiling over the table. "Is that a water stain?"

Grandpa didn't bother to move the newspaper. "Doot it. This old house is sturdy."

Wallace scratched at the back door, needing to go out but not wanting to. Paislee hurried and opened it up—the screen on the porch was also open. Wallace pranced on the top step, then seemed to realize it wasn't going to get any better. Down the stairs, across the grass to the partial shelter of the trees, near the shed. Within seconds he'd done his business and hurried back inside.

Paislee towel-dried his legs and belly so that he wouldn't get matted fur and knots, then gave him a treat. "Good boy."

Wallace wagged his tail and licked her hand—at least one of them was in a better mood.

"Let's go, Brody," Paislee shouted up the stairs. She had her handbag, her keys, and her hot pink slicker to match the hot pink Wellies. She'd packed her nicer boots for the chance that the weather would change.

This was Nairn, and it often did.

Brody hurried down. Tan slacks, blue school polo, hair wetted down but not brushed. She didn't have the time to send him back upstairs.

"Backpack? Homework?"

"Yeah, yeah," Brody said.

"Don't be smart with me, laddie." Paislee stopped him and lifted his chin. "You know I am not in charge of the weather? Otherwise, we'd have a lot more sunshine."

His shoulders sagged. "Sairy, Mum. Edwyn just texted that he cannae come over tonight, that's all."

"Okay." It was a drab day and since she couldn't change it, they'd have to handle whatever came. "Well, we can still watch movies."

He rolled his eyes. "Whatever."

Paislee opened the door and felt like Wallace as she waited for a break in the downpour that didn't happen.

"Bye, Grandpa! I'll come pick you up if it's still raining like this!"

He didn't argue. "Ta. Have a guid day."

A gust of wind brought some rain into the foyer. "Hurry, love!"

Down the stairs they went to the covered carport and inside the Juke.

Brody buckled up. "Did you make the appointment yesterday for the tune-up?"

Paislee blew out a breath. When had she had time yesterday? "No."

He shook his head as if hugely disappointed.

"I'll do it today." When, she wasn't sure. Edwyn not sleeping over explained Brody being upset. "You want tae pick the movie for tonight?"

"It's your turn, though," Brody said, to be fair.

"I don't mind."

"Chinese food?" Brody suggested. "Chicken lo mein? Double fortune cookies?"

Paislee hid a smile as he pushed the boundaries. "I'll see what the budget looks like."

Rain dropped so fast her wipers could barely keep up.

"You're really going tae the castle today?" Brody asked with concern. "Mibbe you should cancel. The roads are curvy and steep."

"I'll be all right." She drove carefully through a puddle. "Sold some cashmere so I'll get paid."

Brody rubbed his hands together. "Just in time for Chinese food."

"Excellent point." Paislee pulled before the school. Teachers with wide umbrellas were herding kids inside.

It was Scotland and nobody actually melted when wet, but it could still be uncomfortable if one didn't dress for it.

She realized that Brody wasn't wearing his slicker just as he said, "Bye, Mum!" and raced out the door, backpack over one arm.

"Tricky," she said. Oh well. Gran would say to pick her battles. If Brody was uncomfortable, then he might choose to wear the raincoat on his own accord.

Twelve was a difficult age, but it was only going to get more complicated.

She next went to Cashmere Crush. The wipers would just clear one deluge before another appeared. Parking behind the shop, she noticed Jerry McFadden in a pickup truck that wasn't his normal delivery lorry.

Zeffer had said that he had taken a leave. To avoid him, no doubt. What could Jerry want that would bring him out in this mess?

Paislee covered her hair with the hot pink hood attached to her slicker and opened the door. She tucked her bag and boots under the front of the jacket and hurried out and up the stairs, unlocking the door and stepping in, thankful for the awning over the back door.

She waited for Jerry, who didn't even have a cap, as he ran up the stairs to join her.

"Morning! What a nice surprise," she said politely.

"Mornin'." Jerry sounded as grumpy as Grandpa.

"I don't have a yarn order," she said.

"No," Jerry agreed, following her. "I need tae speak with you." There wasn't a hint of cheer in his attitude.

Paislee would have liked to attribute his mood to the weather, but she had an idea that a certain GQ detective was behind the visit. "I'll heat the electric kettle and make us tea."

"Got whisky?"

Paislee straightened. "No. I don't have whisky. This is a business."

Shutting the door behind them, she shrugged out of her wet jacket, hanging it on a hook near the door. She placed her dry boots by the chair and leaned over to the small counter to press the on button for the kettle.

Jerry brushed water from his hair. "Zeffer is badgering me. Can I file a complaint?"

Paislee shrugged. "Maybe. Why not just talk tae him instead of avoiding him?"

"I'll tell you why—he's looking for someone tae toss in jail." Jerry was as serious as she'd ever seen him.

She got two mugs from a shelf in the back and a selection of tea bags, taking orange for herself and showing the tin to Jerry. "He's collecting information tae find out what happened tae Jory."

"I hate tae say this, Paislee, but Jory must have been *killed*," Jerry declared, choosing a black tea bag.

She had deduced that for herself. "We don't know anything for sure. Zeffer can't put you in jail if you did nothing wrong."

Jerry paced, purple shadows under his eyes. He exuded tension and worry as he walked back and forth in her small storage room, tugging his bedraggled mustache.

How to reach him? Paislee grabbed his arm as he passed her. "Did you hurt Jory in any way?"

Jerry stopped and cursed. "No! Of course not. Why would I?"

"Then talk tae Zeffer," Paislee said with exasperation. "Tell him what you know, and he will back off. He's annoying but fair."

"Are ye friends, then?"

"No. I am not friends with Zeffer." And yet, there was something between them. Respect? "Want me tae call him for you?"

"Dinnae do that! He's been asking aboot the bagpipes. Where could they have gone?" Jerry asked.

"It's the big question, isn't it?" Paislee dropped the orange tea bag into the mug. "I hope by the time I'm at Ramsey Castle today, they'll have been found."

"You're going tae the castle? In this?"

"Aye. The dowager countess is carrying my cashmere goods in the gift shop. I sold several items so I will bring her more. She's offering me lunch while I'm there."

"Posh!" Jerry teased.

"Hardly." Paislee lifted her hot pink rubber boots.

Jerry smirked. "I'm not much on fashion, but you'll probably want tae change."

"Ha. I might need a boat tae get there!"

"Want me tae drive you?" Jerry asked.

"That's sweet." Paislee shook her head. "I'll be fine." She gestured to the kettle as it whistled at last.

Jerry handed the unwrapped tea bag back to her. "No. You've given me an idea. I'm going tae search the woods around Ramsey Castle."

"Trespassing?" Paislee arched her brow. "For what?"

"It's no coincidence that Jory is dead, and his pipes are missing." Jerry scrubbed his forehead with his palm. "Aye?"

"I believe that may be true, but we don't know," Paislee said.

"If I find the bagpipes and hand them tae the DI, he'll back off." Jerry gripped the knob.

"Or," Paislee raised her brow, "he'll ask how you knew where they were. Do you know, Jerry?"

"No." He turned fiery red and released the door. "You make a valid point."

Paislee wondered if Jerry had something to hide. She studied her friend closely for any sign of guilt on his familiar face, but there was none. "I've heard several rumors about gambling and bets behind the scenes of the competition. Did you lose? You can tell me. I won't judge."

"I dinnae bet," Jerry said. He stared at the floor and the water puddled between them.

"What is it?" Paislee's stomach clenched with apprehension.

Jerry leaned back against the door and crossed his arms. "Jory and I may have gotten into a verra loud argument at the pub the Friday night before the competition Saturday. I'm sure Zeffer's heard aboot it by now."

Her heart sank. "What about?"

"Mattias and I were talking aboot the solo over a pint. Jory, at the bar, overheard and said I couldnae play a tune tae save my life. I told him where tae shove the pipes, I would win come Saturday." Jerry banged his fist to his chest.

"That's not too bad," Paislee said.

"We were all drinking," Jerry said. "Jory was wasted. I challenged him then and there but he didnae have his pipes and wouldnae use any others. It made me wonder, when Clyde said what he did aboot Jory cheating, if it was true."

"Meri McVie also received an anonymous letter stating the same. It tempts me tae believe Clyde was telling the truth," Paislee said. "She turned her note in."

"Did Robert send them, like Clyde thought?"

"I don't know." Paislee cupped her mug, inhaling orange and cinnamon. "How could he have cheated?"

Jerry dragged thick fingers through his damp hair. "Right? I have a call in to a guid friend, Fat Fergie, aboot it."

Paislee spluttered before taking a drink. "Fat Fergie? And he's a mate, is he?"

"Laugh if you dare, the man knows every last thing aboot piping. He makes custom bagpipes. If there was a way tae cheat, he might know."

"You talk with F . . . Fergie, and I'll see what I can discover while at the castle. Please don't go there, Jerry. It might cause suspicion. DI Zeffer has had his officers scouring the property already."

"I willnae. Cheers," Jerry said, then walked out the door. The rain had slowed to a drizzle, but Jerry didn't seem to notice as he hurried to his truck.

Paislee carried her mug of tea through her shop, taking inventory of what needed replenishing, and opened at nine thirty. She worked on her sweater orders between customers. It had stopped raining at half past eleven and Grandpa had texted that he would walk. A braw day after all.

She changed into her cute boots and added a touch of makeup to her pale face. Her hair, red and thin, was in a clip to give it body—a trick she'd learned from Lydia.

At noon she was ringing up a customer for an emerald-green jumper when Grandpa arrived.

The hot shower and walking must have done him good because he greeted her with a smile. He held the door open for the customer and whistled as he made his way toward Paislee at the register counter.

"Hello!"

"Hiya," Grandpa said. "You look pretty, lass."

"Oh! Ta." Her blouse was the light blue of her eyes over slacks.

"I may have been a wee bit crotchety this morning." Grandpa pinched his forefinger and thumb together.

"It's all right," she said. "We all were."

Grandpa leaned his elbow on the counter. "What are ye bringing tae the castle?"

Paislee showed him her large Cashmere Crush bag filled with luxury cashmere items. "Three plaid scarves, one shawl, and one jumper. For the lady herself, a knitted coin purse in the Clan Grant tartan."

"Verra nice," Grandpa said with approval.

"Are you okay with Chinese tonight? Brody requested double fortune cookies."

"Aye. Anything I can do in particular while you lunch at the castle?" Grandpa held up his little pinky and pursed his lips. He'd even trimmed his beard and mustache. Very dapper.

"No." She sighed as she remembered Brody's reminder. "I forgot tae call about the Juke."

"I can set up something with Eddy," Grandpa said.

"That would be lovely. Any time."

"You've got your mobile charged? I'm glad it stopped blustering so that you dinnae have to drive in it."

"I do. The ringer is even on," Paislee said with a rueful laugh. "Call if you need anything."

In a fine mood, Paislee left the shop, driving toward Ramsey Castle. It did sound high and mighty, in a way. Sorcha was down to earth, as was Lissia, but Robert and Patrick seemed full of themselves. Cinda had been sweet, yet Paislee got the feeling that Sorcha didn't approve of the "friendship" Cinda had with Patrick.

And why wasn't Robert married or engaged? Lissia was recovering from a broken heart, according to Sorcha, but what about Robert? Scotland wasn't full of lords and ladies that Sorcha could be so choosy for her children.

Adult children. Paislee and Lissia were probably the same age.

Lydia called and the two chatted hands-free as she drove.

"Lydia, why isn't Robert married?"

Lydia burst out laughing. "What if Sorcha is trying tae set you up?"

Paislee groaned at the idea and drawled, "He *is* the Earl of Lyon."

"Robert is just a guy who wears his kilt like anybody else."

"I didn't get that matchmaking vibe from Sorcha at all," Paislee said. "She'll want someone with a pedigree tae match Robert's. Besides, I have my hands full right now."

"With Hamish. Just be yourself," Lydia advised. "You are Paislee Shaw, creator of cashmere fashion. Yarn *artiste*."

Lydia had always been her biggest fan. Paislee laughed. "I might have cards made up." She turned and drove through the open castle gates. "I'm here."

"Text when you're on your way back. I'm dying tae know everything," Lydia said.

Her friend kept up on the latest gossip but was never mean about it. Paislee was quieter as she collected information and didn't like to repeat things that were unkind. She still told Lydia just about everything, to be locked in the bestie vault.

"Bye!" She ended the call and saw Patrick on horseback riding up to see who had arrived. Two large hounds were at either side of the horse.

She lowered the window, but Patrick just waved her through, his handsome face in a scowl. If Robert was forty, then Patrick had to be midthirties. He gestured for her to park down by the gift shop to the left of the castle.

The gravel still sparkled due to the rainy morning and appeared shiny new. A little drizzle fell as she turned the engine off.

Paislee exited the Juke, almost sorry she didn't have her pink boots on. Patrick didn't care for her, or maybe it wasn't personal. It could be as simple as he didn't see a use for her and knitted cashmere.

Cinda had the door to the gift shop wide open and greeted her with a friendly smile. Paislee unpacked her shopping bag, as well as her purse, her boots crunching on the stones. It smelled of fresh outdoors—earth, grass, pine trees.

And cows. Couldn't get past the cows.

Patrick had gone to the barn, and she could hear him talk to the dogs. Paislee entered the shop. Sorcha grinned and pushed away from the counter, walking toward her in brown slacks and an ivory silk blouse. "You're here! I was going tae tell you not tae come but thankfully the rain stopped."

"So nice tae see you again," Cinda said. "May I help ye with the bag?"

"Of course—thanks." Paislee handed it to the cute blonde in the short-sleeved blue dress.

Sorcha hugged her. Surprised, Paislee hugged her back. Sorcha leaned back as if she had terrible news. "Robert willnae be joining us after all."

Chapter 11

"Oh!" Paislee kept her smile on her face. How on earth was she supposed to react to that? The point of her coming to lunch was to meet the earl and talk to him about the note.

Sorcha didn't look at Paislee but nodded at Cinda. "Cinda, I'm certain you can manage things for the next hour. I've placed an advert in the paper so we might have some phone calls or online orders. Paislee and I will be back after lunch."

Cinda nodded, unable to hide a hint of disappointment. "Well, say hello tae Patrick for me."

Sorcha tipped her head and spoke coolly. "You just saw him this morning at the barn when you arrived for work. Next time, please come straight tae the gift shop."

Cinda stepped back, her mouth trembling as she accepted the rebuke. "Enjoy!"

Paislee felt sorry for the lass. Did she have a crush? Were she and Patrick hooking up behind Sorcha's back?

"Our chef does wonders with the old recipes, giving them a modern twist that Robert goes on aboot." Sorcha guided Paislee out to the hall that led to the dining room.

The kitchen was below this floor in the basement and savory spices wafted upward. Her mouth watered. "It smells amazing."

"And tastes even better. Lissia and Patrick will join us. I'd asked Robert but he backed oot at the last moment when he realized there would be company." Sorcha's jaw tightened.

"I'm sorry! Should I go . . . ?" Paislee glanced behind her, uncomfortable.

"Absolutely not. I've run this castle for decades and I'm not pleased with how Robert is acting right now. Please keep that between us." Sorcha held her gaze, her green eyes as hard as emeralds.

Paislee nodded. "Of course."

"Patrick and Lissia know not tae thwart me, but I believe Robert has forgotten he needs me and my direction. I've brought this castle from the brink of poverty," Sorcha said as they walked. "When Dermot died, there were debts that had tae be paid. Despite my grief, in order tae save the castle, I had tae act fast. Guided Robert into selling off the outer parcels of farmland, and Patrick was a natural with the cattle. Lissia and I went through every item in the attics—if we didnae need it, we sold it as a private seller so nobody would know. We were solvent." The pride she felt was evident in her words.

Paislee nodded. Wait. Were?

She couldn't ask for clarity as they had stopped before a partially open door that Sorcha pushed further, and they entered. A long rectangular table was set with five place settings. Shallow bowls, folded cloth napkins, silver spoons, and a small bread dish for each.

Patrick was on one side, Lissia the other. She was gestured next to Lissia, and Sorcha sat between Patrick and the head of the table. "Robert willnae be joining us," Sorcha said. "Neither will Cinda." She rang a service bell next to her plate.

As if waiting for the summons, a maid entered and served soup from a ceramic tureen with a ladle. Warm rolls were passed around. Small balls of butter were placed on the bread plate.

Lissia looked like she wanted to discuss Robert's absence, but Patrick shook his head at his sister. "Excellent," Patrick said after his first sip.

"This recipe is several hundred years old, and our chef has perfected it with our own mushrooms and herbs grown on the property," Sorcha said. "We should jar it and sell it in the gift shop."

Patrick winced as if discussing such things wasn't done in company. Then he squinted at Paislee. "You were here for the barbecue. Black terrier."

"Yes." Paislee halted midway with the spoon to her mouth. "I was with my son, and my grandfather. Wallace is the family pet. He chased a red squirrel into the forest." She quickly ate the bite and swallowed. Brandy, cream, and chunks of mushroom. "Delicious!"

"It is! We are all aboot pets here," Lissia said. "Dogs mostly, but cats, too. Patrick once trained a squirrel tae do tricks."

"I remember that," Sorcha said with a fond chuckle. "Patrick has a way with animals. Lissia has a green thumb. Robert . . ." She shook her head and looked at her two well-behaved children. "I've asked Paislee here tae discuss what happened Saturday."

The siblings exchanged glances.

"Why is that?" Lissia asked. "Robert said we arenae tae talk tae anybody aboot it."

"Robert is being foolish," Patrick said. "I agree with Mum. If there is anything tae discover it's best tae handle it our way so that the castle isnae touched by scandal that might tarnish the Clan Grant name."

"Exactly," Sorcha said. "You are so right, Patrick. Tae my knowledge, Robert doesnae have anything tae keep from the police so he might as well talk with them. Paislee was here that night, and she heard Clyde talk aboot the anonymous letter." Sorcha turned to Paislee. "Robert said he didnae write anything, anonymous or otherwise, tae Clyde Cunningham. As for Jory cheating? Well, it would make sense as tae how he'd won."

Paislee sipped another spoonful. "Have Jory's bagpipes been located?"

"Not yet," Sorcha said. "The police have been verra thorough in their search around the property."

"I have been, too," Patrick said. "Horseback, truck, and hiking the fields."

The thing was, if the Grants had something to hide, Paislee believed that Patrick would get rid of evidence to help his brother.

No doubt Zeffer thought the same, which was why he'd been on the grounds so often. Yet, they hadn't turned up. Where were Jory's pipes?

Lissia delicately scooped the last of her soup from her bowl. "Paislee, what did ye see when it happened? Jerry was right there on the spot. Arenae you friends?"

Paislee hid a smile and peered into her nearly empty bowl. As much as she wanted to, she could not lick it clean.

Of course, if she was after information, it made sense that the Grants also wanted answers. Jerry, her friend, was under suspicion, and Robert, their head of castle, was a person of interest to Zeffer, since Clyde had accused Robert of penning the notes.

Would clearing one name hurt the other?

Paislee set her spoon down, remembering her granny's lessons on manners. Sadly. "Jerry's been delivering my yarn at Cashmere Crush for years." She shrugged. "I barely know him outside of work."

Sorry, Jerry. She hoped that would lower the Grants' guard.

The maid entered and whisked their bowls away, returning with artistic petit fours on individual dessert plates.

"Coffee? Tea?" the maid asked.

"Nothing for me," Sorcha said.

Paislee followed her hostess's suit and said no thank you.

"I'm sorry that today didnae go as planned." Sorcha sighed. "I asked Robert repeatedly tae join us but . . . well. He is his own man."

"I don't mind at all," Paislee said after a bite of delicate pastry. It was a treat, and she didn't think much of Robert anyway.

"Do you think this Jerry bloke might have done something tae Jory?" Patrick asked.

Paislee kept her expression neutral. There was no way she would help them pin any suspicion on her friend. "Jerry was sitting on the bench below me," she explained with a shake of her head. "He immediately went tae Jory's side, prepared tae do CPR. It wasn't necessary as Jory never stopped breathing."

"And the pipes?" Patrick asked.

"Jerry accidentally hit them with his shoe and so moved them out of the way," Paislee said. "He looked around for a teammate tae give it tae, but they were all stunned. Clyde was on the mobile and didn't realize anything had happened."

"That's so odd," Lissia said.

"I agree," Sorcha said.

"And did the DI question Clyde?" Lissia asked.

"That evening, Clyde was questioned by two different officers. I don't know about later," Paislee said.

"How was lunch with Meri?" Sorcha asked. "You didnae call."

"Good." It had been too busy. "Oh! Meri had also received an anonymous letter saying that Jory had cheated the previous year. She'd turned it in tae the police." Paislee looked at Lissia. "I don't understand how a person could cheat. I've never played the bagpipes, but it seems impossible tae do. I mean, you blow in the mouth part and cover the recorder . . ."

Lissia smiled. "That's called the blowpipe. But that *is* something we could ask Robert. It's always been the snare drums for me. He would know the bagpipe inside and oot."

Sorcha sighed.

Patrick patted his mother's hand. "He'll come around."

"Is there something specific that Robert is . . . apprehensive . . . the police will find out?" Paislee decided to press ahead. "Perhaps a bet gone wrong?"

Lissia averted her gaze and wiped crumbs from her petit four to her plate. Patrick glared at Paislee as if appalled she would broach the subject.

"Robert . . . likes tae gamble." Sorcha shrugged. "Sometimes he wins, there are other times when he loses."

"Gambling is a weakness," Patrick said sternly. "It cannae get oot that the Earl of Lyon was willing tae put up valuable farmland tae pay off his debts!" Anger made him forget that Paislee was there as he shouted the words to his mother.

"Patrick, pet," Sorcha said calmly. "You made it right."

Paislee blinked as she absorbed that news but didn't otherwise react. Sorcha had said she'd sold land in order to pay off her husband's debts, but that would have been ten or more years ago. This must be a recent debt. Was it the fifty thousand that Zeffer already knew about?

"I thinned our herd of sheep instead. We need the farmers on the land," Patrick said, appealing to Paislee. Paislee was beginning to understand his attitude about the place and his brother a little better.

Because Robert was the oldest, he had the title whether he deserved it or not. Her sympathies leaned toward Patrick. He wanted her to know of the family's sacrifice.

A knock sounded on the door and Cinda entered with a smile at them all, but it lingered on Patrick.

"Milady, a message from Robert." Cinda passed the note to the dowager countess. Cinda did not have permission to call her Sorcha? Very interesting.

"Thank you." Sorcha opened the note and scanned it.

Cinda went around the table to wait near Patrick.

Lissia shook her head at the blonde but didn't say anything. Did everyone but Sorcha know that Cinda held a torch for Patrick?

Sorcha paled and dropped the note to the table. "Robert's found the bagpipe."

"Robert?" Patrick asked in surprise. "But I've—"

"Let's go. He's at the river behind the barn." Sorcha stared at Cinda. "Did Finn send this? Not Robert?"

"Aye." Cinda didn't move.

Sorcha's lips thinned. "Thank you. You may return tae the gift shop."

Cinda nodded and slowly left.

Lissia looked at her mother, then Paislee, and back again. She read the undercurrent. Should Paislee be involved?

"Robert hasnae done anything tae deserve such questioning," Sorcha said. "Paislee, come with us. I hope . . . I hope this clears his name. Just because he'd bet that he'd win doesnae mean he had a reason tae harm Jory. If anything, he would want Jory alive tae accept Jory's money. Robert was that sure he'd win."

Patrick, Lissia, Paislee, and Sorcha all stood.

"This way," Sorcha said.

They went out a different exit from the rear of the home that spilled to an outdoor fountain and a separate garage. The open door showed several vehicles, all gleaming and expensive.

"Finn!" Sorcha called.

The outdoorsman waited by the fountain and wore a grim expression. "Milady."

Sorcha stopped abruptly and stared at the man, but he didn't give a clue as to what Robert was doing. "This way."

Had Robert wanted Finn to get them, or had Finn acted without Robert's consent? It didn't matter now.

The river was full thanks to the heavy rains. The side banks were lush and green, mossy stone leading downward to the rushing water.

Paislee was quiet and hoped they'd forget she was there. Lissia was at her mother's side, there if needed but not intrusive.

"Robert!" Sorcha scrambled down the embankment after Patrick—then Lissia, then Paislee, with Finn last.

Robert was bent over the riverbank, tugging the drone pipes. There was rope around the tallest piece and something was stuck on the rock. He pulled and pulled.

"I'm afraid I'm going tae break it," Robert said, his breaths coming in a huff.

"Let it go!" Patrick said.

"I cannae." Robert's teeth chattered.

How long had he been in the cold river water? True, it was only up to his ankles, but his clothes were wet as if he'd slipped.

"What happened, Robbie?" Sorcha asked soothingly. A mum's tone.

"I was walking along the banks when I saw a flash of metal. After so long searching I was sure I had tae be wrong. I dinnae think I am." Robert's lips were blue and Lissia left her mother to put her arm around her brother, lending strength and warmth.

Lissia studied the pipes, then Robert, with a question in her tone. "Are these Jory's?"

"They have tae be," Robert said. "I was hoping you'd recognize them, Liss."

Lissia shook her head helplessly. "I was concentrating on my snare that day. I didnae want tae mess it up for you."

"Paislee?" Sorcha turned to her, her arms around her waist against the chill, and possibly bracing for what they might find.

Paislee did her best to recall the bagpipes that Jory had held so powerfully. They'd been black with silver fittings. "I don't remember exactly, but there was silver flashing as he performed."

Robert nodded. "Aye! This has silver on it."

Finn had scrambled up the hill and now came down again with a large fishing net. "Milord," he said, gently scooting Robert out of the way. "May I?"

"Guid idea," Robert said, body sagging after his huge effort to save the pipes from the river's grasp. "Aye. Thanks, Finn."

Robert stepped back and Lissia loosened her hold on her oldest brother. His teeth chattered and he rubbed his hands together. They were both damp.

"Should we call the DI?" Sorcha asked. "Turn this in?"

Robert's mouth thinned at Paislee's presence. A witness, whether he wanted it or not. "Aye, I guess so." He smirked and inched away from his mother.

Patrick took Robert's precarious place on the mossy bank and reached to help Finn drag the pipes in. "I'm here, Finn."

"Thanks," the groundskeeper said.

Together they untangled the ropes around the single tall piece and the two shorter ones, dragging the instrument to the shore.

"Is it ruined?" Paislee asked. Metal, leather, fabric. The Great Highland Bagpipe didn't appear at all as grandiose as it had in Jory's arms.

"It's *destroyed*," Robert said, as if Paislee was a simpleton. "There's no fixing this mess. It had tae be five thousand pounds' worth of pipes. Why would anybody want tae annihilate them?"

"Robert!" Sorcha admonished.

He waved her away.

"Let's go," Lissia said. "Come on, Mum."

Robert led the way nimbly while Lissia walked at Sorcha's side. Finn was at her other side, in the event she slipped.

Patrick easily hefted the net with the wet instrument across his back and climbed up the bank. Paislee went last, taking a few discreet pictures of the bagpipes. The tallest drone pipe had broken, revealing the insides, the leather of the bag torn.

Paislee had no idea what she was looking at, but Jerry might know if this was Jory's. She texted him the photos. She would let the Grants call Zeffer—they had until she left, and then she would make sure she contacted him herself if they didn't.

The Grants, and Finn, reached the top of the bank. Paislee followed slower as she sent the photos to Jerry. She had no time to send a message to explain them.

Sorcha peered down at Paislee from the top of the slope. "All right, dear?"

"I'm fine." Just then, she slipped a little on a mossy rock, but Finn reached back and caught her wrist. "Thanks."

"Not a problem." He was very strong, Finn was. He adored Sorcha, it was clear, though it wasn't a romantic type of love. More like servant to queen.

People were unique with many reasons for doing things that made no sense to others. Paislee couldn't wait to sit down with a hot cup of tea and her knitting, and sort these threads.

Jory's lady friends. Had Jory made one of them jealous, and they'd gone for the jugular?

Or had Clyde decided to take revenge over the accusation of Jory, his supposed best piper, being a cheat? And then what? Randomly tossed the pipes in the river?

Paislee's phone dinged and she sucked in a breath, hoping that the Grants hadn't noticed her phone in her palm.

She discreetly turned off the ringer, despite her promise to Lydia that she'd keep it on.

Keeping back a pace, Paislee watched the family move toward the castle. Patrick placed the wet bagpipes on the stone bench by the fountain.

There was no proof that Jory had cheated, just two anonymous letters. Gran would say that such a person might be a coward.

Could that type of person also be a killer?

Chapter 12

Patrick made a big deal of phoning the Nairn Police Station, asking for Constable Thorn. He had to leave a message, sending Paislee the clear signal that it was handled.

After being rushed out of the castle before the police called back, Paislee drove to Cashmere Crush. It wasn't quite time to pick up Brody yet. She hadn't been paid. Darn it. She texted Lydia, who'd texted her, and wanted to meet her at the shop. Nothing from Jerry.

Paislee entered from the back entrance as it started to rain again. Lydia was seated at the counter, chatting away with Grandpa. Her caramel curls swooped beautifully to her shoulders, and she owned her black power suit, slacks and jacket, with stilettos.

"Well? What did ye find oot aboot Robert from the dowager countess?" Grandpa asked.

"And hello tae you, too," Paislee chuckled. "While I was there, Robert discovered bagpipes floating in the river. I don't know if they're Jory's, but they were dark and had silver on them."

"That was convenient," Grandpa said as she told them how lunch had gone, with Robert skipping the meal rather than talk to Paislee.

Lydia shook her head. "Too convenient."

Customers milled around inside as if not wanting to leave the cozy space for the rain, and Paislee couldn't blame them.

"Grandpa, would you please go get Brody? I'll order dinner for takeout so it will be ready when you pick me up at six. Better make it six thirty. Okay?"

He pulled on his tam and light rain jacket and blew them a kiss before leaving. After thirty minutes, Lydia also gave up on getting more news and returned to the estate office nearby.

Customers came first and Paislee would need to build up the cash in the register if the dowager countess wasn't going to pay her.

It hadn't been intentional. Or had it? Paislee would never understand rich people. Gran had called the working class the salt of the earth and considered her job as a teacher essential to the community. They were equals.

That night, Paislee followed through on the promised Chinese food because it wasn't her family's fault that the dowager countess hadn't paid her.

"So good, Mum!" Brody said as he ate a second cookie. They continued the tradition of making up their own fortunes. "Here's an idea." He stared at the white paper and then said, "More rain, means more lo mein."

Paislee laughed. "Good thing we live in Scotland."

Grandpa adopted a wise expression as he said, "Tae truly find oneself, one must play hide-and-seek alone."

Brody tossed his fortune at Grandpa with a boo.

Still chuckling, Paislee noted the time. Almost eight. "Are you going tae the pub with James tonight?"

"Tomorrow." Grandpa scraped the crumbs to his palm and put them in the empty container. "His daughter wanted him home for family dinner."

Family was important. James's daughter, Nora, was fifty plus and had children of her own. Paislee turned to Brody. "Ready for the game tomorrow? It's an early one—nine."

"Yeah." Brody rubbed his tummy and scouted the containers. "I'm still hungry."

Paislee passed over extra rice that he doused with soy sauce. It was gone in a few bites. "You better not be growing again! I just bought you new clothes."

"You dinnae want me tae eat?" Brody widened his eyes dramatically.

Paislee thought about it for all of two seconds. "Of course I do. Have some cereal."

"No thanks." Brody got up and put the dishes in the sink. "Movie time?"

"You bet." Paislee grabbed her knitting and the Shaws went to the lounge area.

Brody took one end of the couch and Paislee the other. Wallace sprawled between them, and Grandpa relaxed in the armchair. He'd snagged the remote first, a game the two played. Paislee didn't care. She only watched with partial attention as she knitted.

Inventory needed to be replenished, not to mention the online orders, and now the castle. Well, she'd be more excited about the castle when the dowager countess paid the bill.

The next morning, after a filling breakfast with oatcakes, ham, and lots of orange juice, they piled into the Juke for the football field.

The engine clicked but didn't rev. "Uh-oh."

Grandpa buckled in. "You have an appointment Wednesday."

She patted the steering wheel. "Hear that, my girl? You just need tae be good until Wednesday."

"Try again, Mum. We cannae be late!"

"I know!" Paislee closed her eyes and said a little prayer. She turned the key again. Nothing.

Brody looked at her with panic. They had sliced apples, juice pouches, and cheese squares to bring to the game. A case of water.

The engine caught. Died.

"It's not the battery," Grandpa said. "If it was, then it wouldnae catch at all."

Paislee knew nothing about cars except to take them to Eddy. It was his area of expertise. Just like he couldn't knit a cashmere mock turtleneck, she couldn't do more than open the bonnet.

She closed her eyes and prayed harder. The engine revved to life. "Oh, thank you!" All three exhaled in relief.

They arrived at the football park, and she worried about turning the SUV off. "It will be fine," Grandpa said. "If we need tae, we can call a taxi and get this lovely lass in on Monday. I told Eddy it wasnae urgent."

Things had changed.

"All right." Paislee turned it off and the car sounded normal.

Brody ran ahead with the cooler and she and Grandpa followed, setting out their camp chairs on the sidelines.

She greeted Bennett and Edwyn. The younger Maclean was a carbon copy of his da, blond curls and big jade-green eyes. Bennett brought his chair close to theirs as Edwyn and Brody joined their coach.

"Hey!" Bennett said. "It's going tae be a braw game. Rain forecast for noon, but we should be guid—even if we hit overtime."

"I'm glad for that. Sometimes I fear I might start tae mold," Paislee joked.

"I hear you," Bennett said. "Cannae imagine living anywhere else, though."

The boys were down and then Edwyn, offense, kicked in a goal, with Brody as the assist. The coach cheered and looked back at Paislee, Grandpa, and Bennett. "Dream team right there, mark me words."

Bennett grinned for the coach.

When the coach turned back to the field, Bennett said, "Edwyn is thinking he doesnae want tae play anymore after this year. Can you believe it?"

"Too bad!" Grandpa said. They all enjoyed being spectators.

"He doesn't like it?" Paislee asked. Her stomach tightened with nerves. If Edwyn quit, would Brody? She liked that Brody had a healthy sport to play.

"It's not that as much as Edwyn wants tae try other things," Bennett said. "I want him busy doing things that are constructive. I worry he might decide tae goof off."

"Goof off" could be code for drugs or drinking or girls. Parties instead of practice. Oh, no. Paislee felt his pain—and feared that Brody might feel the same.

"Dinnae mention it, though, okay?" Bennett asked.

"Oh, we won't," Paislee said. Grandpa nodded.

Edwyn scored a goal and the team won.

This moment was bittersweet—enjoying the now while concerned for later. Brody and Edwyn went in Bennett's new jeep to the little bungalow behind the comic book shop/arcade that they shared with Bennett's girlfriend, Alexa.

The only constant in life, Gran used to say, was change.

Paislee and Grandpa went home and she opened the back door for Wallace, making sure he had dry kibble and water.

Grandpa nudged her arm when he realized that she was quiet. "Are you okay?"

"Aye." Her nose stung with unshed tears. "Brody's growing up, that's all. I can't control so much of what's happening."

Grandpa chuckled and peered into her eyes. "You've taught him well. Dinnae worry so much. You cannae change a damn thing."

"I miss Gran and her sage advice. No offense, Grandpa, but telling me not tae worry?" Paislee sniffed and reached for a paper napkin on the table to dab her nose. "I can't help it. What if he and Edwyn grow apart? What if Edwyn and Brody quit football for drugs? What if Edwyn coerces Brody tae drink? What if Brody turns into a cat burglar tae support a drinking habit?"

"Lass. Kids will be kids—it's their job tae grow up. Brody's twelve and not in the bottle yet. I was ten when I had my first wee nip of whisky."

"Ten!" Paislee clapped her open hand to her chest.

"A nip from me da while we were fishing tae keep away the

cold. Dinnae say how long ago that was." Grandpa raised a finger. "How old were you when you had your first wee taste?"

Paislee sank down at the kitchen table, her mind churning back through time.

"Be honest," Grandpa said, taking a chair across from her.

She thought back to her and Lydia, always her partner in good times and bad, drinking wine. "We were fourteen. We snuck her mum's sweet wine from the fridge." Sophia Barron liked a prosecco sugary enough to damage the enamel on your teeth.

"And you survived?" Grandpa teased.

"We had terrible headaches the next day," she said with a laugh. "We didn't drink again until a party that summer. It was never a big deal."

"It's part of growing up." Grandpa shrugged. "Drugs?"

"No. Not even weed."

"Me either." Grandpa tapped the table between them. "Brody's been raised with guid morals, Paislee. You've done well."

Her phone dinged a text from Hamish. He offered to pick her up that evening for dinner. She shot off a text of agreement.

"You can take the car if you like," Paislee said.

"And what are you doing?"

Her blush was painful. "Hamish is taking me tae dinner."

"Oh, is he now?" Grandpa leaned back and crossed his knee with his ankle. He rubbed his trimmed beard.

"Aye." She jumped up and went to the basket of laundry. It was a never-ending chore with Brody's football uniforms.

"Should we have a blether over his intentions? Dinner number three?" Grandpa laughed. "Paislee, love, sit doon. Relax. You look ready tae combust."

Paislee cursed her redhead complexion. She could hide nothing. Instead, she put the basket down and smiled at her grandpa. "I'm going tae get ready. You and James have fun tonight. Call a taxi if you get stuck." She might even take a bubble bath.

"James is driving. Have fun yourself, but not too much fun, if you know what I mean." His brows waggled up and down.

"Grandpa!"

Paislee spritzed a light floral perfume as she pouted her lips at her reflection in the vanity mirror in her bedroom. Fine wrinkles had appeared between her brow and around her eyes. She didn't mind them so much.

Wrinkles were signs of a life well-lived, Gran used to say. Her face had become very well-lived at the end. And loved.

Lydia called, as Paislee had ignored her friend's texts.

"Sexy lingerie? No underwear?" Lydia suggested. "It's time tae get oot into the world, my sweet friend."

The lingerie in question had been bought for the wedding when Paislee had been Lydia's maid of honor. It had been an excuse that allowed Lydia to update Paislee's underwear drawer. So what if most of what she wore was cotton and comfortable?

"We barely hold hands," Paislee said. "Stop rushing me!"

Lydia sighed. "What are you wearing?"

"Blue dress, thin straps, beige pashmina, and beige heels."

"You know what I mean!"

Paislee laughed. "A full slip with a corset. And iron under-wear."

"That's it. I'm coming over," Lydia threatened.

A knock sounded on the front door. "Gotta run—Hamish is here."

This reminded her of when she and Lydia had been sixteen and seventeen, going on dates and grading kisses afterward. Palm sweats. Roaming hands. Now she was a single mum on a third date, nearing thirty, while Lydia was married to her knight, in a second marriage.

What would she say to the naïve girls they'd both been? Be patient?

"Call me!"

"I will." Paislee hung up and ran down the stairs, not caring if she made a squeak on the third and fifth stairs because she was the only one home. She blew a kiss to Wallace and opened the door, saying hello to Hamish and urging him back down the stoop to his car. It was a new model; conservative, like him.

"Hi!" Hamish, with dark brown hair and brown eyes, was incredibly handsome. He stayed fit with golf. He wore a loose short-sleeved button-up camp shirt with a subtle print. Leaves, maybe. Chinos. Hamish looked very good in chinos. Way more relaxed than the suits he wore as headmaster of Fordythe primary school.

"Hello. Thanks for driving. The Juke's acting up a bit, and we have an appointment on Wednesday with Eddy and . . . I'm babbling. Sorry!"

"It's okay. Are you all right?" Hamish drove to the A96, the main road leading toward Inverness.

"I am!" Paislee told herself to calm down and just be in the moment.

Hamish briefly glanced toward her, concern flashing across his face. "I made us reservations at a new steak house on the water in Dairlee."

"That sounds great." An adventure. She sent him a shy smile.

"You look beautiful," Hamish said.

"Ta. Thanks." She blushed and peered out the window, hoping he wouldn't notice. If he did, he was a gentleman and didn't comment. Her phone dinged a text. She saw that it was from Jerry, asking her to call him. Probably about the photos she'd sent him. And he was just now getting back to her?

Jerry could wait. She was on a date and Jory's death wasn't anything that she could make a difference about right now.

They arrived at the restaurant and Hamish let a valet park his car. Hamish clasped her hand as they neared the front door and her skin warmed pleasantly. He opened it for her. The interior was dim but opulent with glossy mahogany pillars and brass accents. The scent of meat cooking made her hungry.

Paislee was reminded of the barbecue at the castle, which had been rustic, while this was something luxurious.

The waiter gave them a romantic table near a long bed of coals with roasts on spits being grilled. A wall of windows showed rocks and the ocean splashing against them.

"What will you have tae drink?" the waiter asked.

She smiled at Hamish. "Wine would be nice. Lydia said that red goes with beef, from when she and Corbin were in Germany."

"That's correct," the waiter said. "I can recommend our house cabernet sauvignon. It will pair well with the steak or the lamb beautifully because of the high tannin content."

"Sounds great tae me." Paislee folded her hands in her lap.

"Make it two glasses, then," Hamish said.

"Perfect. Feel free tae peruse our menu for sides while I get those. You can order either beef or lamb, or both, for your meal." The waiter continued, "You may choose two side dishes."

"How fun," Paislee murmured to Hamish when the waiter left.

"I'd heard aboot this place from some of the parents at Fordythe. I'm glad you were willing tae try it," Hamish said. "I wasnae sure if it would be too heavy."

"I am unapologetically a carnivore." Paislee bared her teeth.

Laughing, Hamish reached for her hand. "Me too."

The conversation flowed beautifully during dinner, and she was sorry when she was too full to eat another bite because it meant that the evening was over.

They had set some ground rules when Paislee had first agreed to a dinner with Hamish. Slow, slow, slow. Friends first. She wasn't looking for a relationship. She couldn't promise anything. Brody came first for her.

If Hamish still wanted to go out to dinner, then, so be it.

They were to pick and pay for the restaurant they selected, so Paislee would choose next. "I don't know how I can top this," she said on the drive home.

Though full, she wasn't the least bit sleepy. She was too aware of Hamish in the seat across from her. His hands on the steering wheel, his shoulders filling his shirt.

"It was a wonderful night," Hamish said in a low voice that sent chills down her spine. "Especially getting tae know you more."

They parked before her house. There was an awkward silence as she considered her options. Should she invite him in? Was Grandpa home? The Juke was in the carport because James had driven Grandpa to the pub.

"I guess I should go," Hamish said. He didn't pressure her but let her take the lead. She really liked that. She really liked him.

"Would you care tae come in?" Paislee blushed. "Not for a . . . just for a drink, or a cup of tea?" She didn't want the night to end.

Hamish immediately agreed. "I'd love tae."

They each exited the sedan and went up the stairs, his cologne teasing her senses. What would it be like to kiss him? His mouth was full, his chest broad.

What on earth was she thinking?

She unlocked the door with shaking hands and went inside. Her mouth was dry just considering what might be next. Wallace remembered Hamish, and while he didn't exactly welcome the man, he didn't bark, so that was good.

Paislee shrugged off her pashmina and hurried down the hall to the kitchen, draping it over a chair. "Would you like tea, or whisky? Tea *and* whisky?" She whirled after turning on the electric kettle.

Hamish was right at her back, now, her front. "Oh!"

She stepped into the counter, banging her hip.

Hamish raised her chin softly and peered into her eyes. "Paislee . . . may I kiss you? It's been all I can think aboot. For months. Mibbe years."

She bit her lip, slightly out of breath. She'd wanted that, too. "Only a kiss, Hamish."

Hamish cupped her cheek and smoothed his thumb over her skin, gently, as if she might take flight. "You dinnae have tae answer, but when was your last physical relationship?"

With an exhale she said, "Brody."

Surprise, followed by understanding, filled his brown eyes. "I see. We can take this any speed you want, Paislee."

He kissed her then. Slow, warm, just the right amount of pressure. Hamish swept her away with desire her body had completely forgotten.

She stood on her tiptoes, kissing him back.

His hand lowered to her hip.

He tasted of the mints they'd shared after dinner. Glad they'd both had one, Paislee leaned closer to him. His chest was just as muscled beneath her palm as she'd imagined.

A crack sounded.

It took her a moment to understand that something wasn't right.

Was that Grandpa home already?

She started to pull back from Hamish, in a daze. And then, she and Hamish were doused with cold water, slimy, and bits of ceiling plaster.

If it wasn't so awful, she'd laugh.

Chapter 13

Like any good Scotswoman, Paislee held her own superstitions—not to the point of Lydia's mother-in-law, but she took this as a literal sign from Above that she and Hamish were not meant to be.

Was it her granny splitting them apart? Her da? Was this the universe's way of saying she should have answered Jerry's texts? Or, and this was probably the right of it, was it a sign that she wasn't done with being Mum yet?

"Are you all right?" Hamish immediately asked with concern. Cool in an emergency, he brushed water from her shoulders and plaster from her hair, never minding that he was also damp.

Wallace barked like crazy at the commotion, racing around the table, plaster in his fur. The front door swung open. Grandpa whistled and sang off-key, loudly, as if to warn them he was coming in.

A few minutes before the ceiling's demise that might have been needed, but right now?

"Grandpa, grab towels, would you?" The ceiling continued to drip, bigger drops in places. Paislee selected a large pot and tried to find exactly where to place it to do the most good. Her ceiling was ruined. Water landed on her beloved kitchen table.

"Hamish! Och, bloody hell. What happened here?" Grandpa went into the downstairs bathroom. "I'll turn the water off." The stop tap to control the whole water supply in the house was under that sink.

"The ceiling. The upstairs bath!" The enormity of what would need to be fixed stole her breath.

How dare she think she was fine? That she could manage? "I'm so glad Brody's not here."

"He's fine. Are you?" Grandpa handed Paislee the last dry towel in the house.

"Yes." Was she? Her forehead stung.

"Angus," Hamish said. Paislee couldn't blame him for his somewhat stunned expression.

"Thank you for a wonderful dinner," Paislee said, dabbing water from the ends of her hair. She imagined she resembled a drowned rat thanks to the deluge.

"Paislee—" Hamish began.

She held up her hand. "Thank you. I don't want tae be rude, but I really need tae wrap my head around this. You should go."

"I understand!" Hamish didn't move away. "I want tae help. Can I do anything? Find you a hotel?"

"The bedrooms are fine for tonight." She watched in horror as another piece of plaster plopped into the sink and on the stove despite the water being turned off. She looked up to see rotted wood spiderwebbing the ceiling.

"You cannae use the kitchen," Hamish said. "It isnae safe."

"I won't!" She urged him toward the front door in a daze.

"I feel terrible leaving," Hamish said, dragging his feet.

"Don't—please. I will figure this out." This was so embarrassing. Yes, embarrassing. She owned it.

"You dinnae need tae be alone!" Hamish said.

"I am not alone, Hamish. I have Grandpa. I need tae look at my insurance." She needed to talk to Lydia, who had convinced her to pay a tiny bit more for her premium in case disaster struck. Did this qualify?

Another plop sounded as wood fell and then another waterfall over the fridge. Paislee was being punished for sure, thinking she could have a life.

She got the message loud and clear.

"Paislee . . ." Hamish said as she gently but firmly ushered him to the front stoop.

"Good night, Hamish."

"I'll call you," he said.

"It's okay. I'll call you when I get things sorted."

"Things like what? The ceiling?" Hamish's brow rose as he gripped the threshold of her doorway, not willing to budge. "Or other things?"

He must have sensed that something in her had changed.

"Now is not a good time," Paislee said sadly.

"I dinnae accept that."

She blinked tears from her eyes. "Find a nice woman who is ready for you now, Hamish. You deserve that happiness."

He shook his head, angry.

Paislee closed the door, slowly, not wanting to hurt his fingers, until he finally released the wood. When it was shut all the way she put her back to it and pressed her hand to her stomach. She felt sick.

Grandpa crossed his arms. "What was that aboot?"

Tears streamed but she wouldn't look at Grandpa until she swiped her cheeks and had them controlled. "None of your business."

"Hamish cares aboot you." Grandpa reached for her shoulder and squeezed it gently.

"I don't have time for a relationship." Paislee pushed from the door toward the bottom step leading upstairs to her room, but held onto the post. She had to brave the mess in the kitchen, not bury her head under the comforter in her room.

"Ye're putting up walls against a guid man," Grandpa declared.

"I need them. I should have done something about the ceiling." She passed Grandpa in the hall to the kitchen and moved the circular table aside.

The rug beneath it was soaked. That could be replaced but the table couldn't be if it was completely ruined.

On autopilot, she went to the back porch and retrieved a mop and the cleaning bucket, bringing them inside.

"I dinnae think it's done falling yet, lass," Grandpa said kindly. "Why not wait until morning tae clean."

Paislee couldn't breathe and dragged the mop handle to the couch in the living area.

Grandpa poured a whisky for her and handed it to her. "Drink it doon, now. You're in shock."

Paislee did as directed, not a question asked. Why? How?

The whisky burned but also cleared the fog from her head.

She still couldn't move, but she recalled where she'd filed the insurance paperwork. The landline rang.

Grandpa answered. "Lydia, love, we've a spot of trouble tonight."

Paislee glared at Grandpa.

"Och, aye, Brody's fine. The ceiling collapsed and water is flooding the kitchen."

"Grandpa!" Paislee said.

"It's true, so?" Grandpa said to Paislee, then to Lydia, "She's upset with me that I told you."

Grandpa gave the receiver to Paislee, who still couldn't get up from the couch. She accepted it grudgingly.

"Hello, Lyd."

"I'm coming over!"

"Don't come over. There is nothing that you can do." Paislee shivered. "I am not being selfish or mean—I just don't know what tae think."

"I understand," Lydia said. "Your insurance will cover new pipes and fixtures. Paislee, I want you tae take pictures of the damage. Dinnae clean! I have the name of several plumbers. You call the insurance company in the morning and see what steps need tae be followed."

"I can do that," Paislee said. The whisky and the advice were just what she needed. "I can take pictures, then mop."

"Do not touch a thing!" Lydia repeated. "The agent will need tae see it at its worst."

"Okay. Don't clean." Paislee nudged the mop that rested next to her on the couch.

Grandpa had heard her and used the second mobile that Brody had forgotten to take with him today to snap photos. Another piece of wood and plaster dropped with a loud smack, almost getting Grandpa. Wallace leapt to the safety of the couch next to Paislee.

"What was that?" Lydia exclaimed.

"More ceiling."

Lydia groaned. "Please come over. You and Grandpa, Brody. Wallace."

"Brody is at Edwyn's. We are fine."

"Are you sure I cannae come over? I'll stay with you and eat chocolate. You willnae be able tae use the bathrooms. You turned the water off?"

There was a petrol station not far from the house that she could use, but there was always the trick to add water to the back of the toilet to flush. She had jugs of water for football games in the pantry.

"Aye. It's fine. Lyd, I love you so much. I just need a minute."

"Send me pictures. I will be there in the morning with coffee and breakfast sarnies, and a list of construction workers as well as plumbers."

"Okay. Thank you." Paislee nodded numbly.

"I'd called tae see how your date with Hamish went," Lydia said.

"It was great. The food was great. We were going tae kiss"—*had* kissed—"and the ceiling fell on me. I think it's a sign that I'm supposed tae be single a while yet."

"Paislee Ann!" Lydia shouted so loud it hurt Paislee's ear. "That is not true!"

"I don't want tae talk about it."

Grandpa handed her another glass of whisky and had one for himself. He spun the armchair so he could face her on the couch.

"I . . . I just am glad that you are all okay," Lydia said. "Wait, did you get hit?"

"Plaster. Water." Just the thing to cool an awakening libido.

"Unbelievable." Lydia sighed loudly. "I will see you in the morning. Seven. Mibbe earlier. I know you willnae sleep."

"It's Sunday," Paislee said.

"Find your insurance. Take pictures. Try and sleep because tomorrow will be a busy day."

Lydia ended the call a little miffed with Paislee, but Paislee couldn't soothe her bestie's feelings. Right now, she felt flayed alive.

She looked at Grandpa. "Lydia said tae take pictures. Find the insurance policy, which she thinks includes the pipes bursting."

Paislee wiped a tear.

"It will be okay. I've been saving my paychecks. I dinnae require much," her grandfather said. "I can help."

"Grandpa!" She patted Wallace at her side. "That's so sweet. I just don't know. I don't know where tae begin." Her mind couldn't handle the shock.

"Lydia will be over in the morning?" Grandpa asked.

"Aye, with breakfast sandwiches. We can move the kettle into here and make tea."

Grandpa shook his head. "Kettle got smashed, love. We will need tae buy a new one."

Her credit cards had just been used to buy Brody clothes for school. She had some room on them, but not enough to pay for a new kitchen. A new ceiling. Pipes.

Her lower lip trembled.

And what if the car needed more than just regular maintenance?

The bag of knitting she'd had by the table was drenched. She could see chunks of plaster on the project, which meant starting over.

For once, knitting didn't appeal to her. She was too frozen. Too numb.

"Grandpa." Paislee got up as if she was seventy-six instead of her grandfather. She replaced the receiver to its base and saw the message light blinking. What if it was Brody? She hit play. Jerry McFadden, asking her to call him and see him on Sunday. He'd left a message on her mobile.

Her phone was in her handbag, which had been on the counter and was now drenched. Could things get worse? "You got enough pictures?"

Grandpa stood, too, and they surveyed the motley kitchen and jagged open boards of the ruined ceiling.

"We can take more in the morning." Grandpa put his arm over her shoulders. "Damn it."

Paislee looked to the swear jar. Also smashed. She let free with a string of curses as more of the ceiling dropped. She started laughing and couldn't stop.

The next morning, Paislee awoke with a crick in her neck and a wee headache from too many glasses of whisky. The telly was still on low and Grandpa asleep in the armchair. Wallace was curled up on the other side of the couch.

She heard a soft knock on the door. Wallace alerted and woofed, avoiding the mess on the floor as they reached the hall.

Lydia was on the other side with Corbin, both in jeans and boots as if ready to get dirty—but stylishly. Lydia had a kerchief tied over her hair and Corbin wore a cap.

"Come in!" Paislee winced at the dim light from behind a cloud.

"Oh, Paislee!" Lydia and Corbin entered. Lydia stared at Paislee. "You have a bruise on your forehead, and your cheek."

She touched the sore areas. "I didn't feel it last night."

"Dinnae think we felt much of anything last night," Grandpa said, shuffling his slippered feet behind her. "Mornin'."

Grandpa's silver-gray hair was sticking up on one side and his eyes red-rimmed. He hadn't put on his glasses yet.

"Probably a guid thing," Lydia said, taking in the round kitchen table scooted up against the pantry. She raised a box of hot drinks. Corbin handed Grandpa a white bag that held food. "Oh, my sweets. This is awful."

"On the table by the couch," Paislee suggested. "There's room."

Corbin brought out his mobile. "Do you mind if I take pictures?"

"Please do. Grandpa got some but we don't know what tae look for, for the insurance. I have the policy on the table. My mobile phone is wet. Doesn't work at all. Dried out my credit cards and cash, though."

"What does the policy cover?" Lydia asked. "I forget exactly."

"I don't know. I don't understand it. I think we can have the pipes replaced but there will be a big deductible."

"Dinnae fash aboot that, now," Lydia said. "We will get things figured oot." She placed the box of coffee on the table. "You cannae live here like this."

"I have nowhere else tae go." Paislee was still in shock. "We have tae make it work."

"Or," Corbin said, opening the bag of sandwiches while Lydia handled hot drinks, "we discussed another option."

Lydia gave a mocha to Grandpa, cream and sugar in coffee for Paislee, and a chai for Corbin, keeping a mocha for herself.

"Thank you," Paislee said. She sipped. The only way she could drink the stuff, and Lydia had even added extra sugar.

"This bag has ham, egg, and cheese. This is sausage and cheese." Corbin offered them wrapped sandwiches.

Paislee couldn't eat. Her stomach was a knot of nerves.

"Please have a bite, especially if you were drinking last night." Lydia crossed her arms. "This will be a busy day and you'll need all of your strength."

Paislee accepted the sandwich and unwrapped it. Her stomach rolled.

"Trust me," Lydia said.

She nibbled a bite of the bread.

"Now. We happen tae have an extra house at the moment," Lydia said.

Paislee laughed and then coughed.

"It's true!" Lydia said. She smacked Paislee on the back.

"How luxurious," Paislee drawled, tears in her eyes.

"The point is that you, Grandpa, Brody, and Wallace can stay at the flat while your house is being worked on," Lydia said. "We're almost moved into ours as we decided tae leave the furniture and keep it as a rental anyway."

Grandpa eyed Paislee and took a big bite of his sandwich. His pride was as grand as hers, and yet he would do what she wanted. They had to have a roof for Brody's sake, if not their own.

Was this about being humbled? Was it a lesson that she needed to learn?

None of that mattered. What was most important was making sure that Brody was safe, and her wanting to do things herself had to take a back seat.

"How can you be moved in?" Paislee asked. "You just bought it."

"Money talks," Corbin said. "The owners had already moved oot, so it wasnae a problem."

"I know it's not your first choice," Lydia said.

Paislee blew out a breath and forced a bigger bite of her sandwich down.

"Thank you, Lydia and Corbin. I will accept the help with a grateful heart. Now, what does this policy even mean?"

She opened the paperwork and passed it to Lydia.

Lydia was an estate agent and familiar with what was mandatory and extra when it came to homeowner policies. She skimmed the page with her fingertip.

"You have something called Buildings and Contents. This

means, and I'm pretty sure the insurance agent will agree, that your appliances will need tae be replaced as well as the counters and the floors."

"This will need tae be gutted," Corbin said.

Paislee swallowed the bread and cheese rising up her throat. She would be strong. She would do what had to be done. If it meant taking on more online orders, then so be it. Instead of taking Saturdays off to see Brody's games, she could work those days instead of paying Amelia. Surely Elspeth would understand.

Lydia grabbed Paislee's shoulders and grinned. "I dinnae know why you're moping, Paislee Ann Shaw."

"What am I missing? My life is in shambles. I appreciate the place to stay but Lyd, this is a blasted mess."

"This is going tae be a brand-new kitchen, Paislee my darling lass. It will be *brilliant*."

Chapter 14

Lydia called in some favors and the female insurance agent came out that morning. She and Lydia had worked together before. Manda Nichols was in her forties and very competent—Paislee knew immediately that she was in good hands. It was a matter of paperwork, and so many pictures of the destroyed kitchen and ceiling.

"You have a place tae stay? I can see aboot getting upfront funding tae cover additional expenses," Manda said.

"I have a place, thank you. Uh—how long will this take?" Paislee had a bad feeling. "A week or two?"

Manda laughed. "Arenae you a doll? It will be a month or two *at least*. These pipes will need tae be replaced throughout the house. We'll hire a remediation team tae dry the water, and prevent further damage."

"Oh—I can't be away that long." Paislee shook her head.

"Yes, you can," Lydia said. "We've already taken over the personal items tae the new house this morning. You bring what you need tae the flat. We *will* make it work."

Paislee gulped.

Grandpa put his hand on her shoulder and squeezed, offering his support. She wasn't alone. Paislee nodded. "Okay."

At eleven, Manda was done with her pictures and had offered to take care of filing the paperwork. Manda winked at Lydia. "I see a safe new waterpipe and drain system for your best friend. I've heard so much aboot you, Paislee."

"Thank you," Lydia and Paislee said in unison as they walked Manda out.

Hamish arrived as the woman left. He got out of the car, wearing jeans, boots, and a Henley.

"He's so cute," Lydia murmured from the stoop. "Hi, Hamish. I hear you had a wee bit of a shock last night."

"It's not every evening that I'm covered in plaster," Hamish admitted. He looked at Paislee as if to see what she'd shared with Lydia or Grandpa.

It wasn't that their dinner dates had been a secret—just quiet. And the kiss? No kissing and telling on her end.

"Hamish. I said that I would call you." Paislee had already emotionally pushed him back to square one.

"I wanted tae help if I could," Hamish said. He wasn't retreating as she'd hoped.

"She's going tae stay at my old flat while her pipes are replaced," Lydia said.

Paislee glared at her best friend. "Want tae take an ad out on a billboard next?"

Lydia laughed. "Dinnae be cross. I know you were fair fond of those old countertops, my love, but this is heaven's way of telling you tae upgrade. Change is nothing tae be afraid of. Hamish, have you met my husband, Corbin? Corbin, this is Hamish McCall, headmaster at Fordythe Primary."

Lydia stepped back to allow Hamish inside the house. Paislee fumed as she understood her friend's message but wasn't sure she agreed with it.

Change. She'd had plenty of change and was sick of it.

She went inside and Grandpa wisely said nothing when normally he had an opinion on everything.

As she shut the door, she jumped when a knock pounded. She opened it, and was surprised—but not really, the way things were going—to see Jerry. He wore a sweatshirt that said JoJo's Goat Farm, jeans, and trainers.

"Jerry!" She stood on the threshold. "Now is not a good time."

"The pictures—where did you get them?" Jerry's body practically vibrated, he was so charged up. "We need tae talk aboot the pictures you sent."

She was itching to go back inside to hear what they were all talking about. Her failures? Her weaknesses?

"Jer. My kitchen ceiling fell. Pipes," Paislee said, somewhat defeated.

"Pipes—that is what I'm trying tae tell you!" Jerry said, red-faced. "Those are not Jory's bagpipes."

Paislee sank against the side wall, and gestured for him to come in. "You might as well join the party." She closed the door, peeking outside to make sure nobody else was going to show up and witness her downfall.

Jerry blinked as if he suddenly realized that she had a full house. He scrubbed his mustache with a wide palm. "Sairy. Didnae mean tae barge in this way on a Sunday. I know you're usually at home. Couldnae figure oot why you'd be ignoring me after sending me the pics, with no explanation."

She'd selfishly decided to enjoy a dinner with Hamish. Was this her punishment? "I'm sorry, Jerry. I've had a . . ."

"Spot of trouble," Corbin said, putting his hand out to Jerry. "Corbin Barron-Smythe, Lydia's husband. That's how the Shaws refer tae their upstairs suddenly in their downstairs."

Jerry snickered and looked past Corbin to the folks clustered around the kitchen table that had been snugged against the pantry to keep it from getting further damaged.

She had good memories over that table and wanted it fixed if she had to learn to sand it herself.

"Sheezus!" Jerry said. "Were ye hurt?"

Paislee couldn't look at Hamish. "No."

"She's got a bruise on her cheek and forehead." Lydia ratted Paislee out. "It could have been much worse."

"True." Paislee's head ached. Too much whisky, too much stress, and too many people around to keep her from having a proper breakdown.

Chin up. She felt Gran's love around her and breathed out, then in.

Of course, the door opened behind her and in walked Brody, Edwyn, and—because she was being punished for something karmic in a past life, the only plausible reason—Bennett and his pretty blond girlfriend, Alexa.

"Paislee! Is everything all right?" Bennett exclaimed. "You have more cars than a car park in your yard."

"Hi, Bennett. We've had—"

"—a spot of trouble," her *ex* friends all said at once.

"Mum?" Brody looked her over. "What happened tae your face?"

There was no sugarcoating from her son, which meant she probably really did look a fright. "I would say come in, but it's getting crowded. The waterpipes burst and we're going tae move tae Aunt Lydia's flat for a while, okay?"

Brody nodded, his eyes snagging at the bruises. Wallace greeted his boy with tail wags and Brody gave him a good pat, picking plaster from the pup's fur. "Did Wallace get hurt?"

"No, son. But his fur is like a magnet for that stuff. We'll give him a good brushing later, at Lydia and Corbin's."

Brody straightened at that, his recovery instant. "We get tae stay at Aunt Lydia's? It's the best! Brilliant!" He elbowed Edwyn. "She has a heated pool."

At least one of them was happy.

"I've got the jeep," Bennett said. He and Alexa had moved to the staircase, out of the narrow foyer. "Let's load up your stuff and bring it over. Between us all it shouldnae take more than a few trips."

"That's really kind of you." Paislee swallowed down that Scots pride. "I accept."

Within thirty minutes, Paislee had prepared a bag for a week's worth of clothes for her and all of Brody's. She packed Wallace's food and dishes, his bed and lead, and toys. The brush for his fur. Scottish Terriers had a double coat—long on the outside, soft and dense beneath it. The special slicker brush, every week in addition to a six-week professional grooming, meant that of all the Shaws, Wallace had the most professional maintenance.

Grandpa was on his own for packing.

"You'll have tae walk Wallace," she told her son. "There's no garden."

"I will!" Brody promised, hand over his heart. "Promise."

She gave it three days before he considered it a chore rather than an adventure. "I will need your help in this, Brody."

Grandpa had his suitcase of clothes and toiletries. It was the sad truth that they'd need to leave some stuff behind.

The important things were pictures and the clothes. Though it didn't seem like too much, the luggage still filled and overflowed her Juke. Lydia's Mercedes was very cute but not helpful. Hamish offered to help, too, but it wasn't needed. Bennett's jeep and Jerry's pickup were enough.

"I'll follow the queue," Hamish insisted. "Tae lug things upstairs."

Paislee smiled at Hamish. He was truly a good man. Now was not a good time. Would it ever be? Was it fair to him?

The caravan crossed Nairn to Lydia's flat. Lydia and Corbin had already tidied it for her. The three rooms were perfect for Paislee, Grandpa, and Brody, giving everyone their own space.

"This is great!" Edwyn exclaimed. "I like this house a lot more than your old one."

Bennett smacked Edwyn on the back of the head.

"Sairy, Paislee." Edwyn grimaced.

"It's okay." Paislee laughed at his honest observation. "It does have a nice view, doesn't it?" She pointed to the picture window of the ocean.

"Sometimes we can see the bottlenose dolphins while we have our morning coffee," Lydia said.

"That will be nice." Grandpa doffed his tam at her, ever the flirt with Lydia.

"Where will you be?" Bennett asked Lydia.

"We finally bought our own place." Lydia hooked her arm with Corbin's. "I've had this flat for years and when Corbin and I got married, we wanted something tae buy together. Our new home is on the bay."

"Lovely area," Alexa said.

"It is the perfect mix for us both. Classic style with modern amenities." Corbin kissed Lydia on the top of her head.

They were so sweet together. To think she'd once thought Lydia and Bennett would be a perfect match, but no. This was better.

Paislee glanced at Hamish. As headmaster, and golfer, and single career man, he belonged in this type of flat, too. Not really her old place. She liked her home.

"This will feel like vacation," she said, to be positive. To keep from crying.

"Vacation!" Brody and Edwyn went to "Brody's room" to get it all set up with his things. The spare bedroom already had a nice TV on the wall.

Paislee read the time on the foyer clock. Half past one. "It's lunch—shall I order something as a thank-you tae you all?"

"You probably want tae get settled," Bennett said. "We should go."

"You don't have tae." Gran would have her head if she wasn't polite to those who had selflessly pitched in.

"I know!" Lydia said. "We have the room by the pool downstairs. Lounge chairs. Why dinnae we move the party there?"

"Party?" Paislee squeaked.

Lydia put her hand on her hip. "There is nothing that you can do right now for your house. Is there?"

"No." Paislee's head spun. There was so much to do that she couldn't even think about it without her body feeling very heavy.

"You will worry, my friend, unless you are occupied." Lydia stepped toward Paislee and gave her a hug.

Paislee sighed and fought tears. She stepped back. "Okay. Let's order in downstairs. Edwyn can borrow a swimsuit of Brody's and the boys can swim."

Hamish looked like he wanted a reason to stay but couldn't find one that wouldn't reveal his feelings for her in a public way.

"I should go," he said reluctantly.

"Me too." Jerry lifted a brow. "But I do need tae talk tae you, Paislee. Aboot the bagpipes."

"Fine," Paislee said. "I don't have my phone anymore."

"You'll get a new one, covered by insurance, thanks tae paying that wee bit extra each month for things inside the home," Lydia said. She scribbled a number on a sheet of paper by her landline, twice, and gave it to Hamish, and then Jerry. "Until then."

Paislee was going to have some words with her bestie. "I will be at the shop tomorrow."

"It cannae wait," Jerry insisted.

Hamish realized that he wasn't going to get a private goodbye. He waved from the door and left. Jerry ushered her to the kitchen. Lydia stepped back but not too far, letting Paislee know she was there if needed.

Jerry might be a big guy, but he wasn't a threat to her. She didn't believe to Jory, either. She nodded.

"The bagpipes werenae Jory's," Jerry said emphatically.

"How could you know?" Paislee said. "It was black with silver, like what Jory played that day."

Jerry took his phone from his back pocket and enlarged the pictures she'd sent to him. "See?"

What was he trying to show her? "The flute thingy is broken."

"The chanter. You're right," Jerry said. "And the drone pipe. We can see the reed inside."

"Okay." Paislee shrugged, still not getting it.

"It's *cane*." Jerry stepped back as if everything should be clear now.

Clear as mud to her. "I don't understand. Please simplify. My brain can't take innuendoes right now."

Jerry showed her the phone. "The reed here is made of natural wood. Handmade by a craftsman."

"So?" But she was getting it, a little. Giant Reed was grown on the Ramsey Castle property and had been for hundreds of years.

Jerry gulped and pocketed his phone again. "Jory believed that *plastic* made a better sound. He only used plastic. It was a big discussion among the pipers, but plastic is cheaper, and some say cleaner. The argument is that synthetic offers more consistency. I dinnae agree. I prefer the cane myself."

Paislee's forehead stung, as did her cheekbone. "Well, it was a shot in the dark. I think you should make sure tae tell this all tae Zeffer."

"That's not everything. You were on the right track aboot the gambling. It seems Robert and Jory had a side bet for fifty thousand that his cane reed would win this competition."

"Did Clyde tell you that?" Clyde was shady and Paislee didn't trust him. "He told that tae Meri, too. Zeffer already knows."

"No." Jerry shook his phone. "I've been at the pub, buying rounds and asking questions aboot Jory. His snare drummer friends knew aboot the bet. That's a fortune."

Paislee recalled the way they'd watched Jory and how they'd gone to the hospital. Cass the blonde, and the brunette. They'd cared the most of all that she could tell. "Plastic reed versus cane reed, for fifty thousand pounds?" At least there was more to it than just a win.

"Seems crazy tae me. What should I do?" Jerry asked. "What if Robert did something tae Jory tae make sure he won that fifty thousand? Maybe Jory wasnae supposed tae die but it went too far?"

Paislee raised her hand. "You don't know that. Please, show Zeffer the pictures I sent you, and bring him up tae speed. I don't have my phone with pictures anymore. You have tae do it."

Jerry shook his head. "Nope. Zeffer wants me tae go tae jail."

Wincing, Paislee wanted to throttle Jerry and have a nice nap. "I have an idea that might get you in his good graces."

Jerry sputtered. "That I'd like tae see."

"Yesterday, Patrick Grant called Constable Thorn about the bagpipes. They think that those were Jory's. You can prove tae Zeffer, with what you just told me about the plastic reed and cane reed, that they don't belong tae Jory." Paislee crossed her arms. "That would be actual evidence in the case."

"How did the Grants find the bagpipes?" Jerry asked. "If Nairn police scoured the property and didnae come up with anything."

"Robert saw them in the river and pulled them out. Well, with Finn's help, and then Patrick's. I took those photos on the off chance you might recognize them," Paislee said.

Jerry's eyes widened with alarm. "Robert found them? He would know that Jory used a plastic reed. What if Robert planted those bagpipes tae get the heat off of himself?"

Jerry had already jumped ahead. Paislee nodded. "I think you should convince Zeffer tae let you look at the bagpipes, if they are in police possession. You would be an expert."

Jerry shook his head. "No. Cannae do it."

"Why not?" Paislee thought it was a great idea. And honestly, she was really tired. Her body ached. "Let me see your phone."

Jerry handed it to her. "Why?"

"Do you have Zeffer's phone number?"

"No."

His mobile number was in her phone. Ruined.

"Has he called you?" Paislee asked.

"Aye," Jerry said. "Unfortunately."

"Maybe it's in your recent calls." Paislee handed the mobile back to Jerry.

Jerry scrolled the numbers and peered up at Paislee. "This might be it."

"Try."

He did, and it went to the Nairn Police Station.

"Leave a message for him tae call you," Paislee urged.

Jerry didn't want to, so hung up.

"I think that's a mistake," Paislee said.

"I'm saving me own skin, thanks." Jerry didn't seem like he'd slept any better than Paislee had. "Please, help me, Paislee."

Lydia slowly walked toward them. "Hey, sweetie, you look ready tae drop. How aboot you come sit doon now?" Her best friend gave Jerry the stink eye.

Jerry lowered his head. "Sairy. I dinnae mean tae be a bother."

With a raised brow, Lydia still came toward them, letting Jerry know it was time for him to go.

Paislee reached for his arm and gave it a pat. It was her fault for sending Jerry the photos when she should have sent them to Zeffer instead. Zeffer would have mocked her and demanded to know what he was looking at, and then say how he wanted proof. She'd hoped Jerry would give her that, and in a way, he had.

"Listen, Jerry. Meet me at the shop tomorrow after I drop Brody off at school."

"Why?" He sounded suspicious. "Going tae have the constables of Nairn waiting tae toss me in jail?"

"That's a wee bit dramatic," Lydia declared. She slid her arm around Paislee for support.

"You and I will go together tae the station and demand tae see the bagpipes. I promise that I won't leave your side."

"Thank you," Jerry said, shoulders bowed. "I hope you feel better."

"Go, Jerry," Lydia said. "It's time. You either put on a swimming suit and join us downstairs, or Paislee will see you in the morning."

Chapter 15

The pool party was exactly what her friends thought Paislee needed—and it did keep her mind off her destroyed ceiling and burst waterpipes. Jerry's stark fear of going to jail stayed front and center. He didn't understand that Zeffer, though cold as a Scottish winter, was fair.

She missed her phone like a missing tooth and constantly reached for it to not be there. She supposed she could borrow the one Grandpa and Brody shared until hers was replaced. Manda had told her to save her receipts if she replaced anything that was ruined in the water damage to be reimbursed later.

Monday morning, Paislee was up far before her alarm clock. Strange bed, strange routine, and she worried they'd all be late to school or work. Hamish's disappointment yesterday when he'd left had reminded her of previous instances where she felt like she'd let him down.

She didn't like it. It was best to be alone for the next few years.

Paislee got up to find Grandpa making his way around the kitchen in the near-dark. "Hey!" she whispered.

Grandpa put his hand to his heart and whirled, his robe flying behind him like a cape.

"Lass, you nearly killed me!" He kept his words at a moderate tone. "It's only five. I was trying tae be quiet and not wake you."

"Sorry!"

"S'all right." Grandpa leaned back against the counter, his silvery hair wild, his glasses just a wee bit crooked on his nose.

"What were you rummaging around for?" Paislee asked in a hush.

"A kettle for tea," Grandpa said.

"I don't think Lydia has one." Paislee admired clean counters in theory, but she hated having to search for whatever appliance one needed. Lydia was a tidy person with all her things put away in the cupboards below.

"No kettle?" Grandpa sounded like he'd just found out there'd be no Hogmanay this year.

"She's got a fancy machine." Paislee opened the next cupboard. "Here it is."

Paislee pulled it from its spot and placed it on the counter by the sink. The Nespresso was sleek and could do just about anything except drive.

Grandpa joined her.

"Why's it so dark in here?" she asked.

"Couldnae find the lights either," he admitted. "Where's the on button?"

"That I can help with." Paislee turned on the light switch, designed to be nearly flush with the wall so it didn't ruin the modern aesthetic of Lydia's kitchen.

"That's better," Grandpa said.

"Lydia has a selection of teas for when I'm over, in this canister." Paislee opened another cupboard with no handle. "Hot cocoa. Black tea. Green tea. Herbal. Anything you could want."

Paislee brought it down and opened it to reveal two dozen assorted pods.

Grandpa scratched his beard. "I want plain. Brodies. Like at home."

"We need tae drive tae Inverness tae replace my mobile at Tesco." She'd gotten her phone through the large store chain that also sold home goods at a great price. "We can pick up whatever else we might need. Another kettle won't go tae waste. Why not make a list?"

Grandpa seemed doubtful but nodded. "I can do that."

"Here." Paislee pressed a button and the machine whirred. Dear God—was it broken? She jumped back in alarm.

Grandpa snickered.

"Oh!" Paislee recalled the tank in back that Lydia had showed her how to operate. "Water. Have tae make sure it has water."

"It's a lot of bother," Grandpa declared.

"It's new, that's all." Paislee filled the canister and tried again. This time it made no awful dying sounds and in less than a minute, Grandpa had a steaming mug of black tea.

She repeated the process for herself.

"Shall we sit on the balcony?" Paislee suggested. It was only half past five and still dark yet.

"Aye." Grandpa followed her out of the kitchen to the right, where a second indoor lounge area had a view of the Moray Firth.

She held her mug of tea to her chest and opened the door. Brine from the sea's salty air reached her nose. The balcony was protected on three sides and had a space heater, four chairs, and a low table, but it was still cold. A solar lamp was between the chairs and Paislee switched it on, providing soft light.

Two blankets were folded on an end table to protect against the chill morning, and she handed one to Grandpa. She'd knitted these for Lydia several years back in soothing ocean blues. The cotton was soft and warm.

"Now, this I could get used tae," Grandpa said.

"It's beautiful. Peaceful. A wee bit out of my price range." Paislee sipped her tea, finally relaxing.

"You know, Paislee lass, that I'd be happy tae do more with the bills." Grandpa peered at her as he held his mug.

She sensed his earnestness. "You take care of Brody and work at the shop. You don't need tae pitch in for a roof over your head. It's paid for, besides." She closed her eyes, breathing in the steam from her tea, not remarking that the roof had actually collapsed on *her* head. That was nobody's fault but time. "You pay for groceries. Treat for takeout." She opened her eyes and smiled at him. "No, Grandpa, you do more than enough."

"And what do I spend my money on?" Grandpa scoffed. "I dinnae have the storage unit anymore."

"Beers at the pub with James." Paislee gave a low chuckle. "As it should be."

"I like tae work," Grandpa said.

Paislee knew that he was telling her the truth, as she was careful to watch him and make sure that he didn't overdo it. "You'll let me know if you want more time off tae go fishing? Relax?"

"Aye," Grandpa agreed.

"Good." Paislee widened her eyes as the fog cleared and the first pinkish rays made their presence. Three dolphin fins could be seen in the distance. "Oh, look!"

Grandpa grinned and snugged his blanket closer around his lap. "Beautiful."

"It really is." She could appreciate this, as a vacation, as a favor, as nature's gift . . . but she had her home, the only one Brody had ever known.

Paislee heard a noise and her Mum antennae quivered. She placed her mostly empty mug to the low table and went inside as Brody and Wallace left his room for the hall.

He'd put shoes on with his pajamas and had Wallace's lead in hand. "Mornin', Mum."

"Morning." Brody looked so sleepy, his auburn hair in all directions. Freckles. "Why don't you go sit with Grandpa on the balcony? The sun's rising and we saw dolphins! I'll take Wallace down." The dog wasn't a big fan of the elevator, but she imagined they'd all get used to it eventually.

Brody ran to the glass door. Paislee shrugged on a heavy cardigan and hoped they didn't run into anyone on the way down or back.

"Brilliant!" Brody said. He waved at Grandpa.

"It's nice. Go ahead, hon." Paislee grabbed a cap and covered her hair.

Brody returned and held his hand out for Wallace's leash. "I'll do it with you, Mum. I promised."

She gave it to him, proud of his decision. "Wallace seemed tae like the fenced dog area for a quick pitstop. We'll ask if Grandpa can take him once more before he comes tae work at noon."

Brody nodded. "I will." They stepped into the hall. "Mum, why was the headmaster at our house yesterday?"

Paislee locked the door of Lydia's flat behind them and went with Brody toward the elevator.

What to say? "Well, he wanted tae make sure that I was okay."

"Oh." Brody kept walking, seeming to accept that.

Thank heaven. Just as she was congratulating herself on keeping it short and sweet, he asked, "But, how did Mr. McCall know aboot it?"

Shoot. "I told him."

"Are ye friends?" Brody persisted.

"Aye, I suppose we are." Paislee picked up the pace, the elevator in sight.

"Have you kissed?"

"Brody!" Her eyes stung as she recalled the ruined kiss. "Where is this coming from?"

"Edwyn said the headmaster likes you. He can tell. Have you ever had a boyfriend?"

Paislee walked faster and hit the button. Then tapped her toe on the floor. What was taking so blasted long for the elevator?

"Not in a very long time."

"You just dinnae want one?"

How much time had he spent thinking about this? Was Edwyn to blame? They'd promised to be honest with one another. Her throat ached as she said, "I don't."

"That's okay, if you do," Brody said, parroting her own words to him. "If you're happy."

"Thank you." The doors dinged and opened. Thank all the angels and saints that the bleeping elevator had arrived.

"Are you?" Brody pressed. He gave Wallace a tiny treat to enter the silver car. "Sit. Guid boy. Mum?"

"I am happy," she said defensively.

"You sound cross." Brody looked at her intently.

Paislee cleared her throat and shoved her hand into her cardigan pocket. "I *am* happy. There's just a lot going on right now."

"With the ceiling."

"Aye."

"And the bagpiper dying."

"That's true." Paislee made a note to self that Brody must have ears like a bat, and she'd need to be more careful in the future what she said and to whom.

"But that doesnae have anything tae do with you, does it?" Brody blew back his auburn fringe as if concerned that she was in danger.

"Not directly."

The doors opened and they stepped into the lobby. There was a new security guard on duty. Paislee ducked her head, wishing she'd brushed her teeth, but Brody, suddenly social, called a hello.

"We're stayin' in me aunt Lydia's flat," Brody said.

"You are?" The guard scrutinized them. He wasn't one that Paislee had met yet, either.

"It's okay, Artie," the receptionist said. "They've been cleared. Brody, Paislee, and Angus."

"Mornin'." Artie dipped his head. "Dog run is tae the left."

They went outside and Paislee wrapped the thick sweater closer to her body.

Brody took Wallace to the gated and fenced dog area and went in with the pup, who had the place to himself, but had to sniff every last thing in case something had changed since last night. At last, Wallace was finished.

In the elevator once more to Lydia's flat, Paislee directed the conversation to homework and safely away from any commentary about Hamish, dating, or boyfriends.

It hadn't occurred to her how much *her* life would evolve as his did.

Paislee's energy flagged but she had so much to do that it couldn't be put off despite her lack of sleep.

"Bye, Brody!" She patted his shoulder, and he waved back before dashing out of the car to the front of the school building.

She drove to Cashmere Crush. Where on earth was Jerry? She couldn't call him because her phone was ruined, and Grandpa would carry the extra for his longer walk to work. Two miles. *Och.*

Paislee entered the shop and tossed her bag on the lower shelf below the register. Would anybody notice if she took a wee nap on the stack of cozy blankets she'd knitted?

A knock sounded at her front door. Not even nine thirty. Jerry would come around back. A tall shadow was visible at the picture window. She had déjà vu.

Her heart racing, she hurried past her tables to the door and opened it. Not Grandpa, but Zeffer.

Of course. Russet hair combed, a sky-blue suit pressed. He smelled like the ocean but in a good way, not the salty brine of fish, but fresh air.

"Yes?" She widened the door and the DI entered.

"Do I have you tae thank for Jerry's garbled phone message?" Zeffer had an accusing tone that rubbed Paislee the wrong way.

"What are you talking about?" She lifted her chin.

Zeffer scooted past her to a tall table and placed his mobile on top. Paislee closed the front door behind him. "This."

He played a message that sounded like Jerry was totally pished and wanted to prove that Robert had tried to pull a fast one. He, Jerry McFadden, was innocent.

Poor Jerry.

Explained why he wasn't at the shop, if he'd been out drinking.

A lot. "He's afraid that you want tae toss him unfairly in jail. So, yesterday, I offered tae go with Jerry tae see you at the station today. This morning, in fact."

Zeffer wasn't listening as he nodded at her. "What happened tae your face?"

Paislee put her fingers to her cheek. The bruise was an interesting shade of purple and green. "Just . . . well, the water pipes burst at the house, and I was hit by falling plaster, that's all."

Zeffer looked alarmed. "That's all?"

"It's *fine*." The last thing she needed was one more person trying to fix the situation.

Zeffer stepped back, lips twitching. "Fine. Put your claws away, Paislee Shaw."

"Sorry. It's been a long week. Longer than that, even," Paislee said. It had been nine days since the competition, and Jory's death.

"Can you explain what he's talking aboot?" Zeffer asked. "How is Robert trying tae pull a fast one?"

"Do you know about the bagpipes found in the river at Ramsey Castle? When I was there for lunch, I took pictures of them and sent them tae Jerry tae see if he could identify them. Good thing since my phone was ruined in the kitchen flood."

Zeffer raised a brow.

"Jerry said that Jory used plastic reeds, preferring the sound," Paislee explained. "Robert uses reed, from cane grown on his property."

"All right," Zeffer said, "I'm following you. Jerry uses cane reed as well."

"The point is that the pipes pulled from the river had natural wood reeds, not plastic, and are not Jory's. If Robert or the Grants said that it was. I don't even know for sure." Paislee shrugged. "I left after Patrick called Constable Thorn."

"Thorn passed the message on, and I talked tae Finn McDonald. When I stopped by, the *entire family* wasnae at home. He gave me the bagpipes they'd found."

Paislee hid a smile at the whole clan being away. "Finn and Patrick both helped Robert drag the instrument from the water. Robert said it was ruined."

Zeffer smoothed his chin in a contemplative manner.

"Well?" Paislee asked. "Did they say it was Jory's?"

"No. Just that it might be." Zeffer smoothed his lapels. "They hinted heavily that Jory's bagpipes looked just like the ones in the water, black and silver."

Paislee nibbled her lower lip. They hadn't lied. Now what was Robert trying to hide? Gambling? Side bets out of control? It wasn't illegal and not worth harming someone over.

"As much as I want tae speak with Robert Grant, Jerry is still a person of interest," Zeffer said. He tapped the phone.

"I'm sorry that Jerry called you drunk. He's feeling uncomfortable by your *unrelenting* attention."

"If he would meet me at the station, I could ask him these questions, tae his face." Zeffer knocked his temple lightly with a knuckle. "See him when he answers."

"Jerry is a good man, and that was our plan this morning. He must have slept in after last night."

Zeffer exhaled.

"How did Jory die?" Paislee asked. She was too tired to play games with the DI.

"His death is verra suspicious." Zeffer picked up his phone.

This wasn't news. "How so?"

"Jory had a gambling problem. Sought help aboot it in a way that made it public knowledge."

That wasn't an answer to her question. Typical of Zeffer, though. "Jory? Not just Robert and Clyde?" Maybe gambling was a widespread problem.

"Aye. For some people it is an addiction," Zeffer said. "They like the thrill of chancing everything on the roll of a die."

"That is not for me." Paislee worked too hard for her money to risk it. "Did you find out if Jory was cheating, as the anonymous letters accused him of?"

"I have not." Zeffer glanced at his watch. "I'm asking around."

"DI Zeffer. Jerry is an expert when it comes tae bagpipes. He can help you identify if there is anything odd aboot the pipes that were found in the river at the castle." She wanted Zeffer to think of Jerry as an ally rather than a person of interest.

"I dinnae think those were Jory's either. A ruse, like you said." Zeffer exhaled. "I will still have them examined, but I believe it'll be a waste of time."

"Tae cover Robert's tracks?" Paislee sighed. "Then why aren't you 'investigating' him?"

"Every time I arrive at the castle, Robert is 'away.'"

She'd seen the family protect him, the heir. The earl.

Just then, Jerry entered from the back entrance. He saw Zeffer and turned around without a word.

"And that doesnae make him look guilty?" Zeffer demanded before taking off after Jerry.

Chapter 16

Paislee's pulse raced with apprehension. Why would Jerry run from the DI? Oh, Zeffer was correct that it made Jerry appear guilty as sin.

She paced back and forth, curious as to what was going on, but there was no window to see out the back door to the alley.

Ten minutes later, Zeffer returned, without Jerry.

The DI was out of breath and his cheeks ruddy. He smoothed his suit over his chest. Paislee handed him a cold can of fizzy water from the fridge. All she had was lime Pellegrino as it was Brody's least favorite. Anything else was consumed fast.

"No luck?" Paislee asked, worried.

"Jerry moves fast for a large man," Zeffer said. "You cannae protest his innocence anymore, Paislee."

"He's scared of you for some reason," Paislee said. "He doesn't believe me when I say you have a heart beneath your tailored blue suits."

"Not amusing, lass," Zeffer said.

She chose not to take offense at his word choice. "I've asked him tae go tae you. Hence his message. *How* did Jory die? No more messing around!"

Zeffer swallowed the water fast, then wiped a droplet from his mouth. "The coroner found inflammation in Jory's lungs."

Paislee didn't get it at all. "Like, he had pneumonia, or the flu?"

"Not that." Zeffer drank again.

"How could inflammation kill him?" Paislee asked. "He was a young man in excellent health."

Zeffer didn't answer. "Another reason I wanted tae talk tae Jerry, who, as you said, is an expert. The coroner has heard of situations where a bagpiper has gotten ill because their instrument hadnae been cleaned properly. Hypersensitive pneumonitis—also known as bagpipe lung."

Not cleaned?

"I need tae find those pipes. If Jerry doesnae come in willingly, then I will charge him with something in truth, just for annoying me. Tell him that when you see him next." Zeffer stared at her.

All Paislee could do was nod as he left in a huff.

"Wait!" Did that mean that Jory had died from the bacteria? Zeffer had specifically said pipers had gotten ill. Not the same as dying. What had been different for Jory? And how could that be on purpose? It couldn't be. The DI really did just need information. Jory had died by natural causes.

Zeffer didn't come back. The shop phone rang, preventing her from chasing after him to tell him about Fat Fergie, Jerry's friend who was also an expert, and perhaps more available than Jerry at the moment.

"Cashmere Crush!" She sank onto a stool and propped her elbow on the high-top table.

"Paislee, it's Hamish. How are ye?"

"Oh—fine."

Why was he calling? She remembered what Brody had asked her about a boyfriend. Did Hamish think that they were a couple? They weren't, though. And she couldn't go there right now.

If the ceiling landing on her head wasn't a clear sign, then she wasn't paying attention.

"Guid," Hamish said. "Guid."

Paislee drummed her fingers to the table. "Well, thank you for calling. Have a nice day!" She hung up before he could say anything else. She was grateful that he didn't call back.

Checking her website for online orders, Paislee was glad to see one for a knitted dog harness with a lead and cap with ear holes for a medium-sized dog, in blue.

Paislee would do whatever was necessary to bring in money, and now that she'd have more expenses, well . . . the insurance was a lifesaver, but the deductible would wipe her out.

She'd probably have to pay on her credit card, only to charge it again.

It was her own fault for thinking that things were going just great. What could go wrong? she'd thought. Never again, she promised herself.

Paislee got to work on the sweater order from the prior week, close to finishing so that she could mail it off.

Customers kept her busy and she managed a partial list of things to buy at Tesco before Grandpa arrived at noon. Mobile phone, kettle. Brodies Tea.

They could go later that night to Inverness, right after work and picking up Brody, as the mobile shop was open till seven. The rest of the place was open past midnight, but the mobile was the most important item. How had she managed without it?

The shop phone rang as Grandpa arrived. She waved at him, noting the pink on his cheeks, and answered, "Cashmere Crush!"

"May I speak tae Paislee?" a familiar feminine voice warbled.

"This is she," Paislee answered.

"This is Dowager Countess Grant."

"Oh!" No longer Sorcha? She'd wanted Paislee to help, but there was nothing Paislee could do if Robert was actively avoiding the police, let alone guilty. "Hello."

"How are you?" the woman asked.

"Wonderful." Paislee wouldn't tell the DC about her ceiling troubles, nor even hint at them.

"I apologize for the chaos on Friday. You left so fast that you forgot tae pick up your money for the items sold at the gift shop."

She'd been given a quick escort out as she recalled, but Paislee could really use the money to help with the expenses. "I did. There is no need tae apologize! How are you after what happened?"

"Finn took care of things for us as we were called away tae London," the dowager countess said. "He met with the police and gave them the bagpipes Robert found in the river."

"Not Robert?" Paislee hadn't meant to say it like that.

"No." The older woman's voice cooled.

Grandpa leaned on the counter.

Paislee put the handset on speaker. She was done being involved in the nobles' problems—she had so many of her own! "Is there something I can help you with? It's been busy today at the shop."

"Well, I hate tae ask if you're so busy," the dowager countess said, "but I'd hoped you'd bring more cashmere goods. I've had many compliments on the coin purse in the Grant Tartan you'd done for me."

That would be ideal. What did she have that was cashmere and fine enough for the castle? She walked with the phone to the front of the shop where she kept her items on display. One cashmere jumper, one cashmere scarf, two cashmere tams.

"When?"

"Today, if possible."

Grandpa nodded that he was okay with it. He rubbed his fingers together in the symbol for money.

"I don't know." Paislee didn't like the feeling that she had to be at the woman's beck and call. "My supply is limited. I'll start coin purses next month."

"I will make it worth your while, Paislee. I understand, being a woman of business."

Paislee sighed. "All right. I can come on my lunch hour, but I can't stay long."

"I'll have our chef make us sandwiches."

"That's okay. You don't have tae feed me." She didn't have

time for more than a granola bar in the car on the way. Something to add to the list for Tesco.

"It will be a reason tae get Robert at the table. I've been working on him tae talk with the constables, and you," the dowager countess said. "Shawn Marcus was over yesterday, with Shannon."

That had probably helped Robert see things differently. Paislee appreciated all that Sorcha was doing to help her son. "Is that so?"

The woman's voice lowered. "They explained how useful you were in finding the true killer, when the police considered Shawn a suspect."

Paislee recalled the field trip to the Leery Estate with clarity. Shawn's cousin being shot to death while she was a chaperone. "I care about my community."

"Yes. I know. I believe that now Robert knows, too."

Goose bumps dotted her skin. Was Robert guilty? Surely inflammation wasn't something that could be given on purpose. "What does that mean?"

"He wants tae talk tae you aboot what happened that day. The bagpipes in the water."

Should she play her hand? Yes. Get things out in the open and hopefully skip the sandwiches, get her money, and come back to the shop. "Those pipes didn't belong tae Jory."

"We never said they did, dear," the dowager countess said.

No, they'd implied it.

Grandpa wrote on her notepad, below the list, *Have her pay ahead for the goods, since you are making the trip?*

"All right, then." She was speaking to both Sorcha and Grandpa. It was a fine idea and might take away the sting from being ordered about.

The tone on the phone was regal. "Be here at one, Paislee. Come tae the front." The dowager countess hung up.

Paislee gritted her teeth. "Nobility. They aren't better than everyone else."

"No," Grandpa agreed. "But their money is guid and that's what we need, eh?"

"True." Paislee blew out a breath, ruffling her fringe—her bangs needed a trim, something she'd learned to do herself to save money. "I was thinking we could drive tae Inverness tonight and shop. Bring Brody. He likes Tesco."

"Brody likes tae admire the fishing poles. Same as me."

Paislee laughed and picked up the sweater she was working on for the custom order in blue. "Almost done."

"It's a braw jumper." Grandpa added a few things to the Tesco list. "If I could I'd shop for you, but you need tae be there in person because of the phone."

"That's sweet, though, Grandpa."

"Let's not get carried away," he said with a smirk. "I am *not* sweet."

She tossed a thin knitting needle at him. "Sour and cranky, that's you."

He seemed pleased as he caught it. "Aye, that's better."

She reached for the needle, and he gave it back.

"What happened with Jerry this morning?" Grandpa asked, rifling through a stack of fishing magazines.

"He wasn't here when I arrived, but Zeffer was."

"Oh?" Grandpa patted the top magazine and eyed Paislee speculatively.

"Yeah. Seems Jerry got tae drinking and thought it would be a good idea tae leave the DI a message, saying that the pipes in the river at the castle weren't Jory's. That Robert was 'pulling a fast one.'"

Grandpa grinned and stroked his beard. "How did that go over?"

"About as well as you could imagine, since Jerry walked in right after, saw Zeffer and then ran for the hills." Grandpa's jaw gaped as he imagined the scene. "Zeffer wants tae talk with Jerry about something called bagpipe lung. The coroner found inflammation in Jory's lungs."

"Humph. Never heard of it," Grandpa said. "Sounds awful, but a natural cause."

"Right? Zeffer says if Jerry doesn't come in then he's going tae arrest him. If we see Jerry again, we need tae tell him that Zeffer isn't messing around."

"Jerry really ran?" Grandpa asked. "I hope he's not guilty."

Customers trickled in and ended the conversation. Paislee packed up all of her cashmere stock in a nice shopping bag to bring to the castle. "Great idea about asking for the money up front. Hope Sorcha goes for it, since I'm now out of cashmere here." It cost her money to buy the yarn, to create her items, that she could then sell.

"You'd best get tae knitting," Grandpa said.

"My work is never done," she lamented. Idle hands—who had idle hands?

Not her.

"Just dinnae let the DC forget your money again."

"I don't think it was on purpose," Paislee said. "Finding the bagpipes had been a big surprise."

"She was too smooth when you said that those werenae Jory's—she already knew. But if Jory had inflammation in his lungs, that doesnae equal murder. You should be safe driving onto the castle grounds. I forgot tae bring the extra mobile but it's at the flat if you want tae take it with you."

"Maybe. I think you're right, about there not being any danger. Robert's avoidance must have tae do with his gambling. He'll be surprised tae find it's not exactly a secret." Paislee read the time. Half past noon, and she would be late if she didn't get moving.

Another customer walked in, leaving Grandpa with two browsers. A woman with a knit cap was admiring several skeins of yarn. A couple, tourists from England, were looking at completed fisherman sweaters.

"It's all right," Grandpa said to her. "Go on. Drive safe."

But it wasn't. Other than Brody, this business was her main concern. This paid the bills, not the Grants.

"You take the couple," she said. "I'll talk tae the woman in the knit cap."

Grandpa nodded. The Shaw style of salesmanship was normally very lax and no pressure but since Paislee had to go, she stepped up her game.

"Hiya," she said to the young woman. "Did you knit your own hat?"

"I did!" The young woman held out her hand.

"It's quite bonnie." Paislee shook it. "I'm Paislee Shaw, owner of Cashmere Crush."

"KiKi Montgomery. I began knitting a year ago and cannae get enough of it. I've been teaching myself online. You can learn anything with videos."

"Well, I'm glad tae meet you, KiKi. We have a Thursday night Knit and Sip where other crafters come together and have a nice blether. Nothing too harmful. Snacks and drinks."

"That sounds smashin'." KiKi faced Paislee with a big smile.

Paislee pegged her to be in her early twenties. "You live around here?"

"Near the wharf," she said. "I've got my certification in yoga and fitness, and work at the golf course."

"That's awesome. Blaise O'Connor is a dear friend who knits, whose husband is the golf pro."

"Shep's amazing. So kind tae everyone. I knew he was married and had a little girl. I didnae know that his wife was a knitter."

"Nairn is a small community."

"That's true," KiKi said. She piled several skeins of soft merino wool in her arms, all a light blue.

"Can I help?" Paislee asked.

"I've got it." KiKi walked toward the counter.

Paislee rounded it to the register and chose the right size bag for KiKi's purchases. She rang KiKi up.

"I will definitely check oot that Thursday night group," KiKi said. "Does it cost?"

"Nope. Free. And fun, I promise."

"What will I need?"

"A dish tae share, if you feel like it. Whatever you'd like tae drink."

KiKi's grin widened. "Brilliant."

Paislee had the idea that another new member might join—so different from Meri, and yet she'd be a great fit, too. That was the best thing about this community, the different personalities with knitting in common.

KiKi paid and waved as she left. "See you soon, Paislee."

Grandpa was now at the register. The couple had each chosen a thick sweater in beige that she just couldn't keep in stock. Her customers loved it and anything she made in that color seemed to sell fast.

That was three hundred pounds in the register, and another fifty from KiKi.

They left and the store was empty again.

"A nice little run," Grandpa said.

"It was!" They smacked hands together.

"You need tae get crackin' on more inventory," he said shrewdly.

Paislee's shoulders hiked defensively. "And just what do you think I do every free second?"

Grandpa backed up until his hip hit the counter. "I know! Sairy for mentioning the obvious."

"It's all right." She grabbed her handbag. "This is a good problem tae have, right? It will slow down over the winter."

"It's just that I cannae help you." Grandpa sounded sincere.

She twitched her lips. "I could teach you."

"No, thanks anyway." His eyes and mouth rounded in true horror.

She laughed aloud. "Don't worry. These need tae be a Paislee Shaw original, according tae Lydia."

"Guid. That's great." Grandpa sounded relieved.

"But the offer's open, anytime."

"Arenae you late?" Grandpa tapped his watch.

"Blazes."

It was one o'clock and she was supposed to be there already.

The shop phone rang.

"You answer it—if it's the dowager countess, let her know I'm on my way."

"Drive safe!" Grandpa reached for the handset.

"I will." Paislee juggled her handbag and the Cashmere Crush bag. "I'll call her tae let her know."

"You dinnae have a phone."

She left and climbed into the car. The engine whirred and sputtered. She tried again.

It didn't start.

Paislee bowed her head to the steering wheel. She couldn't take one more thing.

Chapter 17

With a prayer to *anybody* who was listening, Paislee started the engine again. It caught and she sighed in relief.

Her appointment with Eddy was on Wednesday.

"Hang in there, lass," she told her Juke. "You've got a date with our favorite mechanic in two days." Paislee patted the dash.

She reached for her phone to call the castle but recalled that it had been drowned in her kitchen. Since she was already late, she couldn't stop at the flat for the spare mobile. Instead, Paislee cranked the radio to a local station and listened to music. She wasn't the best singer, but it felt good to belt out songs rather than yell at the world.

Twenty minutes later, she'd reached Ramsey Castle. The gates were imposing but one was open. She looked for Patrick. Instead, Finn waved her through to a spot to park.

She got out and shouldered her bag. "Hi, Finn. How are you?"

"Fine, fine." Finn adjusted a worn checked tam over his mostly black hair. His coat smelled of hay and pine. "And yerself?"

"Good."

He nodded. "This way."

Finn entered the castle through a side door hidden to the right that led to a mudroom rather than the grand entrance.

"Smart," Paislee said, seeing rows of hooks for jackets and a cement slab so that the boots wouldn't track mud inside.

"Aye. This is Scotland and always the rainy season," he chuckled.

Paislee stomped to get any muck off her shoes and followed Finn into the main house and a parlor with a large fireplace and plush couches. Slate was on the floor here, too, and covered with throw rugs.

"I like this room," Paislee said, turning around to admire the bright colors and fabrics. She could be in this space without feeling self-conscious in her jeans. She'd had no idea that Sorcha would want her to be at the castle today or she would have chosen something less casual.

"It's where the family spends the most time," Finn said. "Cozy." He gestured for her to follow him. "The dining room is this way."

"Have you worked for the Grants long?"

"All me life," Finn said. "My da, too."

"Oh? How interesting!"

"Groundskeepers are important tae the running of the property. McDonalds have been doing that for the Grants for over a hundred years."

What a powerful connection to both the family and the land. What wouldn't Finn do for them?

Paislee recalled how he'd been in the frigid river to retrieve the pipes. He might have known that they weren't Jory's. He might have known whose they were in truth, and still not mentioned it or clarified it to the constables. A worthy gatekeeper.

They reached the dining room.

Finn pushed the door open and announced, "Paislee Shaw."

"Stay with us, Finn," the dowager countess requested.

"Naw. Thanks, milady. I already ate, and I've work in the greenhouse."

"You always have work," Lissia teased.

Paislee could identify with his work ethic.

Finn touched his cap and backed out without commenting. A

man of big actions and few words. Paislee admired that, too, and wondered at the secrets he kept close to the chest.

"Come in!" Sorcha stood and gestured to a seat between Lissia and Cinda. Cinda, allowed at the table? Something must have shifted. Robert was at the head, and Patrick to his right, and then Sorcha.

They were all in different styles of clothes in the opulent room—silks and tartan, blazers over pants. Paislee did not fit in here at all.

"Nice tae see you all again," Paislee said, brazening it out.

"And you," Lissia said.

Cinda and Patrick murmured a greeting, staying seated.

Robert stood with Sorcha, confusion on his face.

"Hi, Paislee," Robert said. "Mum didnae mention you would be here. What a lovely surprise."

She could tell that he wasn't pleased. Made her feel a wee bit like leaving. Shawn Marcus's sense of entitlement hadn't been as great as Robert's, who was an actual earl. The Leery title was more a token as a landowner back in the day.

This was legit.

But still, Gran had said that everybody puts their pants on one leg at a time, and they weren't better than anyone else. All people deserved respect.

"Hello." Paislee paused. Would Robert tell her to go? It was incredibly awkward.

No.

"Please." Robert gestured to the seat his mother had and then they all sat together. "You're welcome as Mother's guest."

"Thank you." Paislee smiled around the table. Blue ceramic dishes with a floral pattern were before each person. A cloth napkin was to the side, and Paislee placed hers over her lap as the others had already done.

"I thought we were waiting for Finn." Robert looked at his mother. "Now that I know why you were stalling, can we eat?"

Sorcha pursed her lips and gave a slight nod.

Robert rang the bell near his plate. The staff brought in "sandwiches" that were restaurant quality: thick, toasted artisan bread, grilled onions and mushrooms, thin savory slices of beef. Greens on the sandwich added a peppery flavor.

"Everything is grown on the property," Sorcha said. Her dark hair was up in a clip, and though she didn't wear much makeup, there was face powder and lipstick.

"Even the lettuce," Lissia said. She was her mother's younger twin, though her hand on the eye makeup was heavier. Long lashes as were the style. Lydia managed them beautifully, but Paislee didn't have the time or skill.

"We bake our own bread, harvest our own cattle." Robert bit into the sandwich with a crunch, chewed, and swallowed. At forty, and the heir, he had silver at his temples. Patrick's was silver-free. His body was chiseled while Robert, though not fat, was softer somehow.

"It's wonderful tae be so self-sufficient," Paislee said.

"Aye." Cinda glanced around at them all and smiled hesitantly. "Patrick oversees the meat distribution not only for Ramsey Castle, but those on the farms surrounding this land."

"You make him sound like a butcher," Lissia said with a frown.

Cinda blushed. "Oh! That's not what I meant at all."

Patrick glared at Cinda. "You said you would be quiet."

Paislee wished that she didn't have to endure this awful lunch. The yummy beef twisted in her stomach. Next time, if there was a next time, she would refuse to come. Invent an emergency, if necessary.

Families were interesting dynamics. Robert, as heir, had the head of the table. Patrick, next in line, was constantly a step behind his brother.

And yet, expected to do the work with grace and no complaint. Lissia, as the lone woman of the Grant line, would no doubt marry. In the old days, it would be for money to bring into the family accounts. Would she be allowed to choose her husband with affection?

Cinda's continuous peeks at Patrick betrayed her love for him. Would Sorcha ever come around to approving their alliance?

She couldn't imagine living in such a way. They were nobles, bound by rules and strictures that didn't apply in her modern life.

Paislee sipped her water. Lydia would fall over in a faint to hear Paislee say such a thing as that. Lydia was modern, to Paislee's old-fashioned values. Ramsey Castle, with its medieval furnishings, was downright archaic.

"Everything was delicious." Paislee put her napkin down and looked around the table. Sorcha wanted her help to get Robert to open up, but nobody was talking. She read the time on her watch. Two. Where time had sped earlier today, now it dragged.

She cleared her throat. "Any word about the bagpipes found in the river, from the police?"

Robert winced.

Paislee shrugged. There wasn't a smoother way to bring up the subject as Sorcha wanted.

"Aye," Robert said. "Constable Thorn doesnae think they belong tae Jory. Seems Jory used a plastic reed, and this had cane."

"You don't say?" If he was going to act like she was an idiot, then she could play along, and layered the words in sarcasm.

Robert blushed. He spread his hand and placed it on the table. "It seems like the bagpipes might have been an old set of my da's from the music room. I have no idea how they ended up in the river."

"No idea?" Paislee blurted. The man might be an earl, but he was ridiculous.

Sorcha raised a warning brow at Paislee. "The castle was open tae the public during the competition," she said. "As you know, since you were here. Anybody could have wandered off with them."

"But why?" Cinda asked. Then she bowed her head, having forgotten the "be quiet" rule. It was obvious that whatever story the Grants had concocted, Cinda wasn't part of it.

Patrick dipped his head at Cinda. "Who knows? People get tae drinking and think things are a lark."

"It could happen," Sorcha agreed.

But was it likely? Paislee didn't think so. Whatever. "That's helpful in a way, tae identify them. It means that Jory's are still missing."

"That's right." Robert drummed the table, impatient.

What did he have to be impatient about? He was avoiding the police and making things worse for himself—if he was innocent. Was he? Paislee looked at Robert. "Did you consider Jory a friend?"

"No," Robert said. "I didnae know him. He came onto the scene last year, thanks tae Clyde bringing him into the Clan Cunningham band."

"Clyde said his cousin Ewan was impressed by his playing and suggested Jory join the group. That's what Clyde told me, anyway," Paislee said.

"Aye." Robert reached for his cup. It was empty and he snapped his fingers.

From the shadows, a maid came out with a pitcher of something brown and frothy.

"Ale," Patrick said, tapping his glass. "For me, too, please. Paislee? We brew it on the property as well."

"No, thank you," she said. "I can't stay long." She again looked at her watch. That was probably borderline rude, but it was also the truth. She had so much to catch up on.

"Oh?" Cinda said, in a tone that suggested Paislee was not in her right mind. Cinda might long for a life in the castle with her knight, Patrick, but that wasn't for Paislee.

"I promised my employee that I wouldn't be gone long, as we've been so busy." Paislee snapped her fingers. "I forgot the cashmere in the car."

"You can get it once we finish here," Sorcha said. "You have tae join me in the gift shop anyway."

Paislee sipped her water and hoped she wasn't making a mistake, but she really wanted to leave, and this might get her out of the hot seat with Sorcha. Zeffer hadn't told her to keep it quiet. "I heard that Jory had inflammation in his lungs."

The Grants and Cinda all sat up straight.

"A cold?" Sorcha asked.

"Flu?" Patrick queried.

"Pneumonia?" Robert said.

"He didnae seem sick tae me," Lissia said.

"I'm not sure." Paislee kept the phrase of "bagpipe lung" from the coroner to herself.

"A natural death?" Robert's shoulders eased. Tension deflated from the Grant family and the air seemed physically lighter.

"I think you should talk tae DI Zeffer," Paislee said. "He's simply trying tae find out what happened that day."

"There's been no ruling of foul play," Sorcha insisted. "Correct?"

"Right." Paislee smiled around the table. Now could she go?

Sorcha stood and brushed her hands together. "Paislee, let me help you get the items from your vehicle."

Paislee rose and thanked everyone. "The sandwich was delicious, and far better than the granola bar I'd planned for lunch."

"It was my idea that she stop in and join us for a bite since she was delivering her cashmere anyway, but Paislee, you are *always* welcome," Sorcha said, a brow lifted at Robert.

Robert stood and nodded, a real smile making his features handsome. "That you are. Thank you for the update aboot Jory. That does make me feel better. Perhaps you're right that calling the DI wouldnae hurt."

Paislee smiled and followed Sorcha, glancing back to see Cinda and Patrick touching hands under the table.

Was Patrick leading Cinda on for some reason? It wasn't fair, if so.

"Why not drive around?" Sorcha suggested. "I'll meet you at the gift shop."

"Okay."

Paislee went to her car from the mudroom. It was true that the castle had been open that day of the competition, but she doubted wild revelers had rampaged the music room and tossed the bagpipes into the river.

She wasn't satisfied with the answers but accepted that she might never know. It wasn't her place to demand the truth.

She parked before the gift shop, where Sorcha waited at the door. Paislee brought the bag of knitted goods inside.

"This looks lovely," Paislee said. "You've done it up really nice." The tidy shelves were filled with stock from the jumpers, scarves, and shawls to little jars of jam with ribbons.

"Thank you. Cinda's talents as a shopgirl shine here." Sorcha smoothed a loose hair back from her cheek. "I wanted tae fire her for being too familiar with Patrick, but it seems I wasnae paying close enough attention and she's wormed her way into his life already."

Paislee stifled a rude retort and asked instead, "You don't care for her?"

"She's bonnie," Sorcha said scornfully. "But *poor*. All three of my children are on notice that it's time tae get serious aboot finding a mate. Someone tae be a true partner. If Cinda is Patrick's choice . . . I can only hope that he comes tae his senses. There will be no divorce."

"Will Robert have tae marry someone of his same rank?" Paislee asked, feeling sorry for them.

"There is nobody in Scotland who is his equal, but he's reached oot abroad," Sorcha said. "Italy, France. He'd been engaged tae a lovely lass, but she broke it off when she discovered Robert's temper."

Sorcha stopped at the counter and turned to Paislee with concern in her shrewd green eyes. "I'm afraid I've been entirely too personal—let's talk of something else. I had the cookbook printed, and I'll give you a copy for coming oot today."

"Thank you!"

"The oldest family recipes are in there, from cock-a-leekie soup, to the chef's mushroom risotto, to lamb shank."

"My grandfather is the cook at our house," Paislee admitted. "I don't have the energy tae be creative in the kitchen."

"No. I suppose not," Sorcha said. "You're a businesswoman."

Paislee set her bag on the counter, glad for the subject change. "Several scarves, a jumper, and a shawl. I'll need tae knit more inventory, including the coin purses."

Sorcha opened the register and drew out an envelope. "This has your portion of the sales."

"Thanks." Paislee drew in a discreet, fortifying breath. "I'd wondered if you'd pay ahead for the items I've brought, as my stock of cashmere is now all here." She was proud of herself for asking. Why not? She couldn't sell what wasn't in her shop.

Sorcha blinked but then tilted her head and smiled. "Let me write you a check for the entire total. I think that's fair and wish I'd thought of that beforehand."

They tallied the sales and then the cost of the items. "Thank you," Paislee said. It would be a big help to her bank balance.

"Here's the cookbook." Sorcha handed it to Paislee in a bag. "I cannae thank you enough for coming oot today. The news that Jory's death was natural is a big relief."

"I imagine so," Paislee agreed. Sorcha must have been worried that Robert had done something wrong, besides gambling too much.

Sorcha pursed her lips, fine lines creasing around her mouth. "Robert gambled. He and Jory had a ridiculous bet."

Paislee nodded but didn't confirm or deny what she'd been told. Jerry had been as informative as Meri and Zeffer in that regard. The Cunningham clan snare drummers had known about the bet between the two.

"If Jory's death had been deliberate, then, well"—Sorcha swallowed hard and touched the pulsing vein at her throat—"it wouldnae have looked guid for us here at the castle, would it?"

"No." Not to mention that Jory would have been *killed*. Paislee bowed her head to hide any anger that might show.

"Patrick was prepared tae step in, but now that's not necessary." Sorcha held Paislee's wrist. "Thank God."

Patrick would have taken the fall for Robert?

She couldn't believe it.

The maid came to the door with the handset for the house phone. "Ms. Shaw? It's your grandfather."

Her stomach clenched with immediate worry. "Grandpa?" She needed to get her mobile replaced right away.

"Glad I caught you!" Grandpa said jovially.

She relaxed at his tone. "What is it?"

"Jerry is at some bloke's named Fat Fergie and wants you tae meet him there."

Wincing at the name, Paislee asked, "When?"

"Right now. Here's the address. You've gotta step on it, or Jerry's worried Fat Fergie will change his mind aboot talking with you."

Chapter 18

Check in her handbag, Fergie's address jotted on a piece of scrap paper from Sorcha, now plugged into her satellite GPS, Paislee waved goodbye to Sorcha and headed away from Ramsey Castle to the main road.

Rather than turn toward Nairn and her shop, she went deeper into the forest of the highlands. Near the medieval hamlet of Bruachmary was an old stone house surrounded by tall trees.

She recognized Jerry's vehicle outside the home and her trepidation eased. Jerry came out as soon as she arrived, as if he'd been waiting for her.

"Paislee! Thanks, lass. I owe you one."

"Jerry." Paislee was relieved to see him, free and not in jail. "Did Grandpa give you Zeffer's message? You need tae talk with the DI right away."

Jerry waved his hand dismissively. "Never mind that. I want you tae meet my guid mate, Fat Fergie, in his workshop. Be prepared for a lesson," he chuckled. "He doesnae get much company."

She checked the time on her watch. Three! "You have an hour, Jerry, before I need tae pick up Brody, so let's hurry it along. Maybe we can invite Zeffer here?"

"Naw. Fat Fergie isnae a fan of the cops."

Jerry went around the back of a single-story stone home with a thick chimney and a mossy roof, following a cobblestone path through tall grass that had never seen a mower.

She shivered as if stepping back into time.

Once around the house, they entered a cleared gravel space with a huge firepit in the center. No flames at the moment, but she could imagine a bonfire come Hogmanay, or Saint Andrew's Day on November 30. Her birthday was November 6. For thirty years old she could use a bonfire, too. It reminded her of an old-fashioned courtyard, with buildings for working or living around the central communal fire.

"Fergie," Jerry called, rapping on a closed wooden door of a single-story garage made of stone.

"Come in!" the voice boomed.

Jerry opened the door. Inside was well lit when Paislee had been expecting pitch-black with a candle or two.

Overhead lamps were spotlighted on a worktable, chest-high for her, where three bagpipes were arrayed. A very large man turned around. His hair was as red as a ripe tomato, his cheeks plump and bright, and his chest huge.

Fergie wasn't obese, Paislee realized, but thick with muscle. Like a Viking. Aye, she could see him now, riding on a ship holding a claymore instead of a bagpipe. He moved with grace around the table—jeans, no kilt. His brown shirt was like a pirate's, big and loose, and covered with a half-folded leather apron.

"Hiya! My friends call me Fat Fergie." He pumped her hand.

"Hi. I'm Paislee." She took her hand back. Though he hadn't squeezed, it still stung.

"Aren't you a bonnie wee thing?" Fergie—she would not call him Fat—grinned down at her.

Paislee blushed. "Thanks for taking the time tae see me." She glanced at Jerry and then her watch. What was the point?

"Jerry told me you're not a piper." Fergie gestured to at least a hundred different styles of bagpipes arrayed on various shelves and gold plaques from competitions he must have won.

"No," Paislee said.

"A young piper is dead, and the coppers want tae know what happened?" Fergie seemed nervous as he untied and retied his leather apron.

"Aye." Paislee sidled toward the table to look at the three bagpipes he'd set out. "What's this?"

"Scotland lays claim tae three unique bagpipes," Fergie said. "There are others throughout the world but in relevance for the local competitions, these are what matter."

Jerry was right—Fergie had a teacher's cadence. Paislee reached for her phone to take notes. No phone. She gritted her teeth. "May I borrow a pen and paper?"

"Och, sure." Fergie walked to a desk littered with scrap pieces and pencils. Pens. Scissors. Yarn. Rolls of tape. He was not a tidy man.

Jerry dragged up a stool to the table. "I've asked him tae play a bit of each instrument tae show the difference in sound. You've heard me play the GHB. I dinnae play the border pipe or the SSP, so I thought this was the best way for you tae feel and hear the difference."

She checked her watch. "I don't mean tae be rude, but I must pick up Brody at four. No being late. *Why* do you want me tae hear these three?"

"Fergie made my stand of pipes for me, personally," Jerry said. "We were talking aboot how someone might cheat, and I asked him tae show you what is so amazing aboot the Scottish pipes. I cannae do them justice. It's aboot the music, eh?"

Paislee took a seat. For honorable Jerry it was just that. Since he wanted her to hear the difference, she would be patient.

"Let's get started." Fergie picked up the set of bagpipes to his right. "These are known as border pipes. Been around since the sixteenth century, if no' longer."

The instrument looked delicate in Fergie's large hands.

Fergie pointed to the various pieces. "It's got the chanter, the drones, and a bellows. No blowpipe, unlike the GHB—lass, please tell me you know what those are?"

"Aye!" She gave Jerry a thumbs-up, wanting him to know she'd paid attention. "Great Highland Bagpipes."

"Guid. Now, the GHB is used at the Ramsey Castle competition. Not this dear instrument, though I do love it, too." Fergie patted the bag on the border pipe. "This acts like a fireplace bellows. Rather than use lung power, the instrument is played with pressure from the arm. It had a bit of a revival in nineteen eighty, but never came near the status of the GHB."

"I only used the GHB, and never learned tae play these others," Jerry said. "Fergie is a master. He can play the Irish pipes, the Welsh—hey, he even rocked oot with the Red Hots on an electric bagpipe."

Paislee heard true admiration in Jerry's voice and asked Fergie, "Do you compete?"

"No, lass. I used tae when I was younger. Won plenty but my true calling is creating instruments by hand." Fergie gestured toward the plaques and awards on the walls.

"One of the last craftsmen making pipes in Scotland," Jerry said. "Certainly, the best."

"You're biased, because I made yours." Fergie chuckled and picked up the middle instrument and blew into the blowpipe. The warm sound reverberated off the stone walls.

That explained how Jerry knew Fergie. "Let me guess," Paislee teased, "you're a fan of the cane reed rather than the plastic."

"Oy!" Fergie stomped a large foot. "You're right there."

"What's that called?" Paislee asked, pointing to the instrument in the middle.

"SSP—Scottish Small Pipes. Now, this pipe has been specially fitted with a blowpipe rather than a bellows," Fergie said. "You'll notice the sound is softer."

"It's nice," Paislee said, hearing the difference when Fergie lifted the border pipe and squeezed the bellows, then he switched it out again for the SSP fitted with the blowpipe.

"A bellows instrument prevents moisture from the piper's breath damaging the sensitive reeds," Fergie said.

Moisture. Was that how bagpipe lung occurred? Jory had inflammation in his lungs.

Fergie cleared his throat for her wandering attention. "It also allows greater endurance in long sets withoot tiring the lungs, or your mouth."

Meri had called that respiratory fatigue. Paislee tried to see how this might all fit. A bellows created air, instead of blowing into the chanter. Could that be a way to help someone win?

Fergie tapped the chanter on all three instruments. "The finger arrangement is similar, nine holes, but the chanter is what gives the border pipe a unique sound. The main difference between this and the GHB is the smaller bore. It really is aboot the sound, isnae it, Jerry? Each bagpipe has a personality."

"Aye," Jerry said.

Paislee sat closer to the table. Fergie's love for music was as clear as the water in the River Nairn. "Why aren't these other two pipes at the competitions?"

"Ach, they fell oot of favor a long time ago, like the seventeen hundreds." Fergie reluctantly turned his attention from the border pipe to the SSP. "This beauty is more popular than the border pipe because with the modified blowpipe, GHB enthusiasts can jam, and practice GHB tunes withoot the neighbors hating you."

"Out here you don't have tae worry!" Paislee observed.

"And why do you think I've never moved from the family home?" Fergie laughed. He picked up the SSP, again arranging the pipes and bag across his chest.

Fergie broke into another tune and Paislee clapped when he finished.

The note died off. "The chanter in the SSP has a cylindrical bore, different from the conical bore on the border pipe." Fergie patted the border pipe he'd just laid down, and the bigger instrument he had yet to play. "These both have conical bores."

"What does that mean?" Paislee asked, completely invested in what Fergie had to say. If her music teacher in primary school had been as compelling, she might have tried a little bit harder.

"In plain speaking, the SSP has a chanter that is the same diameter all the way through," Fergie said. "The other two taper from the wide bore at the base tae the smaller bore at the tip."

"What does that do tae the sound?" Jerry asked. Being a musician, the details would matter.

"This is what makes this pipe unique—the chanter on the SSP is aboot one octave lower," Fergie said.

At her confused look, Fergie again played the difference.

"It's really pretty, and soft, as you said," Paislee agreed. "I understand why it's popular."

Paislee enjoyed the notes in a way that she—quite honestly and with no offense to Jerry—hadn't done with the GHB. Bigger was definitely louder.

Fergie set the middle instrument down.

"Aye, I can see why you like it, too," Jerry said to Paislee.

Fergie lifted the GHB. "Now, this is a true beauty. It's the most familiar bagpipe in the world. When people think of Scotland and the pipers, this is it."

She nodded. Fergie was right about that.

"You'll see it has a conical chanter." Fergie showed the pieces. "A bass drone, and two tenor drones." The bass was the tallest of the three. Rope was tied to them. Rope, like had been around the bagpipes in the river.

Fergie adjusted the bagpipes. "In the old days it sometimes only had two drones, but the players in competitions, yes, they had them even in the eighteen hundreds, complained that the two drones had an unfair advantage."

"Competitions that far in history?" Paislee shook her head in disbelief.

"The bagpipes are legendary." Fergie shrugged. "A skilled player can make even these big beasts sound incredible."

"A not-skilled one sounds like ten cats in a room full of rocking chairs," Jerry said.

Paislee raised her hand. "That would be me."

"Everybody starts somewhere." Fergie patted the middle instrument. "I always recommend beginning with this, with the blowpipe modification."

Paislee shook her head. "So, it's possible tae play that way all the time?"

"Aye. But any traditional competition would want the rules followed tae the letter," Fergie said. "It's what makes the event special—all players on an equal field."

"The rulebook for the competitions is verra specific aboot what instruments are allowed, how many medleys must be played according tae band skill level," Jerry said.

"And here I just enjoyed the concert!" Paislee admitted.

At last, Fergie lifted the GHB, and ran his fingers over the chanter. "The bag's sound is manipulated by my arm here. A skilled player can maintain pressure for twenty minutes."

"No way!" There'd been fifteen minutes to play at the castle, and two separate sets. Twenty full minutes?

"The talent is in making sure the sound is fluid and not detectable when you take a breath," Fergie said. He demonstrated, stepping back from the table.

Paislee was enthralled. She'd had no idea that the bigger pipes could be played so reverently.

She scanned the room, seeing different pipe parts on the shelves against the wall, stacked on the floor, and in organized piles. This was a man who loved what he did, and it showed.

She felt that way about her knitting. Would any of this that she was learning be of use to Zeffer? To get answers, they would have to locate Jory's pipes.

"You make it look easy," Jerry said when Fergie finished. "I cannae imagine adding a bellows tae learn, too. Practice, practice, practice."

"In all cases," Fergie said, "it's verra important that the reeds and drones are cleaned when you finish playing."

Paislee put her hand on the table, recalling what Zeffer had said about the inflammation in Jory's lungs. Should she say something? These men were the experts. If only Zeffer were here!

"What is it?" Jerry asked, having been watching her face closely to see her reaction to the music.

"You can't repeat it." She eyed them both sternly.

Jerry and Fergie replied, "I promise," at once.

"The coroner said that Jory had inflammation in his lungs," Paislee said.

"Ah," Fergie said. "Rascal didnae clean his pipes."

"Jory liked the plastic reeds," Jerry said. "Mibbe because he thought he didnae have tae worry as he might've with the natural cane reeds. Rookie mistake."

"But he played well," Paislee said. "Not like a rookie."

"That kind of thing takes time," Fergie said. "Bagpiper lung. It's not instant."

"Is that what killed Jory?" Jerry asked.

"I don't know." Paislee sighed. "It might simply be a tragic accident."

"It's awful." Jerry crossed his arms.

"Please, go see DI Zeffer. He wants tae clarify several things. I think you can answer some questions." Paislee turned to Fergie. "Certainly, you could."

"No!" Fergie said. "I willnae have the law around my door."

Paislee looked at her watch.

"How on earth did it get tae be five o'clock?"

Cursing a blue streak, certainly nothing the two men hadn't heard before, Paislee left to pick up her son.

Chapter 19

Homework, being out of her house, and more work orders meant that by the time Paislee arrived at Lydia's flat at seven, it was too late to drive to Tesco in Inverness and order her mobile phone.

"Who wants cheese toasties for dinner?" Paislee asked after rummaging through what Lydia and Corbin had in their fridge and freezer.

"Let's have pizza," Brody said.

"No pizza." Paislee was exasperated and tired. She'd finished one sweater order at the shop but had two more to fill, not to mention the lack of cashmere inventory on her shelves.

Right now, the dowager countess was sitting pretty. On the other hand, so was her till since Sorcha had paid ahead for the items.

"Lemme make them," Grandpa said. He had bags under his eyes so big that his black-framed glasses couldn't hide them.

"No, Grandpa. I want tae do it. I promise not tae burn them like the last batch."

"This hob is state of the art. Mibbe it willnae allow a pan tae get too hot?" Grandpa had brought their electric kettle from Cashmere Crush to Lydia's and it was plugged in on the counter looking very out of place on the granite.

"I wish," Paislee laughed.

She missed the warmth of their small kitchen with Brody doing homework at the round table, Wallace at his feet.

"Brody's in his room?" she asked, knowing the answer already. The nice thing about this layout was that they were all on the same floor.

"Aye. Complaining tae his mates aboot having tae take an elevator tae walk the dog." Grandpa chuckled.

Paislee heated the burner and prepared the sandwiches. "I hope you like Havarti," she said.

Grandpa tipped his pinky in the air. "Posh cheese. Bet it's delicious." He opened the cupboard to the soups. Lydia had cartons, not cans, of organic chicken noodle or tomato basil. Grandpa chose the chicken noodle.

"That will be perfect. I'll heat it!" Paislee found the appropriate pan, flipped the first three sandwiches, and added the soup to the pot.

"How aboot I switch days off so that you can go tae Tesco tomorrow?" Grandpa pulled the wish list from his pocket and placed it on the counter.

"You and Elspeth can man the store while I zip over. That might be a good idea." Paislee stirred the soup.

Lydia called on the house phone and Paislee put her bestie on speaker. "Hey, love! Hope you don't mind that we're making ourselves at home."

"You know it. Just calling tae see if there's any news aboot your water pipes?"

"Manda hasn't been in touch." Paislee slipped the edges of the spatula under the toasting bread to keep it from sticking.

"Well, these things take time. Did you get your phone sorted?"

Brody wandered out of the bedroom, Wallace on his heels, both sniffing the air as if drawn by the scent of toasted cheese. "Is dinner ready? I'm starving. All this studyin' makes me brain hurt."

"Lyd, I didn't. Hey—want tae join me for a drive tae Tesco tomorrow?" She motioned for Brody to sit at the bar next to Grandpa and piled the sandwiches on their plates.

"Sure. I'll drive."

"I need groceries. They won't fit in your back seat!" Paislee laughed.

"I'll borrow Corbin's beast. See you tomorrow."

Brody and Grandpa ate dinner in record time, and they were all fast asleep on Lydia's plush couch with the telly on.

Even Wallace didn't wake up until dawn.

Tuesday, Paislee rushed against the clock to get Brody to school on time, and walk Wallace, and do the dishes, and . . . and . . . And.

"I'd like the extra phone, please," she said, on the way out.

Brody froze in place, emanating guilt from his pores. "It needs tae be charged."

"What?" Paislee heard her voice raise and reminded herself to calm down.

"I was playing games and forgot tae plug it in," her son said, red-cheeked.

"Brody Shaw. You know better." Paislee was angry because she hadn't checked it herself and now it was too late.

"Sairy, Mum."

"I can't even, Brody," she said. But, it wasn't his fault. They were all trying to do the best they could.

They left the flat in record time. Paislee hurried, safely, to Brody's school. Jenni, Anna, and Edwyn were all waiting for him. Oh, it was so nice that he had such good mates.

"Have a good day today, Brody. I will figure out the phone situation today, all right?"

"Aye. Love you, Mum."

"Love you!"

He hurried out of the car and slammed the door closed. She was so silly-mushy-warm over his voluntary *I love you* that she didn't mind his slamming the door. Leaving the school, she was halfway to the shop and had to stop at a red light. The Juke stalled.

Paislee sweet-talked the SUV and at last the car fired up. She reached Cashmere Crush worn out. It was only Tuesday! Tuesday. Would Jerry show up, back to work now that he had no reason to fear (not that he ever really did) that Zeffer was after him?

Yep. She waved at Jerry, already parked in his delivery truck at her back stairs.

"You're late," Jerry said. "I was getting worried."

"Thanks," Paislee said. "Car stalled but she's okay. Needs a tune-up or something. I have an appointment tomorrow with Eddy."

"Oh, guid." Jerry eyed her car as if he could tell what was wrong with a simple scan. If he could that might save her some money.

Paislee went up the back stairs first, and Jerry followed, carrying a box of assorted yarn.

"I'll need tae add several boxes of cashmere on my next order," she said.

"Can I help you with that?" Zeffer was behind them on the stoop, blocking Jerry's potential escape.

"Oh!" Paislee said, surprised. Zeffer had only once come around the back. He looked good in his blue suit, this one a bright turquoise. The man was not afraid of showing off his lean physique with fitted clothes.

"Well, hell." Once inside, Jerry lowered the box of yarn to the counter.

"Now, do I need tae use cuffs, or can you walk with me like a shining example of guid citizenship tae the station?" Zeffer asked.

Jerry glared at Paislee.

"Hey! I didn't tell him you'd be here," she said. "Per usual, I told you tae talk with Zeffer. I wouldn't go behind your back, Jerry. We're friends."

"I used my incredible powers of deduction over the last year of watching when you showed up, Mr. McFadden. Every Tuesday." Zeffer didn't smile as he gestured to the back stoop. "Shall we? It's just a few blocks."

"Fine," Jerry said, very begrudging.

"Jerry!" Paislee escorted them to the back entrance. "Just tell Zeffer what we learned yesterday at F . . . Fergie's, about the different pipes." The one thing that might interest Zeffer was confirmation of bagpipe lung from not cleaning the instrument properly.

"Sounds riveting," Zeffer said dryly.

The pair went down the cement steps to the pavement.

"Jerry, come see me when you're done!" Paislee said when they reached the middle of the alleyway.

"If I dinnae toss him in a cell for avoiding me," Zeffer said.

Jerry exhaled and kept walking, his broad back to her.

"I mean it, Jerry," Paislee shouted, worried that she couldn't go with him as she'd promised. "DI, be nice, would you?"

Paislee watched them go, arms crossed. She could only hope that they would put aside their differences to find the truth of what happened to Jory during his last days. Ensure it was a tragic natural happening, nobody's fault, and then move on.

The shop was so busy, Paislee didn't hear when Jerry left with his truck. If she was in the flow, she could do a sweater in five days. This was not the flow, getting up and talking with customers, answering the phone, pricing yarn.

She couldn't complain because this was all wonderful income-bringing stuff.

Grandpa arrived at ten till twelve, his walk double from Lydia's house. He said he didn't mind.

Elspeth arrived at noon on the dot, as did Lydia, who parked in the front behind the wheel of Corbin's latest baby. Silver, shiny, with terrible petrol efficiency, but dang it looked cool.

"I'll need a ladder tae get up," Paislee said.

"They have one, right here. Shorty," Lydia teased. She waved at Grandpa and Elspeth.

Paislee left the keys to the Juke on the counter. "If you could pick up Brody, just in case we're late, that'd be great."

"Sure," Grandpa said. "The mobile is still charging, but I brought it."

"Smart of you," Paislee said.

"Bye! Guid luck!" Elspeth called.

Lydia drove to Inverness like she'd been driving a monster truck all her life.

Paislee kept her mouth shut, knowing that Lydia's love for speed was something she tempered with caution.

They reached Tesco in twenty minutes flat where it might have taken Paislee thirty or more.

"Here we are." Lydia grinned. "You excited?"

"It's an added expense that I hadn't budgeted for, so no, not really." They entered the shop.

"Sure, but you will get it reimbursed," Lydia said. "Where tae first?"

"Mobile phone, then I have Grandpa's list."

"I love a list!" Lydia said.

The place was packed. While that gave Paislee a headache, it seemed to energize her best friend better than a double espresso.

They passed a refreshments counter. "Coffee!" Lydia said.

"Tea for me," Paislee said, needing a boost. "But after the phone? I can't believe how much I missed not having it."

"Welcome tae the modern world." Lydia winked.

"I am ten times more modern than those at Ramsey Castle," Paislee said. "It came as a shock."

"Who knew that you'd become a social butterfly." Lydia bumped her arm to Paislee's.

Paislee exhaled loudly. "Attending a command performance, but for the last time. I think Robert is full of himself and his title. The rest of the family all defer tae him."

"He's the Earl of Lyon." Lydia glanced at her with a smirk. "They have tae."

"I may have a wee bit of sympathy for him, as Sorcha told me she's informed all of her children that it's time tae settle down and bring in mates tae help with the castle," Paislee said. "Sorcha still has her hand on the wheel, even if Robert is earl."

"That so?" Lydia asked. "Maybe we can pawn off one of Corbin's cousins tae the younger son."

"Too late," Paislee said. "Cinda the shopgirl has her hooks in him already, according tae Sorcha. She's nice enough, but poor."

The queue for the mobile phone had five people in it and moved quickly. Paislee worried that it would be a hassle, and that it would be more money, and she hated to spend when things were tight, even if she would someday get it back. How long might that take? Months?

"Any prospects for Lissia?" Lydia asked.

"Sorcha has alluded tae Lissia having a broken heart, but even her own daughter isn't safe from needing tae find a partner." Paislee adjusted the strap of her handbag on her shoulder. "It's awful."

"Robert's handsome. Owns a castle. Has a title. What's the holdup?" Lydia asked.

"Nobody in Scotland is his same rank," Paislee explained. They stepped forward. "I guess Robert is looking in Europe for a possible wife."

"I am glad tae have the whole marriage thing in the rearview," Lydia said. "Now, what kind of phone?"

"Same as before. Samsung. I can get my same number, right?"

"Aye, you should be able tae," Lydia said.

Another customer left with a bag of goodies, bringing them closer.

"I want it. Can't possibly try tae remember a new one. I'm going tae be thirty in November." Panic edged her voice.

"It's not bad." Lydia's birthday had been in July. They'd had a wonderful celebration at a fancy restaurant at the golf course. "The right Botox will ensure that I look forever thirty."

"Please don't go there," Paislee said. "You are beautiful."

"I aim tae keep my youthful skin as long as possible." Lydia and Paislee shuffled forward.

"Great," Paislee said. "So, when we're both fifty I'll resemble your mother."

Lydia snorted. "Or, I could share the magic potion."

"No, thank you."

Only one more customer to go. They were done fast and then it was her turn. She and Lydia reached the help desk. "I'd like tae replace my Samsung. It was drowned in a water-pipe bursting accident."

The twenty-something sales assistant gave a sad headshake, her hair tight back from her face in a bun on her head like a ballerina. Tall and willowy, as if on the weekends she was an opera star who only did this sales gig to keep her in pointe shoes. "Homeowner's insurance?"

"Yes," Paislee said. "I'll need receipts because the money will be reimbursed."

"Not a problem," the saleslady said. "Would you like the same mobile number?"

"Definitely." Paislee was beginning to feel better about the whole thing.

"I see here you have the verra basic plan." The saleslady peered up from her tablet. "We're running a special right now. Would you like tae upgrade?"

"No," Paislee said.

"Aye, she would like tae upgrade," Lydia said. "And do you have any deals on a third phone for the family?"

"And you are?" the saleslady asked, taking in Lydia's tall and slender beauty, her style, her bearing. She gave a nod, one beauty to another.

"Her best friend," Lydia said. "Paislee never gets anything nice for herself. It's the little things like *all you can text* mobile sharing that matter." Lydia smiled at the younger lady. "Dinnae you agree?"

"Well . . ." The sales assistant looked at Paislee, and Paislee shook her head.

"I heard an advert," Lydia said. "The special sounded just a wee bit more than what Paislee pays right now, which is criminal."

The saleslady nodded. "I actually have an even better deal that's in store. I can toss in a free phone, but it willnae be the newest model."

"But Paislee's replacement phone would be?" Lydia asked.

"Aye. Top of the line," the saleslady said.

An hour later, a dazed Paislee left the mobile phone desk with two new phones for the price of one, and unlimited data, all for just a bit more than she'd paid monthly before.

As they went to get refreshments, Lydia said, "I'm buying you a new case, too, so pick one oot while we're here."

"No! You've done enough. There is nothing wrong with this case that it came with. Lydia, you have done so much already."

"What are ye going on aboot?" Lydia demanded. "This was fun."

"We are living in your flat, eating your groceries," Paislee said.

Lydia tossed her chin. "That we would have had tae throw away! I wasnae packing food tae the new place. You are doing me a favor."

Paislee sipped a hot tea and chose a chicken filet on a bun. Now that the hard part was over, she was starving. "I can't believe it's four o'clock already."

"Time flies when you get tae spend other people's money." Lydia elbowed Paislee and ordered her double espresso and an egg salad on whole wheat bread.

They went to a table and watched the folks shopping as they ate.

"I won't ever be able tae repay you."

Lydia lowered her sandwich, her gray eyes serious. "We are best friends. There is no owing or repaying."

Paislee sighed, her throat stinging. "Thank you."

"You are welcome."

Her gaze grew sharp.

"What?" Paislee didn't like that look and braced herself. "What are you thinking?"

"Well, I know a way you could help me, if you wanted." Lydia shrugged like it wasn't a big deal, which meant that it was.

"Is it going tae cost me more money?" Paislee asked warily.

Lydia sipped her espresso. "Could be. But you know that it would be worth every penny."

"Like the mobile?" Paislee said.

"Even better." Lydia clasped Paislee's wrist. "I would love tae design your new kitchen."

"*What?*"

"I have this computer program that shows how a space will look after a remodel. I may have been toying with some different layouts that would fit your old kitchen . . ."

"Lydia!" Her stomach clenched at the idea of the cost of her dream appliances, and she almost choked.

Paislee's phone rang and she jumped in her seat, having forgotten about the darn thing. "Hello?"

"Paislee? Zeffer."

Figured. "Yes?"

"I wanted tae thank you for telling Jerry tae talk tae me."

"He told you that?" What had Jerry said?

"It was a little tedious aboot plastic reeds and natural reeds and drones and chanters," Zeffer said. "I have it in my notes. Fat Fergie. Just a nickname. Not one I'd be fond of, but there's no accounting for people's taste."

"Did it help? Jerry is an expert, and F . . . Fergie, too."

"The problem is finding oot how Jory may have cheated," Zeffer continued. "If he did, we need that evidence. It will shed light on how he died, which my instincts are saying wasnae natural, despite the coroner's findings—it lines up with what Jerry said aboot bagpipe lung not being instant. Something else must be going on."

Instincts rather than proof? Well, Zeffer was also growing in his career. "What does the coroner say?"

"Not important." Zeffer hummed then asked, "How did things go for you?"

Paislee thought of Robert's agreement to call and discuss what he knew. "As you know, I had lunch at the castle. I may have said that Jory had inflammation of the lungs. It lowered the tension around the table."

Lydia spewed her sip of espresso she'd been in the act of swallowing. Thankfully it wasn't much, and she wiped droplets from the plastic tray.

Paislee started to laugh.

"What's so bloody funny?" Zeffer asked.

"Nothing. Just shopping with Lydia."

"I'm lost. Have you gone mental?"

"Is there anything else?" she asked, trying not to giggle.

"No. G'night, Paislee."

She grasped Lydia's hand. "Best thing about not having a phone was avoiding Zeffer. What tickled you so much?"

"Lunch at the castle!"

They laughed until tears came to their eyes.

Chapter 20

Paislee was quite proud of herself on Wednesday morning, at Cashmere Crush at quarter past nine. She'd made toast, ham, and eggs for breakfast and even rinsed the plates to put into the dishwasher.

Would she be able to buy one for her home? The machine was downright magical. Lydia knew Paislee's finances and could be trusted to design something within her budget. It might not be the top, top, top of the line but it would be quality as it would have to last.

Humming under her breath, she congratulated herself on proper time management. Maybe this new routine was just what she needed. She placed her new phone with the gorgeous case on the counter and tossed her handbag on the shelf below the register.

Brody on time, and Grandpa having a leisurely tea on the balcony. He didn't work today and planned on taking it easy. Maybe soak in the hot tub or the sauna downstairs in Lydia's luxurious building.

Elspeth would be in at noon. Until then, she would turn on the radio and knit.

Her phone rang at nine thirty. "Cashmere Crush!" she answered in a sweet and happy tone.

"Paislee? It's Eddy."

In that moment, she recalled that Grandpa had made an appointment with the mechanic and told her about it. In all the chaos she'd dropped the ball. *Damn.*

"Eddy!" She tucked her knitting needles into the sweater.

"Are ye on your way?" Eddy asked. "You were supposed tae be here at nine thirty."

Eddy's was five miles outside of town center and not an easy walk back.

"Is there any way you can fit me in later today? Say, noon?"

"Sairy, lass. If ye can be here by ten, then aye, I'll getcha in," Eddy said. "Otherwise, it will need tae be next week."

Nine thirty. It took fifteen minutes. She technically didn't open until ten, though she was usually here at quarter after nine on a good day, which allowed her knitting time and a few minutes of quiet before customers.

The Juke was acting funny. Dare she take a chance to wait? She was grateful for her customers! She'd worked hard to build up a clientele. In the end, she had to be responsible with her vehicle as it ferried her, Brody, and Grandpa around Nairn.

"I'll be there in fifteen minutes," Paislee said. She'd call a rideshare to return to the shop. While it was feasible for her to hike the five miles back, she'd be icky and sweaty, and it would take too long.

Paislee was in the Juke when Jerry arrived in his pickup rather than the delivery truck. She rolled down her window, silently urging him to hurry.

He jumped out. "Hey! I need tae talk tae you."

With a glance at the time on the dash she said, "I'm on my way tae the mechanic. If you follow me, we can talk on the way back tae the shop."

Jerry rightfully looked confused.

"I'd appreciate the ride," Paislee clarified. "I have no way back once I drop it off with Eddy."

"Oh!" Jerry smacked his palm to his forehead. "Yeah, sure."

"Thanks. Follow me!"

She arrived at Eddy's and dropped off the Juke, letting the mechanic know about the vehicle stalling.

"We'll take guid care of her for you," Eddy promised.

"Thank you!" A trusted mechanic was worth their weight in gold, Gran had always said.

Paislee got into Jerry's truck, glad she'd worn jeans and her comfortable flats today. "Hey!" She checked the time on her phone and groaned. "The day had started out so wonderfully."

"What's wrong?" Jerry said.

"Nothing I can fix now." Paislee buckled her seatbelt. "Going tae be late opening the shop, that's all."

Jerry grinned and revved the engine. "I can step on it."

"That's okay!" Paislee laughed. "Be safe, that's fine."

"Car's acting up?" He kept his gaze on the road, his profile showing a thick mustache, smooth chin, and slicked-back hair. A nice nose. She'd never had cause to notice his nose before.

"Yes. It was time for routine maintenance anyway. I appreciate you giving me a ride back tae Cashmere Crush." She faced the front and let go of the stress, searching for the Zen she'd had earlier.

"No problem."

"What did you want tae talk about?" Paislee glanced at Jerry. "Zeffer?"

"Aye." Jerry chuckled. "I poked me head into your place yesterday after the interview and you were hopping so I didnae stay."

"I'd wondered!" Business had been good, and she would ride the wave. Winter would come and it would slow down as it always did.

"I went tae Fat Fergie's."

"Why on earth do you call him that?" Paislee asked. "He's not fat. He's pure muscle!"

"He introduced himself that way." Jerry drummed his thumb

against the steering wheel. "I agree that it's not accurate, or a flattering nickname."

"And I noticed you don't call him that when you're talking tae him."

"No." Jerry stopped at a stop sign, checked for other cars, and then stepped on the gas.

"Well, maybe from now on, he can just be Fergie," Paislee said.

Jerry snickered. "You're such a mum."

"I am." She shrugged, not sorry. "So? Be nice. Basic."

Jerry laughed. "Do you want tae know what me and the DI talked aboot, or should we continue the lesson on guid manners?"

She grinned. "I am all ears."

"After Zeffer pretty much cornered me on the back stoop yesterday, he took me tae his office at the station there."

"His office?" The inspector had taken that over, Amelia had said, last summer. Zeffer shared with some of the others when he needed a space in Nairn. All of a sudden, he had an office? "What was it like?"

"An office. Desk with a name plate. Two chairs—not cozy." Jerry turned the blinker, closer to Cashmere Crush. "Why?"

She'd need to find out from Amelia what was going on. "Were Constable Thorn and Constable Smith there?"

"No, just Zeffer and Amelia. I've seen her on Saturday at your place working if there's a delivery."

Paislee nodded. "She helps me during the summer. Was he . . . fair?"

"Considering I'd been avoiding him like the plague, yeah. Zeffer was decent."

Paislee bit her lip to keep from saying *I told you so.* "Good— what did he ask you?"

"Like you said, he's trying tae pinpoint Jory's actions the day of the competition," Jerry said. "I was the last tae see him."

"Were you able tae help?"

"Dinnae know aboot that." Jerry slowed around a traffic circle.

While Paislee appreciated the need for them to keep speeders from speeding, she also found them very annoying when she wanted to . . . speed.

"I hate that Zeffer can't give clear answers," Paislee said. "Makes me crazy, too."

"Yeah. He's the one tae ask the questions," Jerry said with a rueful laugh. "He's heard aboot Jory cheating at the competition and asked *me* if it was possible."

"And?"

"You saw yesterday at Fa . . . Fergie's, how the pipes function. I suppose that something could be altered in the chanter or drone, but I dinnae ken how, or tae what purpose."

Paislee sighed. "Sorry tae leave in a rush like that. I appreciated the lesson, and Fergie showing me the three bagpipes. He's very skilled. Did you stay?"

"Naw. It was a band practice night for Clan Campbell. Everyone was full of questions, so we didnae accomplish much," Jerry said. "It's unsettling tae have one of our piping community suddenly dead. Even though Jory wasnae a close friend tae any of us, we've known Robert Grant all our lives."

They arrived at the shop and Paislee had to switch from what happened to Jory to focusing on a successful day in sales, both yarn and goods, when she was down to the wire with supplies and time.

"Did you order the cashmere from JoJo's for me?"

"Aye. I'll deliver it tomorrow." Jerry turned off the engine.

"Was there anything else?" Paislee asked, her hand on the door handle.

"Fergie and I are going tae brainstorm possibilities today," Jerry said. "Better we find what happened tae Jory's pipes before Zeffer decides I'm guilty of something."

"Zeffer doesn't operate that way." Paislee opened the door as a thought occurred of the lovely tune Fergie had played on the SSP. "Jerry, would it be possible tae trick someone by using a bellows in the GHB?"

"Not allowed, lass, not allowed. The GHB Competition Council is strict." Jerry shifted, on edge. "We've got tae find Jory's bagpipes."

Clyde Cunningham, pipe major, band director, accuser of Robert. "Have you seen Clyde around?"

"Clyde is laying low," Jerry said. "Hasnae been at the pub. Probably worried Zeffer will snap him up for questions he dinnae want tae answer."

Paislee chuckled. "Maybe talk tae Meri and see if there's an update on the pipes. She's taking this whole cheating thing tae heart." She liked the judge very much, but in truth didn't know her well.

"You think Meri might have put the pressure on Jory somehow?" Jerry asked.

Reluctant to be drawn back in, Paislee shrugged. "I'm more convinced Clyde's behind what's going on, tae protect Clan Cunningham's reputation and his own, if it turns out that Jory was cheating. Somebody has tae know. Where did he buy his bagpipes? Who are his closest mates? The same people who knew about the fifty-thousand-pound bet might know whether he cheated."

"Good questions, Paislee." Jerry smoothed his mustache. "Hey, how are you going tae pick up your car later?"

"I'll take a cab. Not a big deal."

"Call me," Jerry said. "I'll drive ye."

She raised her brow. "You have already played my shining knight in armor today. I'm fine. I have no idea what time it'll be ready anyway."

"You're so stubborn!" Jerry said.

"Thanks for the ride." She waved and shut the door, hurrying up the stairs to the rear entrance and going inside.

Shadows were visible through the front window.

Smiling, Paislee hurried across the floor and unlocked, then opened, the door. "Hello! Sorry tae keep you waiting," she said. "I was dropping my car at the shop."

The local women were friends in their sixties who came in

once a month to choose a project that they'd then work on together. It was sweet. The rest of the morning passed quickly with customers and knitting in spurts.

Meri burst into the shop at eleven, orange hair tamed. "Paislee! Jerry called and asked if there was any news aboot the bagpipes. He asked specifically aboot the GHB being fitted with a bellows, like an SSP, for the competition." Her mouth pursed with disapproval.

"I only know what you're talking about because Fergie showed me the three main bagpipes in Scotland yesterday."

"Fat Fergie." Meri's gaze turned dreamy. "That man was pure magic on the pipes. He doesnae compete anymore but oh, he could make grown folks weep with how he played a tune. He just dropped oot of sight for a while."

"Fergie said that he prefers tae make them, but I saw the certificates and plaques on his wall at his workshop," Paislee said. "I didn't count how many different styles of bagpipes he had."

"A true craftsman," Meri said. "I was never in his league, even before my shoulder injury."

Customers came in and Paislee welcomed them, then smiled at Meri. "Can I get you anything while you're here? We sure enjoyed your company last Thursday and hope you'll join us again."

"I had a guid time," Meri said. "I was actually hoping you could join me for lunch at the pub."

"Oh." What was with everyone and lunch? Paislee often worked through to catch up on projects. "I don't think so. Not today."

"I've got Clyde meeting me, that's why."

"Clyde Cunningham?"

"He's been hard tae find but I tempted him with a meal, just him and me. One-on-one time with a premier judge aboot the competition isnae something he'd turn doon," Meri said.

Paislee sighed. Could she make time for it? She shook her head.

"I hinted in a phone message tae Clyde that I had news aboot the possible rematch. That I may have talked with the Grants."

"And Clyde wants tae know what you know?"

Meri's eyes twinkled behind her silver frames. "You got it."

"What *do* you know?" Paislee asked.

"Blasted little." Meri stepped closer to Paislee. "Well, other than Jory had inflammation in his lungs. They call it bagpipe lung. Not verra common, and not usually deadly."

"Where did you hear that?" Paislee hoped it wasn't from Robert at the castle, since she'd told them, but let it go. Meri had more information than what she'd shared with the Grants.

"I call the police department and ask for updates. It's not much and Amelia is a real sweetheart." Meri patted her hair and Paislee understood why it was usually a mess. "Sorcha is putting the pressure on me."

Paislee felt better that it was something the constables had shared, and not her big mouth. "Wait—what does Sorcha have on *you*?"

Meri waved her hand. "Colleagues of the GHB Competition Council for many years, how they've always hosted the event at Ramsey Castle with no cost for the use of the property—verra light-handed in her reminders, but it's enough. Anyway, I was hoping you'd join me. A second set of ears and all that."

"I can't. I'm really sorry." Paislee pointed to the almost finished blue sweater on the counter. "This is for an order tae ship next week."

"That's all right. It's just that I saw Clyde following me yesterday around Ramsey Castle." Meri scrunched her nose like a rabbit rather than a wily fox. "He was driving his truck."

"*What?*" Paislee thought he was plenty shady herself, so she believed the down-to-earth Meri.

"Aye. Got me thinking what sort of bloke is going tae be on the phone with the competition council, worried aboot the title, when a man on his team is accused of cheating? And then fainted on the field. Was he going tae mention it tae me, or let it go?"

Paislee kept an eye on the browsing customers. "I understand your feelings, but does it matter what happened? Jory's gone. As a judge, is there something you can do *now* that the competition has been . . . postponed?"

"I've half a mind tae file a complaint against Clyde for having his phone on the playing field," Meri said. "He's right that because a year has passed, there is nothing tae be done aboot the title, even with proof—that we dinnae have—of Jory cheating."

Paislee nodded with empathy.

"I watched Jory like a hawk this year, but I didnae see anything," Meri said, despondent. "I didnae know what tae look for!"

"I'm sorry, Meri."

"The integrity of this competition means the world tae me." Meri looked toward the frosted window of the shop.

How to help? Besides lunch? A frazzled mum tugging a little girl by the hand entered the shop. "Welcome tae Cashmere Crush," Paislee said.

"Hey," the young mother replied, not making eye contact as she zeroed in on the wall of pink yarn. "We're just browsing."

"Sure, take your time." Paislee shifted slightly to Meri. "Do you feel like you're in danger?"

The petite judge hefted her chin. "I know how tae defend myself."

Paislee gave an inward sigh.

Another of Paislee's customers, a woman with light brown hair, midforties, pointed to the top shelf of red skeins in various hues from bright red to brick. "Can I see that yarn up there?"

"Absolutely." Paislee went to the back storage area and retrieved the ladder, climbing to the top row. "This?"

"Not that one," the woman said. "The lighter red. Yes, that one there."

Paislee passed it down. "Here you are."

"Oh." The woman frowned. "It's too pink. Sairy! Yes, the one you first touched, please. Let's see that again."

"It's not a problem." Paislee gave it to the woman.

The woman inspected it closely. "I wish I would have brought the sample I'm trying tae match."

"You can bring it back if it's not the right shade," Paislee said.

The woman beamed. "Thank you! I'd like six skeins, please."

"My pleasure." Paislee counted out six rolls of yarn and met the woman at the register. "What are you making?"

"An afghan to match my new throw pillows," the woman said. "If they don't match, I'll be back this afternoon."

"Not a problem at all—in fact, why not bring in the pillow?" Paislee suggested.

"Brilliant!" The woman paid cash and Paislee bagged the yarn, adding the receipt.

"Mum! Can I have this hat?" the little girl said.

"Must you ask for everything?" the harried mother answered. "I just want tae get some yarn tae make a blanket for you. Behave!"

"It's just so pretty," the little girl said, tone teetering on a whinge. "I'm fair fond of the flowers."

"If you're guid," the mother said, quickly picking up rolls of pink merino wool, running her thumb over the yarn as if to test for softness.

The little girl started to cry. "It's too hard tae be guid!"

Meri dropped to her knees, eye level with the child. "I like flowers, too. Do you know there's a pattern tae make them oot of yarn?"

"There is?" The little girl brought her finger to her quivering lower lip.

"Where?" the mum asked. "Is it difficult? I'm just learning, really."

"Over here," Meri answered, directing them to the patterns. "I believe there are different skill levels."

"Can you make me this one, Mum?"

"Instead of the hat?" This was not the first rodeo for the mother and daughter bargaining over behavior.

"Yes, please," the little girl said, tears gone.

Paislee rang up the pattern and the yarn, with mother and daughter both smiling as they left the shop.

The customers all filed out and Paislee's register was fuller than it had been. She exhaled and reached for the sweater to work on.

Elspeth entered. "Oh, quiet morning?"

Paislee laughed and shook her head. "Elspeth, I'm going tae take a quick lunch break during the lull with Meri here. Call me if it gets crazy. I'll just be across the street at the pub."

It was the least Paislee could do for Meri's assistance just now. And it didn't sit right with her that Meri would be afraid of Clyde.

Chapter 21

Paislee and Meri walked out of Cashmere Crush and across the street to the Lion's Mane pub. The food was good, the tavern quaint, and the prices fair.

"I hope Clyde won't be upset that I've joined you," Paislee said, scanning the dim interior of the pub. "Oh, there he is, seated toward the back."

"Too bad if he is," Meri said. "I'll buy and hint that you'd invited yourself. All casual-like so he doesnae suspect anything. The worm."

Which sounded good in theory, but Clyde would have to be blind and a fool to not see how high and tense Meri's shoulders were.

It made her angry at the man. Before Paislee left, she'd find out for sure if he'd been following Meri, and why.

"Meri!" Clyde got up from his seat. He was luckily seated at a table for four. His smile faltered when he saw Paislee.

She didn't take it to heart.

"Hi, Clyde!" She held out her hand. "Remember me? Paislee Shaw."

The sly band director's dark hair was styled heavily with oil so it would flop just right, his swarthy skin had a pale tint, and his handshake held a tremor.

"I do." His expression had a question as to why she was here, but he didn't verbalize it.

"Meri's part of my Thursday night knitters' group and was in the shop for supplies. When she said she was stepping over for a bite, my stomach growled." Paislee laughed and covered her tummy.

"It wasnae that obvious," Meri chuckled.

"I quite invited myself tae clam chowder without realizing she already had a companion."

"It's not a bother," Clyde said. "Please, join us. I just arrived myself."

"I can't stay too long." But Paislee wouldn't leave until she knew Meri was okay.

Meri sat, as did Paislee and Clyde. A waiter brought over three menus with a promise to be right back.

Paislee read the menu but already knew what she was having. "Wednesday's lunch special is a bowl of clam chowder with a roll. I love it."

Her phone dinged a text. She saw that it was from Lydia and not the shop, so she didn't answer.

"You come here often?" Clyde asked.

"I work across the street, so yes." Paislee placed the menu down. "Do you live around here?"

"No," Clyde said. "I'm closer tae Inverness, where I slog at a tech job, boring nine tae six, five days a week." Clyde wasn't as slick as he'd been at the competition but sounded like a normal guy. Who was the real Clyde?

"Married?" Paislee asked casually.

"Naw." Clyde peered up from the menu and then glanced at Paislee's ringless left hand. She could tell that he thought she was okay-looking as he asked, "You?"

"No. Single mum of one boy, twelve going on forty."

His eyes widened. Any idea about a date went out the window as he realized she had a child, which was fine by her. She had zero time in her life and zero interest in Clyde. Ugh. She was only helping Meri get information on the man.

"The Cunningham clan has been playing competition pipes for at least six years," Meri said. "Getting better and better. I really thought you and the band had a shot tae take the title again this year."

Clyde turned an awful crimson.

"I'm so sorry about Jory," Paislee said, making eye contact with the waiter as she put her menu down. She really was on a time crunch.

"His death was a shock." Clyde also put his menu down.

Meri, too. The waiter stopped and took their orders.

"I'll have the lunch special," Paislee said. "And a Perrier."

"Same for me," Meri said. "Except I'll have whatever is on draft."

The waiter gave a selection and Meri went with a lighter beer, then turned to Clyde.

"I'll take the beef pie," Clyde said. "And a dark beer."

The waiter zoomed off toward the kitchen.

Another message vibrated her phone—also from Lydia. She must be at lunch, too, and wanting a blether. Well, Paislee had no time for aimless chit chat today.

Paislee studied Clyde. He had a career, no family, and enjoyed his bagpiping competition. Not exactly a menace to society.

She glanced at Meri when the waiter delivered their drinks. The ball was in the judge's court.

Meri sipped. "Clyde."

"Aye?"

"Were you following me yesterday?" Meri's bid for subtle was an epic fail.

"What?" Clyde said. His guilt was evident as he slurped his large glass of beer.

Neither of them should take on a life of crime.

"Why did you follow Meri?" Paislee asked. Her phone wouldn't stop dinging and she turned the volume down after seeing that the messages were still from Lydia. None from the shop or Brody's school.

"I'd hoped she hadnae seen me." Clyde shrugged, very embarrassed.

"I did," Meri said. "Following too close behind the delivery lorry."

"Blast." Clyde sat back.

"Well?" Paislee asked.

"I was coming from Ramsey Castle," Clyde said. "Were you there, too?"

"No. I live on some acreage nearby that's been in the family for generations," Meri explained. "I knew you had no reason tae be up that way, unless you were at the castle." She sipped. "Had you been invited?"

"No," Clyde admitted. He glanced warily at Paislee. "I was searching for clues as tae where Jory might have lived."

"What do you mean?" Paislee asked. "The newspaper said Jory lived in Dundee and had no family."

Clyde picked up his fork and placed it down again, as if nervous. "Jory mentioned that his family had farmed the land a long time ago."

Meri's nose lifted and light glinted on the lenses of her glasses. "Dootful. I dinnae remember any Baxters."

"Why would he lie?" Clyde asked.

"Why would he cheat?" Meri countered.

The food arrived, breaking the tension.

"Just because he was accused doesnae mean he was guilty," Clyde said. It would be a stain on the competition crown if it was discovered Jory had broken the rules. Worse if Clyde had known about it, too. Even though the title would remain with the clan, it wouldn't be a clean victory.

Paislee tapped her spoon to her bowl. Would a conviction bar the Cunninghams from future competitions?

"That's true. As a judge it's important that I keep an open mind." Meri tore off a piece of roll and dipped it to her chowder. "Do you know how tae contact his family?"

"No," Clyde said. "Jory claimed he didnae have any family left—they'd moved or died a long time ago."

"Friends?" Paislee said. She knew friends could be closer than family from her own situation.

"None that I know ootside the band, and we werenae that tight," Clyde said. "I never saw him unless we were practicing or performing. Then again, we practiced four days a week."

"What did Jory do for work?" Paislee asked. "Was he able tae make his living playing the bagpipes?"

"No," Clyde said with a scoff. "I dinnae know any amateurs who do. Including myself."

"Did you also bet on the competition?" Paislee asked. "You've mentioned Jory, and Robert, but what about you?"

"Sure." Clyde bit into his beef pie, the crust gold and flaky. "On the Cunningham clan. Lots of folks take a chance. It's harmless."

Everyone seemed to agree that it was, so who was Paislee to think differently? He didn't appear worried about it. "You've explained why you were around the castle, but not how come you were following Meri."

He wiped his mouth, clearly still embarrassed. "I wanted tae plead our case for not filing a complaint against the band because of what Jory may have done. I dinnae know if or how he cheated. I'm upset aboot it, tae be sure."

How upset? Enough to harm Jory? He'd supposedly randomly followed Meri yesterday to get her alone for a chat. How much did the title mean to Clyde? Was this accomplishment something that defined him?

"What do the other members of the band think?" Paislee asked. "Do they know about the charge of Jory cheating?"

"I dinnae think so. I received the anonymous note, and talked tae him aboot it, just us," Clyde said. "We were overheard arguing, as you already know, Paislee."

"Did you tell anyone else?" Paislee asked. "Like Ewan, or the girls who play the snare drums? The bass drum player?"

"I may have . . . *acted out* a wee bit later," Clyde said. "Not sure if anybody heard me. I keep hoping it was Robert Grant's jealousy behind the letters."

"How did Jory pay the rent, then?" Meri asked.

"I dinnae think Jory had a career, per se. I know he put in a few nights a week at a bar, slinging drinks." Clyde still exuded guilt.

"Is that the only reason you'd followed Meri?" Paislee pressed.

Clyde drank his beer in several gulps. "I'd hoped tae convince Meri tae tell me who the winners of the competition would be, if, you know, the event is canceled."

Meri gasped. "No. No, I would not, and will not, share that information with you. It is strictly confidential."

"I'm sairy. I know it wasnae a guid idea," Clyde replied.

Was Meri satisfied?

Meri nodded.

Her phone dinged again. Paislee quickly finished her chowder and placed money on the table. "I hate tae eat and run, but my phone is going crazy."

Meri stayed seated. "I'm fine tae visit, Clyde, if you'd like."

"Aye," Clyde said.

"Okay. Meri, stop in at the shop after tae pick up what you need for supplies. Clyde, thanks for letting me intrude."

"No intrusion," he said, also seeming to be relieved to have Meri to himself.

"I will," Meri said.

Paislee left the Lion's Mane just as Lydia called.

"Hey, are you okay?" Paislee asked right away. "What's going on? Did you get a new estate agent award?"

"I wish. I'm fine, but where are you?" Lydia demanded.

"At lunch with Meri."

"Have you even looked at my texts?"

"I have not," Paislee said. "It's only been twenty minutes and I was eating."

"What is the point of having a phone if you dinnae answer it?" Lydia asked.

"If there is no emergency it can wait, aye?" Paislee put the mobile on speaker as she stopped at the street, reading the messages from Lydia asking her to call. They got more urgent with each one. "What is it?"

"Well, you dinnae have tae be snippy," her best friend said.

"Snippy?" Paislee counted to ten. "Lydia, what is it that you wanted?"

"Manda had a free moment tae stop by your house. I thought you'd want tae meet her there tae go over some questions she had regarding the damage."

"You're right," Paislee said. "That would be good. When?"

"I dinnae ken if she's around now," Lydia said with a huff.

"I can't just drop everything, Lydia." Paislee eyed the sky and wouldn't have been surprised to see a gray cloud following her around. Nope. The sun actually dared to shine. Of all the nerve.

"I'm just trying tae help."

Paislee hated needing help. She grew defensive. "Do you want us out of the flat? I can find us a hotel."

"No!"

"Well, what's the hurry?"

"I thought you'd be more comfortable in your own place, Paislee."

Lydia was right. She would be. "I don't even have the Juke today," Paislee said. Oh God—was that an actual whine in her tone?

"Is the car okay?"

"It's at the shop." Paislee squared her shoulders. "Maintenance."

"Oh."

Silence ticked.

"Want me tae pick you up?" Lydia asked.

"That's all right." She would call a cab or walk. "I don't know what time it will be done."

"I was just excited for you," Lydia said. "Wait until you see my idea for your new kitchen."

"Lydia!" Things were spinning out of her control.

"I'm sairy, Paislee. How aboot this . . . you call me when you hear aboot the Juke, and I can arrange with Manda to meet us at your place later at a firm time. Oh. What aboot Brody? Who will pick him up from school?"

"I'm sorry, too." Paislee smacked her palm to her forehead. "I would love it if you could pick him up at four thirty, if I don't have the Juke yet."

"I will, I will. Call me if anything changes." Lydia hung up.

Paislee went into the shop. Elspeth was helping a woman with some yarn. Another customer browsed the few sweaters she had on display.

"Hi," Paislee said, slinging her handbag behind the counter. She wondered if she could afford a full-time employee.

The idea terrified her.

September was winding down from tourist season, so she knew things would naturally slow . . . she just had to go with the fabulous fast flow.

"Hello," the woman said, bringing a beige and orange sweater to the counter. "I love this one. Do you do these yourself?"

"I do."

"It's perfect," the woman said.

"Thank you." Heart warm, Paislee rang the woman up and added a business card. "I make them tae order as well, if you want one for a gift, or in a special color."

The woman's gaze lit. "What a unique idea. I will definitely be in touch."

Paislee answered the phone as the woman left, floating on air. "Cashmere Crush."

"Paislee? It's Eddy. I've got some bad news."

"What is it?" Up, down, sideways. This day was worse than a carnival ride. She had visions of the car being toast. Then what on earth would they do? Lydia didn't have an "extra" car—besides, hers was too small, and that meant a rental . . .

"It willnae be done today, lass," Eddy said apologetically. "I know you need it."

"What's wrong?" She felt a little like a rabbit daring to peek over a hedge to make sure the fox was gone.

"I didnae want tae rush it, that's all," Eddy said. "I promise tae do it first thing in the morning."

Paislee blew out a very relieved breathe. "Okay."

"I know you need tae pick up your son. I feel terrible."

Her chest eased, allowing her to breathe. "I can call a friend, Eddy. That's all right. God, I was a little worried."

"Didnae mean tae scare you. Nothing should be too bad, but I ran oot of time and didnae want tae hurry the job."

"That's all right. Tomorrow is fine."

"You're verra good at bringing her in for regular tune-ups. This Juke might last another ten years."

Paislee exhaled and leaned her hip to a stool. "Have you noticed that Nairn has been busier this year?"

"Aye. We have the Earl of Cawdor and his outreach tae thank. I'm chuffed when I make deposits at the bank, but not so pleased when it takes me longer tae get home," Eddy said.

Paislee laughed. "I understand completely."

"I'll call you when it's done! Thanks, Paislee."

"Bye, Eddy."

Since Elspeth was with a customer, Paislee called Lydia. "Hey."

"Yes?" Lydia answered cautiously.

"I would really appreciate a ride tae pick up myself, and then Brody. Eddy didn't get tae the car yet today."

"Sure!" Lydia said. "I am happy tae help. You know that, right?"

"I do, Lydia. I'm sorry if I was short with you."

"You cannae help it," Lydia teased. "You are what you are, Paislee. Petite. Add the redhead temper? Well . . ."

Chapter 22

Paislee kept an eye out between customers for Meri and was glad when the judge came in around one thirty. Her cheeks were flushed, and Paislee wondered if Meri had stayed to talk with Clyde over a second beer.

"Hey!" Paislee placed the project she was working on aside. "How did it go?"

"Fine, fine. Clyde was happy enough tae talk after you left. Wanted tae pick my brain aboot Robert Grant. I think he has some earl envy," Meri said.

"Why is that?"

"He grew up on the loch in Inverness," Meri said. "His mum was mates with Sorcha during primary, well before she married Dermot Grant, and taught him tae revere the local nobility."

Paislee thought that fit—if Clyde was forty-ish, and Sorcha (and presumably Clyde's mother) was sixty-three. "Are they still friends?"

"His mum passed away. His only brother moved tae London and was glad tae brush the dust off his heels. I guess he doesnae have the same respect for the old ways as Clyde."

Was that empathy for Clyde in Meri's tone? Amazing what a good blether in a pub could do. Maybe Robert should be the one having low-key conversations over a pint.

"Do you think he's sincere?" Paislee asked.

"When I'd suggested lunch, he'd taken the afternoon off so that we wouldnae be rushed." Meri removed her glasses, cleaned the lenses on her soft shirt, and put them on again. "He was very curious as tae whether or not the competition will be allowed a rematch."

"And?"

"My lips are sealed." Meri gave a sheepish grin. "He had a chuckle over my worry aboot whether or not he'd been following me for a sinister reason. It was a completely spur-of-the-moment decision that he regretted immediately."

Paislee briefly closed her eyes. Was Clyde being truthful? Did Jory used to have family near the castle? Sorcha had said they'd sold some land a while ago. Then again, Meri claimed the name Baxter didn't ring any bells. She picked up her needles and yarn. "He wanted tae know the winners."

"I didnae tell him, or aboot what the council had told me and Connor." Meri tucked her hand in her pants pocket. "Clyde had been with Ewan when his cousin had discovered Jory in the pub he worked at and invited him tae be part of Clan Cunningham Piping Band. It was a personal slight tae him that Jory might've been dishonest when Clyde had been rather pushy aboot getting him a slot in the group. Clyde gave up his place as a piper to be the pipe major because of Jory. He had visions of piping-band glory."

Paislee knitted on the sweater, her mouth curling with uncertainty.

"I assured him that I wasnae going tae file a complaint aboot his mobile on the field, though it's against the rules, and gave him a verbal warning."

"That was nice of you." Clyde had gotten a favor from Meri, though the judge had kept the important information close to her chest. Paislee didn't care for the man, but he wasn't dangerous.

"Anyway, I'll see you tomorrow for Knit and Sip," Meri said. "Thanks!"

The judge hurried out of the shop. Not ten minutes later, Lady Shannon Leery walked in, with her son, Shawn Marcus.

Paislee felt a jolt of concern but kept knitting from her seat near the register. He'd tried to sell the building behind his mother's back not that long ago and she'd feared that she would lose her business that she'd worked hard to build.

She'd started off with online orders and built this brick-and-mortar shop for almost ten years now on prized Market Street.

Elspeth's gaze shifted behind the pair for Margot, who managed the medical clinic on the block and who was dating Shawn— to everyone's surprise.

"Hello!" Paislee said.

Margot must be at the clinic as she wasn't with Shawn and Shannon.

"Paislee," the lady said somewhat stiffly. Shannon wore a navy dress that showcased her slim figure; her blond bob wouldn't dare have a stray hair.

Uh-oh. What now? Paislee studied the heir to the Leery Estate. Shawn looked healthier than he'd been in a while. He was taking new medication after a liver transplant and had quit drinking, along with changing his diet.

Paislee had helped with a small incident at the Leery Estate and become friendly with Shannon, though the vibe she was getting now was anything but buddies.

"Paislee. Elspeth." Shawn nodded at them each.

"Yes?" Paislee braced for news of some kind. Bad, good, it would be one or the other the way her day was going. Nothing neutral for her today.

"As you know, we were planning an ice cream shop where the bakery used tae be," Shawn announced. He almost matched his mother, wearing navy slacks. His Oxford shirt was white with small navy pinstripes, and he'd opted to forgo a jacket. It was the end of summer, after all.

"We've heard that, yes," Paislee said. "Brody is very excited."

"Mother suggested that I give you the chance tae pay more for a bigger space before signing the contract." Shawn raised a brow at her.

"What?" Leave this spot on the corner for a bigger corner with a view of the park? It was double the space for her yarn and tables. Shelves.

She was going to say no but bit her lip to keep quiet.

"Mother has an idea tae make your shop grow ten times the size." Shawn spoke indifferently, as if this was all up to his mum, and of no interest to him personally.

Paislee put down her knitting and smiled at Shannon. "You've already done so much! Introducing me tae the dowager countess at Ramsey Castle—"

"You're right." Shannon's mouth firmed with no answering smile.

"I . . . May I have some time tae think about it?" Paislee felt like she was in trouble or something and needed a minute to sort things out.

Shawn peered down his nose at her. "It's an excellent opportunity."

"It is," Shannon said. "No doot."

Though the lady was hot under the collar, her attitude had brought the temperature in the shop down by ten degrees. "I appreciate the offer, but I'd still like time tae think about it."

"I hope you are quicker tae act than what you've been for my friends at the castle," Shannon drawled.

"What do you mean? I've brought up the finest goods as soon as Sorcha asked for them." Paislee gestured to the shelves. "Tae the detriment of the stock in my storefront."

"Is it too much?" Shannon queried sharply.

"No." Paislee didn't have time for games and wasn't good at them anyway. "Have I upset you?"

"Me?" The lady put her fingers to her chest. "Not me. The dowager countess. Sorcha said you havenae been the least helpful in the matter with Robert. When I assured her you would be."

"As did I." Shawn puffed his chest.

Was this a bribe to move her to the bigger shop to help Sorcha, her friend? As if Paislee wouldn't do all she could just because she was part of the Nairn community?

Paislee raised her hand. "I have been tae the castle twice for lunch as . . . *invited* . . . by the dowager countess. It is not my fault that Robert Grant doesn't want tae talk with the police." She glared at Shawn, as he'd been the exact same stubborn way. Male? Nobility? Scotsmen? It was a nightmare, as the men did what they pleased.

Shawn turned toward his mother with a tint of pink to his cheeks.

"I don't know what else you want me tae say," Paislee said. "Sorcha seemed happy enough when I left the other day with the news that Jory had inflammation in his lungs that may have contributed tae his death. Robert told me that he would talk with the police. I have no clue what changed."

She hated to disappoint anyone. It wasn't in her nature.

"I have arranged a dinner for you there tomorrow night," Shannon said.

Paislee shook her head. "I can't. I have my Knit and Sip." Business came right after Brody. Brody! She checked the time on her watch.

She had an hour before Lydia would pick her up, and then they'd get Brody and discuss the house projects.

"Lunch tomorrow?" Shannon seconded.

"I'm sorry," Paislee said. "Tomorrow is not good. I have several appointments."

Her house, her car, and her work. Her stomach tightened with nerves.

Lady Shannon Leery stiffened.

Paislee felt terrible but also resolute. There were boundaries that she wouldn't give on. "I'm very sorry but I can't do more."

Lady Leery stepped away, dialing someone on the phone and murmuring into it. When she returned, daggers radiated from her eyes.

"I was able tae rearrange the meeting for Friday, lunch. Does that suit?" Her tone said there would not be another chance.

There was a lot on the line—her business relationship at the castle for the gift shop, her "friendship" with Shannon, and now this opportunity for growth in the bigger shop on the prime corner of Market Street.

Even if she had to take a cab, Paislee would be there. "Thank you so much, Lady Leery. I will be there Friday. What time?"

She was terrified of making a mistake that could tank her business. Due to the lady's sponsorship, she had a champion for her cashmere goods.

"Half past twelve." Her lips pursed. "You'll be there?"

"I promise."

Shawn and Lady Leery exchanged a look and then both circled the interior of Cashmere Crush.

Paislee saw it from their eyes. Colorful shelves bursting with skeins of yarn. Clothing, pet harnesses, patterns, and two high-top tables. Customers browsing.

It was perhaps crowded, long and narrow with high ceilings, but it wasn't cramped.

"After your lunch at the castle," Shannon said, "we can discuss an upgrade for your business space."

Speechless, Paislee nodded her thanks.

"Well, that was something," Elspeth said when the pair left. "What will ye do?"

"I don't know." Discuss it with Lydia and Grandpa. "Elspeth, let's close up early so that we can both go home at four."

"You dinnae have a car?"

"No. Lydia's picking me up."

"I can stay until six," Elspeth offered. "I wait for Susan, and we walk home together so it's not a bother."

"Okay. Thank you—but only if you want tae. Any progress on the service dog for Susan?"

"Not yet," Elspeth said. "Lots of queries floating aboot. She's put in several applications."

"What a day! Elspeth, do you think we have enough business tae warrant another employee, or the bigger space?"

Elspeth smiled. "Sometimes you just take the leap, and the growth will come."

What would Gran say?

Lydia honked outside the front window.

"See you tomorrow at Knit and Sip. Thanks again!" Paislee grabbed her bag and hurried out the front. Lydia had Corbin's special SUV with all the bells and whistles. She jumped up to get inside.

"Thinking I might sell my little sports car for one of these." Lydia grinned and revved the engine.

"That would be dangerous," Paislee said with a laugh.

"I got ahold of Manda, and we can meet tomorrow around one, if that's okay—I'll drive so you dinnae need tae worry aboot the car."

"Thank you." She reached across the ultra-spacious console for Lydia's arm. "I mean it, Lyd. You're the best."

"No problem." Lydia changed lanes after checking her mirrors.

"Brody is going tae be the coolest kid on campus when his mates see him picked up in this," Paislee said.

"You could buy one," Lydia said. "Get an upgrade on the car as well as your kitchen."

"Leave my Juke alone! She doesn't need any bells and whistles. I like getting in and not risking a pulled muscle." Paislee laughed. "Eddy thinks the Juke will be good for another ten years. I won't mind Brody driving it."

"Fair," Lydia said.

Lydia arrived at the school; Edwyn, Jenni, Anna, Sam, and Brody waved. Brody had his cap pulled down and his hair was long enough it was in his face.

Making a mental note to get him a haircut, Paislee admired how spry he was as he leapt up to the rear passenger seat.

"Aunt Lydia! Did you buy a new car? It's brilliant. I love it."

"This is Uncle Corbin's," she said. "But I like it, too. You think he'd notice if I kept it for myself?"

Ten minutes passed with casual after-school chitchat.

"I've got lots of homework, Mum, so I'll go straight tae me room. Can you walk Wallace for me?"

Paislee almost said no, that he'd agreed, but Lydia cut in on Brody's behalf with, "What kind of teacher is going tae weigh you doon on a Wednesday?"

"They're in secondary now," Paislee said. "Yes, I'll help." She turned to Lydia. "Wallace is getting used tae the dog run on the property. He was very confused at first, not having the whole back garden."

"Change is guid." Lydia parked before the front door of her flat.

"Thanks!" Brody was out of the door and inside within seconds.

"I wish I had that much energy," Lydia said. "Was that sweet Jenni all grown up that he was standing with?"

"Aye." Jenni was a cutie.

"She's blossomed," Lydia said diplomatically. "Has more curves up top than me."

"You're beautiful." Paislee sighed and opened the door. "Brody says they're just friends."

"The blinders will be off before you know it," Lydia said.

"Haud yer wheesht." Paislee got down with a jolt and shouldered her handbag. She looked inside for her son, who was already in the elevator.

Change. It was happening whether she wanted it or not. Since Brody wasn't waiting, she said, "Lyd, Shawn Marcus and Shannon Leery made me an offer today, tae change my space and have the chance tae grow into the old bakery."

"I thought they'd signed an ice cream parlor? That's a guaranteed moneymaker no matter what time of year." Lydia shifted on the leather driver's seat.

"I guess the ice cream parlor would take my spot?" Paislee shrugged.

"That makes no sense," Lydia said. "The bakery is already plumbed and fitted for food and drinks."

"That's what I thought, too."

Lydia's mouth gaped. "Hey, what does Shannon want from you?"

"I already did it!" Paislee cried. "Shannon requested my help with Robert Grant. I told Robert about Jory's inflammation in the lungs and the last I knew, Robert was going tae talk with the police about Jory. Why hasn't he, then?"

"Oh." Lydia tapped the steering wheel. "She's putting the pressure on you."

"You got it." Paislee was getting a crick in her neck from staring up into the SUV from the pavement.

"Not nice. Or fair," Lydia said. "What do you think?"

"I've been busy, aye, but is it enough tae warrant a move?"

"You consider change the enemy," Lydia said. "It doesnae have tae be."

"Change? I don't mind a wee bit now and again, but this is a big deal."

"Want me tae come up and we can talk aboot it over a glass of wine? I left you a bottle of German chardonnay."

"Tempting, but no. I've got tae get dinner. Every free minute I need tae be knitting." Paislee lifted her tote bag with two partial projects. "It's a great problem tae have."

"I'll be here at eight thirty tae pick up Brody and you in the morning!" Lydia promised.

Paislee bowed her head. "Totally forgot that part of not having a car. Thanks!"

She waved and Lydia drove off with a jaunty honk.

Paislee went inside and up to the tenth floor and Lydia's flat.

Grandpa had something cooking on the hob that smelled of brandy, butter, and mushrooms. Her eyes watered at the job she didn't need to do. He had the Ramsey Castle cookbook open to the page for the wild mushroom soup.

"Thanks, Grandpa." She walked to the lead hanging on a hook on the wall and took it down.

"Already walked Wallace," Grandpa said.

She put it back and gave the dog a treat, then patted her grand-father's back.

"How'd Brody get the shiner?" Grandpa asked.

Paislee felt all kinds of silly for not paying closer attention and buying the "having to do homework" story.

"I don't know. He didn't say." Paislee placed her bag on the foyer table. "I'll ask."

"Dinnae be too hard on him," Grandpa called.

Paislee knocked on Brody's closed door.

"Doin' homework," her son said.

"Coming in," she replied, twisting the knob.

Brody was sitting cross-legged on the bed, shoes off to the side. He kept his head down, his hair not long enough to hide the red mark on his cheekbone.

She sat down at the small desk that held a laptop. He had a tablet for schoolwork as well. As much as she hated it, technology was the way things were done now.

"Hey," he mumbled to his tablet.

They had a deal—being honest with each other, no lies. There were times when this was painful, but for the most part, it worked. Would it as Brody got older, with his opinions and world experi-ence?

"So. Look at me, love. What happened?" She tapped her own cheekbone.

Brody's entire body turned the color of a ripe strawberry as he raised his gaze. "I dinnae want tae talk aboot it."

"It's all right tae tell me," Paislee said in a calm voice.

"You promise not tae get mad?" He stretched his legs out, taller by the second, or so it seemed to Paislee. His auburn hair was get-ting darker, his brows, too. He still had the freckles that she loved so much.

She chuckled. "I can't promise that."

He stiffened. "Naw, thanks, then."

"I promise tae listen." She shifted so that she was looking at him with all the love in her heart.

After a minute, Brody nodded.

"Are you in trouble at school?" Paislee asked.

"Naw." Brody shrugged. "Happened after."

"Okay." Paislee blew out a soft breath. "I'm assuming it wasn't just a scuffle, or you wouldn't have tried tae hide it."

"No." Brody's chin hefted. "It wasnae. Nelson tried tae grab Jenni, you know?"

Sweet Jenni with the curves that had sprung up overnight. As much as raising a boy was a challenge, she couldn't imagine a girl. "Oh?" She sent a prayer for strength to Jenni's mum.

"Yeah," Brody said. His chin jutted firmly. "She pushed him away, but he didnae stop. I hit him. He hit me back."

Paislee's thoughts jumbled and collided. Violence was wrong. A guy grabbing an innocent girl, also very wrong.

Brody smacked his small fist into his opposite palm. "If he does it again, I'm gonna break his nose. Then his fingers."

Paislee held up her hand. "No, you won't."

"It's wrong! You know that, Mum."

She counted to ten. "It is. You defended your friend against a bully."

"Nelson's a dobber." He raised his fist.

"Brody, stop. If it happens again, you must tell the headmaster at school."

"No way." His chin grew even more stiff. "Willnae be a wee clipe."

Paislee exhaled. What was the right thing to do here? Oh, how she missed her granny. "Do you really have homework?"

"Aye." Brody raised the tablet, which showed math of some sort. It was like a foreign language to her. She would prefer a foreign language, because she'd be more confident that she could assist with the homework.

She stood. "I need tae think about this, Brody."

"I'm not sairy."

Paislee could see that. She nodded and left, softly closing the door behind her. Grandpa whistled in the kitchen. She walked to the pantry where they kept the whisky, pouring one for her and one for Grandpa.

"That bad?" Grandpa clicked the glass to hers. "Must be over a girl. *Sláinte*."

They drank and she blinked tears from her eyes. "He was defending his friend, Jenni, from a handsy bully, which I agree was the right thing tae do. Violence isn't the answer."

Grandpa stirred what was in the pot, then poured them each another. "Yer grandmother would agree—but she didnae go for bullyin'."

"Brody's only twelve."

"You've taught him right from wrong," Grandpa said. "You've got tae trust that he will make the best decision possible under the circumstances."

Nose stinging, she sipped and bowed her head. Would she ever be confident that she'd done a good job raising him?

Chapter 23

Thursday morning, Paislee had a headache—from stress and lack of sleep. She'd been knitting on the couch long after Brody and Grandpa went to bed to make progress on a blue-and-white jumper in a large weave. She'd finished her other projects and felt good about that, at least.

She'd turned her ringer off on the mobile so she wouldn't be distracted by text message notifications. If somebody wanted to talk to her bad enough, they could call Lydia's landline.

Breakfast was a quiet affair of cereal, tea, and juice. Grandpa offered to take care of Wallace. "Thanks, Grandpa," Brody said.

"You got it," Grandpa said.

Paislee missed the convenience of opening the back door and letting the dog have the run of the garden. She made sure to pack the insurance paperwork in her bag so that she had it for Manda this afternoon.

Lydia gave Brody's shoulder a light punch and called him Slugger when he entered the car—once again, Lydia had borrowed Corbin's SUV.

Her Mercedes had such a small back seat that Brody would have to fold his legs to fit these days.

"Be good," Paislee told her son when they dropped him off at the school.

Edwyn, Anna, and Jenni were all waiting for him, a pack that was learning to stay together against bullies.

"Bye," Brody said, no promises.

"What on earth am I going tae do?" Paislee complained as Lydia drove toward Cashmere Crush. "About Brody?"

"He's a hero," Lydia said. "At least in Jenni's eyes. Mine, too. It's nice tae have a protector. I agree, Nelson's a dobber of the first order."

"It's awful that she needed one," Paislee said. "That's the problem."

"You're right."

Paislee leaned back against the seat and closed her eyes, her head aching. "Thanks, Lydia, for the ride." How would she ever repay her best friend? "Want me tae buy you a coffee?"

"If I thought you had time tae enjoy a drink with me, I'd say yes, but I see your needles poking from your bag of yarn and know you didnae get much sleep."

"You notice too much." Paislee sat up and widened her eyes, pinching the bridge of her nose.

"I love you, my friend. On second thought, mibbe *you* should have a coffee, too." Lydia got into the lane of a popular drive-through.

"I don't like coffee!"

"A strong tea, then."

She ordered and Paislee paid. Truth be told, she didn't object overly much when Lydia added pastries to the order.

"Sugar and caffeine." Lydia smacked her lips. "Promise me that you willnae work too hard today?"

Unable to do that, Paislee waved goodbye and took her second breakfast into the shop, entering through the front door rather than the back.

The phone was ringing as she entered and she hurried, spilling hot tea on her hand but not dropping the cup or getting the yarn wet.

"A bloody miracle," she muttered.

The phone rang again.

"Cashmere Crush!"

"Paislee—it's Eddy. Wanted tae let you know that the reason for the car stalling was a corroded wire."

"Oh." Didn't sound too bad. Or expensive. "Can you fix it?"

"It will be done. Just a reminder, though; the brake pads are even more worn."

"Is it dangerous tae drive?"

"Should be awright through the winter," Eddy said. "Put it on your spring budget. That one will be around seven hundred pounds."

Yikes. "You know how I think," Paislee said with a laugh.

"Not a mind reader," Eddy chuckled. "I have sisters with bairns."

Paislee, handset tucked between her chin and chest, opened the safe and put the money for the day in the register. "When will it be ready?"

"You can pick it up any time after one," Eddy said.

"Thank you so much!" She hung up. The brake pads would be around seven hundred, give or take, and would require some maneuvering since the credit card just might be maxed with the kitchen and water-pipe repairs. How on earth did people manage?

The idea of moving to a bigger store just was too much.

Paislee finished her pastry and tea, then washed her hands, pulling out her project. Just as she got settled, a knock sounded. She put it down to open the back door. Jerry was barely visible behind a large box.

"My cashmere!" She eagerly let him in.

"Yours when ye pay for it," Jerry said with a chuckle. He placed it on the counter. "This is dear."

"But so soft and worth it." Paislee opened the box of fifty skeins. Black, brown, and beige. Ivory. Sage. Grant clan red, and a variety of blues.

"How are ye?" Jerry stepped to the side.

"Fine." Paislee looked up, satisfied that this would get her through the next few weeks, so long as Sorcha was happy. "How did it go with Fergie yesterday?"

Jerry held out his arms, palms up. "Fergie was verra surprised when I asked what you'd suggested. He said no way would it be possible tae rig a Great Highland Bagpipe with a wee bellows withoot it being visible."

"Well, then," Paislee said. "It was just a thought. When Fergie played any of the instruments, it was pure magic. Tae win a competition, it's got tae be about the *sound* of the GHB. Creating gorgeous melodies. Cheating wouldn't be obvious."

"The win, the win. The cash prize is nothing," Jerry said. "The title is more important."

"The side bet of fifty thousand pounds between Robert and Jory isn't nothing." Paislee closed the box. "Maybe more so than clan pride, or band pride."

"You're right. I just dinnae understand having tae cheat for something." Jerry gave her the bill and she sucked in her breath at the high figure, which was simply the cost of doing a high-end product. It took an up-front investment. "A crooked victory takes away the pride."

"Because you're a good man, Jerry," Paislee said. She wrote him a check for the full amount, hoping that today would be another busy day.

"Ta." Jerry pocketed the check.

"No, thank you." What could she do as a token of gratitude? "Would you like a scarf, Jerry? A cap?"

"I cannae afford no cashmere," Jerry said.

"Merino wool," Paislee said. "I have some wonderfully soft skeins that you will love. A gift from me, anyways, for all you do."

"That's verra kind." Jerry leaned on the counter. "I would love a cap. Thanks."

Paislee smiled. "I'll get tae it next month, before winter. So. Meri coerced me tae have lunch with her and Clyde yesterday. Clyde claimed Jory had grown up around that area, but Meri didn't recognize the Baxter name."

"Baxters around Ramsey Castle?" Jerry shook his head. "Never heard of them."

"Clyde was following Meri up near that area. He wanted tae

talk with her about the competition, spur of the moment. He's shady." Paislee counted the skeins to make sure the order matched, and it did.

"Back up! Clyde was following Meri?" Jerry asked. "Why would he be up there? He lives near Inverness."

"Clyde was supposedly searching for Jory's childhood home but I'm not sure I believed him," Paislee said. "Then again, he was probably telling the truth about the anonymous letter, so, maybe he's just impulsive. Locating the bagpipes will hold answers."

"Tae see if there's something tae cause that inflammation, like mold." Jerry sighed sadly. "I hate tae think that being lazy cut Jory's life short."

Paislee raised a brow. "Is there a record tae find where Jory bought his bagpipes? Would Clyde know?"

Jerry shrugged. "I can ask, but Clyde and most of the members of Clan Cunningham arenae mates of mine. Always pushing the envelope. Even the lasses will try and take advantage for the win."

Meri had said the same.

"Anything more from Zeffer?" Paislee put the box of cashmere on a shelf in the back since it would be for projects and not for sale. "I've been too busy tae check in with him myself. He's not one tae just call you for an update."

"I can see that," Jerry said. "And no. Nothing. How's your car?"

"Done today! Lydia will bring me tae pick it up. I'm supposed tae meet the insurance agent at the house. I dreamed of a new kitchen, but this wasn't how I imagined getting it."

Jerry snickered. "Only you."

"Hey!"

"Just teasing," Jerry said. "See you later, Paislee."

Grandpa showed up at eleven thirty with sandwiches to share from the restaurant he now passed on his way from Lydia's to Cashmere Crush. Elspeth arrived at noon and flirted with Grandpa over a quarter of a cheese, ham, and onion hoagie.

Paislee was ready when Lydia arrived in the Mercedes to drive to the house. "Here you are," Paislee said. "I like you in this car."

"Guid thing, since Corbin does, too," Lydia laughed. "He says I can borrow his anytime I want, but he thinks this car is sexy."

Paislee laughed and buckled in for the mile drive to her house.

When they got there, Manda waited in the front. They walked through and the insurance agent pointed out places in the wall where water pipes might need to be replaced. The house had a stale smell from the water damage that the agent promised would go away once everything was fixed. "I've got a crew coming tae bring in huge fans. Trust me, Paislee, it will be like new."

At the end of the tour, Paislee was very overwhelmed.

She had a deductible, and once that was met, insurance would cover the rest. There were still more costs to come. Not everything would be covered by insurance. The upstairs bathroom technically would need only the pipes under the sink. Manda said she might consider an update, but it wasn't necessary. New pipes and flooring, paint. There was some wiggle room in how the money might be dispersed but not much.

"It will be okay," Lydia told her when it was over, and Manda had gone back to the insurance office.

"How?" Paislee was on the verge of a meltdown. Lydia urged her out to the back porch and fresh air. They sat on the steps and watched the birds in the wild cherry trees until Paislee could breathe again.

She wanted to help Brody with university, and this would wipe her savings to the negative. The credit cards would be maxed. It wasn't responsible to live so out of her budget. "What am I going tae do?" Paislee asked aloud.

"Maybe you should consider taking the bigger shop," Lydia said.

"What?" Paislee turned to her bestie. "Are you mental?"

"Just listen a minute," Lydia said, raising her hand. "That is the choicest lot on the block. You could really grow and expand Cashmere Crush. That means more income."

"I would need tae hire another person full-time." Her body hummed and her stomach ached.

"Not a bad thing." Lydia smiled at Paislee. "You can focus on your bespoke products."

"I'm the only one who knits." Paislee flexed her hands. "Only one of me."

"Again, not a bad thing," Lydia said. "You are an artiste."

"I need tae pay the bills. So many bills." Her brain hurt.

"You can raise your prices," Lydia said.

Her phone dinged—a message from Hamish wondering what she was doing Saturday night. She'd be eating cheese on toast for the rest of her life.

Paislee didn't answer his text—not to be mean, but she couldn't handle one more thing. Not even one. She stood. "Let's go get my car."

"Who was that?" Lydia asked, also standing.

"Nobody."

"Liar!" Lydia shook her head. "Unbelievable that you willnae tell *me*."

"Hamish," Paislee said reluctantly. "He wants tae go out tae dinner on Saturday." She opened the door to the kitchen and the scene of the disaster *last* Saturday. A sign that she was meant to be single.

"Say yes, Paislee. You deserve some fun." Lydia followed her inside. "We can take Brody tae the movies."

"No. No, no." Her life was not just spinning out of control, but cycloning. She would come back tomorrow to get the rest of her clothes and any perishables as it was clear it would take months for the house to be finished.

"You cannae push him away," Lydia said. "Hamish cares for you."

"Yes, I can." Paislee stubbornly lifted her chin and led the way down the hall to the front door. She grabbed a small picture of her, Gran, and Brody from the wall and put it in her bag. She didn't feel her grandmother right now, and that made her even more sad.

Lydia drove to Eddy's, listing Hamish's good qualities the entire way. Paislee had to tune her out and jumped out of the Mercedes as soon as it was parked. "Thanks for the ride. I'll see you later."

Paislee went inside to pay Eddy. She noticed that her best friend waited with a well-intentioned net by the car, as if to make sure that Paislee didn't fly off.

She paid and discussed what would need fixing in the spring, tucking it away for a future problem to worry about. "Thank you, Eddy." She palmed the keys to the Juke. Her phone went off again. Zeffer texted to see if she'd talked to Robert Grant. He had some questions.

Well, she couldn't answer either man, or her best friend. In order to cope she would need to compartmentalize.

Lydia stood outside the Mercedes, arms crossed. "Well?"

"Lydia. Thank you for everything, but I have two sweater orders that must be completed. I've been coerced into lunch tomorrow with the Grants at Ramsey Castle. My son has a black eye that I still don't know what tae do about." She took Lydia by the shoulders and stared up into her steady gray eyes. "Please understand that Hamish needs tae be last on my list."

At that, Lydia nodded. "The subject will be tabled—but it's not over. You were my rock during my wedding, and I will be that for you."

Relief filled her body because she knew that Lydia meant every word. "See you for Knit and Sip?"

"Yep. I'm bringing stuffed peppers and warm sourdough from a bakery near the estate office," Lydia said. "Love you."

Paislee made it back to Cashmere Crush and finished one of the sweater projects. Elspeth and Grandpa took the front for customer service and Paislee sat in the back, focused on getting the work done.

Grandpa left with the Juke at four thirty to pick up Brody. By six, the ladies were all there, including Meri. Her friends, her circle.

Who was in Jory's circle?

Paislee put down a cashmere scarf she was working on in Grant clan colors. "I feel like an idiot!"

"Why?" Lydia said, immediately coming to her defense.

"I just had an idea about where the bagpipes might be." Paislee shook her head, angry at herself for not following through earlier.

Who would have your back in a bad spot?

"Where?" the ladies chorused.

Paislee looked at Lydia, then Meri. "The lasses who went to visit Jory at the hospital. The snare drummers. One of them was named Cass, and they were good friends of Jory's. Meri, do you have their phone numbers and addresses, as judge?"

Meri tapped her roll of yarn, merino wool in a burnt orange color to match her hair. "I dinnae, offhand."

"Mibbe we can track them down." Lydia raised her mobile, which had every app possible because of the estate business she did. "What are their names?"

"I only know the one, Cass, with no last name." Paislee remembered them both being tall, one blond, one brunette. Slender but strong, obviously, to carry the snare drums.

Meri smiled. "Not tae worry. I dinnae have that personal information—but Clyde, as Clan Cunningham band director, sure will!"

"What are the chances that he'll give it tae you?" Paislee asked.

"Certain enough that even I would place a wee wager. I've just done him a favor, havenae I?" Meri sipped whisky from her tumbler. "I gave him a verbal warning rather than file a formal complaint, so he owes me one. I can call him in the morning and collect."

Chapter 24

Friday morning, Paislee drove Brody to school. He and Edwyn had plans and Brody would stay the night at Edwyn's.

This left her evening free to catch up on the sweater order from last week and start the next. She felt a little like an automaton—one thing complete, begin the next in queue.

"You're sure you didn't have any problems with Nelson?" Paislee asked Brody one more time. She slowed to a stop before the school.

"No, Mum." Brody's bruise had changed from red to a light purple with the beginnings of green around the cheekbone. Hers was healed but she recognized the hue. "He's stayin' away from Jenni, like we told him."

"That's good, then." Paislee put the Juke in park and unlocked the doors.

"Dinnae fash!"

"Impossible," she said with a low laugh.

Brody shut the door and waved, granting her a half smile through the window.

"Love you!" Brody mouthed, then hurried to his friends.

Oh!

She grabbed a napkin from the console and dabbed her eyes.

He knew just how to reach her. Paislee loved her son so much that it physically hurt her. What wouldn't she do for him? To grant him the space he needed to find himself was going to be very hard.

Once at Cashmere Crush, Paislee unlocked the door and went inside. Grandpa was going to be here at half past ten so that she could knit and go to lunch at the castle. Elspeth would put in a six-hour day.

Was it fair to have them work so many hours? They both claimed to enjoy it and it wasn't as if they didn't have breaks or were expected to be on their feet all day.

While she knitted, Paislee mentally went over the cost of a full-time employee as well as the increased rent to pay at the corner bakery, if she decided to go for it.

The costs of the new kitchen.

Paislee powered through her nerves and finished the third sweater at ten, when she opened the door for business.

Zeffer greeted her, his hand lifted to knock. "Good morning," he said. "I was wondering if you'd had car trouble again."

Ritchie the florist waved from across the street. "You open?"

"Aye," she answered.

Zeffer stepped back out of the way when Ritchie raced across the street, dodging cars, to deliver a dozen red roses in a clear vase with fancy greens.

"An admirer?" Zeffer's brow rose.

"None of your business," she said tartly.

Only one man had ever sent her flowers before: Hamish McCall, and it had been from the Fordythe school secretary, really.

She peeked at the envelope, which read, *Thinking of you, H.* So sweet. More sweet and thoughtful than she deserved. "Thank you, Ritchie—these are lovely."

"Dinnae forget tae cut the ends with fresh water in a few days tae make them last longer." Ritchie scanned Zeffer's blue suit with approval. "See *you* later." He darted back across the street, taking his life in his hands.

"Your cheeks are red, Paislee." Zeffer's lips twitched.

"Can I help you, DI?" She brought the flowers to the long counter with her register. Zeffer followed.

"Aye." He was at her back, so she rounded the counter to put it and the flowers between them. "I remember when you used tae answer your texts."

"I've been incredibly busy." And she remembered when the only death that touched her was by natural causes. Before Zeffer had entered Nairn to spy on her grandfather.

"Son's in secondary now." Zeffer leaned an elbow on the counter, a man relaxed and in no hurry to leave. "Takes more time?"

"That's not it," Paislee said. "Not all, anyway."

He waited, his sea-glass green eyes searching her face until she squirmed like a gummy worm on a crochet hook.

Should Paislee tell him that she suspected Jory's friends knew where the bagpipes were? Meri was supposed to call this morning as soon as she had the information. This was something that might interest Zeffer, but considering how he was hounding Jerry, she didn't dare mention Meri McVie's name. It was best to see for herself first. She wasn't a hundred percent correct on her ideas.

Stepping back, Paislee asked, "Have you found those blasted bagpipes yet?"

"Tsk, tsk," the DI said, shaking his finger.

"After the bagpipe lesson the other day, I'd wondered if it might be possible tae hide a bellows in the bag, even though it would be against the rules of the GHB Competition Council—but Fergie said it would be too obvious."

"What is Fergie's surname?" Zeffer asked. "Unless 'Fat' is the real deal. I once knew a bloke named William Williamson. Parents can be cruel."

"I don't know." Paislee moved a rose stem more to her liking in the arrangement. The scent of the roses was headier than perfume and the petals soft to the touch. She had to distract herself or risk blurting out the unsubstantiated idea of where they might be.

"The bagpipes as of yet havenae been located," Zeffer said at last.

"I wish you'd find them soon." Paislee shoved away from the counter and went to her shelves of merino wool, selecting a skein of beige, and another of cocoa. "I have a lunch date today at the castle that I really don't want tae go tae. I simply don't have time for it."

Zeffer, quick as a cat, was at her side. "Why are you going tae the castle?"

"Lady Shannon Leery is friends with Sorcha Grant, the dowager countess." Paislee orbited around Zeffer to the high-top table where she put the yarn down. She had a pattern in mind that would require a 5mm needle. "She said I'd helped her son and now she wants me tae do the same for Robert. I don't like Robert any more than I liked Shawn. However, Shawn is a decent human being now, so my judgment was unfair."

"Your instincts were right on. Shawn was trying tae swindle you." Zeffer leaned in. His cologne was very subtle—sandalwood. "Is Robert doing the same?"

"How can he be? We have nothing in common. The Earl of Lyon doesn't want a gift shop in the castle, and his mother is selling my bespoke cashmere items there despite it because she wants tae bring in cash. I guess these estates are expensive tae run." She tilted her head to stare at Zeffer. "I don't *need* tae be in the gift shop. It would be nice, but not necessary."

Oh, how extra money would come in handy.

Zeffer swiped his hands together. "A kind word aboot Cashmere Crush by the upper crust would do you better than an advert in the paper. So, I'm calling you on that. It's important for you tae be on guid terms with the DC. As for Robert Grant? He's a noble pain in the arse and I dinnae care what the lady says aboot clan pride being what drives him. The earl has lost farmland because of his betting habits. His mum is pulling oot all the stops."

"Lost farmland?" She thought of how Patrick had taken care of the lands. How self-sufficient they were.

"Aye. They all protect him and the 'Clan' name, but they're fools," Zeffer said. "That's not the kind of secret you can keep. Unhappy tenants are rarely quiet."

"I suppose not." She crinkled her nose. A customer walked in with two young children, a boy and a girl.

Zeffer gave a low growl, realizing that she had to move away from his questions about Robert. "Please call me when you have a minute." He nodded at the trio and strode toward the door.

"Find the bagpipes!" Paislee called as the door shut behind him. She smiled at the woman and the kids. "Welcome tae Cashmere Crush."

At ten thirty, Meri arrived. She'd been expecting Grandpa, but the woman's orange hair was a bright spot. "Morning! Any luck?"

"Clyde wasnae happy tae give me their contact information, but he did," Meri said. "He reminded me, though, that Constable Thorn had already talked tae them." She read from a scrap of paper. "Cass Penders and Sandi Sinclair."

Paislee nodded, recalling that as well. She knew in her bones that if Lydia needed Paislee to tell a white lie, she would do it without question. Your best friends were family of choice. Jerry had just said that *all* the Clan Cunningham members were loose with the rules. "Good job!"

"Thanks." Meri placed the paper on the table next to the vase of red roses. "Beautiful flowers!"

Paislee smiled. She hadn't had two seconds to let Hamish know she'd gotten them. What would she say? "They're from an old friend."

Meri didn't press the issue. "I called Sandi but had tae leave a message, and then Cass, who answered. I said that I wanted tae honor Jory's name with an award for newcomers in the piping competition."

"That's smart," Paislee said. It would play on the heartbroken young woman's sympathies.

"I asked Cass if I could come over and talk tae her in person, so she gave me her address. I have an appointment at eleven. I hope she'll lower her guard enough that I can ask aboot Jory's bagpipes."

"Meri, you can't go tae her house! It's a sham and you're a judge." Paislee looked at the clock. Ten forty. Where was Grandpa? She hoped he was okay on the walk to the shop. Did she have time before that blasted lunch at the castle?

"I feel tricked, Paislee. Besides, depending on how Jory died and if he cheated or not, *might* mean suggesting such a scholarship in truth. I'm gathering information."

"You can't go by yourself," Paislee said. What if something went wrong? She strummed her fingers on the counter. Zeffer would not approve of her going to Cass's house.

In the end, Paislee didn't have time to go to lunch at the castle. If she was able to find the bagpipes and hand them to Zeffer, then she could have the rest of the day to knit her sweaters and scarves to bring money in.

Having weighed her options, Paislee said, "Let me come with you. I need tae drive tae my flat and check on my grandfather, and then we can go tae Cass's."

Grandpa arrived just then, opening the door with a happy whistle. "Sorry tae be late, Paislee. Lost track of time. Hello! Have we met?"

"Meri McVie, judge for the competition." Meri offered her hand and Grandpa shook it.

"Aye. Of course, that's why you look familiar! We were there. You know." Grandpa waggled his bushy silvery brows. "When Jory collapsed." He loved a good gossip.

"We hope tae find the pipes," Meri said, "and have Jory put tae rest." The judge pocketed the address to Cass's house.

"You know where they might be?" Grandpa asked. He noticed the roses. "These are verra nice. For me?"

"We can enjoy them together," Paislee said, wishing she'd thought to hide the card from *H.* "Grandpa, I have my phone if you need me. God willing we'll find the pipes so I can cancel my lunch date at the castle. I'll keep you posted on where I am."

"Be careful, lass. Lasses," Grandpa graciously amended.

Meri chortled. "You're a love!"

Paislee read the address from Meri and saw that it was less than two miles from downtown. Having learned by now that a gift or two helped when arriving with questions, Paislee brought chocolates and a bottle of wine left over from the Knit and Sip party last night.

Meri grinned. "Bribe Cass with treats. My kind of bribe," the judge said.

"I doubt you've ever taken a bribe, let alone offered one," Paislee said as they left the shop via the back entrance. She unlocked the Juke and climbed behind the wheel as Meri, holding the wine and chocolate, got in the passenger side.

"Not really," Meri admitted. "I guess that's why I'm so upset aboot not knowing that Jory might have cheated. I believe that talent should win the day."

Five minutes later, Paislee parked before a row of brick townhomes two stories tall. "Here we are."

Meri read from the paper. "Number three on the corner."

The women exited the car, Paislee praying that the women would know where the pipes were at so she could give them to Zeffer and reclaim her life. She knocked and a tall, pale brunette woman in her early twenties answered with bleary eyes. A blonde just as tall was at her other side. She recognized the snare drummers.

"I'm Cass," the blonde said, "and this is Sandi, come on in. Hi, Meri. I would say nice tae see you again, but we've been bloody miserable since . . . since . . ."

Sandi dragged Paislee inside and then Meri. "I'm so glad that you're honoring Jory's memory." The brunette slammed the door behind them.

Paislee, alarmed, offered the chocolate to Cass while Meri gave Sandi the wine.

"Thanks." Sandi relaxed a little.

"I'm Paislee Shaw." Paislee looked around the spacious entryway. Boots, female and male, were lined up beneath a coatrack. An umbrella stand held three umbrellas. To the left was a sofa and low table, to the right was an open door that revealed the snare drums and the body equipment to hold them. The room with the sofa also had a small piano and several guitars. Music was a featured part of their lives, it seemed. Just like with Fergie.

"What happened tae Jory?" Cass asked, her eyes so red they had to hurt.

"I dinnae ken, pet," Meri answered.

"We cannae move forward with a service until the constables give us the go-ahead." Sandi's grief held an angry edge to it, while Cass's was softer. Both were suffering. "I've been checking the papers every day and there is no news."

"Not a mention," Cass said. She broke down with more tears.

"I'm so sorry for your loss," Paislee said. Her own eyes welled in empathy.

"We loved him. *Loved* him," Sandi said.

"He lived here?" Meri asked, nodding at the menswear and boots in the foyer. "I thought he had a place in Dundee."

"He moved in with us last year," Cass said. "After an ugly breakup from a woman who didnae understand his needs."

"Aye. We all three shared a room." Sandi bristled, eyes daring them to say a cruel word.

"Oh." Meri straightened as she realized that they weren't just friends, but really, really close friends.

Cass jutted her chin defiantly.

"Mibbe we could sit doon?" Meri suggested.

Sandi nodded and led the way to the sofa. Paislee and Meri took an end while the lasses shared a large, cozy armchair.

Paislee noticed the bagpipe backpack against the wall near the sofa. JB was engraved on the handle. Could it be? It was a testament to her relief that she blurted without thinking, "Is that Jory's bagpipe?"

Meri turned, body tense as she saw the bagpipe's case. "When did ye get that? The constables have been searching for it."

So much for Meri's cover story!

Cass hiccupped through her tears. "Stupid Clyde didnae care at all aboot what happened tae Jory. Sandi and me were so mad that we drove back tae the castle after the hospital."

Sandi raised her fist. "Tae have it oot with Clyde!"

"You were at the barbecue?" Paislee hadn't seen the lasses but with all of the people eating and talking, she could imagine them being stealthy.

"Aye," Sandi said. "Clyde blethering on the phone instead of helping his supposed star piper. We were furious. Our Jory deserved better."

Cass curled one leg over the other as she sat forward. "Clyde was a monster tae Jory that day. What if that had something tae do with Jory's death? I willnae ever forgive Clyde, if that's true. I told Ewan already that I need a break from the band."

Sandi nodded. "I did, too. I just cannae get over how cold Clyde was, you know?"

Meri ruffled her orange hair. "Do you know if Clyde asked Jory if he'd cheated, before the competition started?"

"It's bollocks," Cass said to the carpet, not looking at Meri.

"Robert Grant was jealous of Jory's win. We agree with Clyde that he must have made it all up. We told that tae Constable Thorn," Sandi declared, arms crossed over her thin chest. "You cannae believe it, Meri. Jory Baxter deserves tae be honored, not vilified."

"Did Jory cheat tae win last year's competition?" Paislee asked, watching them closely.

"Jory would never!" Sandi said. Her voice lacked conviction.

Did they suspect what their roommate and lover was up to, or did they know for sure? Paislee looked at Meri, and then at the bagpipes. The answers would be inside, she knew it.

Meri inched forward on the couch, her hands folded. "Cass. Sandi. You should turn the bagpipes in."

"Why?" Cass asked with suspicion. "They are the last thing we have of Jory's. Clyde asked for them, too, but we said we didnae know a thing aboot them. He sounded verra nervous. Serves him right if that Constable Smith bloke is riding his arse."

"Didn't the constable ask if you had the bagpipes?" Paislee asked.

Sandi sniffed. "Not exactly," she said. "We were at the station, and he was more concerned aboot the fifty-thousand-pound bet Robert forced Jory tae accept, over the plastic reed and the cane reed. With our Jory dead, Robert dinnae have tae pay, does he?"

"Jory would win. We had plans tae travel, the three of us, with the cash." Cass jerked her thumb toward the pipes. "They've been there since we took them from the castle. I hope you kick Clyde off the competition tour forever, Meri."

Paislee had the feeling that if Zeffer had been on the interview instead of Constable Smith, the bagpipes would have been in the evidence log already.

"Cass. Sandi." Paislee's mind whirled. "You could be in a lot of trouble for not turning these in tae the police."

"Trouble with the cops?" Sandi squeaked.

"Aye," Meri said.

"We dinnae need that," Cass said.

"Why not let us bring them in for you?" Meri suggested. "Or we could call the officers and have them come here?"

"No! No," Cass said. "You can take them tae the police."

Sandi and Cass looked at one another. Sandi nodded. "But we want them back when they're through, okay?"

Paislee stopped herself from jumping up and grabbing them, but just barely. If she could get these to Zeffer, then who knew what shape they'd be in by the time the lasses got them back. "Thank you. We will be very careful."

"Paislee, who are you exactly?" Cass asked. Despite her grief she wasn't totally oblivious that Jory may have done something wrong, and yet they didn't care if they had the bagpipes, which made Paislee doubt her theory that the tool to cheat was inside. She was glad that she hadn't told Zeffer after all.

"I saw you at the competition," Sandi said.

"She called for the ambulance," Meri explained.

"I'm on the committee." Thankfully they didn't ask what committee.

"Thank you so much, dears." Meri stood and went to the backpack, moving it from the wall. It was clear that the judge knew how to handle the GHB. "Again, I am so sairy for your loss."

"You better not give those tae Clyde Cunningham. Swear?" Sandi said.

"We willnae and that is a promise," Meri said.

Paislee nodded. The girls opened the chocolate and wine, and she and Meri left.

Unlocking the hatch of the Juke, Meri put the bagpipes in the back and then came around to the passenger seat. Paislee feared any minute the girls would come running out to demand the instrument.

Throat dry, she got behind the wheel and started the car.

"Now what?" Meri asked. "Constable Smith? Or Constable Thorn?"

"I'd like tae call DI Zeffer first. See how fast he can find someone tae examine the bagpipes so that we know if Jory was cheating somehow. As a judge, Meri, what do you consider a winning tune?"

Meri considered this with a head tilt. "Duration of the song, the attacks and rolls of the pipes and drums. The combined beauty of all instruments. The GHB is the star in the competition."

"So, what if Jory somehow discovered a way tae prolong his ability tae hold a note?"

"That Jory might have access tae extra air? It burns me up. I need tae see inside that bagpipe meself," Meri said. "I can identify what's wrong."

Meri would be an expert. Paislee's phone rang and both women jumped. She answered via Bluetooth. "Hello?"

"Zeffer's at Fergie's," Jerry whispered loudly. "You better get here right now. He wants tae question him, and Fergie doesnae want Zeffer on his property. It's goin' tae get ugly!"

Paislee looked at Meri, who could hear everything as the sound came through the Juke's speakers loud and clear. "Stall, Jerry. Meri and I have the bagpipes."

"Hurry!" Jerry said and ended the call.

"Meri, do you mind if we stop at Fergie's?" She recalled the directions to the medieval town where Fergie lived. His workshop. Would Fergie be able to examine the bagpipes right there?

"Not at all," Meri said. "We must find oot what happened in the competition that has always been aboot talent. If there's a problem, I want it fixed."

"You did great in there." Paislee left the townhomes.

Meri sighed. "I hate tae say this, but I think those lasses knew Jory cheated."

"I agree with you," Paislee said. "But maybe not how. They sure had a grudge against Clyde. A woman scorned is one thing—but two?"

"How can I reward that behavior, by allowing them tae compete next year?" Meri grew quiet for the rest of the drive. The Juke was much smoother after Eddy's magic.

Paislee arrived at Fergie's fifteen minutes later, where Meri perked up.

"Fergie was quite the musician," Meri said. "Tae think he's hiding his talents oot here in the woods. Why?"

"Freedom, I suppose." Zeffer being at Fergie's brought a warning chill to her body. "Was he ever in trouble with the law?"

"I dinnae ken. Then again, I didnae suspect a young champion tae cheat. I'm dooting meself right now." Meri sighed, her tone depressed and disappointed both.

"Och! What's this?" Paislee asked in alarm.

Zeffer's blue SUV was in the front of Fergie's overgrown property. Jerry was pleading with Zeffer, his face ruddy with emotion. Fergie had his head bowed. In shame?

"Wait here, Meri." Paislee jumped from the Juke after putting it in park. Her shoes slid on the gravel and layer of pine needles.

Jerry saw her first and his body relaxed.

"Zeffer!" Paislee cried to the DI, who had his back to her. "We have Jory's bagpipes."

"Paislee, what on earth?" Zeffer whirled to her. "How? Where?"

She ran around to the back of the Juke and popped the hatch. "In my car—hang on."

"Jerry, Fergie—dinnae move a muscle," Zeffer demanded. "This had better be guid, Paislee."

"It is." Paislee dragged the backpack from the hatch and lugged the case around to the front of the car. "These are Jory's bagpipes. Who better tae tell you if something was wrong or abnormal than an expert?"

She breathed heavily after the exertion and watched the DI, then Jerry, and Fergie.

"I thought Jerry was an expert," Zeffer said. "But all along it was Fergie."

How he said the words didn't sound so great. In fact, another idea fell into place. Fergie, the expert. The craftsman. Artist.

"I'm an expert, too," Meri declared.

"Please, Zeffer?" Paislee reached for the DI. "We can find out right now if Jory was a cheater."

Chapter 25

Meri unzipped the backpack-style case before Zeffer could yell at her not to and dragged the bagpipes to the grass.

"Jerry!" Meri said. "You saw his instrument last. Are these Jory's?"

Jerry stepped closer to them, giving Zeffer a wide circle, to peer at the pipes on the grass and soft pine needles. "Aye, I think so. Look at the silver scrollwork." He knelt to examine them.

"Get back!" Zeffer didn't shout—he didn't need to. Paislee froze, and Jerry immediately sprawled backward.

"I know those are Jory Baxter's bagpipes," Fergie said in a quiet voice. "The leather and the drones. The silver. You'd find oot sooner or later. That scrollwork is mine."

"Yours?" Jerry stumbled a little as he righted himself to a standing position. "Why didnae you say that you'd made them?"

Fergie didn't answer.

"Dinnae touch those!" Zeffer scowled at Meri, who backed up with her hands out to her sides. Then to Fergie, he said, "I ran a background check on you, sir. You had some trouble with the law."

"That was ten years ago. I did my time," Fergie said, broad, strong shoulders hunched. "Five years behind bars."

"Oh," Meri said. She brought her fingers to her lower lip.

"Death caused by careless driving," Fergie said in a hard tone. "I pled guilty and kept me nose clean ever since."

"Fergie." Jerry tugged his mustache in dismay.

"I lost the gift I hadnae cherished enough while behind bars." Fergie exuded sorrow. "Now, I pour my energy and talent into making them."

"You'd dropped oot of sight," Meri said.

"The accident happened in London. That's where I served me sentence. It's not easy tae find work after jail." Fergie kicked the gravel when he stepped toward the pipes.

Zeffer put his hand up to both Meri and Fergie. "Dinnae touch anything else or you will be charged with interference."

"How?" Meri asked. "There is nothing visible, no extra air."

"Technology," Fergie said. "Electronics. In the chanter and the drones, you'll find sensors tae give that wee bit extra volume and power withoot going over the top. Completely adjustable. Just enough tae win."

Jerry's mouth gaped. "I dinnae understand."

"I got the idea while in prison, actually." Fergie shrugged. "We were allowed tae play but not the GHB. The electric version. I was familiar with the setup because of my time playin' the electric bag-pipe with the rock bands. You'll find several tiny devices inside."

"You helped Jory cheat," Jerry said. "The whole time I was coming tae you for answers! You already knew. I cannae believe you let me whinge on and on aboot it."

"Aye." Fergie sighed.

"You didnae win that way, did you?" Meri sounded like she'd faint.

Fergie raised his chin as if that thought would be too much. "I did *not*."

"Why?" Meri demanded.

Fergie rubbed his fingers together. "Dosh. Jory paid me well."

"Jory didnae come from money," Jerry said. Now that he was over the hurt, he seemed furious. "How did he get it?"

"Jory worked hard at the pub—he was a natural with customers and had a lucky streak you wouldnae believe when it came tae betting," Fergie said. "It's where I met him."

"How long ago was that?" Zeffer asked.

"Two years now." Fergie blew out a breath. "He was the bartender at my local drinking hole."

"Was he guid at piping already?" Meri asked.

"He had talent, aye." Fergie seemed reluctant to talk and yet he answered their questions.

"Did he want tae be better?" Meri asked.

"Yeah." Fergie placed his hands behind his back.

"How did you come up with the cheating scheme?" Zeffer asked. "Was it his idea, or yours?"

"A collaboration. We got tae talking." Fergie studied the ground. "Aboot where we'd grown up. My kin have always been in this hamlet."

"What about Jory's?" Paislee asked, recalling what Clyde had claimed about looking for where Jory had said he'd grown up.

Fergie clenched his jaw but then said, "Jory was born on Ramsey Castle land."

Paislee looked at Meri, who shook her head. Clyde had said Jory had let that slip. "I never saw him or his family," Meri said. "I've been in my family home all my life. The Baxters?"

"He didnae go by Baxter, then," Fergie explained. "But McDonald."

"Like Finn McDonald?" Paislee asked. Finn and Jory were both black-haired but that wasn't saying much in the Highlands of Scotland.

"Perhaps," Fergie said. "Lots of McDonalds around that area."

"The McDonalds," Meri nodded. "Now them I know. They were a hardworking lot."

"They were," Fergie agreed. "According tae Jory, anyway."

"What happened?" Paislee asked.

"Robert's da turned them oot after a hundred years on that

farm." Fergie held the tone of a man who thought that to be an awful move.

"Why?" Zeffer asked.

"Who knows the way of nobility?" Fergie shrugged. "Probably a need for funds. They have cattle on that property now."

"I'm sure they were compensated," Meri said, coming to the Grants' defense.

"Did Jory say?" Paislee asked.

Fergie nodded, but not happy. "It wasnae enough tae get that branch settled in a brand-new place when all they'd known was farming."

Paislee remembered how Sorcha seemed to rely on Finn for everything. The lady of the castle would trust Finn. So why had he stayed on, when the rest of his people left?

"Jory was a McDonald," Meri said slowly. She removed her glasses and pinched her brow. "I just cannae fathom it."

Fergie shrugged. "He held a wee grudge."

"And so Jory wanted tae beat Robert in the annual piping competition, because of what Dermot, his da, did?" Meri said. "That was so long ago."

"Jory's parents passed away." Fergie shifted his weight from one leg to the other. "His cousins moved tae England tae find jobs that werenae on the land. He returned here with a different name."

"For what purpose? Tae take on the Grants?" Paislee asked.

Zeffer gave her an arched brow.

She'd meant to keep her mouth shut but the question had popped from her mouth.

"He was only a wee lad of five when his family was forced oot," Fergie said.

"*Bought* oot," Zeffer clarified.

"Five," Fergie repeated firmly. "Brought up on stories of the guid old days."

"And I assume that his new life wasnae as grand?" Meri said.

"No," Fergie confirmed. "They were poor as church mice."

Paislee pictured a young Jory growing up, learning to hate the Grants from his own family. Would that be enough of a reason to return and create such an elaborate hoax? "I still don't understand why he would target Robert," Paislee said. "The older earl has been gone for ten years."

"Since Jory couldnae get at the old earl, Robert, as heir, was next on the list," Fergie said, as if this made perfect sense.

"Did Robert know Jory, personally?" Zeffer asked. Zeffer remained determined to find out answers about Robert Grant.

"I'm not sure if they'd met as kids." Fergie scuffed the dirt. "Aboot six months ago, Robert came tae the pub where Jory worked, and wanted a rematch, just the two of them. Imagine it— the grand Earl of Lyon in a small country pub, calling oot the bartender."

"Did Jory agree?" Zeffer asked.

"He didnae want tae, but Robert was manic. Frenzied, and offered a lot of money. Fifty thousand pounds that his cane reed was better than Jory's of plastic. Both men were awful that night, too pished to play. Jory hadnae activated the sensors. Robert was suspicious. They agreed that the winner of the fifty thousand pounds would be the champion at the Ramsey Castle competition."

"Did you see this yourself?" Zeffer asked.

"Aye," Fergie said. "I was at the pub. I knew that, sober, I could help Jory win and beat Robert and the Grant clan."

"And me," Jerry interjected, his face red with anger. "Helping Jory cheat closed us all oot of the competition, not just Robert."

"Aye." Fergie didn't look at Jerry or Meri but rather at the forlorn bagpipes. "Guess that's so. It wasnae personal tae you, Jerry."

Zeffer phoned the Nairn Police. "Zeffer here. I need a large evidence bag, several actually, brought tae Fergie Monohan's house." He reeled off the address.

"Not personal?" Jerry replied. "You have a talent for making beautiful bagpipes and now I cannae view mine the same way. Why?"

"I told you," Fergie said. "Money."

"Bollocks," Jerry said.

Fergie rubbed his large palm over his face.

"There has tae be a better reason," Meri said.

Both people were disillusioned that their hero had brogues of clay.

"Believe it or not," Fergie said. "I needed cash, simple as that."

What could make someone do something immoral? Cheating wasn't against the law. The loss of Jory's home had affected the piper adversely. What did Fergie do for income? Was creating bespoke bagpipes enough?

Paislee studied the stone house behind Fergie. "You told us that this property has been in your family for generations," she said. "Paid for?"

Fergie stuffed his hand into his wild red hair. "That's none of yer business, lass."

"You're right," she said. "I'm sorry."

Jerry glared at Fergie with contempt. The large man finally said, "I wasnae able tae work while in jail, obviously. I have no family tae help me. I asked Robert for a loan until I got on me feet again. He declined. I found another agent with higher interest."

Zeffer gave her a minute nod. Motivation.

Cheating the system wasn't jail-worthy but it was something Meri and the GHB Competition Council would need to be aware of moving forward. Meri gestured to the pipes. "DI Zeffer, I'd like tae see the inside when you're done with this. Tae know how tae stop a cheater in the future."

"We will attempt tae find any of Jory's kin," Zeffer said. "For now, we have a forensics team that will take it apart carefully, piece by piece."

"I'll take it," Fergie said, somewhat defiantly. "I made it."

"You *sold* it. It doesnae belong tae you," Zeffer countered, unfazed.

"What will this mean for the competition?" Jerry asked Meri.

"I need time tae think," Meri said ruefully. "These folks are at the top of their game and practice tae be the best."

"It's not fair," Jerry said, stepping away from Fergie.

"No." Meri sighed deeply. "A bad fish can ruin the barrel."

"Can ye take away the title from Clan Cunningham?" Jerry asked.

Meri turned her focus on Fergie. "Did Clyde know that Jory was cheating, or suspect, before he'd received the anonymous note?"

"Dunno," Fergie said. "Ewan and Clyde often drank at the pub together. Happens tae be the same one I do. Connor Armington, too. Ewan's house is closer tae the pub and plenty big. It's where the Cunninghams practiced. Clyde would crash there—they all would, if they'd had a lot tae drink. I never heard aboot it."

"The day when Robert came tae the pub," Zeffer said, "did he leave peacefully, or was there a row?"

"Robert wouldnae listen tae reason," Fergie said. "His brother, Patrick, finally had tae drag him home. There was no fightin'."

Paislee could see it now and felt terrible for the brothers. One an earl, the other in charge of cleaning up after the earl.

Zeffer turned to Jerry. "Do ye bet?"

Jerry shook his head. "The amount of money was often too rich for my bluid."

"You, Fergie?" Meri asked.

"Aye." Fergie shrugged. "Nothing illegal."

"On Jory's performance?" Meri crossed her arms.

"Aye."

"With the rigged bagpipes?" Jerry asked.

"Aye."

"A weighted gamble in your favor," Jerry said with disgust.

"Perhaps." Fergie pointed to the bagpipes on the ground, the black drones shining, the silver scrollwork glistening. "The beauty of the hidden sensors was that if he didnae want tae use them, he didn't have tae, with nobody the wiser. Jory, by the end, was most adept."

"Did you make them for others besides Jory?" Meri asked in horror.

"No. Not much of a secret, then, would it be?" Fergie shrugged.

A van arrived with two officers to collect the bagpipes.

Zeffer joined them, murmuring quietly.

The tallest of the officers brought a large plastic evidence bag and placed it to the side to take pictures of it first.

Paislee was very curious as to why Zeffer was making such an effort over an instrument that was used for cheating—nothing more sinister.

Unless . . .

Did Zeffer have a reason to be suspicious? Was Robert Grant involved?

Zeffer saw her watching him and gave a half smile after checking his watch. "Dinnae you have a command performance at Ramsey Castle today?"

"I do." Paislee checked the time. Shoot. "I'm going tae drop Meri off at Cashmere Crush on the way."

"Hmm," Zeffer said, "see if Jerry can do it."

"Why?" Her defenses rose.

"Must you always ask so many questions?"

"Aye." Paislee crossed her arms.

"Why?" Zeffer sounded impatient.

"I could ask you the same question." Paislee snorted. "I have rotten luck getting answers, but in this instance—why do you want me tae have Jerry take Meri tae her car when she came with me?"

"I cannae tell you much," Zeffer said.

"Then forget it!"

He blew out a breath.

She remained firm.

"I need tae go over a plan with you." Zeffer again read his watch. "You have thirty minutes before you need tae be at the castle."

It would take fifteen. Paislee didn't like the sound of his voice at all. It was bossy and, well, a wee bit controlling. As if he knew something she didn't (besides the obvious things) and that he just expected her to go along with him without question.

She hadn't missed him when he'd been away. "I thought you'd finished your time in Nairn with Craigh sorted," she whispered.

His sea-glass eyes grew chilly.

"I'm surprised that you haven't moved tae Inverness or even Aberdeen," Paislee continued. "Maybe Glasgow? Edinburgh? Somewhere your talents can be more appreciated than our little shire."

He gave her a wolf's grin. "Nairn has grown on me. I'm fair fond of it."

"Do you golf?"

"Huh?"

"I mean, it's a good pastime and very popular." Paislee couldn't see him in a golf polo or casting a fishing rod. "I don't think you're the fishing type."

"I have no idea where you're going with this," Zeffer said. "I dinnae golf."

"Then I don't see what our Nairn could hold for you."

Zeffer gritted his teeth. "Let's stay focused on Ramsey Castle. Jory Baxter's death."

"Jory McDonald—probably a cousin to Finn McDonald. Sorcha's right-hand man."

"Exactly." Zeffer nodded.

"Why are you so interested in those bagpipes?" Paislee demanded.

"I'm not," Zeffer said.

She rolled her eyes. "Please. I know you. Your interest goes beyond proof that Jory was cheating, when Fergie said he was already and told you what you'd find inside the bag."

"You're verra clever," Zeffer said.

"And right?" Paislee asked.

"I wish I could tell you more."

"I am not going tae do you a favor unless you do," Paislee said.

She'd grown a lot since she and Zeffer had first sparred and her pulse sped with excitement. She was no longer the lass who would let him walk all over her.

Zeffer walked with her to the edge of Fergie's property. Fergie watched the constables with wary eyes.

"Will you please ask Jerry tae return Meri tae her vehicle at your shop?" Zeffer asked, his tone polite.

"Once you are clear with me what you want." She crossed her arms.

Zeffer scrubbed his chin. "There is a possibility that the inflammation in Jory's lungs could be a reaction tae something on the Ramsey Castle lands. My team needs tae test inside the reeds, the chanter, and the drones tae zero in on what it could be."

"Why?"

"For answers, Paislee."

She snorted. "If Jory died from natural causes, why are you going further with this?"

"I never said that he did," Zeffer replied.

"Oh, well, hell's bells." Paislee sighed.

"I am investigating all avenues," Zeffer said.

"And you suspect the Grants of hiding something from you?" Robert in particular.

Zeffer leaned close and whispered in her ear, sending shivers down her spine. "I want answers, and I want *you* tae wear a wire tae get them."

Chapter 26

Paislee's mouth dried. "You want me tae wear a wire?"

"But," Zeffer said, "that would be entrapment, and it would be illegal. I dinnae even know what kind of information I'm looking for."

Paislee's shoulders eased. No wire. Zeffer was unsure if there was even a crime. "I'm not in danger?"

"No," Zeffer said with certainty. "Unless you're breathing in allergens on the sly?" He leaned toward her chest, his ear to her heart. "I dinnae hear any congestion."

"Funny man," she said with a frown. She backed up a step. "Who would you like information from? Sorcha? Finn?"

"Robert. In the past week he has evaded all but one interview—over the phone. He claimed tae have a cold and couldnae leave his home." Zeffer appeared very doubtful.

"Maybe he did have one and was simply being thoughtful. Was the inflammation in Jory's lungs caused by a cold virus?" Paislee's knowledge of such things didn't go beyond the basics.

"No. The coroner wants tae call it bagpipe lung and be done with it. It's similar tae something that farmers get in the barn from hay mold, or mushroom growers on a mushroom farm. Dandelion puffs? They are breeders of wee little spores." Zeffer shuddered.

"Did you know that teenagers have been known tae breathe in the puffs tae get high?"

"No!" If Paislee ever saw Brody do such a thing, there would be serious consequences.

"Ends up in their lungs, making them sick, silly sods."

"Would everyone react the same way tae the"—Paislee cleared her throat—"mold?"

"Another excellent question. I hope tae get answers while you're at lunch. Please keep your phone on in case I need tae call you."

"That's not very discreet," she said. "Listen, I just want tae make an appearance tae keep Sorcha happy, and my cashmere in their gift shop."

"Smart." Zeffer tapped his temple.

"Aye." Paislee was overwhelmed by all that was in front of her. She'd hoped to hand the pipes to Zeffer and skip the lunch at the castle, but it wasn't going to happen that way. "I have a lot of expenses coming up since the water pipe burst."

"Ouch. One of the downsides of homeownership," Zeffer agreed.

"You have a house?"

Zeffer's brow rose. "Do you think I live at the police station?"

Paislee blushed. "Of course not."

"In fact, I'm in the market for a new place in Nairn. I'd like tae get Lydia's information from you."

Lydia sold high-end properties. Wait, Zeffer planned to live in Nairn? Where had he lived before? She'd never given it a thought!

He was too fastidious to reside anywhere other than a luxury home. "Oh!"

"Is that all right with you?" Zeffer smirked.

"Not my business!" Paislee assured him quickly. But it would be odd, to see Zeffer at the market or grocery. Would he shop at Tesco?

His designer suits were custom-made, and she just couldn't see it. Ned the dry cleaner had taken care of Zeffer's suits while he'd spent more time in Nairn well over a year ago.

When he'd had an office, before Inspector Macleod.

"Are you taking over the inspector's position?"

"No." Zeffer gave a pleased expression. "There is enough crime now in Nairn tae warrant a full-time detective. I requested the transfer."

"Hmm."

"Can we get back tae the castle?" Zeffer asked.

"Yes." Why on earth would Zeffer choose Nairn when he'd seemed so disparaging once upon a time? Paislee put it from her mind.

"I want you tae find oot if Finn and Jory are related in truth. Would Jory have a reason tae visit the barn, or a place where mold might be?"

"All right," Paislee agreed. "But Finn only joined us for lunch one time. I think Sorcha insisted but he wasn't comfortable."

"I've run background checks on Finn McDonald. Clean as a whistle. He's a mycologist. Everyone respects him, even Robert and Patrick."

"What does that mean?"

"He's a mushroom specialist," Zeffer said. "Went tae university."

"And Patrick? Does he have any secrets? Besides his affair with Cinda, that is—worst-kept secret in the world."

"What affair?" Zeffer asked. "Cinda who?"

"Cinda Dorset, gift shop manager." Paislee was glad to know something that he didn't. "Cinda's always giving Patrick looks of longing. Sorcha knows about it and is against it. Robert and Lissia also know that their marriages are expected tae bring in money or a good name. Something tae help the clan and the castle. Cinda is merely a pretty, but poor, shopgirl."

Zeffer ground his back teeth together. "Nobility. But that's what I'm talking aboot. Robert thinks he's better than the average

Joe, which is why he refused tae come tae the station. If I had even a shred of solid evidence, I'd make it happen anyway. I dinnae."

"Evidence of what?"

Zeffer raised a brow. "Just keep your ears open. You have guid instincts aboot people. What do you think of the family?"

"I like them. Sorcha has spunk. I feel bad for Cinda, in love with Patrick. I think Patrick is cruel tae carry on with her if he won't marry her. But he's . . . steadfast."

The constables loaded the van. The shorter one gestured at Zeffer. When he left, Paislee went to Jerry and Meri. They all ignored Fergie, shutting the large man out.

"Hey. Jerry, can you drive Meri tae her car at Cashmere Crush? I have tae be at the castle, in—yikes!—twenty minutes. It will take all of that tae not be late. I was late last time and can't do that again."

"Sure," Jerry said. "Meri, is that okay with you?"

"Yeah. Appreciate it. You have a solid head on your shoulders, Jerry, and I'd love tae discuss ways we can prevent things like this happening in the future of the competition. I'm tempted tae ban Clyde Cunningham permanently."

"He didn't know Jory was cheating," Paislee said.

"True," Meri relented. "But I think Jory's girlfriends did. Should the clan be banned, or just them?"

"Girlfriends?" Jerry repeated. "Plural?"

Meri held up her hand. "I only judge in the competition."

Jerry and Meri both waved at Paislee.

"Take care, and let us know how lunch goes," Jerry said.

"I will." She got into her car and rolled the window down when Zeffer hurried toward her. "Yes?"

"I've asked the team tae put a rush on testing the bagpipes. Call me on your way back tae the shop? I'll be nearby if you want tae grab a coffee and go over it while it's fresh in your mind."

Grab a coffee?

"Uh," she stammered. "I'll try."

When she was on the way to the castle, Paislee called Lydia. "Something is going on with Zeffer—he's moving and looking for a house in Nairn. He's going tae contact you, Lydia. Which means he has money."

Lydia chuckled. "Interesting. Well, I'm happy tae help him. What else did you find oot?"

Paislee sighed. Where to start? She only had—gulp!—fifteen minutes. "Fergie created electronic sensors in the pipes as a way for Jory tae cheat. Jory had a relationship with both snare drummers at the same time and they all lived together. They were keeping the bagpipe away from Clyde on purpose because they didn't like him. Jory is actually a McDonald, and was raised tae have a grudge against the Grant family."

"That's incredible," Lydia said.

Paislee finished at lightning speed, almost to the castle. What could she tell the Grants that wouldn't get her in hot water with Zeffer?

"I'll call you later, Lyd!" She hung up and dialed Zeffer. "Hey— can I tell them about Jory cheating?"

"Yes. Definitely. I'd love tae be a fly on the stone wall."

Paislee laughed at the image of a fly in a blue suit. "I'm here."

"Be careful."

She drove through the gates. Finn was there to greet her with a wave. It was hard to believe that the man who looked very salt of the earth in worn denim and an oversized jacket was a learned scientist. Just goes to show that one shouldn't judge.

Paislee hopped from the car.

"Hi, Finn." Paislee smiled and lowered her voice. "I have a quick question. Did you know that Jory Baxter's last name was really McDonald?"

Finn clamped his jaw tight and glared at her. "No. Jory *McDonald*. Ye're sure?"

"Aye." Paislee gestured toward the mudroom of the castle where he'd taken her in before. "Why don't you come in with me for lunch, so I can deliver the news all at once?"

"News?" Finn gulped. "Guess I better."

Finn didn't say another word as they entered and arrived from the mudroom to the foyer. The same maid from before brought Paislee to the dining room. There was Sorcha, and Robert, Lissia, Patrick, and Cinda.

"Sorry tae be late!" It was two minutes after one.

Robert stood. "Is this a bad habit? Or do you get a thrill tae make the Grant family wait for you, a nobody, Paislee Shaw?"

Sorcha gasped. "Son!"

"Somebody's hangry," Lissia quipped.

Cinda gave a nervous chuckle. Patrick drummed his fingers to the table.

"I apologize. That is certainly not it." Paislee was fed up with Robert's elitism and watched him closely as she said, "I was at Fergie Monohan's house. With Jory's bagpipes."

Robert's gaze sharpened. "You found them?"

"Who is Fergie, and why would he have them?" Patrick asked.

"He didn't." Paislee raised her hand. "Let me start over a bit." She took a breath and tried to line up her thoughts in an order that made sense.

Sorcha watched her closely, speculatively.

Paislee wouldn't cower. "It seems Jory used tae live on Ramsey Castle grounds with his family, the McDonalds."

The Grants now shifted their attention to Finn.

"I didnae know," Finn said. "I dinnae watch the blasted pipe competitions. Never liked them, never will. Always work tae do around this place." He hefted his chin. He wasn't at all apologetic.

Was he telling the truth?

"Did you see Jory on the property before the competition?" Paislee asked.

"If I did, I didnae know—I wouldnae have recognized him as kin," Finn said.

"What is the point of these questions?" Robert asked coldly.

"Jory hired Fergie tae create hidden electronic sensors in the GHB tae give him more staying power on the notes he played."

Paislee watched Robert closely. She knew Zeffer would want every detail of the earl's reaction.

"Electric bagpipe?" Patrick said with sincere confusion. "Cannae believe it."

"Cheater!" Robert slammed his fist to the table. The food had yet to be served as it was only five after one. "I won that competition." He paled. "I lost money—but I didnae really. What will the council do? Mum, we need tae talk tae Meri McVie immediately."

"Meri was there with me at Fergie's. Twelve months have passed since the title was awarded so they can do nothing."

Robert turned ghostly white.

"Oh, son," Sorcha said, her fingers to her chest. "What did ye do?"

"Nothing." Robert jammed his fingers through his hair, his eyes clouded. "I'll fix it."

Patrick rose. "I will *not* sell off another parcel tae pay your gambling debts, brother!"

Cinda stood at his side, clinging to his arm.

"You will do what I tell you," Robert said, not even giving Patrick the courtesy of looking at him.

"You are ruining everything, Robert!" Cinda said. "I just want tae marry Patrick."

Patrick and Cinda left, for the first time arm in arm in front of his mother.

"Come back!" Sorcha was torn between following them and staying to find out more from Paislee. "Please, sit. Let's eat and discuss this news like reasonable adults."

"Electronic sensors?" Lissia stood. "I'd always wondered how— I knew he had tae have cheated—Jory, I mean. He was a cheater in other things, so it made sense. Fergie, superstar piper, helped?" She shook her head, pale. "I need a moment. I'll go tae the kitchen and tell them we're ready tae serve. Steak and mushroom pie."

"I'll go with ye," Finn said, obviously uncomfortable.

"Thank you, Lissia, Finn," Sorcha said. "Paislee, I'm so sairy. I wouldnae blame you if you left, but please, join us. I cannae believe this."

Paislee wondered if she was talking about Patrick and Cinda, or whatever debt Robert may have accrued, with the castle at stake. Property versus pride? She took a seat by Cinda's empty chair. Sorcha fidgeted in misery.

"What did Lissia mean aboot Jory being a cheater in other things, Mum?" Robert asked.

Sorcha shook her head. "It doesnae matter."

Robert rose and reached for the decanter of whisky in the center of the table, pouring them all two inches, and adding another two to his glass. "They were together?"

Paislee declined, putting her hand over her glass.

"Lissia had feelings for him that didnae go anywhere, that's all," Sorcha said. Paislee recalled Sandi and Cass saying how Jory had moved in last year after an awful breakup.

They were all seated when Lissia returned. Her cheeks were red but her hand and voice steady. Finn followed her.

Robert's nostrils flared.

Sorcha put her hand on Robert's with a shake of her head.

Had Lissia and Jory had a physical affair? Had Finn known about it? Maybe even covered for Lissia, or Jory? Jory's other girlfriends hadn't minded sharing.

No, Finn's loyalty was to Sorcha. Even over his possible cousin, Jory? Family ties were hard to break. What would Finn get from Jory winning the competition over Robert, the earl?

A behind-the-scenes tweak of the nose? Nah. It didn't make sense.

Finn handed out individual pies to Robert and Sorcha, and put one on Patrick's plate. Lissia passed pies to Paislee, Finn, and Cinda. "For when she returns," Lissia said.

She'd promised Zeffer to ask Finn questions but had only managed one before Patrick and Cinda had walked out.

"The chef is teaching me how tae make water pastry," Lissia

said. "The pastry edge on my efforts wasnae as pretty so I had him do the rest."

"I'll take that one," Sorcha said. Such a mum thing to say.

"Mum," Lissia teased, "I already had Finn give it tae Robert."

Robert glared at the pastry crust. "Seems fine tae me."

"Family got the ugly crusts," Lissia said.

Finn stood and studied the pies on the plates, then glanced at Lissia.

Paislee dug her fork into the savory beef and mushrooms. The crust was crisp yet soft. Herbs and gravy oozed on her fork. It was too hot to eat.

"Finn and I collected the mushrooms this morning, aye?" Lissia asked. "The corner of the barn is guid and dark for growing your new variety of mushroom."

"You can do that?" Paislee asked in surprise.

"He's a mycologist," Lissia said.

"He's a wee bit of a mad scientist," Robert said.

"He's verra skilled and we are lucky tae have you, Finn," Sorcha said.

Robert ate a bite. "Nice pie. Finn, will ye pass the gravy?"

Finn, who had just sat down, gritted his teeth. He got up and passed the gravy boat to Paislee, who passed it to Robert. "Would you like me tae pour, too?"

"Ah, calm doon, man," Robert said. "You're verra testy. Is it because Jory is your cousin that you didnae know, and now he's dead?"

Sorcha glared at Robert. "Son. That's rude and in front of a guest."

Paislee sipped her water and noticed Lissia's glares as Finn sat back down again. She put a piece of perfect crust into her mouth and swallowed.

"What *is* it, Lissia?" Finn asked, slamming down his fork.

"I dinnae believe you," Lissia said in a very cold voice. "I think you knew that Jory was a McDonald. That he was on the property when he shouldnae have been."

"Lissia," Sorcha said, her tone stricken at her daughter's attack on a loyal member of the staff. "You are oot of line."

"Liss, come on," Robert cajoled. "Finn is family."

"No, he's not," Lissia said. "He is not a Grant. Mother, what would Father think of Finn's stash of money in the barn beneath the mushroom shelves?"

Finn gulped a bite of pie and washed it down with whisky. Sweat formed on his brow.

Robert groaned and shook his head. "No. I dinnae believe it. Lissia, love, you are oot of your mind. Mental."

Her phone rang on vibrate and it was Zeffer. She answered without saying anything, putting it on speaker, setting the mobile on the table and covering it with the cloth napkin—she hoped that Zeffer could hear what Robert might confess. Or Finn. Finn had stolen money?

"I am not wrong," Lissia said. "I checked again this morning. A metal chest full of cash. I think he and Jory had a plan tae humiliate the Grants as payback for sellin' the farmland from under them."

At that, Sorcha stood, her body trembling. "Show me where the money is. I'm sure there is an explanation."

"Is there, Finn?" Robert asked.

Finn started to choke and gag. He spit the pie to the napkin. "It's no' right."

"What's *wrong*?" Paislee asked, loud enough for Zeffer to hear. She swallowed her second bite of pie.

Robert raced around to Finn, who was coughing and gagging. He sucked in a wheeze.

"What can I do?" Robert asked.

Sorcha stood. "Call emergency services, son. What isnae right, Finn?"

Lissia laughed and pointed at Finn's plate.

"Did you do something tae the pie?" Paislee wished she hadn't had any. Would two bites make her ill?

Robert gagged but called 999.

"You, Robert, are fine," Lissia said. "And you, Mum."

"Why?" Sorcha demanded.

"Finn knew Jory," Lissia said. "They are McDonalds. He stole from us. There is thirty thousand pounds at least in that chest. He betrayed us, Mother."

Zeffer, brought by a harried maid, reached the dining room. Medics and two constables entered the room.

"How did you know tae be here?" Paislee said.

"The blowpipe contained mushroom spores of the variety found on Ramsey Castle property," Zeffer replied. "Otherwise known as death cap."

Paislee's stomach clenched. "Only Finn's?"

"Did ye eat some?" Zeffer asked, searching her face.

"The crust."

Lissia laughed maniacally. Paislee raced for the nearest bathroom, unable to keep the two bites of pie in her tummy.

Chapter 27

When Paislee returned from the bathroom, mouth rinsed and face patted dry, Finn was being loaded onto a gurney.

Sorcha clasped Finn's hand. "Be careful with him," she told the medic. "I'll be there soon. I'm sure Finn will have an explanation."

Patrick and Cinda had come back and were crowded in the room, Patrick demanding answers from Robert.

Robert appeared to be in shock by the events. "Stop pestering me, Patrick—I dinnae know what's happening."

Patrick gritted his teeth. "Did Finn eat a bad mushroom?"

"Lissia dosed his pie with it." Robert shook his head. "I dinnae ken why!"

"Sister?" Patrick turned to Lissia, who was resisting being cuffed. She was a strong woman and hard to hold onto.

The medics wheeled Finn from the dining room to the hall and out the front door. Sorcha swiveled away from her poisoned groundskeeper to her children.

"Lissia, are ye mad?" Sorcha demanded. "Finn would never betray this family. You should have asked him aboot the money."

Lissia stopped struggling in response to her mother's tone.

Zeffer motioned for the police officer to give Lissia some room even as he blocked the doorway to keep her from escaping.

Paislee was just glad to see him and his team so quickly and prayed that Finn would survive. That she hadn't eaten enough to be poisoned.

"He had tae know aboot Jory being a McDonald, not a Baxter," Lissia said, repeating her prior words.

"Why do ye think that? It's been nearly thirty years since the McDonalds moved tae Edinburgh tae start anew. Your father paid them handsomely for their farmland," Sorcha said. "More than the going rate at the time. We were expanding from the orchard tae cattle. Not that you would know that. You were just born yerself."

Sorcha stepped closer to her daughter, her cheeks ravaged. "Mum!"

"Finn is a guid friend tae this family," the dowager countess said. "You better pray he survives."

"Aye," Zeffer said from his post. "Or it will be two charges of murder and not just one."

"Murder?" Robert gasped. "We are the Grants." He sounded superior and Paislee cringed, as did Cinda.

"Jory's blowpipe was filled with deadly mushroom spores," Zeffer said with confidence. "The same kind that have been found on this property."

"How?" Robert asked the room in general, but Lissia answered, sounding too proud. Something she had in common with Robert.

"I collected the amanita mushroom spores when I was oot gathering mushrooms for the table," Lissia said. "Easy tae dehydrate them. I was learning from Finn, who didnae suspect a thing."

"Why?" Patrick asked.

"I've been planning my revenge since last year," Lissia said, not the least contrite. "I was verra surprised when Jory fainted. The poison is supposed tae take several days before it attacks and by then it's too late."

"Jory's lungs were compromised, and he had an allergic reaction tae the mushroom itself," Zeffer said. "It accelerated his death."

"I had no idea Finn was involved until the last few days," Lissia continued. "I suspected he had something tae hide and did a little snoopin'. The money in the chest was just the beginning."

"Oh, darling, please. Dinnae say another word." Sorcha raised her hand and blinked quickly.

"Jory was a bad man. He hurt Robert—he cheated, and I knew that I couldnae let him ding our clan pride again, right, Mother? It was my duty as a Grant tae stop him."

Sorcha glanced at the door and Zeffer. She said nothing.

"Did you write the anonymous letters, too?" Paislee asked.

Lissia nodded. She wanted to be quiet, but she also wanted to tell her story. "I did! I did write them, wanting the competition stopped, or at least Clan Cunningham oot of it. Then the bet between Jory and Robert would be canceled, the castle in the clear again."

"Hush, Liss," Robert said. "Mum, we need tae call our solicitor."

"The bagpipes from the music room?" Paislee asked.

"My idea!" Lissia cried and slumped over. "Jory deserved tae die. You dinnae think I'm smart, but I knew plenty aboot the mushrooms on this property. Finn taught me himself. I knew I could get away with it for Jory. I'd hoped tae kill Finn, and Cinda, she's not family. Neither is Paislee. They had tae die."

"But you didnae get away with anything," Patrick said sadly. "Jory is dead. You've just confessed tae planning murder."

Cinda glared at the uneaten steak and mushroom pie. "It's poisoned?"

Zeffer gestured to the constables. "Collect all the pies."

Paislee broke out into a sweat.

Sorcha's shoulders bowed but then she straightened. "First, I'm going tae the hospital. Second, I'm calling our solicitor. DI Zeffer, will you take Lissia tae Nairn for questioning?"

"I'll go with Lissia," Patrick offered.

"No company allowed," Zeffer said.

"I hate mushrooms," Cinda said on a sob. She sank to the chair and bowed her head to the table.

"It's not the mushrooms' fault. It's the intent with which it was used," Zeffer said.

Paislee agreed (to herself) with Cinda. It would be a while before she could eat a mushroom of any kind.

"How do ye feel?" Zeffer asked Paislee, once again studying her face.

"I only had two bites, mostly crust. And"—Paislee gestured to the bathroom where she'd already tossed her cookies—"I think I'm fine."

Zeffer nodded. "You're probably right. Just be aware if you start tae have symptoms."

Paislee left Ramsey Castle with a heavy heart and rolling stomach.

Later that afternoon, after fielding phone calls from Lydia, Meri, Jerry, and even Hamish, she lost herself in the rhythm of knitting at Lydia's flat. Friday night it was just her and Grandpa, who'd stayed home from the pub after hearing of her adventures. She'd missed her appointment with Manda.

"A close call," Grandpa said. "Never thought you'd be in danger at Ramsey Castle."

Paislee nodded. "Lissia had targeted Finn because she blamed him for covering up for Jory on the property. The rest of us weren't family, me and Cinda, which put us in the firing line." She gulped and her stomach whirled.

"The DC and the earl had no idea what Lissia was plannin'?" Grandpa pressed.

"No. It's chilling."

"A mental breakdown because of tarnished clan pride," Grandpa said.

"It will be a lot worse for them now." Paislee finished a sweater order and started on a scarf. "It's similar tae what happened at the Leery Estate. If we've learned anything, Grandpa, it's that nobility are regular people with both good and bad."

The phone rang and Grandpa got up to answer it.

"Brody? Sure, lad, hang on." Grandpa passed her the handset.

Alarmed that her son would call on a Friday night with Edwyn, Paislee answered, "Hello?"

"Mum, can you come get me? I dinnae feel guid."

"Sure. I'll be right there," Paislee said. "What's wrong?"

"My stomach hurts."

"Okay." She put the knitting aside and grabbed her handbag and keys. "Can I talk tae Bennett?"

"Yeah."

"Paislee?" Bennett's normally strong voice wavered.

"It's me. What's going on over there?"

"I thought it was just Edwyn eating too fast, he does that when he's growin', but I think it's the flu. All of us are doon with it. I dinnae have the strength tae drive."

"I'm on my way."

She hung up and turned to Grandpa. "Sounds like the flu bug is going around. This is your last chance tae cheek it for a hotel. You might be okay at the house. Oh, no plumbing. Never mind."

"I'm strong," Grandpa protested. "I can help."

The last thing she needed right now was everyone getting sick. Yes, her grandfather was healthy, but still. She opened the fridge. Orange juice and fresh fruit. Then the pantry. Lots of broth and rice. Noodles. Bread for toast.

Medicine in the bathroom cabinet.

"I'll be back shortly. Maybe stay in your room?"

Grandpa had a few choice words about that.

Paislee picked Brody up, Alexa and Bennett at the front door, waving them off with pale faces and bleary eyes. She felt his forehead as she got him buckled up. It was burning to the touch.

"Oh, hon. I'm sorry that you don't feel good."

"And I cannae play in the game tomorrow," Brody complained.

Paislee would call their football coach to let him know that he'd be out two players. When they arrived at Lydia's flat, Brody didn't have the strength to get out of the car, so she went around to his side and slipped her arm around his waist to help him.

Artie the security guard opened the door for them.

"I hope he feels better soon—we can have groceries delivered tae your flat if ye need it," the guard said.

"Thank you."

Tomorrow was Saturday, which meant that Amelia would be in. Hamish. Oh—she needed to answer him about the date. Out of the question, and she could blame Brody's being ill and avoid deeper reasons.

Grandpa had broth boiling on the hob and saltine crackers on a plate. A glass of clear water. Brody went straight to his room with a groan.

Paislee gave him medicine to lower his fever and a cool towel for his forehead. Wallace wanted to be in his room, too.

Could dogs get the flu?

It was probably too late, and they'd all have to ride it out.

She joined Grandpa at the counter. He'd made a wonderful cock-a-leekie soup and now served her a bowl.

"An ounce of prevention," he said with a wink.

"It's delicious," she said, after a soothing bite. She hadn't eaten since, well. This was like Gran's and untangled the knots in her tummy.

"I like tae cook for you," Grandpa said. "And for Brody. Your granny taught me this verra recipe."

"You cooked together?" Paislee asked, surprised.

"I wasnae around as much as I wish I'd been. It was different then, ye ken? I worked on the fishing boats and came home when I could. Hard labor. Until I hurt my back. Then, I fished. Now, I fish for enjoyment but it's a skill I had tae make sure we never went hungry."

"And you've taught Brody." She patted Grandpa's wrinkled hand. "Thank you."

"Ye're welcome, lass. I see so much of your da in Brody."

"You do?" That made her grin. They hadn't really talked so much about her father, who had died in a boating accident when she'd been sixteen. Her mother had moved away, stricken by grief, to America. She was married now and hadn't cared enough to come back to Scotland.

Paislee was only human and kept her mother in her prayers, but there was a wee bit of a grudge she held, too. Gran had been the one to offer help when Paislee found herself pregnant. Gran had encouraged her and believed in her.

"What happened tae the photo albums I know Agnes kept?" Grandpa asked.

"Oh, they've got tae be in one of those boxes in your room." Paislee scrunched her nose. "We might as well tackle some home improvement, eh? Lydia's got the whole new kitchen planned."

"Mum!" Brody called in alarm.

Paislee hurried to his room and helped him to the bathroom. She spent the rest of the night at his side, knitting and texting.

Hamish understood and sent well wishes for Brody to feel better. Zeffer wanted her at the station in the morning.

She'd think about that, but Brody came first.

Jerry and Meri were both shocked that Lissia Grant had killed Jory with mushroom spores and tried to kill Finn, Paislee, and Cinda.

Zeffer texted that Finn was stable but being kept in hospital. The money in the metal chest was his savings. Finn McDonald didn't believe in banks.

Lissia was being charged with murder for Jory, and attempted murder for Finn. Cinda wasn't pressing charges. Did Paislee want to? Robert had ordered all of the mushrooms in the castle pantry to be burned in a big fire outside.

Sorcha had been so busy protecting Robert she hadn't realized that Lissia was a danger to others until it was too late.

Epilogue

Monday morning, they were all feeling better from the flu. Forty-eight hours had felt like a week, but the Shaw family had taken care of one another through thick and thin.

Brody went to school with a spring in his step, Jenni waiting for him. Edwyn was staying home another day just to be safe.

Brody said it was because he'd gotten a new video game and wanted to play it.

Paislee laughed and kept Edwyn's secret. Today she had an appointment with Zeffer at the station. She'd warned him that she only had a few minutes before she needed to open the shop.

He'd agreed to be mindful of her time.

Paislee enjoyed their banter and parked in the lot by the police station. Zeffer met her in the lobby. Amelia waved at her.

"Thanks for coming. Glad you're better." Zeffer's nostrils flared. "You arenae contagious, are you?"

"I hope not, for Amelia's sake," Paislee said.

"Thanks?" Zeffer led her to his office. It wasn't the one he'd originally had, as Inspector Macleod had taken that over.

This was smaller and, like the other office, he hadn't put any personal touches on the walls. What made him tick? What was his story?

Paislee hadn't cared much beyond keeping Grandpa out of trouble, but now that was over, and she could lower her guard.

"Have a seat," Zeffer said.

She chose the hard plastic foldout chair that faced his desk as he went around to the opposite side. This office had no window.

"How's Finn?" she asked.

"He will recover. He's decided tae take his money and retire with his cousins in Edinburgh."

"Can't say I blame him," Paislee said.

"Same." Zeffer studied her over steepled fingers.

"What?"

"I need your statement regarding what happened on Friday. Both at Fergie's and the castle."

"All right. Can I email it tae you later? My handwriting is appalling."

Zeffer chuckled. "Fine. Just drop it by today, so that I can add it tae the case file."

"Is that all?"

"No. I just wanted tae say . . . thank you . . . for your willingness tae help. Not that you did much, but . . ."

"Hey!" Paislee said. "I kept the phone on speaker so that you could hear what was happening."

"Yeah. Brilliant—and since I didnae ask you tae do it, you have guid instincts." Zeffer rubbed his smooth-shaven chin.

It must have almost killed him to say thank you—so why had he? She was suspicious of him, no doubt.

"What do you want, DI?" She glared at him. "I already told Lydia that you might be interested in a house, so . . ."

"Thanks."

Her phone dinged. Hamish, asking how they were all feeling.

He was a nice man, a good man, and didn't irritate her to distraction. Not that he was too nice—they'd certainly had their squabbles.

Now, they were getting to know one another with the occasional date.

Next, her phone rang. Manda the insurance agent, probably about meeting this week since she hadn't been able to on Friday.

"I have tae go. If you just tell me what it is you are really after, Zeffer, then we can cut tae the chase."

His eyes glittered.

"Go, Paislee, go. I'll be right here."

And why did those words make her skin tingle?